THE SHROUD

NEOTERIC PRESS
www.neotericpress.net

This book is a work of fiction. Names, characters, places, and incidents either are products of the author's imagination or are used fictitiously. Any resemblance to actual events or locales or persons, living or dead, is entirely coincidental.

Set in Times New Roman and Arial Narrow
Designed by Cathy Roberts

Cover art by Marc Moellinger

Manufactured in the United States of America

ISBN 978-0-615-35215-2

To our parents,
Dr. Taylor Meloan, and Jeri Meloan.

Acknowledgements

I'd like to thank: my wife Julie Jay and son Tyler, who have each played their own special role in bringing this book to fruition; My brother, for invaluable hours of brainstorming, discussion, writing, editing, and helping to make this story all that it could be; Carl Sagan, without whose work this book would surely have never existed; Michael Carr, for his truly stellar editorial skills; And lastly, to Christine Susan Smith, my real life "Altman," for tirelessly challenging my entrenched inner reductionist, and showing me the other side.
--Steven Meloan--

Here's to Cathy Roberts, my wife and intellectual partner in all endeavors. She keeps the home fires burning and provides a reality check when I'm rocketing out of the solar system; My brother, for the spark of the story, much writing, and great flashes of insight. I'd also like to thank Carlos Castaneda for introducing me at an early age to the notion of something mysterious beyond the veil. And to the synchronicities that regularly whisper in my ear.
--Michael Meloan--

Special thanks to Dr. Paul Curlee, Patty Bongiovanni, Diana Rhoten, Dr. Ransom Stephens, Lilla Weinberger, Patty Westerbeke, and Jane Zimmerman for their insightful readings of the manuscript, and early encouragement.

Additional thanks to the following for their encouragement, insights, information, and general inspiration: Scott Adams, Dr. William Barnes-Gutteridge, Deepak Chopra, Peter Crosman, Kay Dangaard, John Diamond, Pia Ehrhardt, Tracey Ellis, Rod Flagler, Arielle Ford, Joe Frank, Thaisa Frank, Dr. Dean Hamer, Jan Heiss, Ethan James, Dr. Bruce Lipton, David McCracken, Dr. Edgar Mitchell, Robert Rico, Terry Rossio, Dr. Peter Russell, Dr. Norman Stroh, Dr. B. A. Troesch, Renée Vogel, Dr. Ruth Weg, Kathy Zaffore, and the Sonoma State University Library.

Illustrations

Genome Sequence Graph on page 140 generated using PatternHunter,
Larry Miller, University of Waterloo, Ontario, Canada (others involved with
Pattern Hunter are Bin Ma, John Tromp, and Dr. Ming Li)
Stereogram on page 352 www.garybeene.com/images/gbsirtsmain1.gif
Stereogram on page 353 altered from www.Ice.hut.fi/~ikalliom/stereo.txt
Stereogram on page 353 generated dynamically at
www.kammerl.de/ascii/AsciiStereo.php

Not everything that counts can be counted,
and not everything that can be counted counts.
—Albert Einstein

I

Chapter 1

Frère Jean was the first to wake. Smelling the smoke, the aged monk sat upright in bed, his hand instinctively clasping the iron key and the gold medallion on the chain around his neck. He threw on his robe and deftly moved toward a thick hemp rope hanging from the tower. After hauling on it once, twice, the heavy bronze bell began to toll. Three other monks burst into the chamber, eyes wide, with rough wool blankets draped across their shoulders. Without a word, all four hurried to a stone-and-wood chamber already half engulfed in flames. At the room's center, still untouched by the blaze, stood an ornate silver chest on a low stone pedestal.

With their blankets, the other monks beat back the flames enough that Frère Jean could insert the key and open the chest. He lifted out the contents: an old, stained bolt of linen, already singed from the heat. Tucking it beneath his robe, he hobbled out of the burning room toward the monastery's rear entrance, where the horses were stabled. From the village came the thunder of hoofbeats and cries of alarm.

As the other three monks stood around him, illuminated in the moonlight, Jean removed the gold medallion from around his neck. It bore the embossed image of a many-limbed oak tree. He looked into each man's eyes. Then, approaching the youngest, he placed the medallion's chain over his head, took the bolt of cloth from beneath his robe, and tucked it into a longish leather pouch with a shoulder strap. All eyes were on the strong young monk as he slung the pouch over his shoulder and covered it with his tunic.

"You are being entrusted with what will one day be recognized as the Church's most valuable material possession," the old man rasped, still laboring to catch his breath. "It is the most sacred earthly connection to the spirit of Jesus Christ. Deliver it to the abbot of Chambéry. The gold oak will confirm your mission. God be with you. Now, go!"

The young monk jumped on the back of a waiting horse and galloped into the night just as the invading horde rounded the corner leading to the front of the monastery. The horsemen swarmed inside, throwing silver goblets, figurines, and other artifacts onto blankets and howling into the darkness.

As the three remaining monks tried to save the monastery, a phalanx of horsemen struck them down with mace and sword. Frère Jean was felled by a single blow from a chain-mailed fist.

* * *

The camera pulled back to reveal a scene of flaming destruction. Suddenly, the image froze—a ghostly abbey engulfed in flames. Looking exhausted, Dr. Robert Strickland stopped the DVD player, rubbed his eyes, and glanced at the clock on a nearby desk. It was 1:42 A.M.

Strickland gathered up the stack of papers strewn across the couch beside him. The top page was printed on fine parchment, with the gold crossed keys of St. Peter—the symbol of the Papacy. Yellow markings highlighted several paragraphs pertaining to "ethnogenomic sequencing" and "dating analysis," as well as a proposed time frame for "delivery of the sample."

After slipping the pages into an unmarked manila folder and locking it in a filing cabinet, Strickland pressed the DVD's eject button and returned the disk to its case. Dropping it into the desk drawer, he turned out the light and headed upstairs to bed.

Chapter 2

The alarm came on gradually, with the slowly building strings of Górecki's Third Symphony. Strickland sat up and swung his feet over the side of the bed, closed his eyes, and meditated for several minutes, going into the zone almost immediately. Sometimes there were colors, other times complete visions, and occasionally, a glimmer of scientific insight.

A preprogrammed pot of coffee was already steaming on the counter as he entered the kitchen. Pouring a cup, he took a few sips, then went to the condominium's front door. Brisk morning air wafted in as he retrieved the *Washington Post* from the front stoop.

Twenty minutes later, he had finished his bagel, coffee, and paper. He counted out fifty push-ups while listening to public radio, then showered and dressed, and tossed two medical journals and several thick texts into his briefcase—a detachable hard-shell saddlebag from his BMW motorcycle. Then he zipped up a full-length red Kevlar jumpsuit and donned a silver full-face helmet.

Pulling out of the underground parking lot, he rolled the handgrip back and felt the surge of acceleration. He loved the feel of riding a bike—so different from being in a car, where the mind was apt to be on everything but the driving. A bike demanded complete focus, and paid it back in exhilaration.

He had ridden an old Triumph Bonneville back in medical school at NYU. The chaotic traffic required a Zen-like immersion—the ability to flow amid the confusion without being touched. After a long day cloistered in the library, he had hungered for the fast evening ride home through the Village.

Strickland pushed the BMW hard through the semicircular transition from the beltway to Highway 355, heading south toward Bethesda. Leaning steeply into the turn, on the way out he twisted the grip and surged into the heavy traffic streaming toward northwest D.C.

As he pulled into lot B of the National Institutes of Health's Genomic Science Center, two female grad students in white lab coats waved from a distance. Waving back, Strickland circled into a reserved space marked DIRECTOR, ETHNOGENOMICS.

As he unzipped his suit, a young man hurried up to him. "Dr.

Strickland!" he said excitedly. "My paper's been accepted by the *Journal of Molecular Genetics*! I think your suggestions about the role of surfactant protein D made the difference."

"You had all the necessary ingredients," Strickland replied, pulling off his helmet and gloves. "We just cleaned it up a bit. It's an impressive line of research, Wesley—congratulations. When you finish your degree, you should consider working full-time for the NIH."

"I'm . . . not sure where I'll be living," Wesley said. "My wife wants to move to the Bay Area."

"Ah, the lure of California gold." Strickland grinned. "On the other hand, there's something to be said for the relative freedom of government work, shielded from the demands of shareholders. It's a tough choice these days—and, thankfully, not one I had to make at your age." He glanced at his watch. "Afraid I have to run," he said. "Congratulations again on your paper!"

He was barely through the door of his cluttered office before George, his administrative assistant, caught up with him.

"Dr. Strickland, don't forget, you have the quarterly budget meeting today at ten," he said. "I've e-mailed you the presentation file."

"Maybe I should just send you," said Strickland, smiling. "At this point, you probably know the data better than I."

"I just supply the numbers," said George. "You do a far more impressive dog-and-pony show."

"Lucky me."

Strickland thumbed absentmindedly through the stack of phone message slips on his desk. Their very existence indicated a certain type of caller: bureaucrats who wanted "ear time," not e-mail.

Afterward, he headed down the hall toward the lab, past a half-open door whose nameplate read, Dr. JORDAN RANDALL, DEPUTY DIRECTOR.

"Bob— perfect timing!" said a voice from within as he passed. "I want to run something past you." A short, solid man with thinning russet hair filled the doorway.

"What's up, Jordan?" Strickland said.

"There's something unusual going on with one of the new sequencing systems. Seems to be generating matches outside the specified target areas—it's quite strange, really. We don't have any wiggle room left on the

AIP trigger project, so I'd like to get your take on it."

"Okay, let's have a look."

The two men descended a concrete staircase into a sprawling basement complex filled with genetic sequencing machines, stainless steel tissue storage cauldrons, and sentinel-like tanks of liquid nitrogen. The windowless, fluorescent-lit space looked and felt like a bunker, and rows of equipment filled it with a droning low-frequency hum.

Strickland logged on to the computer network's master console, checking the programs that controlled sequencing operations. A computer graphic with multicolored overlapping bars depicted the genetic region in question.

Sensing something important, a number of graduate students gathered to watch as Strickland typed in cryptic commands. He took his time in the analysis, evaluating the data from several different perspectives, and gradually most of the students drifted back to their work at state-of-the-art computer workstations interspersed across the cavernous lab.

Finally, a high-resolution 3-D graphic appeared. Absently dragging his fingers through his unkempt salt-and-pepper beard, Strickland studied the display, then bolted up from his chair.

"Look at this!" he said to Randall, who was busy at another workstation. "You're right, we seem to have a hit inside chromosome eleven. It's not clear whether this is a software bug, a data error, or . . . something else."

Strickland brought up a color display of a spiraling DNA molecule, along with a tabular listing of the adenine, thymine, guanine, and cytosine base pairs below it. As an added analysis tool, he presented the region in karyotypic form, as dark- and light-colored bands.

"The structure is definitely unusual," said Randall. "It almost looks like code for a transcription factor."

"Exactly what I was thinking," Strickland said. "Given its proximity to areas associated with anterior pituitary function, this might be the reason acute intermittent porphyria is sometimes triggered by the menstrual cycle. And notice that it's only a few centimorgans from the M51X gene—also found in patients of Dutch descent. This could be the activation switch we've been searching for."

"Possibly so," said Randall. "Let's simulate transcription and see if we can track the mechanism."

Strickland checked his watch. "*Shit,*" he muttered. "I was due in the budget meeting ten minutes ago. I have to get over there." He turned back to Randall. "Jordan, this is truly exciting. Why don't you carry on, and we'll touch base afterward."

He began closing the nonessential windows on the screen to give Randall more room for the simulation process. As he positioned the cursor at the karyotype window, something in the patterns of dark and light brought to mind a photo of an odd petroglyph he had once seen in an archaeology text. The cave wall had been filled with repeating sequences of vertical brown and black bands of varying widths, rather like Morse code. No one had ever managed to decipher whatever ancient, rudimentary language appeared to be locked within the patterns.

Lost in thought and gazing at the on-screen karyotype, Strickland suddenly realized that the dark and light bands of this region of the chromosome formed a perfect Z—only an anomaly of the presentation, of course, but interesting nonetheless. He clicked on the window, and the pattern collapsed in on itself.

Chapter 3

As Strickland entered through the back door of the mahogany-paneled conference room, all conversation stopped, and the five men and two women seated around the large wooden conference table turned to face him.

"Our scheduled time is nearly half over, Dr. Strickland," said a man with sculpted hair, looking at him over a pair of half-frame reading glasses.

"Something promising just happened in the lab," Strickland replied, refusing to play the chastened schoolboy.

"Press releasable?"

"No, much too early."

"Then let's get down to business, shall we?"

Strickland passed him a flash memory stick with his department's quarterly financial data, and the first page of the presentation was soon projected on a large white screen. With a jiggling red laser pointer, the man highlighted key expenditures, probing and challenging each one.

Strickland defended the items essential to his work: the semiannual upgrades to the analysis workstations, and the latest in sequencing hardware. It was a familiar dance. In the end, his department would likely get its usual increase, and the assembled bureaucrats would come away having justified their existence. The two groups were members of very different tribes, grudgingly sharing finite resources.

Then it was someone else's turn to be grilled, and as the meeting dragged on, Strickland found it harder and harder to stay focused on the budgetary minutiae being discussed. His mind drifted back to the unexplained sequencing discovery and where it might lead.

* * *

After the meeting, Strickland headed back to the lab, where he found Randall still seated in front of the console, running simulations.

"Fill me in, Jordan. What have you got so far?"

"I'm simulating the translation of these new sequences. From the preliminary runs, it's not a data glitch—it's the real thing. I haven't completed the entire scenario yet, but I'm already getting some promising results. Unfortunately, this new region appears to be part of a group of expressors."

"As always, the puzzle expands," Strickland said.

The two men fell into an easy, familiar rhythm of work—exchanging ideas and bouncing theories off each other to explain the data at hand. The hours flew by, and when they finally passed their badges over the proximity reader at the lab's main entrance, it was 2:27 A.M.

"I think we made some major headway tonight," Randall said as they walked out into the crisp night air.

"These are the times I like best," said Strickland, zipping up his jumpsuit. "Reminds me of when we were residents, solving cases that had everyone stumped. You just feel *alive*."

"Right, nothing like it—but I did miss homework duty tonight."

"Apologize to Mary and the kids for me. When I get going on these things, I just can't stop."

"I'm not complaining," Randall said, slapping a Kevlar-padded shoulder. "Nowhere I'd rather be. Ride safe."

Riding north on the Rockville Pike, Strickland was in the buzzed trance that often followed a new and promising lead in his research. There was almost no traffic, and he cranked it up to 110 for a short stretch, then pulled it back down to an easy 75. The green-tinged street lamps flickered across the seemingly endless sprawl of industrial parks. He passed a tow truck, its yellow and red beacon lights dancing across the wooded hillside as it winched up a fallen car.

* * *

After a few hours' sleep, Strickland woke, unable to stop thinking about the potential porphyria trigger sequence. He padded out to the courtyard of his condominium building, slipped on a mask and snorkel, and floated facedown in the warm waters of the big oval swimming pool. Focusing on slow, even breath, he watched the ghostly intertwining patterns of light on the pool bottom. The iridescent shapes were impossible to lock on to—constantly in motion, merging and morphing in response to every tiny disturbance on the surface.

As he lay still, the water calmed, and the hypnotic beauty and symmetry of the shapes intensified. He had always believed that every aspect of nature held answers, if only we could interpret the data. Everywhere you looked, tantalizing secrets were on display—from the mysterious way birds flocked and moved en masse, to the elegantly programmed social behavior of insects, to the streaming of cytoplasm within a cell. Each reflected fundamental scientific principles, yet the overarching insights often felt just out of reach. All you got was the teaser—the intuitive sense that extraordinary treasures lay veiled right before your eyes.

Chapter 4

Now that the porphyria trigger investigation was well under way, Strickland and Randall had delegated the final analysis work to their postdoc researchers. Connie Franklin, one of the Ethnogenomics Center's most promising postdocs, had just approached Randall and asked him to review her work. Thumbing through the data on her computer workstation, she gave a running commentary as the multicolored graphics flashed past.

"We've narrowed the search to several exon areas on chromosomes eleven and sixteen," she explained. As she clicked on the regions in question, the relevant base pairs appeared on the screen. "Here it is," she said. "That sequencing anomaly was an amazing bit of luck. We might never have investigated this area using standard procedures."

"Right," Randall said, "and who would have expected anything there? As one of my med school profs used to say, 'When you hear hoofbeats, think horses—but never count out zebras.'"

Just then a large, elegantly wrapped package arrived at a nearby secretarial station. A woman signed for it, looked at the attached card, and said, "It's for Connie."

"Thanks," said Franklin, continuing with her presentation and trying to maintain a professional demeanor, though her eyes kept cutting across the room.

"Go ahead," Randall said, "see who it's from."

The package was a bouquet of white roses from Franklin's boyfriend, now finishing his dissertation at Berkeley and soon to join the NIH. Dangling from the neck of the elegant vase, a large tag in Day-Glo blue text read, "*A product of FloralFire, a division of Celeronics Corporation.*" And beneath this, "*Turn out the lights!*"

By now three of the department's secretaries had gathered around Franklin, admiring the arrangement. At first glance, the roses, though lovely, appeared unremarkable other than a subtle luminescence.

As the clamor arose to turn out of the lights, Randall gave the nod, and the room was thrown into darkness—except for an unearthly bluish glow from the roses. And amid much oohing and aahing, as eyes adjusted to the darkness, the reticulated light from the layered petals produced a subtle array of colors from deep purple to electric aquamarine.

Randall smiled. The glow was produced by luciferin, the bioluminescent substance found in fireflies. FloralFire, using an altered version of the rose mosaic virus, had developed a cost-effective way to insert the gene into flowers. More recently, the company's gene delivery technologies had transcended the plant kingdom, and its latest triumphs included bioluminescent goldfish and butterflies.

Randall remembered the early corporate frenzy of gene patent applications, with FloralFire in the thick of it. Before the legal system caught up with the technology, broad-ranging patents were awarded to a handful of early genomic companies. As a result, those firms began demanding licensing fees every time a patented gene was used in industry. Eventually, basic patent awards were restricted either to drug treatments derived from a given gene's function or to technologies useful in discovering and manipulating genetic data. But the early patents remained in force, having withstood numerous legal challenges.

As the lights came back up and a self-conscious Connie Franklin was besieged by well-wishers, another of Randall's postdoc students approached with an update on his portion of the porphyria work.

"Dr. Randall, we have a problem with the X3FP gene," he said hesitantly. "I checked the GenPat database, and it's owned by Geniac, Inc."

Randall took off his reading glasses, narrowing his eyes.

"I just wanted to give you a heads-up," the student said quickly, backing almost imperceptibly away. "If we're going to do any major work on X3FP, we'll need to file a licensing agreement."

Strickland glanced up from a nearby computer.

"Damn it, these frivolous patents have to be overturned," Randall grumped. "We've got to be savvier about business and politics. We need to be *activists*!"

"There's a problem, I agree," Strickland said. "But we can't do everything. We've chosen to focus on research, and I believe that's where we should put our energy. We can provide information and opinion, but it's ultimately up to the government, and society as a whole, to make policy."

"I just don't buy that," said Randall, his face flushed.

"Well, to be fair," Strickland said, "without FloralFire's work on the luc gene, I doubt that we'd be nearly as far along with technologies like bioluminescence-activated destruction of cancer. As you and I have seen time and time again, it's impossible to predict where these discoveries are going to lead. But companies aren't going to do the essential early development work if they fear being immediately overrun by competitors, with no way to recoup their investment. I'm no apologist for big business; it's just reality."

"I say, left to their own devices, they'll focus on the licensing end of things, and research and diagnosis be damned," said Randall. "Why should they do any actual work when they can collect money for doing nothing?"

"That's a bit cynical, don't you think?" said Strickland.

"It's just reality."

Strickland nodded to Randall with a slight smile. Their debate had a familiar ring, and the usual outcome. Though that was it for this round, they had been arguing science and philosophy for decades, since their internal medicine residency at Washington University in St. Louis.

From the beginning, there had been a culture clash between the two. Randall was the product of a Midwestern fundamentalist upbringing, and Strickland had chided him early on, calling him strident and narrow-minded. And Randall, for his part, had been more than a little wary of his newfound colleague's bohemian lifestyle. Strickland tore around St. Louis on a beat-up motorcycle and was known at the hospital as a womanizer and likely recreational drug user.

As Randall sat down at one of the lab's workstations to send an e-mail concerning the X3FP license, he glanced across the room at Strickland. He distinctly remembered their first meeting. At the orientation meeting for new residents Strickland had arrived late, wearing torn jeans and a T-shirt, with his jaw set and a dark, troubled look clouding his face. As a religious person, Randall felt compelled to engage him later—to try to ease a perceived deep-seated inner pain. But it soon became apparent that religion would be a delicate topic between them.

Strickland was widely read in everything from Buddhist sutras, the Quran, and the Upanishads to the Mayan Popol Vuh. And his verbal skills were formidable, dismembering opponents with surgical precision. Leave the slightest flaw in your argument, and Robert Strickland would cut you off at the knees. In their first conversation, which quickly turned into an argument, the agnostic Strickland had quoted Biblical Scripture to counter each of Randall's assertions about faith.

But somehow, the trial by fire of medical residency had brought them closer together despite their philosophical differences. Recognizing Strickland's brilliance, Randall began to engage him in late-night conversations during their twenty-four-hour shifts. Ultimately, their relationship proved symbiotic. Randall believed that he had, little by little, offered Strickland insight into the experience of an abiding faith that transcended mechanical Aristotelian logic. And beyond sharing his knowledge, Strickland had helped Randall become more open-minded and willing to see the world from differing viewpoints.

But through it all, the overriding bond between them had been science. After one particularly heated exchange on the role of the scientific researcher, Strickland suggested that Randall read a biography of J. Robert Oppenheimer.

"This guy's story embodies every imaginable conflict regarding science and the scientist," Strickland said. "He lived it all."

Ironically, in later discussions they each used Oppenheimer to bolster their own worldview. Strickland saw in him the ultimate complex melding of scientist and philosopher—a pacifist who looked beyond his own beliefs to help build the ultimate weapon of mass destruction.

"He was convinced that if America didn't build it, the Germans would," said Strickland. "And he was also convinced—or at least he hoped—that the bomb would save more lives than it took."

"He may have believed that early on," Randall argued, "but the path he chose changed him. For my money, he made the classic Faustian bargain. He achieved the ultimate in power and knowledge but, arguably, paid for it with his soul."

"I think that's a bit melodramatic," said Strickland.

"Look at his face in pictures taken shortly before he died," Randall said. "His eyes are haunted. You feel like you're staring into the depths of a broken man—a man who concluded that he had pursued supreme knowledge but instead produced a monster of biblical proportions."

"There may be some truth in that," Strickland said, "but the whole Joe McCarthy witch hunt, accusing him of being a Communist, and then revoking his government clearances, is what truly did him in. Oppenheimer did what he felt he had to do, and suffered the consequences."

Chapter 5

Robert Strickland's bike was in the shop with a blown clutch, and he was walking home alone late at night through Manhattan's Lower East Side. The dark, empty streets had an oily sheen.

An unexpected chill had descended on the city, and four men were gathered on a street corner, warming themselves by an oil drum filled with burning debris. Strickland made hard eye contact with one of the men as he passed, and the man looked away, back into the flames. After four years at NYU School of Medicine, Strickland felt a certain mastery of the streets of New York.

As he passed a dead-end alleyway, three strongly built young men stepped from the shadows. They were faceless in the dim light. Strickland spotted an exposed knife blade glinting from the cuff of a leather jacket.

"Your money and your watch," one of the men said. His voice was deep yet strangely hollow.

Strickland's heart quickened, his mind racing. And then he remembered . . .

Suddenly he was weightless, rising slowly from the ground. The men stood far below, drifting from his consciousness, though he was still vaguely aware of some grave danger.

For a moment, his concentration waned and he began falling. Then he regained focus and started to rise again, up alongside the ornate cornice of an early 1900s brownstone. Strickland examined the delicate texture of the stone carvings; they seemed profoundly beautiful. But in this state of fascination, he failed to notice an array of high-tension wires looming overhead. At the moment of contact, a popping shower of blue sparks rained down from his illuminated form. His body tensed, but to his amazement, there was no physical sensation as he ascended *through* the wires. He felt only a sense of exhilaration at having crossed a threshold.

* * *

Strickland awoke with a feeling of almost cosmic well-being. Momentarily disoriented, he scanned the bedroom of his Rockville condominium. The glowing clock face read 3:23 A.M. Throwing back the covers, he slipped into a bathrobe and walked down the hall to his study. He checked e-mail, but the only new message was from a reporter at the *Times,* apparently seeking a tour of the Ethnogenomics facility. After reading the first few sentences, he forwarded the message to NIH Media Relations, then deleted it from his in-box.

Next he logged on to the Ethnogenomics Center's extranet system, to retrieve the latest notes on the metabolic trigger research. He read through his own entries, Randall's observations, and those of the postdocs. The puzzle was almost complete, but as always, the final pieces were proving elusive. There was still at least one more key insight out there in the ether—he could feel it.

Strickland rubbed his puffy eyes. The dim light of the computer screen bathed the study in a ghostly hue. He stood and stretched his back, then flicked on the desk lamp and stared distractedly at the framed photos on the bookshelf. One of the shots, faded now with the years, showed his sister Susan and her young daughter, Grace. Strickland had taken it on the beach in Key West, during a break from his medical training. Grace was waving in that exaggerated preteen way. He smiled at the memory.

During his second year of residency, Grace had come down with what appeared to be a bad flu. They sent her home from the emergency room with orders to "drink fluids and get plenty of rest." But the next day, her mother brought her back in, feverish and disoriented. Something was obviously very wrong. Grace was next diagnosed as suffering from a severe urinary tract infection and was put on IV antibiotics. But the medication had little effect, and she began exhibiting bizarre mood swings and was soon only semilucid. The psych resident suggested that it might be the beginning symptoms of schizophrenia. Then her condition spiraled rapidly out of control. She began having seizures and then laughing and crying uncontrollably. She was sedated, and further blood work was ordered, as well as a spinal tap and an MRI. By the time her urine turned dark red and the attending physician finally made the proper call, Grace had already sustained severe brain trauma. She never regained consciousness, and died a few weeks later.

Grace had suffered from porphyria, an inherited disease resulting in the improper breakdown of an intermediary substance in the production of hemoglobin, the essential oxygen-carrying element of blood. The condition was rare and, with its confluence of wildly dissimilar symptoms, easy to misdiagnose. Tragically, her neurological damage had been made even worse by the antiseizure medications in the ER. Strickland had wondered in later years whether he would have made the proper call himself.

He walked over to the bookshelf to take a closer look at the picture. Grace seemed like a perfectly healthy young girl, already beginning her metamorphosis into womanhood. But even then the mechanisms had been slowly ticking away toward the moment when they would trigger a cascading chain of biochemical disasters. Susan was devastated, and never fully recovered from the blow.

Over the course of researching the disease, Strickland discovered that it tended to be found primarily in people of Dutch extraction. During his investigation, he became fascinated with genetics and with diseases specific to different ethnic groups. He found himself spending every spare moment in the library, accessing the latest papers on the subject over the Medline system.

After finishing his residency, he knew what he wanted to do. He applied for, and won, a postdoctoral fellowship at the NIH. Having always felt ill at ease with the intimacy of the doctor-patient relationship, he proved to be a natural for the solitude of research.

In his second year at Bethesda, Strickland's research helped identify several new gene defects in the heme pathway, which were ultimately responsible for the manifestation of porphyria. And he went on to help develop an inexpensive, easily administered blood test for the disease. When he heard through the NIH grapevine that there was talk of developing a department chartered to study ethnically specific genetic diseases, he used his porphyria work to lobby for the directorship. In the process, he coined the term "ethnogenomics." Within its first five years, his department had discovered over fifty new disease-causing gene mutations. Eth-gen became a stand-alone center at the NIH, comprising over a hundred researchers.

Strickland turned away from Grace's wild, enigmatic smile and stared out the window to the courtyard below. A ghostly plume of steam rose from the glowing swimming pool. He checked the clock again: 4:47 A.M. Fortunately, he had never needed much sleep—an invaluable physiological boon during his medical training.

He opened the metal pool gate and was soon floating facedown with mask and snorkel in the warm, luminescent waters, embraced by the familiar glowing latticework of rippled shadow and refraction. Letting his eyes go out of focus as he melded with the dance of light, he felt all sense of place and time fade away. Ideas moved through his mind with a fluidity and ease that transcended linear thought.

Finally falling into bed as the first rose tints of dawn gathered in the east, he drifted into several hours of deep, dreamless sleep.

Chapter 6

Jordan Randall typed the ID number of the requested skin sample into the lab's main database, then imported the DNA sequence data from the sample into the RES-5000 3-D computer graphics "reanimation" system. It was the final step in a complex and now regularly occurring analytical process.

Using the vast body of knowledge that had emerged from the Human Genome Project, it was now possible to produce a head-only computer-generated representation of a given subject based solely on the subject's DNA. Single-nucleotide polymorphisms (SNPs) were key to the process, providing data on the myriad traits that had come to be recognized as "the individual." The RES-5000 could render overall facial features—cheek, chin, nose, lips, forehead, hair and eye color, complexion—and even a synthesized voice based on larynx structure.

Genetic reanimation had become the hot new tool in forensic pathology. All it took was a strand of hair, a drop of blood, or a tiny skin sample to visually identify a victim or criminal. For both altruistic and revenue generating reasons, Strickland's lab had begun regularly performing such analyses.

Skin cells recovered from under the fingernails of a recent murder victim were the source of Randall's current genetic analysis. The crime's circumstances were similar to another murder case for which there was already a detailed suspect description. The RES-5000 image would either reinforce the connection or lead the investigation in a new direction. The technique was still considered somewhat experimental by the courts—roughly the same order of reliability as a polygraph test—and could be used to free or convict only with other corroborating evidence.

Strickland walked in and glanced at the subject materializing on the high-resolution monitor. "Just look at that face," he said. "A born killer if ever I saw one."

"You can't really tell," Randall replied solemnly. "I've seen enough to know."

"Just kidding, of course," Strickland said, grabbing his leather folio and heading back out the door. "I'm off to present our latest milestones to the Directors' Council. Back in an hour or so."

"Okay. You know where to find me—in here, playing God."

* * *

The impact of their work was increasingly troubling to Randall. Among other things, the entire basis of health insurance—a pooled and shared risk—was rapidly falling by the wayside. It was an increasingly simple matter to determine that someone harbored a predisposition to a disease process that would almost certainly manifest. And from an insurance carrier's perspective, why offer coverage on an already smoldering house?

With such issues in mind, Randall had made himself regularly available to the members of SEW (Scientists for an Ethical World), offering his expertise and advice. The organization of concerned scientists and some private citizens was attempting to guide the course of research and public policy in areas where science seemed to be rapidly outpacing cultural and ethical perspectives.

Randall stared up at the face still displayed on the lab monitor. Between his work in the sciences, driven only by the goal of discovery, and his faith-based focus on ethics and social justice, he sometimes felt split between two very different worlds.

* * *

By the time Strickland returned from the Directors' Council meeting, both he and Randall had missed lunch. Over coffee and sandwiches in the cafeteria, SEW came up again.

"If you'd get involved, even on an occasional basis," Randall urged, "your inputs would have tremendous impact."

"I just don't see it as my role," Strickland said.

Randall sighed. "I can't fathom that position. Look at what's happened just as a result of your work—parents who can't get health insurance, because their child tested positive for the porphyria gene."

"Again, a matter of public policy. I agree that it's wrong, and I'm more than happy to say so. But I see my efforts better concentrated elsewhere. With any luck, while they're busy arguing these issues, we may discover a cure, and the whole controversy will be moot."

"Right, and then the cost of *delivering* the cure will become the issue," said Randall, "and we'll be right back where we started."

"As I've said, I can't anticipate every possible repercussion of my work. I can exchange ideas and occasionally offer opinions, but I have to focus my time and energy."

Randall was about to counter this last point, but thought better of it. After this many years, he instinctively knew when such debates had played out and, if pursued, would lead only to acrimony. But even with their differences, there was no place he would rather be, either personally or professionally, than working alongside Robert Strickland.

It had been a long and unpredictable ride. After completing his medical residency, Randall had stayed on at Washington University in St. Louis. The genetic sequencing center there was putting the school on the scientific map, and Randall's undergraduate degree in bioinformatics made him a particularly valuable commodity. The massive quantities of information pouring out of the Human Genome Project made information processing—storing, enhancing, and interpreting data—the next wave of genomic investigation, and he was ultimately recruited by Washington U. as an assistant professor of medicine and bioinformatics. While there, he established himself as an innovator in computer graphics imaging for genomic data, pioneering many of the bedrock technologies used in 3-D reanimation systems, and becoming recognized among the handful of world authorities on the subject.

But when Strickland became director of the Ethnogenomics Center, his first recruiting call was to Randall. Randall would never forget the infectious, almost childlike enthusiasm in that voice on the line. Already well along the tenure track from his software work, he had understandably been reluctant to leave, but as Strickland outlined his goal of uncovering countless disease processes, with exciting clinical applications, he was soon hooked. And the position guaranteed Randall a pure research focus—no formal teaching, regular meetings, or scheduled distractions of any kind. It had been perhaps *the* watershed decision in his career.

Chapter 7

Taking a break from his summary work on the porphyria investigation, Strickland wandered into the lab to find Randall sitting at a workstation. "So *this* is where you get your hardware ideas," he said, grinning down at the copy of *Popular Science* on the desktop.

"Oh—glad you mentioned that," Randall said. "I almost forgot to show you . . ." He leafed through the magazine to the classifieds in the back. "One of my postdocs pointed this out. . . ."

Randall opened to a page marked with a sticky note. A half-page ad began,

> *Genomic Banking & Clone. Why let the ages separate you and your beloved pet? We offer complete cloning packages for all major species, with convenient payment plans. Call now for a free brochure and tissue preparation packet.*

"Yeah, a new twist on the puppy mill," Strickland said. "These labs are popping up everywhere—often in developing countries where there's almost zero government regulation. And I'm betting at least some of them are gearing up for full-scale human work."

Randall sighed. "It's a disturbing trend."

"But there's really no way to control it—it's the nature of the beast." Strickland paused on his way out. "By the way, when you reach a good break point, can you drop by my office? I've got something important to discuss with you."

"Give me half an hour."

Chapter 8

Strickland was poring over a stack of documents at his desk when Randall stuck his head in the door.

"Close the door and have a seat, would you, Jordan?"

Randall sat down, immediately struck by the seriousness and formality in his tone.

"We're about to receive an anthropological specimen for analysis," Strickland said. "I wanted to make you aware of some things beforehand."

"Any specific prep work involved?" Randall asked, already forming a mental list of supplies to check.

"The usual for dried blood samples," Strickland replied, "except that this specimen is particularly ancient."

"Even so, it sounds fairly routine. Why all the drama? I have to say, I almost felt like I was about to be canned."

"This involves the Vatican."

"The *Vatican*? What on earth would they . . ." A wave of realization passed over his face. Strickland was staring intently at him. "My God . . . is it the Shroud of Turin?"

Strickland nodded. "The Church would like us to do some analysis work."

"Of what nature?"

"The scope is pretty open-ended. Obviously, DNA analysis, with an emphasis on ethnogenomics. But they're also interested in chronology. Past carbon dating of the Shroud has been inconclusive, and the source of endless controversy and debate. Previous investigations reported the stains on the cloth to be blood, but they'd really like us to start at square one—see what we can find initially and then make recommendations for further analysis. 'Amaze us,' is what one of their representatives told me. Those were his actual words."

Randall paused. "Why didn't you tell me about this sooner?"

"There's been some dissension within the Holy See about releasing the sample—and about the analysis. Things have nearly fallen apart more than once. Neither side wanted the work acknowledged until it was an absolute certainty."

"And now it is?"

"It is. But it's still highly confidential. Only you and I, Director Burnham, and whatever essential support staff we require, are cleared to know."

"I've always been intrigued by the Shroud," Randall mused. "I even planned to go see it one day. . . . And now it's coming to *me*."

"I hope you're not disappointed by what we find."

"I don't expect to be," Randall replied, grinning.

"I think you're a bit too settled in your skin," Strickland said peevishly. "Some of your beliefs may prove completely wrong."

"If we're talking about faith, it's not a matter of right or wrong. It's more of a personal orientation."

"But if we're talking about the historical validity of the Shroud, there definitely *is* a right or wrong, true or false. And that's what we're being asked to determine."

"True," Randall replied. "And I'll grant you that overzealous belief can sometimes get in the way of uncovering scientific truth. But belief can also be a powerful force for personal growth. It's all a matter of knowing when and where to apply it."

"And our analysis of the Shroud of Turin isn't one of those when-and-wheres."

"Agreed. I'm just saying my intuition leads me to believe that the Shroud is a valid artifact. The Vatican obviously feels the same way or they wouldn't be exposing it to this level of scrutiny."

"We'll find out. Thankfully, our predispositions are irrelevant to any final determination."

"I'm with you a hundred percent," said Randall. "But belief is clearly what's driving the investigation; otherwise, nobody would be interested, one way or the other."

"I'm as interested as anyone," said Strickland, "and I do believe that a couple of millennia ago, a guy named Jesus in a backwater of the Roman Empire was a highly evolved spiritual teacher. But I'm not so sure about the whole 'Son of God' notion or the Resurrection. Previous carbon dating on the Shroud came up with a time frame in the Middle Ages—about the same time it first surfaced historically. It all sounds a bit suspicious."

"But there are just as many counter theories," Randall said, "one of them being that the cloth fibers are contaminated by a coating left behind by bacteria. It's theorized that the previous study may have inadvertently dated the coating and not the fibers beneath it."

"That's what bothers me," Strickland said. "No matter what facts emerge, people who believe will always find a way to keep on believing."

"That's probably true, but there's a reason for that. The Shroud goes much deeper than its ultimate validity as a historical artifact—in the same way that, to a Christian, a cross is much more than a couple of pieces of metal or wood. In the end, they both act as a physical bridge to the power of Jesus Christ and all that he stood for—inspiring states of transcendence and heightened spiritual awareness in the believer."

Strickland just nodded thoughtfully — his tacit acknowledgment that this was a debate that could never be won or lost.

Chapter 9

A week later, three emissaries from the Vatican arrived at the NIH complex. Strickland and Randall greeted them discreetly in the lobby—it was 6:30 in the evening, and most of the support staff had already left for the day. The youngest of the visitors, a tall, thin-featured man, stepped forward. "Dr. Enrico Rutigliano, chief science attaché of the Holy See," he said, smiling warmly and shaking their hands. The encounter seemed entirely congenial, but as Randall ushered the group through the lobby, he thought he saw the bulge of a weapon beneath the suit jacket of the stocky man flanking the attaché. The man silently remained behind as they approached the security metal detectors.

For some reason, Randall found his eyes repeatedly drawn to the young Vatican representative's gold tie clasp, which bore the image of an oak tree etched into its polished surface. He noticed that Strickland, too, glanced at the image.

Inside Strickland's office, the Shroud sample was removed from a padded briefcase that had been specifically molded for the purpose. It was a small, stained piece of rough-woven cloth, secured within a climate-controlled Plexiglas box. To the uninformed eye, it was nothing more than a small swatch of rag. But Randall felt his hands tremble slightly as the papal emissary passed it to him.

* * *

Strickland had already instructed NIH building maintenance to install a fingerprint recognition system and motion detector in one of the labs, with only himself and Randall programmed for access. The sample had arrived just before the beginning of the Columbus Day weekend, and neither of them felt entirely comfortable leaving it unattended for three days. Before leaving for the day, they each tested and retested the biometric security system. Finally satisfied, and having agreed to check the Shroud sample on alternate days of the long weekend, they began packing up their work.

"By the way," Randall said, "Mary and I are having a barbecue Sunday afternoon. Can you and Jennifer make it?"

"Thanks, Jordan, but Jenny and I aren't seeing each other anymore."

"Sorry to hear that."

"Don't be," Strickland said matter-of-factly. "I've got plans for the weekend. But thanks for the offer."

Randall knew better than to probe further. It had been years since Strickland's divorce. In the interim, there had been liaisons with numerous postdoc women passing through the NIH. But his old friend seemed to keep an emotional distance that prevented anything serious from ever taking hold.

He recognized Strickland's "plans" comment as code for his usual downtime outing: a long motorcycle ride along Highway 81 through the Blue Ridge Mountains. It had been a favorite haunt since his arrival at the NIH.

"Give my best to Mary," Strickland said, heading out the door with his hard-shell case full of motorcycle gear.

"Will do. Ride safe."

On his way out, Randall double-checked the room containing the Shroud sample. He stared in at the Plexiglas container for a long moment, then reset the motion detector and locked the door.

Chapter 10

Strickland carefully stomped his boots, one at a time, at the main entrance of the Ethnogenomics Center. The first rains of autumn had come with a vengeance, and there was mud everywhere. While making the transition onto 355, a big rig had forced an old Buick monster into his lane, but he had survived thanks to some quick evasive maneuvers—a benefit of his years riding in New York City.

After hanging his helmet and jumpsuit in the office closet, Strickland headed for the lab's coffee room to warm up, and bumped into Randall. Together they confirmed that the new security system had operated properly over the long weekend; then they caught up on personal matters.

"So, how was the barbecue?" Strickland asked, unwrapping a teabag and bobbing it in his cup.

"Great. Wish you could have been there. Mary invited a girlfriend from work—I think you would have liked her."

Strickland nodded but said nothing.

"How was Eighty-one?" Randall asked.

"Amazing. The fall leaves are so gorgeous they're a road hazard."

After briefly reviewing their schedules for the day, Randall grabbed his coffee cup and thrust a stack of documents under one arm. "Well, duty calls."

Both had instructed their administrative assistants to keep their calendars as open as possible in the coming weeks. To avoid arousing suspicion, the Shroud work was secretly brought under the umbrella of a project already under way: helping the Egyptian government research the genealogy of two recently discovered mummies. Burial artifacts and various markings indicated that the mummies were immediate members of the royal family of Tutankhamen. It was the lab's job to corroborate that hypothesis at the genetic level.

Chapter 11

As they settled into their analysis of the Shroud sample, Randall seemed to approach every new task with a heightened sense of reverence, like a monk delicately arranging sacred artifacts. Strickland found it a little annoying at times.

Within days, they had corroborated the work of previous studies—the stains on the cloth were indeed human blood: type AB, Rh+. At one step in their initial analysis, Randall suggested delegating some routine lab work to a grad student, but Strickland reiterated that they were to enlist support staff only on a strictly as-needed basis.

Randall smiled and pulled out the necessary labware. "Oh, well," he said, "this'll be a nice review of Biochem 425—remember that?"

"Seems like another lifetime, but I remember it well," Strickland said.

After a panel of blood work, the Shroud sample entered into the dating phase—something of vital interest to their client.

"I'm actually a bit surprised they sanctioned this study," Randall said, typing at a nearby analysis workstation. "You might think they'd want to back away from any further controversy."

"There *have* been some recent power struggles within the Vatican," Strickland replied. "Between the older, hard-line traditionalists and a newer generation of science-oriented moderates. Keep in mind, the pope now has his own astrophysicist. And in 1996, John Paul II publicly declared evolution to be 'more than a hypothesis.' He even apologized for the Church nearly burning Galileo at the stake four centuries ago. But my sense is, there are still plenty of medieval forces left in Rome—and I'm pretty sure they're adamantly opposed to investigations like this."

"Well, so far, things seem to be going fairly smoothly, with no interference or oversight of our work," said Randall.

"Exactly. *So far.* If history has shown us anything, the old guard in a given arena rarely sits idly by while their world comes down around them."

"Well, I'd hardly call this work fodder for bringing the walls down around them," said Randall.

"That remains to be seen," said Strickland.

Chapter 12

In his early research on the Shroud, Strickland learned that carbon dating performed during the 1980s had indicated an approximate origin date of AD 1300—about the same time the artifact first surfaced in historical records. But later analyses, including those by the inventor of the most common form of carbon dating, had cast doubt on these findings. Some proposed that the tested Shroud sample had been contaminated by a "bioplastic" coating—a microthin veneer produced by bacteria over the course of centuries. Other carbon dating performed on extremely old cloth fibers proved similarly skewed by such coatings, the catch being that the two layers could not be effectively separated without destroying both.

But recent genomic discoveries offered an alternative to radiocarbon dating, making it possible to read a built-in "molecular clock" in historical artifacts that contained sufficient intact DNA.

Strickland had been born since the days when DNA was believed confined to the cellular nucleus. But in the mid-1960s, extranuclear DNA was discovered within the mitochondria—the tiny organelles supplying energy to the cell. It was found that mitochondria replicated themselves through a process of simple asexual fission, duplicating their DNA once they reached a certain size, then pinching themselves in half. Research also revealed that the mitochondria of the sperm cell remained outside the egg during sexual reproduction. Thus, except for any random mutations, one's mitochondrial DNA (mtDNA) was identical to the mother's, the maternal grandmother's, and her mother's, remaining unchanged from generation to generation. Since mtDNA remained unaltered by the sexual union of DNA, the passage of time could be tracked through an analysis of its natural mutation rate.

Accurate calibration of the mutation rate for mitochondrial DNA had been made possible by the discovery of various well-preserved "icemen." A prime specimen found in a Canadian glacier was carbon dated at 550 years old, and since the specimen was frozen solid, there was no possibility of a bioplastic coating. Another iceman, found in the Italian Alps near the Austrian border, was dated at 5,300 years old. By studying the differences in mtDNA sequences in various iceman samples, a mutation rate-of-change formulation was created that allowed such mutations to be used as a secondary means of determining a sample's age. The technique was validated in subsequent iceman discoveries—through both carbon dating and the analysis of period-specific materials such as stone, iron, and bronze found alongside the icemen.

Using these well-honed techniques, Strickland and Randall began the task of extracting and processing DNA from the Shroud sample. Because red blood cells contained no nucleus—thereby maximizing their storage capacity for oxygen—they also possessed essentially no DNA. Knowing they might later want to sequence portions of the Shroud's nuclear DNA, the investigators focused their analysis on the disease-fighting white blood cells.

Strickland and Randall stared at the computer workstation monitor as it displayed the initial mtDNA sequence data.

"We may actually be looking at portions of the genetic code of Jesus and Mary," Randall marveled.

After many hours of processing, the Gen-Chron workstation sounded its completion tone. Strickland entered a password, and the results of the dating estimate for the Shroud sample appeared on the screen: "1,983 years old, error factor ± 40 years."

"Incredible," Strickland breathed. "We're actually in the zone!" The excitement in his voice was a surprise, even to him.

Chapter 13

Because the Vatican's prime directive was to go beyond previous studies, Strickland and Randall felt compelled to expand the scope of their investigation. In a recent journal article, Randall had read about a Bedouin tribe of the Negev Desert in southern Israel who were direct descendents of Israel's biblical-era inhabitants. They were also known for having remained rigidly isolated from the outside world.

Recent genetic-disease studies had focused on groups that were physically isolated by geography or culture. Iceland was a prime example, and various genomic studies had been combing through Icelandic government medical records since the late 1990s. Being geographically isolated and with little immigration, the country offered an invaluable window on the genetics of disease. Normally, the vast genetic variability found within large populations made locating a disease-causing mutation a bit like searching for a needle in a haystack. But with an extremely homogeneous gene pool, it became far easier to pinpoint such a mutation. If a disorder occurred in such an isolated group, and those afflicted with the disease all shared a common mutation, it was a safe bet that the pernicious gene had been found.

The Bedouins of the Negev had served just such a purpose in the journal article, shedding new light on the mechanism of the gene defect responsible for hereditary inclusion body myopathy, a degenerative disease of the muscles.

After lengthy discussions with the study's authors, Strickland and Randall decided that the tribe's genome might provide invaluable additional data for their study. The Negev group had remained isolated for centuries, even from Bedouins in the surrounding region. The hope was that there might be sequences buried in their DNA that could be found nowhere else on earth. If some of those sequences were also found in the Shroud data, it would provide a critical frame of reference for the sample, pointing back to the time and place of Jesus.

Since Randall had a working wife and two school-age children, Strickland was the obvious choice for the trip. As a physician, he was amply qualified to perform any DNA collection procedures, and a summer during med school working at a New Mexico Indian reservation clinic had acquainted him with some of the privacy and cultural concerns of indigenous peoples.

Randall suggested one of his star postdocs, Connie Franklin, to assist Strickland on the trip.

In the days before the trip, Strickland, Randall, and Franklin busied themselves preparing and packing supplies. The collection effort was being conducted under the auspices of the World Health Organization, and in return for the Bedouin group's cooperation, WHO had promised them stores of food and basic medical supplies.

* * *

After a long layover at London Heathrow, Strickland and Franklin arrived at Ben-Gurion International, tired and jet-lagged, just in time for evening rush hour. The interminable cab ride into Tel Aviv was followed by a quick snack at the hotel café before they stumbled, exhausted, into their rooms.

Early the next morning, they rented a Land Rover and drove to the local World Health Organization office. There they were introduced to Asiyah Saleh, a middle-aged Palestinian nurse wearing a black blouse and hijab head scarf. She had a sharp, birdlike nose, weathered features, and a crisp, businesslike manner, all of which seemed at odds with her soft, mellifluous voice. Strickland detected a gentleness about her, particularly in her eyes.

Saleh directed them to the apartment of the young man who was to be their guide—Ahmed Habib. He was bearded, tall, and strongly built, with the thick hands of a workman. Born into a nomadic Bedouin tribe, Habib had grown up in the desert before coming to Tel Aviv for university studies.

Franklin, along with Saleh and Habib, had simply been told that they were visiting the Bedouin tribe to gather information about a gene mutation suspected of playing a role in degenerative diseases of the muscles. The Bedouins they planned to study inhabited an area of the Negev some seventy-five miles outside Beersheba. While other Bedouin tribes had become more modernized, even going so far as to use cell phones, this group was reminiscent of the American Amish clans, avoiding all unnecessary mixing with the outside world.

Chapter 14

As they left the city behind, the sky lost its brown haze and turned a deep, almost cobalt blue, reminding Strickland of photographs he had seen taken from the edge of space. The party speeded along Highway 60, the major artery into a sere landscape that glowed in a dramatic palette of alien colors, from ochers to rusts, to brilliant reds. Soon they were within sight of the rugged brown hills surrounding Jerusalem, and then the spires and towers of the fabled city itself.

Franklin wrapped a scarf around her blond hair, which was flying wildly in the wind. Strickland caught himself gazing at her for a long moment. Apparently sensing his attention, she glanced over and smiled, then grabbed the roll bar overhead and turned her attention back to the dream landscape before them.

Strickland wished he had time to see Jerusalem in depth—the Jewish Quarter and the Western Wall, the Muslim Quarter, and the Dome of the Rock. As an undergraduate, he had taken a comparative religion course at the urging of an old high-school friend and had been struck by the common philosophical threads that ran through all faiths. He had since concluded that the rituals and belief systems of each were merely conduits toward attaining states of spiritual transcendence and personal compassion. But on an intellectual and historical level, he was still fascinated by the dogma, practices, and struggles of each.

The surrounding terrain became ever more barren as they continued their journey. They neared Hebron, which meant passing through both Palestinian and Israeli checkpoints. Armored military vehicles were everywhere, flanked by concertina wire barricades. It seemed amazing that the cradle of so many of the world's religions should be so torn by strife and violence.

Entering the checkpoint, Strickland watched as a group of Israeli soldiers herded a busload of Palestinian workers through the security zone. The animosity between the two groups was palpable. The soldiers held their M16 rifles vertical to the sky, fingers poised on the triggers.

After searching the bus, the Israeli soldiers gave the okay, and a fortified gate was opened. Just then a Palestinian boy on the other side, eyes blazing with resentment, hurled a jagged rock through the opening.

It just missed one of the soldiers, clattering to the ground beside him. The soldiers instinctively spun around, leveling their weapons in the perceived direction of the thrower. Strickland and Franklin held their breath, fearing the worst. But the rock-throwing boy had melted into the crowd, and the soldiers slowly lowered their weapons and waved the bus through.

Several hundred yards farther along, they passed through the Palestinian side of the checkpoint. A man wearing a kaffiyeh headdress glanced first at Saleh, then at Habib, and finally at Strickland and Franklin. He was clearly confused about where to place them in his worldview.

In checking their papers, he discovered that Strickland and Franklin were U.S. citizens, and zeroed in on them. He stood close to Strickland, looking him in the eye.

"What is your business here?" he asked, his mouth curling at the edge.

"I'm a scientist," Strickland replied.

The guard eyed Franklin next. "And her?"

"She also is a scientist."

The man rested his hand on the Ingram Mini submachine gun slung over his shoulder. "So, as a scientist, you seek the truth?" he asked with a smug expression.

"In a sense," Strickland said, holding the man's gaze.

"And if you are an American, then you must also believe in *freedom*."

Strickland offered no response.

"Look around you," the man said, gesturing at the barbed-wire enclosures. "Is this freedom?"

By now, the growing line of drivers behind them were honking angrily and shouting at the guard in Arabic.

Finally, the guard handed their passports back and waved them through, though he spat on the ground as they pulled away.

The Land Rover crawled for several miles through the dusty lines of traffic leading out of the city. Franklin was visibly drained by the checkpoint encounter.

"Are you all right?" Strickland asked, patting her on the shoulder.

"Yeah, I guess," she sighed, looking out at the bustling crowds. "Seeing all this up close is a very different experience from reading about it in the paper or watching the news. We need to know more about what's *really* going on in the world—with more one-on-one contact between different cultures."

"I'm with you there," Strickland said. "No matter what the source, media always comes filtered, with a built-in cultural bias. There's just no substitute for actually being there."

* * *

After leaving the city, their mood gradually lightened. Franklin tapped Strickland on the shoulder, pointing excitedly to the distant sands, where a caravan of Bedouins on camels was making its way toward Beersheba. Then, to the east, they spotted the massive cliff-top fortress of Masada, home to Herod the Great, and site of the Jews' revolt against Rome.

At dusk, they turned west into the Negev, heading down a succession of increasingly rougher roads. There were fewer and fewer cars as they continued into the gathering darkness. Saleh leaned into Strickland to be heard over the roar of the wind.

"We will arrive in about one hour," she said, gazing into the distance.

Sometime later, they entered a vast basin bordered by violet-gray mountains. "We will stop here," Habib announced, and with his help, they set up their camp at the edge of the Bedouin village. The young man made initial contact with the Bedouins, reiterating the earlier agreement made with the WHO. He was ushered into a large tent and did not return for over half an hour.

Finally, Strickland was brought to meet the tribal leader—a tall, sinewy man with a deeply lined face and piercing eyes. As Strickland approached carrying a canvas sack cinched with a drawstring, the elder watched him intently. Strickland slowly opened the bag, withdrew a large, ornate brass teapot, and handed it to the chieftain.

The elder rubbed his leathery hands over its polished surface, then looked up at Strickland and smiled broadly. Opening his palm toward the tent, he said, "*Shukran.*"

Walking to the tent, they passed a young girl, laughing and chasing after several other children. For no apparent reason, she turned and smiled at Strickland, holding his gaze for a moment. Something about her eyes reminded him of his niece, Grace. He smiled back, but she had already darted away to join her shrieking playmates.

Inside the main tent, Strickland reiterated through the interpreter that his work involved scientific research that would lead to cures for many kinds of disease. (That was true, after all, he reminded himself, even if not in this particular instance.) He explained that the tribe had unique characteristics that were highly valuable to science. The tribesmen were initially reluctant—they had already aided one research project; why should another be necessary?

"This study is also extremely important," Strickland said dramatically. "No other tribe can fulfill this destiny."

The elders looked back and forth among themselves with serious expressions. Strickland added that he had stores of dried fruits and nuts, in addition to the agreed-upon supplies, to donate to the village. The tent fell silent as the tribal leader probed Strickland with his eyes. Almost imperceptibly, he nodded. Then he clapped his hands together, and a woman delivered a stone pot filled with a bitter-tasting mint tea.

After a dinner of lamb stew and flat bread, Strickland returned to the camp to prepare supplies for tomorrow's collection effort. Before going to bed, he, Franklin, Habib, and Saleh sat around a crackling campfire. Strickland prepared more of the mint tea, using a silk bag the tribal elder had given him. His appreciation for the brew had somehow changed over the course of the evening—now he tasted a hidden sweetness, with an aftertaste of some fruit he couldn't quite place.

After the tea, Saleh went to her tent, and soon Habib went to his. Only Franklin and Strickland remained. In the moonless darkness lit only by the little brushwood fire, she told him about growing up on a hog farm in Iowa, and the culture shock of coming from a school of a hundred students to UC Berkeley. She tossed her head back and laughed at his story about losing a bet during medical school and having to walk five city blocks in lower Manhattan, wearing nothing but a tiny Speedo, flip-flops, and a straw cowboy hat.

Franklin pulled a blond lock away from her face and looked over at him for a long moment, as she had earlier in the Land Rover. Then she gazed thoughtfully into the fire, stirring it with a stick.

As he stared into the flames, he heard himself say, "We'd better hit it. Tomorrow's going to be very busy."

"You're probably right," she said, looking over at him then back into the fire. "Good night," she said, as she stood.

"Good night," he replied.

Strickland watched as she disappeared into the darkness. As he extinguished the dwindling campfire with handfuls of sand, a sudden and profound sense of loneliness came over him. He had often structured his life around solitude, but lately there was an emptiness to it. Many of his most cherished activities had somehow lost their appeal—even riding the BMW just didn't give him the same sense of exhilaration.

Unable to sleep, he leaned back against a large rock, still warm from the sun, and folded his arms behind his head. He was soon captivated by the silent presence the landscape seemed to exude. There seemed to be an almost palpable energy, as if thousands of years of human consciousness and spiritual struggle had imbued the very rocks with power. He stared up into the dark vault of sky. The Milky Way formed a broad, glowing swath like diamond dust flung against black velvet. A meteorite flashed in a long, bright arc and was gone in an eyeblink. Beyond it, the slower, feebler track of a satellite marched across the autumn constellations, eventually disappearing behind the distant hills.

* * *

Strickland was flying again, levitating outside his old brownstone in the East Village. He could hear a fire bell clanging, and a strange animal wail. As he rose in the air, a jagged piece of metal on the fire escape ladder snagged his trouser leg, holding him fast like a tethered balloon. This complication played havoc with his focus, causing him to fall and then rise again as the ladder's rough edge dug into his thigh. Suddenly, he awoke.

A bleating goat outside was nudging his leg through the tent's nylon wall, its bell clanging with each movement. As the animal sought an opening, Strickland saw its silhouette projected on the tent cloth by the rising sun, and now he could also smell its earthy tang.

He crawled out of the tent and stood up, taking in the desert morning. A bright haze lined the horizon, and he could feel the dawn chill being driven back by the already blazing sun. Before him stretched a sea of white tents against the sere, yellow-brown sand. The village was arrayed in a sprawling circle, with spokelike passages leading to a central tent, larger than the rest.

"*As-salaam alaikum,*" Habib greeted him, gesturing to a bowl of toasted bread soaked in a hot brown liquid. Sensing Strickland's trepidation, Habib said, "Courtesy of the sheikh. For whatever reason, he seems to like you. A traditional Bedouin breakfast—*gourass* bread soaked in tea and goat milk. All the major food groups." He smiled. "And *bonn,*" he said, raising a small china cup, "made from green coffee beans ground with ginger."

"Why not?" said Strickland, stretching his back. "When in the Negev . . ."

In the distance, a line of camels laden with cargo crested a long dune, their guttural groans audible even at this distance.

"Good morning," Franklin said, behind him. She surveyed the timeless scene. "Wow . . . definitely not in Iowa anymore."

"Well, they do have goats," Strickland remarked.

"Yeah, I knew I smelled something familiar when I woke up."

Franklin accepted a bowl of the traditional breakfast from Habib but did not sit next to Strickland. Soon Nurse Saleh appeared and sat beside her.

After Franklin and Saleh had eaten, Habib excused himself to arrange their day with the tribal chieftain. He returned several minutes later.

"There's really some kind of connection between you two—or at least he seems to think so," Habib told Strickland. "I think he views you as a peer, a sheikh from America. He says that his people are entirely at your disposal."

"Please thank him for his graciousness, and for the delicious breakfast."

"I think you'll have the opportunity yourself. He's invited us all to dinner in his tent tonight. Oh, by the way, you'll need to do the sampling of the men, with Ms. Franklin and Nurse Saleh handling the women."

"I'll get everything ready," said Franklin, finishing the last of her *bonn* from the china cup. "Good stuff," she said to Habib. "Has a nice kick."

* * *

The tribe had previously been genetically studied, so there was little apprehension in the process. The sampling consisted of scrubbing the inside of the cheek six times with a rough textured swab. But one elderly man seemed hesitant to enter as Strickland pulled back the tent flap.

"Please come in, it's very safe," said Strickland, with Habib translating.

As the man entered, Strickland caught a brief glimpse of the young girl he had seen the night before. She stood patiently near the opening.

The old man spoke to Habib, who translated for him. "This is my granddaughter," he smiled. "She is waiting for me."

The man sat down and tentatively opened his mouth. He winced slightly as Strickland scrubbed inside his cheek.

"That's it!" Strickland said.

The man nodded appreciatively. As he left, the little girl stared in at Strickland and smiled beatifically, then took her grandfather's hand and walked away.

* * *

That evening, they wended their way along one of the passages in the encampment, to the large tent in the center. Habib led the way with a kerosene lantern that threw flickering shadows on the tent walls as they passed. Everyone they saw nodded respectfully in deference to their position as dining guests of the sheikh.

Inside the octagonal tent, the air was scented with cinnamon. Flickering candles lit a low wooden table set with dishes of roasted lamb, rice, kofta, freshly baked bread, and bowls of thick red and green broth. The sheikh's piercing eyes glinted in the dim candlelight. He gestured to Strickland, patting the pillow beside him. Habib sat on Strickland's other side to translate, and Franklin and Saleh sat across from the three men.

Habib introduced everyone. "Abdul-Bar," said the sheikh, bowing slightly to each of them with his hands on his heart. They replied in kind.

"Bob," Strickland said. "*Bub!*" the elder repeated back with relish.

Despite the language barrier, Abdul-Bar proved to be a charming dinner companion, regaling them with tales of his adventures and conquests in the desert as a young man.

"I learned very early that the desert has a soul . . . a power," he said, his eyes glinting in the golden light. The wise man *merges* with that power and learns the ways of its strength. The fool does not, and is destroyed."

Strickland found himself occasionally averting his eyes from the old chieftain as they conversed—his gaze was almost too soul searching. It was clear why the man had risen to his position of leadership, for he possessed a palpable energy and charisma.

Across the table, Franklin and Saleh conversed at length about the role of the World Health Organization, and their mutual interests in disease prevention in the developing world. Strickland found himself momentarily pulled in by the discussion, then the sheikh spoke directly to him, pausing to let Habib translate. "I can often see into men's eyes," he said without a hint of egotism. "I sense that the desert also speaks to you, and that this journey is about more than just your science."

Strickland looked back at him without speaking, and the old man placed his hand on his wrist. At once, Strickland felt a palpable warmth enter his body. As he looked into the old man's eyes in the flickering candlelight, he felt suddenly disoriented, though not unpleasantly so, as if time and space were slightly out of phase.

"You will find what you seek," the old man announced. "But not here, not yet."

Chapter 15

As soon as Strickland returned to the lab, he and Randall went to work on the Bedouin tissue swabs. Back in his familiar surroundings and regular routine, the encounter with Abdul-Barr seemed like a dream, an altered reality stemming from the exotic desert setting and the personal charisma of the tribal leader. He soon put the incident out of his mind, and settled into processing the collected data.

In an attempt to cover as large a genetic cross-section of the tribe as possible, he had sampled twenty-six of the Bedouin men and boys, and Franklin had sampled twenty-four women and girls. To further maximize data diversity, he had restricted the analysis to tribe members who were no more closely related than first cousins.

A few days back from the trip, Franklin caught Strickland and Randall in the hallway. "When can I get started on the Bedouin sequence analysis?" she asked Randall.

The two men exchanged a wary glance, and Randall said, "I'm afraid that for confidential reasons, only Bob and I will be working on that project."

Franklin cut her eyes at Strickland. "Okay . . . I have other work to do," she said tersely, and walked away. As she rounded the corner, Strickland saw her glance back.

* * *

Using the massive genetic databases at the Ethnogenomics Center, Strickland and Randall narrowed their focus to regions of the human genome containing SNPs found only in Middle Eastern populations. Then they looked for variations unique to the Bedouin tribe—not found in other modern-day inhabitants of the region.

After a week's worth of database analysis, the two scientists peered at the computer monitor as the final results were displayed. A distinct sequence unique to the sample group appeared, then three, then five, then a rapid succession of a dozen more. Several of the unusual sequences were located on the same chromosome, while others were scattered throughout the genome. When the analysis was finished, they had registered thirty-one sequences unique to the Bedouin tribesmen—far more than expected.

The next step was to search for those same sequences within the Shroud sample. Any matching sequences would further tie the sample to the time and place of the biblical Jesus. Because the extremely fractured nature of the Shroud DNA would make locating these regions through traditional sequencing analysis too costly and time intensive, Randall ordered custom-manufactured DNA chips containing the sought-after sequences. Like one side of a Velcro strip, the sequences were microscopically etched into glass on the chips and would bind only with a specific set of sister DNA sequences from the Shroud sample.

Several days later the chips arrived. Strickland and Randall applied a prepared solution from the Shroud sample to the chips, then waited for the laser probe to excite any fluorescent-tagged Shroud DNA that might be bound to the chips.

After several seconds, the equipment displayed its results, indicating seven distinct matches.

"We've got hits!" Randall blurted.

Strickland stared in silence at the workstation screen.

Chapter 16

Strickland sifted through several phone messages on his desk, then shuffled absently through a stack of funding proposals. Unable to concentrate, he stopped and stared out the window, thinking again of the sequences from the Bedouin tribespeople and their matches within the Shroud DNA. It seemed inconceivable. He had assumed that the investigation would merely corroborate previous research on the Shroud, and that would be the end of it. Now he scarcely knew *what* to think.

His workstation played the familiar two-tone announcement of incoming e-mail. Something about the address looked familiar. He clicked on the entry, and a window popped open.

> To: Robert.Strickland@eth-gen.nih.gov
> From: Sara.Bender@nytimes.com
> Subject: Genomic Sciences Book
>
> Dear Dr. Strickland,
>
> As I mentioned in a previous message, I am writing a book on the implications and repercussions of genomic discoveries. In the course of researching the societal impact of genetic disease testing, I read your article in *Nature* about the ethnogenomic roots of Porphyria. I found it fascinating. It would be very helpful to discuss some key topics with you—ranging from the responsibilities of the scientist to the effect of these new technologies on society at large. I look forward to talking further with you!
>
> Best Regards,
>
> Sara Bender
> Staff Writer, New York Times

He flagged the message for NIH Media Relations but didn't forward it this time.

A half hour later, his office phone rang. He waited for his assistant to take it, then glanced at his watch: 5:42 P.M.—George had already left for the day. The phone rang three more times. He considered letting it roll over to voice mail but finally picked up.

"Strickland."

"Hello, Dr. Strickland, this is Sara Bender from the *New York Times*."

"I just got your e-mail," Strickland said. "You're pretty quick on the follow-up."

"I guess it's the reporter in me," she said. "When I find an intriguing story, I dive in."

Something in the tone of her voice made him soften a bit. "I was surprised when you mentioned the *Nature* article," he said. "That was pretty technical stuff."

As he spoke, Strickland entered Bender's name into a search engine and received over 30,000 hits. The first few entries were from the *New York Times* site, detailing her various journalistic awards for coverage in Chechnya and the second Gulf war.

"I spent my first two years at Columbia as a bio major," she explained, "before I discovered the school newspaper. Also, organic chemistry and I were not friends."

"Organic has been the demise of many," Strickland said.

"Well, it was certainly a catalyst for change, though I might not call it 'demise.'"

He laughed. "You're right—poor choice of words."

"I'd be happy to drop by the NIH and verify my existence, and also discuss some of the issues I mentioned in the e-mail."

"Umm . . . to be honest, our schedule's pretty tight right now," he said.

Not to be so easily deterred, she said, "My goal with this book is to demystify some of the hysteria surrounding genomic discoveries. But there are obviously some issues of genuine concern—like privacy, and how genetic information will be used further down the road. Also, I'd like to examine the role and responsibility of the scientist in this whole process—that's truly fascinating to me. One of my all-time tragic heroes is Robert Oppenheimer."

"You're good, aren't you?" Strickland said.

"How so?" There was no mistaking the bristle in her tone.

"If I were suspicious by nature, I might think you'd done your homework on me and came prepared to jazz me up."

"What you hear is what you get, Doctor. You'll find that I'm a pretty straight shooter."

Strickland paused, then quietly checked his online calendar. "Okay, here's what I'm willing to do. Why don't you meet with me and my deputy, Dr. Jordan Randall, over lunch. How about this Friday? I'll order out for pizza."

"Okay, pizza it is," Bender said.

"We tend to eat late around here," Strickland added. "Let's make it one forty-five. I'll have a visitor's badge waiting for you in the lobby."

"Okay, I'm looking forward to it," she said. "By the way, I like mushrooms and bell peppers."

"Hmm, I'll be sure to note that. See you then."

Checking his watch, he realized she had timed the call perfectly to hit the dead zone—when support staff had typically left for the day and people tended to answer their own phones.

He returned to the search engine query and pulled up a grainy image of Bender in a flak jacket, standing next to the burned-out shell of an armored vehicle. In the distance, the billowing smoke of post invasion Baghdad filled the sky. In addition to her rugged beauty, there was something compelling about Bender—something deep and probing in the eyes. Against that violent, chaotic backdrop, they created a haunting visual.

Chapter 17

After the call to Strickland, Sara Bender gathered up her notes and placed them in a manila folder marked "NIH." She walked distractedly to the window and gazed out at the expansive view of Central Park, where an errant gust of wind passed like a wave through a stand of large willows. The phone rang.

"Sara . . . can you hear me?" a familiar male voice said, the connection cutting in and out.

Her face lit up. "Yes. Where are you?"

"On a plane, heading for Dallas. I'll be there a couple of days. Our phone negotiations broke down, so I'm going to try a face-to-face. If I bring in this deal, we'll go to St. Barts. How's that sound?"

"That would be nice," she said, gazing out the window again. "I think we need some time—"

"I know," he interrupted with a distracted urgency. "Look, I'll be at the Four Seasons if you need me." The connection began breaking up again. "We're about to push back from the gate. I—" Then the connection went dead. Sara held on for several more seconds to see if it might come back, then slowly put the receiver down.

She walked down the hall to a small room in the back, her footsteps echoing along the hardwood floors. Climbing onto an exercise bike, she began pedaling vigorously while staring out at the windswept trees below.

Chapter 18

Riding home from the NIH, Strickland found himself violating the cardinal rule of motorcycling—his mind was not on the road. He eased the handgrip forward, bringing it down to a safer sixty-five.

At home, he ordered out for garlic shrimp pasta and salad, then poured himself a glass of cabernet. Sprawled on the couch, he sipped his wine while flipping through the TV channels, producing a jarring montage of light and sound.

A woman's face suddenly flashed past, and a wave of emotion swept through him. He backtracked several channels until he relocated the news report. His ex-wife's image filled the screen.

". . . We're speaking with Marian Jensen, chief economic strategist with Morgan Stanley," the reporter was saying.

Strickland studied the nuances of Marian's face as she delivered her rapid-fire encapsulation of the current state of various economic sectors. It was an insightful thumbnail analysis of the forces driving the current markets.

He had immediately been attracted to Marian's intellect and intensity. She was the antithesis of the struggling artists and actresses he had dated in the East Village during his medical training. His girlfriend at the time had dragged him to a small gallery opening where she was displaying some of her work. In the end, she spent most of the evening working the room, and he spent most of his time talking with Marian. Within a month, they had moved in together.

In certain ways, they couldn't have been more alike. They were both consumed by the academic rigor of their chosen fields. Marian was midway through her economics PhD at NYU, while Strickland was nearing the end of his internship.

She was exciting and supremely self-assured, and he had been drawn to that sense of confidence from the moment he met her. Marian was perhaps the first woman he ever dated whom he considered his intellectual equal. But she was tightly wound, and driven by career aspirations—like him. The following year, Strickland began his residency in St. Louis, and Marian joined Chase Manhattan's economic forecasting division.

They limped along that way for the next three years, dividing their time between the two cities. They broke up briefly during Strickland's first year of residency, then patched things up, and got married in his second year, each convinced that the geographic impasse would somehow resolve itself.

And when Strickland completed his residency in St. Louis, resolution was finally in sight. But the death of his niece was the critical nudge in the direction of research, and he applied for a fellowship at the NIH. They hashed over some different scenarios—she might look for something in D.C, or he might try to find training closer to Manhattan. But they were each pulled by the power centers of their chosen fields, and unwilling to resist that pull.

Their weekends together became fewer and further between. And when they did get together, they often descended into petty arguments. In the end, they simply stopped communicating. There were a few halfhearted tries at reconciliation, a few sessions of couples counseling, but nothing seemed to help. By the time they filed for divorce, it was little more than a formality.

Strickland continued staring at Marian's face on the screen. He tried to see behind the eyes, to imagine what was going on in her life. Occasionally, her mouth softened at the corners, hinting at a certain girlish vulnerability. It reminded him of the first time they kissed. But just when he seemed to catch a glimpse of something true, the camera cut back to the blonde news anchor.

* * *

When the food finally arrived, Strickland had just logged on to the NIH extranet, which allowed him access to the lab's gene analysis systems. He stopped long enough to scoop the pasta and salad onto a plate, then sat back at the computer.

By nine that evening, he had again compared the Shroud and Bedouin sequences. The seven matches between the two sets could be found in no other known genetic populations anywhere in the world. In conjunction with the mitochondrial DNA analysis, there seemed little doubt: the Shroud DNA was of ancient Middle Eastern origin. The implications sent a tremor through him.

Before bed, Strickland sat out on the balcony, gazing at the lights dotting the suburban landscape beyond, letting his mind clear. He sat upright, closing his eyes, and went into the zone almost at once. A diffuse blue spot appeared in the center of his vision as he focused on his breath, letting go of all extraneous thought. His concentration held, and he maintained the state for more than an hour.

Chapter 19

Strickland and Randall spent the early afternoon in the conference room, compiling and organizing their notes on the Bedouin and Shroud sequences. Strickland closed the door when Randall began synopsizing their findings on the whiteboard.

Moments later, George knocked and entered with a large pizza. "This was just delivered in the lobby," he said. "Hope you were expecting it."

"Oh, I forgot all about it," said Randall. "The reporter from the *Times* is coming today, right?"

"We'll see," Strickland said with a note of mild irritation. "She's already late."

"Oh, well, if she doesn't show, more for us. Mind if I start?" he asked. "I'm starving."

"Sure, go ahead."

After wolfing down half a slice, Randall went back to the whiteboard, noting in tabular form the chromosome locations and base pair sequence lengths common to the Shroud and Bedouin samples. He paused to take another bite of pizza. Just then, after a perfunctory knock, the door opened again and George ushered Sara Bender into the room.

Strickland stood as she entered, sizing her up. With long black hair and olive skin, she was even more attractive than her online pictures had suggested.

She extended a hand and smiled warmly. "Hello, Dr. Strickland— Sara Bender."

"Good to meet you," Strickland said evenly, shaking her hand. Randall hastily put down his pizza slice and wiped his hands on a napkin.

"And, Dr. Randall, also good to meet you," she said. "Sorry to be late. My rental car's nav system was broken, and I've always been a bit dyslexic when it comes to reading maps."

"Not a problem," Randall said, gathering his notes into a pile and moving them off to one side. "But it's a good thing you arrived when you did. I've got a hearty appetite today."

Strickland pulled out a chair at the large oval conference table, and once their visitor was seated, he served her a slice of pizza on a paper plate.

"Um-m-m, this is really good!" she said.

"Considering we're not in New York?" Randall said.

"I didn't say that," she replied, smiling. Then, seeing Strickland glance down at his watch, she said, "I imagine you're both on a tight schedule, so I'd like to get started with some questions while we eat, if that's okay."

"That's fine," said Strickland.

She switched on a digital audio recorder and set it on the table between them. Strickland saw her glance up at Randall's summary, and shifted his chair toward her, forcing her to turn away from the whiteboard.

"Okay, first off," she said, "why don't you tell me a bit about how genomic discoveries coming out of labs such as yours will affect the health care field? Once this information becomes readily available, won't insurance carriers demand it? And then won't people with 'problem' genes be forced to pay higher rates, or perhaps be denied coverage altogether?"

"You're right about that: it's a serious problem," said Randall. "And I'm not sure what the solution is. The government will probably have to intervene to some degree and guarantee a person's right to coverage."

"But whether they do or not, it will become increasingly difficult to keep genetic data confidential," Strickland added. "The time is almost here when reliable genetic information can be harvested from the barest remnant of a sneeze or from the cellular debris left behind by almost any kind of human encounter. So the 'Big Brother' scenarios are already beginning to kick in."

"If you're saying that genetic information essentially *can't* be kept secret, then it would seem that we have to devise some means of keeping people with 'different' genes from being discriminated against," Bender said. "It'll be almost like the Civil Rights movement all over again."

"That's an interesting analogy," said Strickland, taking another slice of pizza. "People *will* have to be protected. . . . I'm just not sure how."

"What about recent proposals for a moratorium on certain controversial areas of research, while a global body hashes out the issues and formulates policy?" Bender asked. "Any thoughts on that?"

"I think that's a reasonable approach in certain instances," Randall said. "Of course, it would depend on the specifics of the research."

"But in general, it won't work," said Strickland, "and here's why:

It's a lot like disarmament strategies proposed during the Cold War. For all the good intentions, somebody will always think they can get a leg up by continuing the research. So there'll be constant churn going on behind the scenes. And some developing countries, desperate for capital, will become havens for renegade researchers, who will continue to do as they please no matter what restrictions are in place."

"That sounds awfully cynical," Bender said.

"It's just reality," said Strickland.

He and Randall looked at each other and started laughing.

Bender glanced at them quizzically.

"You should join our debate club," Randall explained. "You're already using the same language, and the arguments end pretty much the same way!"

"Except that Jordan and I can go on for hours," Strickland said. He offered Bender and then Randall the last slice of pizza. Both shook their heads. "Would you like to see the lab?" he asked.

"Definitely. Is it in this building?"

"It's the entire basement," Randall said.

As they stood to leave and Randall turned to the whiteboard and began wiping it clean, Strickland noticed Bender looking back over her shoulder, eyeing what remained of the summary.

They took the elevator down to the basement, emerging into a bustling hive of grad students and postdocs. As Bender followed into the heart of the low-ceilinged room, she narrated the scene into her audio recorder: "The sprawling facility hums with white noise and intense focus. Postdoctoral fellows hunch over genetic-sequencing stations, preparing samples for analysis, using three-dimensional computer graphics software to interpret the massive quantities of data being gathered."

She positioned her recorder on a nearby countertop and turned to Strickland. "I know that genetic defects are now being repaired using gene therapy," she said. "Could you give me a brief overview of that technology?"

"That's the Holy Grail at the moment," said Strickland. "All this new knowledge doesn't mean much if we can't do anything about the problems we uncover. And many new viruses are being crafted to deliver these altered genes. But getting systemwide distribution of the fix is sometimes difficult, because a given virus may not be able to reach all the body's cells. And custom viral vectors can have unforeseen and sometimes even deadly side effects."

"Viruses are designed by nature to inject genetic material into cells," Randall added. "That's how they replicate. So using them as a delivery vehicle for altered genes was a natural early path. But more recently, we've begun perfecting artificial chromosomes—small, entirely new chromosomes that seamlessly replicate within the cell. These provide a far more efficient and targeted means of delivering multiple genes into a cell."

"Meanwhile," Strickland said, "the knowledge that has come out of the Human Genome Project has enabled us to use drugs to control the *expression* of existing genes. We call this class of pharmaceuticals *transcription-modulating drugs*. Genes interact in fantastically complex ways, potentiating and suppressing one another's actions. We're now focusing on regulating these processes in a targeted way with drugs— for example, in the treatment of the insulin resistance found in type two diabetes."

"Sounds very futuristic!" said Bender.

"Yes and no," Strickland said. "Ironically, salicylate, the active ingredient in aspirin, acts through transcription modulation. This is a drug that's been used in folk medicine for thousands of years, yet we've only recently understood *how* it works. With the new knowledge base of genomics, we can design drugs based on their specific actions at the DNA level, rather than relying on simple trial and error."

"Could transcription modulation be used to moderate brain chemistry—say, in people with monoamine oxidase imbalances?" Bender asked.

"That's possible, in theory," Strickland said, looking at her with greater interest. "Of course, there's still the whole blood-brain barrier to worry about."

A phone rang, and one of the postdocs interrupted them. Strickland excused himself to take the call. He returned several minutes later, checking his watch as he approached. Meanwhile, Randall began gathering up some paperwork left behind earlier in the day.

"This has been a fascinating visit," Bender said, taking the cue that her time was up. "I really want to thank you both!" She began stowing her recording gear in her travel pack. "By the way," she added, "I did a bit of research online, and was thinking of dropping by a local place called India Garden before I head back to the airport."

"They're actually quite good," Strickland said."

"Great. I was hoping the online guide was right." She paused. "This afternoon has already raised a number of follow-up questions that are nagging at me. I'd love to keep the momentum going. If I could interest either of you in a quick bite . . ."

Randall began stowing his stack of paperwork in a briefcase. "I'm afraid I've got homework duty with the kids tonight," he said. "I'll have to beg off."

Bender extended her hand. "That's okay, Dr. Randall. It's been a fascinating afternoon. Thank you again for your time!"

"I enjoyed it, too," he said, smiling. "Hope to see you again." He snapped his briefcase shut and headed toward the stairwell.

"I'm really excited about this material," Bender said to Strickland.

"You seem to have a good grasp of the issues," he said. "As for dinner, afraid I can't make it, either."

"I understand completely," she replied. "But I'd love the opportunity to visit your lab again . . . "

"To be honest, we're a little overloaded with our current projects at the moment."

"I can see that." She scanned the huge, open lab space with a thoughtful expression. "Have you ever visited a place for the first time and felt that it seemed distinctly familiar? It's a strange experience, almost like déjà vu."

Strickland stopped moving.

"I had that feeling as soon as I saw your facility," she said. "Maybe it's the reverberation of an alternate path—if organic chem and I had gotten along a bit better." She glanced down as if suddenly embarrassed. "Anyway, I'd hoped to observe more of your day-to-day operations—in addition to posing some follow-up questions. It takes a certain level of immersion to discover the heart of a story."

Strickland studied her face, probing her intent. "I suppose we could work that in somehow," he finally said. "Call my assistant, George, at the main number. He tends to know my schedule better than I do."

He walked her to the lobby, where the guard collected her visitor's badge. "Thank you again, Dr. Strickland," she said, shaking his hand and smiling.

She began to walk away, then turned. "Oh, let me give you my card with my cell number," she said, "in case we end up playing scheduling tag."

Taking her card, he watched her walk quickly out the large glass doors of the main entrance. The evening sky was deep violet, and the first stars—planets, actually—were emerging above the horizon. Strickland lingered as Sara made her way along the grass-lined walkway leading to the parking structure. Then he glanced down at the card, dropped it in his coat pocket, and headed back to the lab.

II

Chapter 20

Strickland set his hard-shell saddlebag inside the front door of the condo. Another storm was on the way, and he had made it home just in time. He pried off his boots, one foot against the other, leaving them on the ceramic tiles of the entryway.

The weeks following his trip to Israel had been a blur. He and Randall had entered into an intense, seamless rhythm of research so focused that he could scarcely remember the last time they had argued. But to hold together the Ethnogenomics Department as well as maintain some level of project secrecy, Strickland had essentially been working two jobs for many weeks straight.

Padding barefoot into the living room, he sorted through the day's mail, tossing the letters into piles on the dining room table: junk, bills, personal, professional. In the courtyard below, he watched as the first sprinkles of rain formed delicate intersecting circles in the swimming pool. Soon, he knew, they would be shutting the pool down for the winter. He opened a couple of overdue utility bills, then glanced back at the haze of steam drifting up into the gray night, and the intersecting circles of light on the pool bottom. The rain was still just a light sprinkle. He felt exhausted, but even so, a late-night swim before bed felt right.

The water was perfect, warm enough even in this weather to provide an almost complete absence of tactile input—like a sensory deprivation tank. He floated facedown with a mask and snorkel, watching his own presence reflected in the patterns of light on the pool bottom. It was one of the classic conundrums of science: the observer altering the thing observed. Strickland closed his eyes, floating free in water that seemed to suspend all thought. Almost involuntarily, he began to enter a meditative state. His breath fell effortlessly into sync with the low hum of the water pump.

But then details of the Shroud study began edging into his consciousness. He found himself reviewing the results from the past weeks. He and Randall were delving deeper into the sequence data, using the latest in comparative genomics and advanced search engines to analyze the sample's SNPs. Having already gone as far as they could with broad dating and ethnicity, they were now concentrating on the particular physical attributes of the individual. Such polymorphisms enabled them to focus on traits as specific as eye and hair color, overall build, and even height—adjusted for the nutritional norms of the time. Contrary to what many believed, genetics did not equal fate. Physicality wasn't entirely etched in stone or chemistry. There was an inextricable interplay between DNA and environment. Genotype plus environment equaled phenotype— the physical manifestation of the genes. Or, as one lay publication had put it, "Genetics cocks the gun, and environment pulls the trigger."

* * *

Strickland found himself dragging through the next morning, his schedule of the past weeks slowly beginning to take its toll. Though he had slept soundly after his late-night swim, he still awoke feeling groggy and out of sorts. And as the day wore on, that feeling manifested as irritability. He snapped at one of the postdocs over a trivial procedural error, one no worse than many he had made in younger days. As the young man walked away, sheaf of lab work under his arm, and tail between his legs, Strickland thought he heard, sotto voce, "What an asshole."

"Bob, glad I caught you," Randall said, catching the door to Strickland's office as the postdoc left. "I've been meaning to touch base on a few things." Strickland composed himself, not wanting to dump on Randall the way he had with the young man before him.

"Come on in, Jordan," he said. "Pull up a chair."

"God, you look worked," said Randall. "You've got that vacant, medical-resident stare."

"It's the hours," Strickland said, sipping his third or fourth cup of coffee. "The board's riding my ass again for the upcoming quarterly budget figures, I'm trying to keep all of our other projects on schedule, and then there's the little detail of the Shroud work."

"Feel free to delegate some of the load," Randall said. "I'm at a stage where I could assign some of my more routine work to one of the postdocs."

"I appreciate the offer, but most of it's in midstream or close to being resolved. It would take too much time and effort, for both of us, to pass it off right now. Afraid I'll just have to ride it out."

"I hear you, but consider it a standing offer," Randall said. "Oh, by the way, I got a voice mail yesterday afternoon from Sara Bender, the reporter from the *Times*. She said she'd left you several voice mails and e-mails but hadn't heard back."

"Shit. I passed on those because I wanted to think about them; then I forgot." He paused, then said, "What did you tell her?"

"I said you'd been buried in budget meetings but that I'd remind you once you came up for air."

"Good," Strickland said. He was momentarily distracted by the image of Bender turning and offering a business card the night of her visit.

"Also, I've been reviewing the original memos and directives from the Vatican," Randall continued, a hint of trepidation in his voice. "Since this is somewhat uncharted water, they were understandably vague in terms of any completion criteria for the project. But we've essentially reached the limits of where we can go with our SNP findings using the NIH databases and our own ethnogenomics DBs. Maybe it's time to touch base with them and see when they'd like our final report."

Though he fought it, irritation began edging into Strickland's voice. "Jordan, they clearly said in their original request, 'amaze us.' If we suggest that we've taken this investigation to its logical conclusion, that will define the boundaries of the project."

From Randall's expression, Strickland could see one of their epic debates brewing, and he wasn't in the mood. "Look, the end may be in sight," he added. "You're probably right about that. But *we* should be the ones to define it. If we suggest that we might be done, they'll either agree and be disappointed, or agree and be relieved. That shouldn't be our role— to offer either disappointment or comfort."

"I guess that's where we sometimes differ," Randall said. "I'm out to expand a body of knowledge, not stir up a hornets' nest. And I worry that if we take this study too far, that's exactly what we'll do. For me, the Shroud represents a physical connection with the divinity of Jesus Christ. And Jesus is at the core of faith for some two billion people around the world. That's something you seem able to ignore."

Strickland's eyes narrowed, but his voice remained even. "Maybe you have an inherent conflict of interest in this study, Jordan. Your beliefs may be getting in the way of a balanced assessment of the project."

"And you're *not* biased?" Randall countered. "You always talk about 'pure' knowledge, as if there were such a thing. Everything exists within some context. There are societal repercussions to almost everything we do."

Strickland heaved a weary sigh. "You're right, Jordan," he said with obvious insincerity.

"Bob, I simply want to consider the consequences of what we're doing," Randall continued. "And I want to make sure the Vatican is on board with wherever we take the study."

"I think the only point of contention here is a matter of *degree*," Strickland said. "I don't think we've reached our endpoint yet."

"And how will you know when we've reached it?" Randall asked. "If we're to surprise them, what are we going to surprise them *with*?"

"It'll come to me," Strickland said, smiling weakly.

Randall patted his friend on the shoulder. "I had *no* idea what I was getting into when we first met," he said.

Strickland downed the dregs of his coffee. "Jordan, I've cranked the throttle full-on many times, but you've never known me to hit the wall, have you?"

"Doesn't mean the wall's not there," Randall said, the humor in his voice tempered with concern. "By the way," he added on his way out, "don't forget to call Sara Bender."

"Right—thanks for the reminder."

Chapter 21

Strickland spent the morning reviewing budgetary paperwork for the upcoming quarter. As usual, the acquisition of new hardware was a tooth-and-claw fight. He thought back to a statement made by an angry NIH administrator during the Senate hearings on the original Human Genome Project's funding: that the entire fifteen-year enterprise was slated to cost approximately the same as a single B-2 bomber. And yet they still had to grovel for the money. Basic research was always a low priority in any enterprise, and nowhere more so than in the sciences. "Show me the money," was the mantra of business and government—if it wasn't quickly profitable, or at least imminently newsworthy, it wasn't worth pursuing.

Just then his e-mail program signaled the arrival of several new messages. Scanning down a list of various NIH broadcast announcements, he noticed a message from Sara Bender and opened it.

> To: Robert.Strickland@eth-gen.nih.gov
> From: Sara.Bender@nytimes.com
> Subject: Follow-up Visit.
>
> Dear Dr. Strickland,
>
> I hope you don't mind, but I contacted your colleague, Dr. Randall, in hopes of arranging the follow-up visit we discussed. I have a number of additional questions, and I'd also like to spend an hour or so observing the various activities of your lab.
>
> My calendar is fairly flexible in the coming weeks, and I'd be happy to work around your schedule.
>
> Best Regards,
> Sara Bender
>
> P.S., No pizza required.

Strickland read through the message a second time. It was warm but at the same time brief and businesslike. She knew when to bear down and when to pull back.

He took out the wireless PDA in his lab coat and checked his calendar for the week. There were no free slots. He glanced back at the e-mail message, then used the stylus to cut his weekly Shroud update meeting with Randall from two hours to one, and transmitted the update to his online calendar, alerting Randall to the change. Then he hit the reply button on the e-mail.

> To: Sara.Bender@nytimes.com
> From: Robert.Strickland@eth-gen.nih.gov
> cc: Jordan.Randall@eth-gen.nih.gov
> Subject: re: Follow-up Visit.
>
> Dear Ms. Bender,
>
> There's an hour opening this Thursday afternoon at three. Let me know if that works for you. I'll notify the front desk. You know where to find us.
>
> Robert Strickland

He reread the message and hit send. Then he pulled up a Web browser and entered "Sara Bender" into the search engine, and the same post-invasion Baghdad images popped up. But scrolling down further, several entries of a more personal nature caught his eye. One described a charitable fund-raiser, with Bender's name alongside those of New York's mayor and several high-profile real estate moguls. He clicked on the link and saw a photograph of her standing in a line of stiffly posed men in tuxedos, and bejeweled women in couture gowns. The caption described the mayor's annual AIDS fund-raiser. The man standing alongside Bender was listed as her companion, Tom Aruldoss.

Strickland's computer suddenly announced new mail. The message was from Bender.

"Done!" it said. "See you Thursday. Best, Sara."

Chapter 22

Sara Bender printed out the final revision of her latest article for the *Times*. To meet the deadline on her book about the genomics revolution, she had arranged to stay closer to home. It was arguably a step down from being on assignment in various international hot spots, but it was the only way to carve out time for the book. She believed in the importance of the topic. And if it sold well, it would open up a new world of career options.

She scanned down the article one last time before e-mailing it to her editor. It detailed a horrific massacre involving ethnic cleansing in Gujarat, India. Warring tribes in the area—one group Muslim, the other Hindu—had been slaughtering one another for centuries. In the most recent incident, a mob of Hindus had cornered a group of Muslim women and children in a deserted building. The mob had thrown gasoline-soaked rags through the shattered but barred windows. The cornered Muslims begged for mercy, imploring, "What have we done to you?" But to no avail. The mob torched the rags, chanting, "Kill the Muslims! Kill the Muslims!"

In the end, over thirty people had been burned alive, with another twenty critically injured.

Bender shuddered at the details of the incident. Although she had covered war zones around the globe, the human capacity for cruelty never failed to catch her unprepared—particularly when organized religion was fanning the flames. And the fact that the victims were peaceful civilian women and children made it all the more heinous. How could such hatred develop between people so closely related by birth, history, and custom—to the point of *murder*? In the distant recesses of her mind, Bender imagined having a child of her own someday. But it was sometimes hard to imagine bringing new life into such a world.

Having muted her office phone for the morning, she began reviewing her voice mail. She deleted several messages related to a Thursday afternoon retirement mixer for a powerful editor she barely knew. She had always hated office schmoozing—one of the reasons she had chosen to be a field reporter. Also, she sensed that the invitation from Robert Strickland, for the same time slot, was not open to negotiation.

The final message in the voice mail queue was from her boyfriend, Tom. They had been shuffling their schedules for weeks, trying to arrange a trip to St. Barts. Tom's commercial real estate deal had come through, and the commission had been even bigger than expected. It amazed her that even during difficult financial times, some niches in the economy seemed perpetually immune to any real hardship. But Tom bristled at such intimations, insisting he was worth every penny. "I work hard for my money!" he declared flatly. "If everyone could do what I do, they'd be doing it."

Tom had suggested several new time slots for the trip. They were now looking three months ahead. Even though they lived under the same roof, they sometimes went days barely seeing each other. She had hoped that working closer to home would bring them together, but so far it hadn't.

Sara checked her calendar, then called Tom's direct-dial number. It kicked into voice mail, indicating that he was on the phone.

"Hi, it's me," she said. Then she suggested several time slots. But even as she did, Sara had the feeling that somehow, no matter what date they agreed on, their schedules would nix the trip before the day arrived.

How could they even consider having children when they couldn't even find time for a brief getaway?

Chapter 23

An ice storm in Chicago had thrown air traffic off schedule all across the country. Sara Bender's flight from JFK into Dulles was delayed by nearly two hours, and stranded travelers were strewn across the New York terminal's floor space, sleeping across seats and against the walls. She tried calling Strickland from the terminal, which was taking on the look and feel of a refugee encampment, but the massive cell traffic in the area had overloaded the local network. Incidents like this made the fragility of a high-technology–dependent civilization glaringly apparent. Whatever humankind's advances, nature was still the master.

Even though she had left home at 4:30 in the morning, the cab finally got her to the NIH an hour past her appointment. As she walked into Strickland's office, she found herself once again apologizing for being late. Randall was polite but reserved, assuring her that she shouldn't worry about it. Strickland was even more remote than during her first visit.

Bender had prepared a number of follow-up questions, but it was soon apparent that her window of opportunity had passed. She was handed off to Connie Franklin, her guide while exploring the lab below.

As the two women silently descended the concrete stairwell to the Ethnogenomics Center's sequencing lab, Franklin said, "You'll have to forgive Dr. Strickland and Dr. Randall." Her voice echoed down the concrete corridor. "When they get immersed in something, it's as if the rest of the world didn't exist. When I first started here, I assumed Dr. Strickland didn't like me—he's sometimes hard to read. But if it's any consolation, you're the first journalist who's ever been invited back."

"Thanks for the insight," Sara said, smiling.

They emerged into the windowless lab, and Bender scanned the massive space. "This must be a fascinating place to work," she said. "In some ways, it reminds me of our newsroom: intense concentration, brutal deadlines, and some tightly wound personality types."

"Always those personality types," Franklin said, grinning. "Still, in spite of it all, the work really is fascinating."

"I'll bet."

"But I can hardly imagine the experiences you've had," said Franklin. "I've read some of your work. It's very powerful."

"Thanks! But I'm sure each realm has its own rush and rewards."

"True, but our work is pretty painstaking and solitary," Franklin continued. "I can count on one hand the number of trips I've taken in the past five years—a few technical symposia along the Eastern Seaboard, and then a trip to Israel."

"Oh, are you Jewish?" Bender asked, intrigued.

"No . . . it was a sampling expedition—an indigenous tribe in the Middle East, being analyzed as part of an ongoing disease study." She seemed suddenly distracted by the memory, then abruptly changed the subject. "This group is working on various stem cell studies," she said as they passed a workbench filled with microscopes and digital analysis hardware. "They're trying to uncover, at the DNA level, what makes such cells totipotent—capable of being transformed into any cell type. This has important applications in our research into the genetic differences between various ethnic groups. If we can coax a given stem cell line into any tissue type of our choosing, we can explore the facets of that particular ethnicity's unique genetic characteristics much more easily."

Although Bender was familiar with the principles being described, she let her host continue uninterrupted. She had learned early on to let interview subjects describe things in their own words. *Then* ask questions.

"As you probably know, every cell of a given organism contains the genetic code for that entire organism," Franklin continued. "But once cell differentiation occurs, it's very hard to regain access to certain portions of the genome, and the functionalities they code for. But stem cells have it all. They're like babies, capable of being molded in all kinds of different ways. For years we were constrained to a limited number of cell lines, established before Washington decided to cut off any further funding of stem cell creation. But many of those lines were established using antiquated techniques, so the quality was poor by current standards. The constraints have now been loosened, but the technology still seems to attract endless controversy. We're just holding our collective breath that the new laws aren't somehow overturned."

They passed a workbench housing a large binocular microscope. A woman in a white lab coat sat alongside the device, busily jotting down notes. "Want to take a look?" Franklin asked Sara. "May we?" she asked the researcher.

Bender sat down and adjusted the twin eyepieces. As the image edged into crystalline focus, she marveled at the ball of cells floating in its nutrient solution. "Wow . . . that's incredible," she breathed. "Where do these come from?"

"They're discarded from in vitro fertilization procedures—mostly low-grade cell clusters that weren't suitable for implantation. That's the irony of certain activists' concerns. They want to regulate the production of new stem cell lines, saying that the process destroys human life. Yet, such IVF clusters are being destroyed every day. With studies like these, we may someday be able to cure diabetes, Parkinson's disease, blindness, spinal cord injuries, and more. Sometimes I wonder whether the anti–stem cell activists really comprehend the logical contradictions in their thinking. And then, in my more cynical moments, I think they're engaged in an intentional campaign of disinformation."

Bender stood up from the microscope, still in awe. "That's amazing," she said, "and it resonates for me personally."

Franklin looked confused.

"Who knows?" she added, smiling wistfully. "At the rate I'm going, IVF may be in *my* future."

Franklin's eyes warmed. "Are you in a relationship?" she asked.

"Living together. I'd never thought much about kids before. Just figured it would magically happen when the time was right. But now . . ."

"I hear you," Franklin said. "I'm the last of my girlfriends without kids. Of course, they didn't take the PhD and postdoc route—just simple stuff, like MBAs or law school." She grinned. "But I can't tell you how many of my women friends have had to drag their husbands, kicking and screaming, into parenthood. And the funny thing is, those are the guys who often turn out to be the most doting fathers. It's strange."

"You nailed it," Bender said. "Men seem to take a lifetime to grow up—and half of them never really get there."

"Well, at least you have a boyfriend," Franklin said. "The men around here are either emotionally stunted, monofocused on their work, or both. I was engaged to a guy out in California—another postdoc—but the distance thing finally got to us."

"I'm really sorry," Bender said. "I do see a lot of parallels between your workplace and mine—the intensity is much the same. And men like

Dr. Strickland—he seems . . . *complicated.*"

Franklin smiled. "Agreed. I admire him, but he's enigmatic, for sure. In general, I try to keep my personal and professional lives as separate as possible." She paused, considering her words. "A certain type of charismatic man was intriguing in my twenties. But as I get older, the thrill of daily navigating a minefield loses its luster."

Based on Franklin's carefully worded comments, Bender speculated that Strickland was a regular topic of conversation among the women in the department. She also guessed that he was hardly aware of most of them. And the word "minefield" had long ago popped into her head when she thought of him.

"So that's pretty much our standard tour," Franklin said as they found themselves back at the stairwell door.

Bender had welcomed getting the tour from another woman. Even in such a clinical setting, there was a palpably different sense of things from the female point of view. She couldn't quite put her finger on it—less data-driven, more big-picture?

"I really want to thank you for your time," she said.

"Oh, it was my pleasure!" Franklin replied. "So, am I supposed to escort you out, or were you going back up to see Dr. Strickland and Dr. Randall?"

"I still feel bad about showing up late," Bender said. "I'd really like to swing past and thank them again."

The two women ascended the concrete staircase, emerging into the more warmly lit office area on the main floor. They checked Strickland's office and the nearby conference room, then headed to Randall's office. Franklin raised her hand to knock on the door. But just as she did, the sounds of a heated argument boomed through, loud and clear.

"God damn it, Bob, I'll contact the Vatican if I have to!"

Franklin jerked her hand back as if she had touched a hot pan. A second later, the door swung open, and Randall emerged, his face flushed with emotion.

They were all momentarily frozen in silence. "Um, Ms. Bender was just on her way out," Franklin said when she found her voice.

Randall appeared noticeably flustered. "How was the tour?" he asked Bender with strained decorum.

"Very informative," she said.

He glanced back at the open office door. "Well, if you'll excuse me . . . ," he said, and strode off down the hall.

Strickland emerged next and nodded to Bender. She glanced down, and he turned to obscure her view of the stack of papers under his arm.

Franklin, clearly chagrined at having brought Sara into the middle of such an exchange, interjected, "Ms. Bender was on her way out and wanted to say good-bye."

"Yes, it was really fascinating—thank you so much," Bender said, doing her best to ease the tension in the air. "I have a much better sense of your day-to-day operations now."

Strickland seemed to be probing Sara's face as she spoke, as if searching for some hidden meaning beneath her words. Then Randall returned from down the hall to stand nervously behind the two women.

"Well, I know you both have a very busy schedule," said Bender, "so I just wanted to thank you again for these visits. It's been a pleasure." She turned and shook Randall's hand.

"I'm sorry we didn't have time for lunch today," he said.

"Not a problem, Dr. Randall. I understand completely," she replied. "I appreciate the follow-up. Next time either of you come to Manhattan, be sure to give me a call. I'll take you to my favorite pizza place—John's, on Bleeker in the Village."

She turned and shook Strickland's hand, but there was little warmth in the exchange, and again he seemed to be probing her eyes.

Bender turned finally to Franklin. Her first impulse was to hug her, but she resisted and they shook hands as she thanked her again for the tour.

"Oh, one other thing," Bender said on her way out. "Once I've gotten a bit further on my manuscript, I'd love to get your input on the sections that result from our conversations."

"We'd be more than happy," said Randall, while Strickland looked back noncommittally.

What did you make of that?" Strickland asked him afterward. "Think she overheard our conversation?"

"I hope not," Randall said, his face grim.

Chapter 24

Sara Bender sat at the desk in her Manhattan home office. A spectacular view of Central Park spread out below the east-facing window, but to the amazement of all who visited, her desk faced a blank, undecorated wall. She had read somewhere that Hemingway, even after graduating from the poverty of ramshackle Parisian studios, had always arranged his workplace this way. The implicit message had stuck: nothing should distract from your work.

She continued reviewing the notes and transcripts from her visits to the NIH. During the first trip, she had recorded a free-association description of her thoughts and observations while touring the lab. ". . . The expansive facility hums with white noise and intense human focus. Postdoctoral fellows hunch over genetic-sequencing stations." There was a temporal gap in the transcript, followed by recollections she had made afterward in her car. ". . . Whiteboard data details genomic disparities between a test subject and ethnic tribal populations." She replayed the audio passage: *test subject* . . . Her visual memory was vivid. She could still picture the whiteboard graph in the conference room where she had shared pizza with Strickland and Randall. The vertical axis was labeled "Subject #1." Odd. Typically, a study like this would compare a smaller genetic population with a much larger reference group. But this graph detailed a single test subject against a larger group. *Why?* Were they trying to pinpoint a specific disease gene or genes? If so, why not sample multiple subjects with that disease? It didn't quite add up. And then she remembered Strickland steering her field of view away from the chart.

Poring over her notes again, Bender came upon a handwritten paragraph detailing the tour given by Connie Franklin. The annotation "Trip to Israel" had been scribbled in the margin. She got up and stretched, arching her back as she gazed at the leaden sky and bare winter trees. Something about the scene below made her think of Strickland. What an odd parting they'd had, with Randall swearing and threatening to "contact the Vatican." What on earth could they have been discussing? Beneath the obvious emotional weight of the moment, Strickland and Randall had both seemed strangely guarded. They had once again been reviewing tables of data—hard copy this time, so she hadn't been able to see much of it. But on the top sheet of Strickland's paperwork, she had definitely registered a single column stub that read, ESTIMATED DOB.

Why on earth would they be interested in the date of birth for a single test subject? And why had Strickland again wanted to keep her from seeing it?

Bender picked up her notes and began pacing about the room. Her eyes fell again on the handwritten entry "Trip to Israel." As she considered the text, the noon bell at the church on Seventy-first Street began ringing. She suddenly stopped pacing, as a wave of realization passed across her face. Then she sat down, pulled up the e-mail program on her computer, and began scanning the address book entries.

Chapter 25

Strickland finished dinner and began halfheartedly cleaning up. It was already 9:30 as he rinsed off the plates and dumped the unfinished glass of wine down the drain. As he flipped the disposal switch, the pungent bouquet of Petite Sirah rose from the sink.

It had been another long day at the lab. For every bit of new data they gathered, for every question answered, it seemed as though five new questions arose in its place. The Shroud project felt like a shimmering mirage on an endless expanse of open road. For each mile traveled, the ghost image moved that much further away. There were endless directions they could go, with no clear signposts along the way.

Strickland rubbed his eyes—he had finally hit the wall of mental exhaustion. During his medical training, he had sometimes gone for days with almost no sleep at all. But now, in his late forties, there were new physical limits. He needed to let the project go for at least a few hours, if only to regain some clarity and perspective.

He sat down before the television and began flipping mindlessly through the channels. As was often the case, he saw little worth watching. He finally settled on the tail end of *Becket,* a film he hadn't seen in years. In it, Peter O'Toole played the volatile King Henry II of England, who appointed his boyhood friend and whoring comrade, Thomas Becket, to be archbishop of Canterbury. It was a seemingly brilliant tactical move by the king, designed to better control the church by installing his own man at the helm.

Inexplicably, Becket begged his friend to appoint someone else. "Do not do this, my lord!" he said. But Henry would not be dissuaded. In the end, Becket became a solemn man of God—and the perceived enemy of the king. It was a path that eventually cost him his life.

Strickland had always found the story to be a moving tale of transformation and personal discovery. While it occurred within the grand sweep of high government and organized religion, the story was really about one man's unlikely spiritual awakening.

Just as he began settling into the film, there was a knock at the front door. Peering through the curtains alongside the door, Strickland perceived a dimly lit male figure—no one he immediately recognized. He flicked on the porch light and looked through the fish-eye lens in the door. He could barely believe his eyes. Certain people acquired an almost dreamlike quality through absence and the passage of time. And for him, Mark Altman was just such a person.

He opened the door, and there stood his old friend, muscular and broad shouldered, wearing a denim jacket with a worn leather collar. With his chiseled features and brawny build, he could have passed for a Quebecois lumberjack of yore.

"Hey, man, it's great to see you!" Altman said, throwing his arms around Strickland. "I was in the area and thought I'd drop in."

By his friend's demeanor, an onlooker might have guessed they had last seen each other a few weeks ago rather than the twenty years it had actually been. But as they hugged, Strickland realized that it really *did* seem like mere weeks.

In high school, Altman had been a blustering New York jock. He and Strickland had ridden motorcycles together, either tearing down the back roads of upstate New York or cruising for women in the city. But after graduation they had gone separate ways, heading off to different colleges.

Altman had reappeared four years later, utterly transformed, with long flowing hair and a scraggly beard. He explained to Strickland that he had dropped acid numerous times and, in the process, had discovered his "true path." In his sophomore year, to his parents' chagrin, he had changed his major from business administration to comparative religion.

Altman's conversations had been laced with excited tales of astral planes and spirit guides. For Strickland, it was all a bit much, and in many ways, he had longed for the old back-slapping, beer-drinking, tail-chasing incarnation of his friend. On the other hand, there was something extraordinary about Altman, particularly in the eyes, which were wild and alive with an almost primordial energy.

Strickland was in his first year of medical school at that point, and wondered about the neurological implications of his friend's transformation. Had he sustained organic brain damage from the drugs? Had they rewired his neurochemistry in some way? Or did it all somehow go deeper?

One evening during the unexpected med school visit, Altman had insisted that they take off their clothes and "streak" the neighborhood. "Let 'em see the *real* you!" he had urged with a wild and gleeful cackle.

Strickland's girlfriend at the time was studying in the living room, and cut her eyes disdainfully at the two young delinquents. But something about his friend's wild new spirit was infectious, impossible to resist, and the next thing Strickland knew, he and Altman were sprinting stark naked through his East Village neighborhood, waving wildly at passing cars.

After the streak, Altman bought a fifth of cheap whiskey at a corner market, and the two friends sat reminiscing about old times. "This is pretty good stuff," Strickland remembered saying at one point, feeling closer than ever to his friend.

Altman's eyes flashed like a wild animal's. "No, it's not! You're an *ass*! This stuff is shit and you know it!" Altman's eyes had stayed locked angrily on to Strickland's. Then, just as suddenly, he broke into a broad grin and started cackling again.

That same evening, Altman had gone off on a wild exposition about the shifting duality of all things—men, women, good, evil, the physical and the spiritual—and how each was part of some greater but indecipherable whole. "You see this fist?" Altman said, clenching it menacingly in Strickland's face. "If I were to punch you in the nose right now, you'd experience it solely on the physical plane. But in reality, neither of us is even solid matter. We're just a manifestation of cosmic forces and subatomic particles. And you'd feel what we call pain, but even that's just neurotransmitters coursing through your brain—it's really not *pain* at all. We're just wired to recognize that particular flickering pattern of neural firings. But it could just as easily mean *joy*. It's all in the wiring, my man, and it's all an illusion. So . . . where is the real you and the real me?" he finally posed.

"Uh . . . where?" Strickland had asked cautiously.

"Here!" Altman said, and snapped his fingers between their faces. And once again he erupted into peals of laughter.

After that encounter, Strickland had occasionally heard from Altman, but the communications were brief and often cryptic. There was mention of a troubled marriage, a divorce, and several wild career changes. And then, eventually, the letters had stopped.

But now here he was again, in the flesh, as if he had simply gotten sidetracked some twenty years back and had taken the long way around the block. From his latter communications, Strickland expected him to look prematurely aged and beaten down by life. But he looked surprisingly youthful—clean-shaven, with an almost glowing energy about him. The wildness in his eyes had subsided to some degree, replaced by a knowing calm.

Altman explained that he had just accepted a new job, teaching science at a high school outside Boston. As each caught up on the other's life, Altman wandered through the living room, pausing before various family photos on the mantel.

"Hey," he said, picking up a documentary film on the Shroud of Turin from atop the television, "does this talk about the Order of the Oak?"

Strickland said no, and though he tried to mask his interest, Altman seemed to pick up on something.

"It was a mysterious brotherhood of Franciscan monks," Altman explained. "I first learned about them in a religious iconography class. Back in the Middle Ages, the group became convinced that the Shroud was something more than just the supposed burial cloth of Jesus. It seems their founder, Frère Jean, had a vision where an angel told him to guard the relic with his life, saying it held an importance to mankind beyond all knowing. Ultimately, the monks were instrumental in seeing that the cloth was spirited away from invading armies during the early fifteen hundreds. After that, they worked to protect the Shroud during centuries of warring factions—influencing events when they could, finding safe havens when they couldn't. They saved the Shroud from a long string of wars, sackings, and fires and ended up transporting it to various secret locations at several pivotal moments in history. After a time, the group's influence seemed to fade, and eventually the Catholic Church took control of the cloth. There's reportedly some remnant of the original followers, but their membership seems more sentimental than anything else."

Even though he was somewhat familiar with the story, Strickland found himself listening intently, for there was something in his friend's enthusiasm—a sort of quiet fire—that he found utterly compelling.

"So, what led you to get this?" Altman asked, setting the disc back down on the television.

"I'm not sure, really," Strickland replied. "I was watching some late-night TV and caught the tail end of it. Guess I was intrigued enough to order the disc."

The hours flew by, and Strickland realized that his earlier mental exhaustion had vanished. His friend's energy was contagious. But around two, he finally asked Altman where he was staying for the night.

"I hadn't actually considered it," Altman admitted. "When I made my plane reservations, I noticed that it was a hell of a lot cheaper to fly into Dulles than Logan. I suddenly got the wild idea of coming to see you, then catching the train up to Boston. I figured I'd just drop by for a few hours, then find a hotel nearby."

"Well, it's a little late at this point," Strickland said. "If you don't mind the couch, you're welcome to crash here."

"You're on."

Strickland tossed down some blankets and pillows from the hall closet, then turned to cut the lights.

"It's good to see you, man," Altman told him.

"It is," Strickland said, feeling a warm wave of nostalgia. "I'm really glad you came."

In the morning, Strickland rented a Honda VFR for Altman from a local motorcycle dealer, and they took a ride along the winding back roads of the Maryland countryside. It was a crisp winter day—forests of bare trees arrayed against a vivid blue sky, sun strobing through the overhanging branches. The brisk wind took Strickland back to the days when he and Altman had first known each other. He marveled at how centered his friend seemed—so different from the wild man he had been just out of college.

After the ride, Strickland asked him about religion and spirituality and the theories that had tumbled so madly from Altman's lips the night they streaked in Manhattan.

"That was just the whiskey talking," his friend said, smiling enigmatically.

There were still traces of the old, wild Mark Altman, ever elusive and contradictory, but there was a new undercurrent of silent understanding. "None of that shit really matters," he added, looking deep in Strickland's eyes. "In the end, we each have to stay open to the signs and find our own way."

Several weeks later, Altman sent Strickland an article on the Order of the Oak, with a graphic of its golden oak tree insignia.

Chapter 26

Sara Bender read and then reread the e-mail message to Strickland. The wording had to be just right—cautious and respectful. She wasn't sure where all this would lead, but if she was right, it could be a rare opportunity.

Over the years, she had come to trust her instincts as a reporter. And from what she had just learned from a Vatican contact, her hunch was quite possibly on the money. If she played it just right, Strickland himself might confirm it. She had left out any mention of the trip to Israel—no sense jeopardizing Connie Franklin's position at the NIH.

Bender read the last line, took a deep breath, hit send, and the message window collapsed.

Chapter 27

The e-mail arrived a week to the day after Sara Bender's visit to the lab. In retrospect, Strickland had registered something in her face as she left that day—perhaps before she knew it herself. Even though no one had ever accused him of intimacy, he was often adept at reading people.

> To: Robert.Strickland@eth-gen.nih.gov
> From: Sara.Bender@nytimes.com
> Subject: Your Study.
>
> Dear Dr. Strickland,
>
> I wanted to thank you again for arranging my follow-up visit. As you will recall, when I dropped by your office on the way out, I inadvertently interrupted a discussion between you and Dr. Randall. I couldn't help but overhear parts of your exchange. While I'm extremely sensitive to the confidentiality of any scientific study, I feel compelled to discuss something with you.
>
> During my first visit to your lab, I noticed data on the whiteboard that seemed related to a genetic study out of the Middle East. At the time, I assumed it was simply a disease study with an ethnic focus. But during my second visit, I saw additional data listing physiological attributes of what appeared to be a specific person, including ethnicity and date-of-birth estimate.
>
> During your heated discussion with Dr. Randall, I heard mention of the Vatican. On a hunch, I contacted several sources in Rome. Please be assured, I did not mention you, Dr. Randall, or the NIH. My sources are well aware of my book project, so questions on the subject fall perfectly within that scope. I simply asked whether the Vatican had ever considered a follow-up to their 1978 study of the Shroud of Turin, using the latest genetic analysis techniques. At first, my queries were met with a resounding silence. But through a trusted source inside the Vatican, I eventually learned that such a study on the Shroud is either in the planning stages or already under way.
>
> I can't help but wonder whether you and Dr. Randall are conducting

such a study. Please be aware that as a journalist, I've risked criminal prosecution more than once to protect my sources, and that I have the utmost respect for your privacy in this matter.

Sincerely,
Sara Bender

"Shit!" Strickland muttered.

Chapter 28

Jordan Randall looked up from his computer workstation as Strickland entered his office. Strickland's jaw was set, his eyes intense. He closed the door and sat down opposite Randall's desk.

"Sara Bender knows about the Shroud study," he said.

Randall gasped. "Are you sure?"

"I just got an e-mail from her. At this point she's still fishing, but she's put enough of the pieces together to know she's onto something."

"But she has no real proof."

"Jordan, think back to the lessons of scandals like Watergate or Iran-Contra. This isn't going away. She's a seasoned investigative reporter, with extensive contacts in the biotech world as well as the international community. In her e-mail, she even referenced a source inside the Vatican. If we deny this and she has even a shred of doubt about our veracity, it will only make her dig deeper. Eventually, it'll cycle back to the Vatican, and that will be the end of the study."

Randall looked back grimly. "Maybe this *should* be the end of it," he said. "Maybe this is a sign we've gone far enough."

"With all due respect, why is it that believers are always looking for signs? What happened to the scientific method? Maybe this is just a random occurrence—plain old bad luck. And bad luck that we brought on ourselves by arguing too loudly, which we're now on the verge of doing again."

"Whatever the cause," Randall said, "I still think it's time to consult others—either Dan Burnham or Dr. Rutigliano at the Vatican."

"If we do either of those things, I can assure you of the outcome: it'll be the end of the research."

"Then so be it."

I'm not ready for that," Strickland countered.

"Then what do you suggest?"

"I want to propose a nondisclosure agreement with Bender. The NIH has used them countless times in studies with large monetary potential, where we were going up against the major pharmas. Bender's already hinted that she's willing to cut a deal. And what does any reporter really want? Access and information. And what do we want? Time. So we give her what she wants, but with a delay clause, and buy ourselves what we need in the process."

"You really think Burnham will go along with that?" Randall asked.

"I hadn't planned to tell him."

Randall looked at him as if beholding a strange new life form.

"Look, call it what you will, Jordan—intuition, a hunch, or who knows what—but something tells me this isn't over yet."

Randall stared back, his face grim. "Fine, Bob, I'll go along with this for now," he said, "but I can't say for how much longer."

Chapter 29

Strickland rifled through his desk drawer until he found Sara Bender's business card. He was about to call her office number but opted for the handwritten cell number instead. He wanted a dedicated digital line that couldn't easily be monitored.

"Hello?"

"Ms. Bender?" he said. "This is Bob Strickland."

"Dr. Strickland!" she said. "I was wondering if it might be you. I saw the Bethesda area code on my phone."

Her relaxed and open tone caught him momentarily off guard.

"Did you get my e-mail?" she asked.

"I did."

"And . . . ?"

"I'm not at liberty to discuss any of our research until it's completed and published," he said.

"I fully understand the need for confidentiality in research," Bender replied. "I'm merely proposing that I be allowed to observe the investigation as it proceeds."

The warmth in her voice reminded him of the old television show *Columbo,* in which the canny old detective feigned a folksy sense of geniality to lull his quarry into letting down its guard. And in a sense, the technique had already worked—Bender had assumed that the investigation was under way, and he had waited far too long to deny it.

"Dr. Strickland, I'm not some muckraking tabloid journalist," she added. "It's really very simple: if this is what I think it is, I'd like to be the first to cover it."

"Okay, let's talk terms."

"Robert, this isn't blackmail." She caught herself, realizing she had called one of the nation's leading scientists by his first name. "I just want the exclusive right to report the story—when you and Dr. Randall decide you're ready."

Chapter 30

Sara Bender draped her winter coat over a chair and set a tasseled princess hat on the dining room table. She had just returned from her niece Jessica's birthday party in Central Park. Sara's sister, Judy, had scurried about the gathering for a good two hours, handing out party hats, serving cake, and ministering to the occasional scraped knee or bruised feelings. The gathering brought back fond memories of childhood in upstate New York.

Sara had always viewed her younger sister's domestic life as a distant and alien world, but lately such gatherings evoked a bittersweet longing in her.

The party had been held at the petting zoo in Central Park. She had invited Tom, but as usual, he was embroiled in a work project—a high-rise office complex planned for downtown Atlanta. To compensate for his absence, he had arranged for a lavish gift to arrive during the party, presented by a "singing prince" courier. As intended, the assembled little girls went wild.

In the earlier phase of their relationship, Tom had wooed Sara with similar gestures, and with similar effect. But Tom's lavish gifts and extravagant overtures were beginning to feel like consolation prizes. Sara wanted to share a life with him, but that didn't seem to be happening. Worse, he saw her career as partly to blame. Since his work generated the bulk of their income, he suggested that she either cut back to part-time or stop working altogether. That way, whenever he was available, they could be together.

As she hung her coat in the hall closet, the intercom sounded downstairs.

"Ms. Bender, a FedEx just arrived," said the concierge.

"Thanks, Malcolm. I'll be right down."

As she emerged from the elevator, Malcolm smiled. "Hey, Ms. B., how are things?"

"Hanging in," she said, picking up the envelope. "How about you?"

"My band just cut its first CD, so it's all good. Would you like a copy?" he said, holding up a packaged disc.

"Definitely," she said, taking it. "How much do I owe you?"

"It's on the house. But it would help if you came to our show next week." He handed her a flyer for the gig at the Bowery Ballroom.

"I'll be there if I possibly . . . no, I'll *be* there," she said.

"Thanks Ms. B.," he said. "I'll put you on the guest list."

As Bender walked away, she scanned the information on the document-size package, noting the return address: *R. Strickland, 1178 Bennington Court, Rockville, MD 20847.*

Chapter 31

"No more chores!" Randall chided, cradling the phone on one shoulder. "With a temperature of 103, I want you in bed—doctor's orders. No, no . . . leave that to me. I'll see you soon." He hung up the phone, then went down the corridor to Strickland's office. "Bob, Mary's come down with a god-awful flu. Afraid I'll have to take off early to pick up the kids. . . ." He paused to look at the torn FedEx envelope on Strickland's desk. His eyes narrowed. "Is that what I think it is?"

"It just arrived," Strickland said, checking the initialed and signed clauses of the nondisclosure document. He motioned for Randall to come in and close the door. "Sara's agreed to all the terms we defined: twelve hours of access per week, beginning next week, and no publication of any material pertaining to the project until the work's been formally received by the Vatican and accepted by a journal of our choosing. She included a handwritten note, saying she's 'looking forward to working with us.'" He looked irritated. "*Working* with us? So now she's a genomic scientist?"

"Give her a chance, Bob. Things could be a lot worse. She's clearly bright and knows the issues—at least from a lay perspective. You and I can practically make book on how the other will respond to a given question. I almost welcome having someone around with a fresh perspective."

"I'm still wary," Strickland said. "But what choice do we have? We'll have to make it work."

"Life is littered with Faustian bargains," Randall said.

"So I've heard."

Chapter 32

Sara Bender hung up the phone. She had just rented a one-bedroom apartment on the edge of Georgetown, sight unseen, and buyer's remorse was already setting in. The agent had assured her it was in a good neighborhood with a bit of character, and that the owner was anxious to fill an unexpected vacancy. She had talked the broker into a month-to-month agreement, even though he wanted a year lease.

Sara hadn't mentioned the move to Tom yet, but she knew it would set off a bomb. He would be against it, or he'd want her to get a bigger place in a better neighborhood, and he'd want to pay at least part of the expenses. She would hold firm, though—their finances were separate for the most part, and she preferred it that way.

Sara had first met Tom at a charity fund-raiser she was covering for the *Times*. He was tall, suave, and princely, from a blue-blooded Philadelphia family, and had an MBA from Wharton. She soon realized that charity events were his only real access to people outside his direct social sphere. Tom was charming and smart, but Sara found most of his social set spoiled and self-absorbed.

Two summers ago, on a trip to Paris, she had insisted on staying at out-of-the-way places—worlds away from Tom's choice of the George V, and refreshingly so. They met a touring mime troupe from Leipzig, a former Silicon Valley entrepreneur who went broke and moved to Paris to reinvent himself, and an odd little man who claimed to have been a CIA assassin for the fabled Phoenix Program during the Vietnam War. For her, the most memorable rides were on the unpaved roads.

Bender crossed off the last remaining items from her checklist. She had arranged a two-month leave of absence from the *Times,* with an option for an additional month. Her editor had probed for more information on this sudden tangent to the book project, but she explained that she had signed an NDA and couldn't reveal anything more. All she would say was that it could move things "in an amazing new direction."

Bender gathered up her essential tools of the road: audio recorder, laptop, portable printer, cell phone, and high-resolution digital camera. Then she began packing her clothes. She chose mostly casual wear but included several pairs of slacks, and two evening dresses just in case.

As she latched the first suitcase, she heard Tom at the front door.

"Hey, honey!" he yelled. She heard him toss his keys into the brass bowl by the door, then rummage in the refrigerator.

Tom entered the bedroom sipping a glass of white wine. "So how was your . . ." His eyes narrowed, surveying the room—bed strewn with clothes, half-packed suitcases. Ever the dealmaker, he went poker faced. "What's up?" he asked nonchalantly.

But Sara could see through it, and a part of her enjoyed watching him squirm. "Remember that lab I visited at the NIH?" she asked.

"Oh, yeah, yeah," Tom said, "the biker doctor."

Sara marveled that this was all that had stuck from her description of Strickland and Randall.

"Well, I've discovered they're working on something potentially big—important enough that I want to cover it as it develops. And the only way to do that is to spend some dedicated time in D.C."

Tom set down the glass of wine. "How much time?"

"Several months."

"What about your job?"

"I've taken a leave of absence."

"So that's it?" he said. "You didn't even plan to *discuss* it with me?"

"I had to act fast. Plus, I knew you'd try to talk me out of it."

"That's probably true. But most couples discuss important moves."

"You're right, but I need to do this. I'd tell you more about it, but I can't—I've signed an NDA."

Tom looked again at the array of clothes on the bed. "On some level, this is about us, isn't it?"

"No. It's about *me,* and my career," she said. "If the deal of the century came along and it required you to spend months away from Manhattan, tell me you wouldn't go for it."

"You're right, I would," he agreed. He hesitated, looking directly at her. "I know we have busy lives—probably *too* busy. But I want this relationship. . . . I want *you.*"

Sara had been with Tom in social settings when he was closing a deal. She knew how he worked—the turn of phrase, the earnest eye contact. Their relationship had been on cruise control for the past year or more. And yet, she felt that the next move was his. As old-fashioned and anti-feminist as it sounded, there were still two magic words that would take their relationship to the next level: "Marry me." But so far, she hadn't heard them.

Chapter 33

Bender clicked through the volumes of spreadsheets in the Ethnogenomics Center's main conference room, marveling at the information Strickland and Randall had compiled from the Shroud sequences.

"This is amazing," she said, scanning through the data. "I had no idea you could derive so many specifics simply from base-pair data."

"Up until very recently, you couldn't," Randall said. "This is pretty much the state of the art."

"Of course, phenotypic projection has varying degrees of accuracy," Strickland added, "depending on such factors as nutrition and lifestyle."

Bender was only halfway through her second week in the lab, but she was already immersed in the exhilarating rhythm of the place. The twelve hours a week she had been promised seemed barely enough, and at the end of a day, she found herself reluctant to leave, wondering what new details and revelations she might miss. To justify her presence, Strickland and Randall had told their staff the half-truth that she was researching a book about the broader topics of ethnogenomics.

After four hours of shadowing Strickland and Randall through their hectic schedules, Bender finally pulled on her coat and gloves.

"Well, my sled and huskies have arrived," she said, wrapping a long burgundy scarf around her neck and tucking it in at the edges. "See you both tomorrow!"

Randall smiled warmly, while Strickland offered only a distracted wave.

* * *

After Bender had left, Randall smiled mischievously. "So, what do you think?"

"About what?" Strickland asked.

"Is she the Faustian bargain you imagined?"

"Too soon to tell. All we've seen so far is the upside."

"So you admit there *is* an upside."

"Like I said, too soon to tell."

Chapter 34

Bender spent much of her time away from the lab editing and organizing, which included volumes of background information along with her descriptions of the Shroud project's experiential aspects. Strickland and Randall regularly engaged in heated philosophical arguments, but these exchanges, rather than impeding progress, actually seemed to fuel their collaboration.

Arriving early Monday on her fourth week, Bender entered the lab just as Randall was beginning the final phase of a forensic DNA project using the RES-5000 3-D reanimation system. The computer had just rendered the face of a Caucasian male in his mid-thirties on the large color screen. The default facial expression was calm and relaxed, as if the subject had just awakened.

"Glad I arrived early," Bender said, looking up at the large wall-mounted display. "I'd read about your work with the RES-5000 in the *Journal of Image and Graphics*."

Randall's eyes lit up. "You continue to amaze!"

"So who's this?" she asked.

"A suspected murderer," he replied grimly.

"It's strange that someone accused of murder could look so . . . beatific."

"Maybe he would have been, if life had simply taken a few different turns," Randall said, adjusting several contrast controls on the system. "This visual rendering is based solely on DNA. Life experiences can affect what I would call a person's soul, in ways that science doesn't have the tools or the language to describe."

"Interesting notion," Sara replied.

"Philosophical considerations aside, this work is vitally important," he added, making further adjustments to the system. "As often as not, we end up vindicating someone during a criminal investigation, or allowing someone already incarcerated to go free."

"That's the double-edged sword of science," noted Strickland, who had just walked in. "People are freed by the technology, true. But sloppy data gathering or poor controls in the lab also run the risk of false positives. The technology's only as good as the discipline of its application."

"But look at how many opportunities there were for errors using the older forensic techniques," Randall said. "That was so hit-or-miss, it was practically a joke."

"Precisely, and everybody understood that," Strickland replied. "Now DNA analysis is viewed almost as if it had the stamp of God. If a DNA test says so, that's the final word—and that can be a dangerous supposition."

"I thought you guys were kidding when you first mentioned your debate club," Bender said. "And, Robert, it's interesting to see you taking Jordan's usual role as the scientific ethicist."

Strickland smiled. "A good debater can eviscerate from either side of an issue."

"Sounds like it could get brutal," she said. "Does it ever get out of hand?"

"Oh, he pisses me off from time to time, but I love him anyway," Strickland said, glancing over at Randall.

Watching him as he spoke, she realized she had never seen him smile so warmly.

Randall started wrapping up his forensic project, gathering notes and powering down the RES-5000. Then he began the transition to the Shroud project. He brought up a high-resolution digital image of the Shroud, provided by Dr. Rutigliano when the project first began. He and Strickland had amassed enough data that it was becoming possible to compare the image on the Shroud with certain physiological traits that had been gleaned from the Shroud's sequence data.

"Our base-pair data from the Shroud sample indicates a male of approximately five ten to six feet tall and weighing between a hundred and sixty and a hundred and eighty pounds," Randall said.

"How does that compare with the physical image on the Shroud?" Bender asked.

"It's a very close match."

"Of course, physiological traits have to be weighed against nutritional and lifestyle factors," Strickland said.

"Right. But if this is indeed an image of Jesus, who was a carpenter by trade and probably engaged in a lot of pushing and pulling and lifting, it makes perfect sense that he'd have a broad back and large pectoral muscles.

And that's exactly the appearance of the man on the Shroud."

"On the other hand, that would likely be seen in almost anyone doing heavy physical labor during that time," countered Strickland.

"True," said Randall. "But there are other supporting attributes as well. The prominent nose indicated by the sequence data and pictured on the Shroud is in keeping with some Semitic characteristics from the region. And then there are the corroborating genetic sequences that we found during the trip into the Negev. Countless bits of evidence indicate that the Shroud is a valid relic—or a forgery of almost unbelievable sophistication," he continued. "For example, virtually every historical image of Jesus—from the time just after his death right up through the Middle Ages—pictures the crucifixion nails being driven through the palms of the hands. Yet, anyone knowledgeable in human physiology and biomechanics knows that such a placement couldn't possibly hold the weight of a human body. As gruesome as it sounds, the only nail placement that makes sense in terms of simple physics is through the wrist—specifically, through the radius and ulna. And that's exactly where the wounds are on the Shroud. Also, note that there are no thumbs showing on the image. Driving large nails through the radius and ulna would undoubtedly sever the median nerve, which controls the flexion . . ." Here Randall's voice quavered. ". . . the extension of the thumb." He gazed back at the Shroud image, suddenly overcome with emotion. "The cruelty . . ."

Bender gazed at the image. "Maybe that's why I find it so hard to believe in God," she said. "I've just seen too much—villages hit by rocket-propelled grenades, small children blown to bits, and then people on the other side crediting divine guidance with the accuracy of their attack. What kind of God would permit a world like that?"

"The kind of God who's not a hoary grandfather figure with a serious mean streak," Strickland said. "Doling out his favors, subjugating us to his will, and then punishing us for violating that will."

Bender turned to him, clearly surprised. "Somehow, I never pegged you as the religious philosopher type."

"I draw a sharp line between religion and spirituality," he replied. "Spirituality unites, while theology typically divides. Organized religion has too many implicit agendas—power, territoriality, moral dictates. I see true spirituality as untainted by those concerns. In some sense, it's just a subset of the broader quest for knowledge. The goal of spirituality is more a pursuit of the divine, with the cultivation of states of transcendence, oneness, and compassion. What we call religion is really just a cultural template established by a particular society, with complex dogmas and rituals to help induce those states of transcendence and compassion. The institutions really just serve to create a sense of belonging to a given group. But too often, the institutions end up being used—whether intentionally or not—as a tool for tribalism and xenophobia. That's how we end up with religions of fear, filled with gods of moral judgment, and believers proclaiming, My God's bigger and better and shinier than your God.'"

Sara gazed at Strickland with rapt attention. "That's a great encapsulation."

"It's not just off the cuff—I think about this stuff," Strickland replied. "Einstein explored the idea of primitive, tribal, vengeful images of God back in the thirties, in an editorial letter to the *New York Times*. Sadly, not much has changed in the world since then. Maybe we're just not ready for a new kind of spirituality—a God of 'cosmic religious feeling,' as he put it."

"Well, we'd better *get* ready," Randall countered. "I remember, back in college, reading Arthur C. Clarke's science fiction book *Childhood's End*. It posed the idea that, due to the slow pace of evolution compared to the rapid pace of technological development, all advanced civilizations in the universe eventually reach a tipping point where their technology outdistances their development as a race. And they either come up to speed very quickly or ultimately destroy themselves. It's as if technological development is a timing device and, at the same time, a test. The test begins at the point that you're able to build weapons of mass destruction. We're at that point now and have to consider very carefully the paths we take."

"What amazes me is the endless ethnic strife around the world," said Bender. "I think every war I've ever covered came about over ethnic, religious, or territorial disputes."

"What else is there?" Strickland said. "Look at virtually every other animal species. They exhibit similar territoriality and tribalism. We're not all that different—we're just better at rationalizing our aggression."

"That's right," Randall said. "We need to somehow recast our perceptions to fit with our scientific knowledge—like we did once we realized the earth wasn't the center of the universe. Genomic science increasingly demonstrates that what we commonly refer to as 'race' is, for the most part, a misnomer based on superficial characteristics like skin color, hair texture, and facial attributes. Actually, there's far greater genetic variability *within* a given ethnic group than *between* them. But at a visceral, animal level, we can't seem to get past those superficial differences."

"But there *are* specific genetic differences between various races and ethnicities," Strickland said. "That's a good part of what we're all about here. Those differences may be small within the greater scheme of the human genome, but groups with sufficient knowledge and ill intent could leverage them. Somewhere down the line, there may be the potential for *smart* biological weapons that target a specific race or ethnicity."

Randall's face grew grim. "An ironic word choice: '*leverage,*'" he said. "But this isn't high finance. It's the potential to slaughter an entire ethnic group. This is why I'm an advocate of careful ethical analysis in the work we do. I feel as if we're on the verge of a second nuclear era, where our technology once again is almost beyond our ability to handle it responsibly. People worry about terrorists and hate groups getting hold of nuclear or radiological weapons, but that's just the tip of the iceberg." He sighed. "Something has to change in our *hearts,* while there's still time."

"On the other hand," Bender said, "aren't there inherent risks in *all* scientific endeavors—with unintended pitfalls, sure, but an inarguable forward march in spite of them?"

"Thank you," Strickland said, smiling.

"Of course," Randall admitted. "But we have to guard against the sin of hubris."

"What kind of hubris are we talking about?" Strickland asked.

"Scientific arrogance. Look, I'm not suggesting we shouldn't push the envelope. After all, heart transplants and in vitro fertilization were once considered 'playing God.' We just need to weigh carefully the consequences of what we do. And that's exactly why I helped form SEW."

"SEW?" Bender asked.

"Scientists for an Ethical World. It's a loose consortium of scientists, ethicists, and futurists, with an orientation toward helping to responsibly guide the application of new technologies. Of course, not everyone agrees on the need for such guidance," he said, shooting Strickland a look.

Strickland smiled back. "I leave the hand-wringing to you," he said. "I've chosen to stay focused on research. But I agree, these issues are important, and I'm glad you're involved."

"SEW was recently instrumental in lobbying against the sale of tropical fish that had been genetically altered to make them bioluminescent," Randall continued. "On the surface, that sounds relatively harmless—and obviously entertaining. But it's a perfect example of the subtleties of such issues. Several marine biologists in SEW pointed out that aquatic mating habits are often powerfully driven by coloration. Salmon, for example, change colors while spawning. If you add brightly colored luminescence overnight to a species that has never possessed it before, who knows what effect it might have—on that species or others."

"Fascinating," said Bender.

"And this isn't the first time we've seen the march of civilization come back to haunt us," Randall said. "Did you know that multiple sclerosis symptoms were never reported in the medical literature before the industrial revolution? Something we've introduced into the environment is affecting people who are genetically susceptible to the disease. And now we're seeing something similar with autism, where the incidence of the disease has increased severalfold in the last few decades—for equally mysterious reasons. The biological landscape is extremely subtle and complex."

"But meanwhile, we have half the developing world refusing to grow crops that have been genetically altered to resist drought and disease," Strickland argued. "Even though genetic manipulation has been practiced, through selective cross-breeding, for thousands of years."

"But never to the extent of fundamentally altering an organism overnight," Randall said.

"Fair enough," Strickland smiled at Bender. These issues are complex. And the debates are virtually endless, particularly when Jordan and I are involved. Let's call it a draw for now."

Chapter 35

Bender pulled her bathrobe around her and sipped at a steaming cup of tea. She had decided to spend the morning consolidating notes and organizing her office workspace. The volume of information related to the Shroud project was already enormous, but she had been careful to transcribe everything daily to keep her stack of hard copy at a manageable level. To avoid any single point of failure, she also e-mailed attached files to an online archival facility. She had never forgotten the story of a colleague who had gotten her laptop snatched while passing through Ataturk International in Istanbul—two months of work vanished in an instant.

Out the window of her second-story apartment, the sky was a featureless sheet of gray. The sheen from an earlier rain still coated the bare white poplars below. It was Sunday, and during such downtimes in D.C., loneliness sometimes settled in. Maybe it was the first-world comfort zone. On assignment in a conflict-ridden hot spot, it was a second full-time job just staying fed, healthy, and out of harm's way. But here there was time to ruminate, and the adrenaline level was generally much lower.

Staring out the window, she wondered what Tom was doing, and picked up the phone, then caught herself. Instead, she checked her e-mail. There was a note from her editor, wishing her luck on the "secret project."

"Thanks, Ron," she wrote back. "Things are going well. Looking forward to telling you all about it. (Well, you might have to read the book.) Best, Sara."

Finally, she gave in and dialed her home number in Manhattan, thinking Tom might still be reading the morning paper. But it rolled over to the answering system, and she hung up. She started to dial his cell number, then aborted the call halfway through and set the phone down.

You need to go out, she told herself. *Get some fresh air.*

Bender put on sweats, then headed to the jogging trail that wound along Rock Creek Parkway. The air was brisk, and the run cleared her head. As if in affirmation, blue patches began breaking through the dome of gray.

Reaching the end of the trail, she decided to cool down by walking along the shops on M Street. She stared in the window of an upscale photo gallery, admiring artful black-and-white images of D.C. history—President

Nixon shaking hands in the Oval Office with an obviously high Elvis Presley, and the hundreds of thousands gathered on the Mall in 1963 to hear Martin Luther King Jr.

"This stuff is good," a familiar voice said, "but if you're looking for Chelsea, I'd try P Street." Bender turned to find Robert Strickland standing beside her.

"Oh, hi!" she blurted. Then she caught herself and turned the enthusiasm down a notch.

She and Strickland began speaking at once, then stopped at the same time. They both burst out laughing.

"Okay, let's start the scene over," he said. "After a marathon at the laptop, you needed a break and some street energy."

"Something like that," she said, smiling.

"Even after all these years, I still enjoy the museums. There's always something new. Afterwards, I usually come over here for a beer, then wander along the river."

It felt odd to encounter Strickland in this setting. He seemed unguarded, almost a different person. The sky had begun to gray over again, and a chill ran through her, so she untied the sweatshirt from around her waist and put it on.

"Want to stop in Dean & Deluca's for a cup of something?" he asked.

"Yeah," she said. "I'd like that."

As they moved toward the café, Bender scanned the bustling market. "I sometimes drop by D & D's in Soho when I'm in that part of town," she said. "This one's very different but quite nice."

"Yeah, I like the jazz quartet that plays on weekends."

They found a small table near the back and were soon trading New York stories.

"So, is Danceteria still in business?" he asked.

"It *is*," she said, laughing in surprise.

"I went there a few times. But I used to go to CBGB at least once a month."

"They had a long run," Bender said. "Believe it or not, I recently went to a rock club in the Bowery—the concierge in our building has a band that's playing around town, and they're really pretty good."

"That's great. It's been a long time since I was at a show like that. Sometimes I really miss New York."

Over several refills, they covered everything from avant-garde classical music, to the sad state of current rock, to online file sharing. But during a lull in the conversation, Bender caught Strickland checking his watch. The gesture reminded her of her first visit to the lab, and she suddenly found herself wanting to get away, before their old dynamic somehow returned.

By the time they were back on M Street, it was already dusk and the streetlamps were flickering on. "Where are you parked?" Strickland asked.

"I'm not," she said. "I ran here, along Rock Creek Parkway."

"I don't think going back that way's such a great idea at this hour. Plus, it's getting pretty cold—why don't I give you a lift?"

"Great," she said. But as they crossed the street, and Strickland headed for a big BMW motorcycle, she began to have second thoughts.

He unlocked his helmet from the bike. "There's only one hard hat, so you need to wear it," he said, handing it to her. "If I get a ticket, *c'est la vie*—I haven't had one in a while." And as Bender swung her leg over the back of the bike, he said, "Put your arms around my waist."

As they wound along the bustling evening streets of Georgetown, she began to relax. Strickland was clearly a seasoned rider, slowing to the perfect speed for each turn, then accelerating back out. She found herself following his body language, leaning into the curves and then straightening up again. It reminded her a bit of horseback riding when she was a girl. Odd that in all the places she had visited, she'd never ridden on the back of a motorcycle before.

As they pulled up in front of her apartment building, Bender hopped off the bike, unfastened the helmet and ran her fingers through her hair.

"It was good running into you!" Strickland said.

"It was. I really enjoyed it," she said, smiling. A moment of dead air followed. "Well…see you back at the lab," she said.

With a nod, Strickland put on his helmet. He started the BMW and waved, then pulled away from the curb. She watched the red taillight disappear around a far corner, and only the distant sound of the engine remained in the cold night air.

Chapter 36

Sara Bender had blocked out Monday for online research on the Shroud project. She wanted to better understand pseudogenes, DNA methylation, and gene amplification, all of which Strickland and Randall had mentioned in passing. But before she could begin, the typical half hour's worth of e-mail awaited. She ran down her in-box, deleting many of the messages, sight unseen. Then she spotted one with an address that jumped out at her.

To: Sara.Bender@nyt.com
From: Jason.Newcomb@vatican.va
Subject: Me and You.

Hey Sara,

Just wanted to check in.

Things are really interesting here. My research is going well, but there are the usual turf battles, as in any large institution. Thankfully, I'm on the political periphery, so I'm more like a fly on the wall. But I've learned whose egos to stroke to gain access to the materials I need.

I'm hoping to get a renewal of my fellowship, but with recent budget cuts, iconography is not exactly a top priority. Plus, you know me, I've never been one to hold my tongue. So who knows how much longer I'll be welcome around here. The pope does have a group of well-educated and fairly open-minded science advisers. I've had some great discussions with them. But more often than not, the nails that stick up get hammered down.

Regarding the study we discussed…if true, I'm surprised it was approved. I can only assume there are wildly differing motivations from the various internal camps. It's really hard to know what's going on beneath the surface. But you can sometimes feel a gathering sense of change in the wind.

Well, I'd better get back to work. My "mentor" will soon be back to check on me.

XOXO, Jason

P.S. I'll be on the east coast in spring. Let's get together!

She had met Jason at Columbia, in her sophomore Introduction to Reporting class. He was sensitive, funny, and smart. Sara had a crush on him from the moment they met, but somehow they hadn't clicked romantically. In frustration, she threw herself at him one night after a late movie. He returned her kisses, but it was a halting, awkward encounter. Soon they drifted apart.

He finally came out to her during their junior year, saying he hadn't really been sure himself until then. Afterward, Sara would see him around campus with his new boyfriend, and he seemed truly happy.

He told her that just before entering college, he had seriously considered the priesthood. But after coming out, he had a different perspective. "I couldn't imagine giving up my sexuality just when I'd finally figured out who I was."

At first he had dabbled in journalism, then drama, but finally settled on religious history, specializing in the field of iconography, and eventually earned a PhD from Harvard Divinity School.

"I'll still get to spend time in the Church," he had explained, "but without the obvious downsides."

She moved Jason's message to a special mailbox she kept for personal e-mail. She didn't plan to mention that she was on assignment at the NIH.

* * *

Crunching along the winding snow-covered paths to the NIH the next morning, Bender came around a steep curve and almost stepped on a wild rabbit. The creature froze at first, but when she stopped, it seemed to regard her more calmly. Its whiskers began to move, and its big, liquid eye looked right into hers. There was something almost transcendent in the moment. It was as if she was truly *seeing* a rabbit for the first time. She felt a sudden and profound connection, beyond that of potential predator and prey. Or maybe it was nothing more than sleep deprivation, she thought, laughing wryly to herself. She and Tom had stayed up arguing until late into the night.

Eventually, the rabbit seemed to tire of the interaction and hopped around a little snowbank to disappear down a hole. Trudging up the hill to the Ethnogenomics Center, Bender returned to considering her late-night disagreement with Tom. He seemed increasingly resentful of her being in D.C. and had begun saying things like "Maybe we need this time apart, to get a better sense of where we're going."

Just days before, Tom had told her how important she was to him and how much he missed her. Had he made this more recent pronouncement out of childish petulance? Sometimes she wondered whether it was even worth trying to figure out the inner workings of men.

Inside the building, Bender grabbed a cup of tea from the break room, then headed for the lab—and walked into the middle of one of Strickland and Randall's frequent "discussions."

". . . But we still haven't answered the ultimate questions about the Shroud," Strickland was saying. "Was it the actual burial cloth of Jesus? And more importantly, who, or what, *was* Jesus?"

"I don't think anyone can really answer those questions," Randall replied, "at least not scientifically. At a certain point, it all boils down to a matter of intuition and belief. We've added several new pieces to the scientific puzzle, and in all likelihood, that's all we—or anyone else—can do."

"I'm not sure I buy that," Strickland said.

"Then what do you suggest?" asked Randall. "We've done mitochondrial dating and gross physiological typing, not to mention the Negev tribal study. Where else would you have us go?"

Bender glanced at the RES-5000 display panel on the wall. "What about a genetic reanimation?" she interjected. "I'm actually surprised that hasn't come up."

"It's certainly occurred to me," Strickland said, turning to focus on her. "But I knew we weren't far enough along datawise. Plus, I've learned to choose my battles. I suspected there would be plenty of other minefields along the way."

"What would it take to perform a reanimation on the Shroud data?" she asked.

"We're about seventy percent there," Strickland said. "The lab's sequencing systems are tied up during the day on other projects, but if we commandeered them at night and ran them all in parallel, we could probably get the necessary data in two to three weeks—that's assuming we manage to get enough nonfractured sequence strands. After all, according to our tests so far, this is two-thousand-year-old blood."

Bender noticed that Randall had remained conspicuously silent. "What do you think, Jordan?" she asked.

After a pause, he said, "I've thought long and hard about this. It sits at a place of great difficulty for a man of both science and faith. In general, I agree with Bob: the role of the scientist is to forge ahead. And I believe that's why God gave us the ability to apply our minds toward such tasks. On the other hand, the discoveries we make here could have profound consequences, in ways none of us can predict. History has taught us that time and time again."

"But as you've already agreed, there are inherent risks and unknowns in any scientific endeavor," she said.

Randall fell silent again for a moment, then said, "Even though it may seem antithetical to the scientific process, I think the heart sometimes has to be followed in these matters. My head tells me to be careful, but my heart urges me on. I feel that very strongly."

"So we're agreed regarding reanimation with the RES-5000?" Strickland asked, clearly hoping to seize the moment.

"I think we are," Randall replied.

Chapter 37

Strickland sat in his breakfast nook, browsing through the *Washington Post*. Normally, he would have been well into his work at the lab, but an early storm had hit, and the entire eastern seaboard was snowed in. The Maryland State Police had issued an advisory recommending against any unnecessary driving. He had already stored the motorcycle for the winter, but even the Jeep would have been dicey on a day like this. He had briefly accessed the NIH extranet from home, but the storm eventually knocked out his Internet access.

The large wooden mantel clock struck nine just as he poured himself a second cup of coffee. The clock's twin chimes produced a beautiful low, droning harmony, which soon faded back into the soft chatter of the device's inner workings. Strickland's father had been a collector of antique clocks, and this was the most impressive of the ones still working at the time of his death.

In his childhood, clocks and watches had endlessly fascinated Strickland. He had marveled at the perfect logic of their design, with each spring, wheel, and gear working together in an almost unfathomable harmony.

His father, also a physician, had often been emotionally remote, but he enjoyed working with his hands, and spent long hours helping Strickland build detailed models of airplanes and cars. These activities were among the few close times they had spent together.

One of his father's clocks had long been missing the alarm hand, and as a result, it was impossible to know when it would chime. Young Strickland had experimented by setting it at random and then trying to deduce the precise moment it would go off. The process was endlessly fascinating to him. It was a complex system, yet completely predictable given sufficient knowledge.

The clocks seemed almost alive, and indeed, he had used his father's stethoscope to listen to their rhythmic ticking and whirring, trying to discern more of the mysteries within. Finally, one summer night, he took apart another of the clocks in an attempt to repair the broken one. But while the transplanted mechanism had appeared to fit perfectly, the clock no longer kept time properly afterward, and it stopped chiming entirely. In desperation, he returned the part to the original clock, but it, too, seemed damaged by the undertaking. His father was furious, saying he'd ruined them both. But young Robert had felt almost compelled to do it, and was certain he had gained something invaluable in the process.

Strickland had always been a loner as a child, intelligent but painfully shy. As a result, he became a voracious reader, retreating into the realms of Jack London, Robert Louis Stevenson, and H. G. Wells. He marveled at how simple letters, and the words built of them, could conjure up entire worlds that seemed as real as anything around him. At the library, he wandered the aisles of books intended for older children, sometimes unable to fully decipher the vocabulary, yet certain in the knowledge that he one day would.

Later, in the fifth grade, he came across an old issue of *Life* magazine in the library archive. It featured the developing science of DNA. He marveled at how such a machinelike process could be the basis for all life. Thinking back to his father's clocks, he wondered how complicated something had to be before it somehow became "alive." And where was the soul in such a construct? When something became sufficiently complex, did a soul simply arrive?

One hot summer day, Strickland sat in the backyard, observing the frantic activities of an ant colony. He illuminated the small anthill with a magnifying glass, imagining the ants to be soldiers under the glare of a desert sun. Then, urged on by a neighbor boy, he gathered the light beam into a white-hot point. The ants scattered in disarray, but those caught directly in the beam began to fizzle and smoke and curl until a passing breeze blew their desiccated bodies away.

Strickland felt terrible about what he had done. Did ants, too, have a soul? He later posed the question to the family minister, who said he should stop wasting his time on such thoughts and keep his energies focused where they belonged.

It was the gaps in scientific theory that most intrigued young Strickland. And the more he learned, the more these gaps troubled him. The evolutionary transition from single-celled organisms to more complex life forms was easy to imagine, but the initial leap from simple organic compounds to the complexity of self-replicating DNA was almost unfathomable. And the subsequent leap from simple, instinctive life forms to self-aware mammals, and all the way up the ladder to Einstein, Mozart, and Shakespeare, boggled the mind.

As an undergrad, Strickland read a book about the life of Alan Turing, the British mathematician and early philosopher on the world of computing. Turing asked questions that no one before him had, such as "Can a computer think? And if so, how would we really know?"

Turing suggested that if a computer's response became complex and believable enough to be indistinguishable from a human's, then it could be said to be thinking. This criterion, known as the "Turing test," was used to evaluate many early programs intended to perform humanlike tasks. One such program was a computer-based psychoanalyst. The program might ask, "What brings you to see me?" If the patient typed in, "I have problems with my mother," the computer might reply, "Tell me about your mother."

To Strickland, such software seemed little more than a parlor gimmick, an imitation of consciousness. It was like comparing an impassioned concert pianist to a player piano. Even if its performance could be made indistinguishable from the real thing, did the automated piano, in playing its sonata, experience a sense of rapture, of having approached the divine? But he had to admit, many lower life forms seemed little different from automata. Ants performed complex social interactions, but there was scant room in their world for variability, adaptability, or self-awareness. They were essentially hardwired in their responses—arguably little different from a Turing machine.

But if such organisms were not truly conscious, did they feel no pain, hunger, or longing? Was their existence simply an array of chemical messages and responses? And if so, when was the line crossed toward true consciousness—and how? At what point did the capacity for experiences like longing, love, music, and poetry come into play? And conversely, what if a computer should become sufficiently complex—did it, at some ill-defined point, stop merely simulating a living thing and actually *become* one?

* * *

The next morning at dawn, Strickland awoke to a dazzling azure sky. The snow from days ago was all but gone and the ground bone dry in many places. He thought back to his undergraduate chemistry days—the theory of phase changes in a substance, and how, under the right conditions of temperature and pressure, snow could, as if by magic, pass into a vapor state without ever having melted.

Wanting to make up for lab time lost during the snowstorm, he decided to skip breakfast. Heading out the front door, he heard a tiny fluttering sound coming from behind the living room curtains. Setting down his leather briefcase, he pulled back the curtains to find a small moth trapped in a spider's web. With its nimble limbs, the spider was busily wrapping the still-struggling insect for a winter ration. There was something horrifyingly methodical about the process, like watching a dispassionate torturer at work. Yet he knew that the spider felt nothing whatever—it was simply operating on instinct.

The image carried Strickland back to his childhood, watching a similar event with his father. His father had insisted that he observe the spider's handiwork, patiently explaining that nature was not always kind but that there was a plan behind it all. He told the boy how local ranchers had once slaughtered coyotes as a matter of course, believing they were protecting their flocks of sheep. But the ranchers had unwittingly upset the balance of nature, dooming the overpopulation of sheep to cruel starvation once winter came.

Strickland let the curtain fall back into place. But halfway out the door, he paused and set down his briefcase. Pushing the spider aside with a pencil, he extricated the struggling moth from the web, peeling away the strong gossamer strands, and brought the insect outside, where it flew erratically up into the blue sky.

Chapter 38

Once they made the decision to sequence the Shroud DNA, Strickland and Randall completely immersed themselves in the project, and all other concerns seemed to fall away. Bender, sensing this dynamic, pulled back to become more of a passive observer.

To gain access to the necessary sequencing hardware, Strickland reallocated the resources of several other projects—a move that couldn't help but raise eyebrows among the senior researchers. But the center's charter anticipated work involving sensitive government projects and research partnerships with the private sector, and in such situations, where security concerns or intellectual property rights came into play, it was sometimes necessary to establish discrete cells of activity to minimize exposure of the bigger picture. As part of this dynamic, Strickland and Randall recruited doctoral students to handle some of the more routine tasks. Most seemed flattered, but also a little mystified, to be working under their direct supervision.

Soon they had commandeered over half the lab's large-scale sequencing machines. As one of the original pioneers in digital reanimation technology, Randall was in charge of cataloging and tracking the progress of this phase II analysis of the Shroud sample.

Bender sat quietly and watched as Randall archived the DNA samples and pored through the workstation's subdirectories, labeling and organizing the digital information. She marveled at his methodical focus combined with a sort of quiet reverence, as if he was assembling the pieces of something that went beyond scientific inquiry.

Chapter 39

Much to Strickland's annoyance, he had been called across town to an interagency meeting at the Department of Health and Human Services. It was a command performance—certain bureaucratic functions couldn't be ignored.

Rocking from side to side in a D.C. Metro car, he watched as a half-asleep infant sipped from a cup of formula offered by his mother. Strickland thought back to his first time encounter with a straw. Not knowing quite what to do, he had blown Coca-Cola all over his mother's new summer dress.

As a boy, he had marveled at how things *seemed* to operate in a certain way, and yet, with more information, a given perception could be turned completely on its head. For instance, when you sucked on a straw, it *felt* as if you were drawing the liquid into your mouth. But in reality you were creating a vacuum, and the atmosphere, like a giant, unseen hand, was pushing down on the liquid, forcing it up into the straw.

When he was about twelve, while playing in the backyard, Strickland experienced a simple but earthshaking epiphany. His father had recently bought him a beginner's guide to stargazing, and he had begun reading about the planets and constellations. There had been numerous fires raging in the wooded foothills near their home that summer. After several seasons of drought, the underbrush had become bone dry, ready to explode into flames from the first errant spark. Strickland stood with his arms outstretched as tiny flakes of ash drifted down like snow from the orange-brown sky. It felt like the end of the world. He stared directly up at the midday sun, which had been reduced to a glowing red ball. And suddenly he knew in his gut that it was a star—like any other, but simply closer. Before that moment, he had, of course, known it on an intellectual level, but now he *felt* it at his core. And the feeling persisted, long after that summer's fires had died out. Afterward, it was like a reassuring secret: in the middle of the day, in brightest sunlight, Strickland felt himself bathed in warming starlight.

His stargazing book also detailed the history of celestial theory. In the pre-Copernican world, when it was still believed that the earth was the center of the universe, theories abounded as to the mechanics of celestial orbits. Some proposed elaborate concentric crystal spheres containing the stars. But to explain the movements of observable objects in the heavens, such theories grew ever more unwieldy. A small number of celestial bodies—what were later shown to be planets—seemed, inexplicably, to reverse direction at regular intervals. As a result, layer upon layer of celestial spheres were added to the theory, like an ever-growing cosmic onion.

Finally, Nicolaus Copernicus, an astronomer and Catholic cleric, proposed that the prevailing view of the heavens was incorrect. If the earth was simply shifted from its intuitively obvious position as the center of the heavens to become just another of the many planets orbiting the sun, all the observable phenomena of the night sky suddenly fell into perfect order. And the theory of celestial spheres came crashing down.

But this profound shift of thought took hundreds of years to become universally accepted, in the process threatening the very lives of many of its proponents. The reality of our celestial existence—that the earth turns on its own axis while simultaneously orbiting the sun—was completely counterintuitive.

In the backyard that summer, with ashes drifting down around him, young Robert Strickland considered the notion that everything might not be as it seemed. There was little reason to believe that today's understanding of the universe was any more final than the theory of celestial spheres had been. What if our current scientific theories were also incomplete, perhaps in profound ways? What if there were forces and principles beyond current understanding or testing? And what if, somehow, both viewpoints—what science told you and what you felt deep down—were correct in their own way? Maybe, at least in some instances, each was simply a different way of looking at the same thing.

Chapter 40

Strickland began the morning by updating Randall on yesterday's meeting in D.C., then moved on to a number of departmental scheduling issues. But during the discussion, it became increasingly obvious that Randall was distracted and out of sorts. He seemed hazy on the details of a budgetary issue that had been plaguing them for months.

Strickland finally interrupted his own narrative: "So, what's going on, Jordan?" he asked.

"I didn't sleep too well last night," Randall said, rubbing his eyes. "Had the craziest dream . . ."

Strickland pulled up a chair, resting his arms over the back. "Tell me about it, Dr. Randall."

"Seriously, it was quite disturbing," he said. "I don't recall the whole thing. All I really remember is, there was an explosion of some sort . . ." He stared out the window. "I was there in a room with the Shroud, but not just our little swatch of it—the entire thing. The room was stark white tile, an almost clinical setting."

Strickland watched Randall as he relayed the dream. His old friend spoke as if describing something that had actually occurred.

"Suddenly, there was a massive explosion, and the room erupted in flames," Randall continued. "I tried to save the Shroud, but the heat was too intense. I was finally driven back by the flames. . . . That's all I remember. There was a sudden shift of time, or place—I'm really not sure. And then it was back again."

"The Shroud?" Strickland asked.

"Yes. But not like before. It was suddenly pure white, shimmering, as if newly formed—almost as if woven of a different fabric . . . and completely untouched by the flames."

Strickland brought his fingers together, forming a steeple beneath his chin. "Classic symbology: trial by fire, the savior's ultimate renewal, and then a cleansing of the soul. Oops, I'm afraid our time's up. See you next week."

"Okay, joke if you must," Randall said. "But it felt very powerful at the time. I didn't get back to sleep for hours."

"I know. I'm just kidding," Strickland said. "This project is heavy stuff, particularly for someone of your background and orientation. But we have to stay focused. In the end, it's all about the data. We need to dispassionately gather the pieces, try to fit them together, and see where it all leads."

Randall sighed. "I know. But this work straddles two worlds that I normally keep rather separate. I guess it's affecting me more than I'd like to think."

But detailing the dream must have helped clear Randall's mind, and he seemed newly focused. "By the way," he continued, "I've been meaning to tell you something very important—about our IT infrastructure. Because we've been reallocating some of our processing resources, I've been updating the security software on our various servers. In the process, I discovered an apparent break-in on Vishnu."

"That's one of our oldest servers, right?"

"Exactly," Randall said. "Due to its slow processing speed, we've been using it as an archive for e-mail and various NIH publications."

"Then why's it even on the Net?"

"Other systems hyperlink to some of our past publications. I'm afraid it's not the best possible arrangement, but it's become a bit of a dumping ground for older data that's still useful and needs to be kept online."

Strickland looked concerned. "Any corruption of the files?"

"None at all," Randall said. "I've run comparisons from last month's disk backups, and they all check out."

"Nevertheless, we need to get those e-mail files out of there."

"Agreed, and done," said Randall. "But rest assured, the directories were all configured for *root*-level access, and the mail files were asymmetrically encrypted. It would have taken someone with a root password to get in—and even then they'd have to get past the encryption to access any actual messages."

Chapter 41

Sara Bender had just returned from an afternoon run along the Rock Creek trail. After the biting air outside, her apartment felt like a sauna. She peeled off her sweats, down to T-shirt and running shorts, then spent several minutes doing cool-down exercises. As she leaned up against the living room wall, stretching out her hamstrings, she eyed the answering machine's display—no messages.

Her interactions with Tom hadn't really gotten *worse* since she came to D.C., but they certainly hadn't improved. The best she could expect was a late-night phone call or two each week, and a few e-mails. Usually, by the time they had caught up on the details of their work life, it was too late to get into anything deeper. They were almost like business partners now, she thought. But then, what was the business?

Tossing her towel and sweats into the laundry hamper, she sat down at her computer to check e-mail. A handful of messages appeared in the in-box. Her messages from the *Times* had slowed to a trickle. She mentally sang a John Lennon line: *No longer riding on the merry-go-rah-hound...*"

Sometimes she wondered if the book project had been the right move. Ron, her editor at the *Times,* had been supportive, but maybe he was simply reacting the way he thought she wanted him to. And then the Shroud project had fallen into her lap, potentially steering the book in a whole new direction. Bender had always trusted her intuition about a story, but this was definitely uncharted territory. Even though Strickland could be prickly, he was more or less on her philosophical wavelength. She genuinely liked Randall, but she had always been a bit suspicious of devout believers. Together, though, the two men presented a fascinating dynamic. Still, she wondered where to take the story once the research angle played out.

Scanning down the list of spam messages, Bender noticed a new e-mail from Jason.

To: Sara.Bender@nyt.com
From: Jason.Newcomb@vatican.va
Subject: Big V.

Hey Sara,

It's late here, but I need to vent a little. There's seemingly no rhyme or reason to the bureaucracy at the Big V. I'll request a document one week and have it approved, then request a seemingly innocuous companion document the next week, and be told that it's "not available for review." And I'm a visiting academic fellow. Imagine what it's like for anyone else trying to do serious research.

I just get bits and pieces of this, but there's a palpable sense of the old and new guard here. The old guard clearly feels under siege—and is hunkering down. It's as if the world is simply changing too fast for them. There are those actively seeking change—liberalization on issues like stem cell research, women in the priesthood, dropping the celibacy requirement, gays in the clergy, etc. But most are just trying to stay out of the fray. The old guard clearly wants to hold onto power (and the past) at any cost. It's like a modern-day echo of the struggles Galileo faced.

But when it's good, there's nothing like it. This place is truly a treasure trove of religious history. And there's a genuine spiritual vibration here. At times, I can really feel it.

By the way, the project you asked about seems real. I've heard further rumblings. Did you find out anything more? I can't imagine there was universal consent, or even knowledge of it. Maybe it just squeaked by as a result of the controlled chaos. But someone around here was clearly interested in seeing it go forward. Maybe there's hope for this place yet—in terms of becoming more intellectually open, and moving into the modern era.

Anyway, back to my candlelit cave…

Love, and later,
Jason

Chapter 42

The men gathered in a dimly lit room with wood-paneled walls. The space was bare but for a table in one corner, with an antiquated personal computer on top. The screen was washed out from years of use, making it difficult to read except in low light.

In the past, before a more modern facility was built on another floor, the room had been used by novices for solitary liturgical research. Now few even remembered that the computer was still here, and the room's location, in a seldom-trafficked basement of the Palace of the Holy Office, offered the assembled men the privacy they required.

The group formed a semicircle around a young man seated in front of the computer screen. "You have something for us?" the elder of the group rasped.

"I believe so," said the young man as his fingers flew across the keyboard. He accessed an Internet search facility and entered a group of search strings. A scattering of Internet postings scrolled down the screen. Most were nonrelevant variations on the entered search items.

"These are the postings of interest," said the young man as text trickled down the screen.

They all drew closer, and one hurriedly put on reading glasses.

From: DarkStar3.14159@gmail.com   Message 14 in thread
Subject: What's Manny up to?
Newsgroup: rec.music.gdead

"PigPen" PigPen999@gmail.com wrote in a message:

I'm heading down to Mexico this summer, maybe I'll just keep going, check out Belize and pay old Manny a visit. I've got some killer produce to share with him.
No way, Pig. Manny's keeping a low profile these days. He wants no hassles or interaction with the gov't of Belize. Plus, I hear if you even walk ashore uninvited, you'll end up staring down the barrel of a gun. Attempt a visit at your own peril.

P.S. Only an idiot would trek through Central America while holding. It takes big $$s to bribe your way out of a 3rd world jail.

The elder scanned the computer screen, then reacted angrily. "Why are we being shown this? What possible relevance can it have?"

"Please, Father, bear with me." He clicked on the "Next Page" button, and a second page of text appeared.

> From: JamBoneTrombone@gmail.com   Message 15 in thread
> Subject: What's Manny up to?
> Newsgroup: rec.music.gdead
>
> Speaking of Manny, check this out…some friends of mine (did I just say that?) recently hacked into a government system. Believe it or not, they guessed one of Manny's old passwords, and the account had root privileges. And amazingly, it was still active (guess it's good enough for government work). They followed some hyperlinks, and ended up on a system filled with 64 bit encrypted e-mail. The Feds still don't seem to realize how easy that is to crack.
>
> Anyway, thinking they might find something good, they picked through it. Man, there was some strange stuff—about the Vatican, carbon dating, "the sample," "blood work." It was like they were going out of their way to be sketchy. It all got my buddy's Spider Sense going. Remember that Dead interview, where Lesh was talking about how Jimmy Herring looks like the face on the Shroud of Turin? What if these Feds are doing some kind of DNA work on the Shroud? Imagine what a guy like Manny could do with data like that? No more cloning poodles for bored billionaires.

An anxious rustling filled the room. For several seconds the assembled men stared in silence at the glowing text.

"This could be what we have been praying for," the elder said. He patted the young man on the shoulder. "You have been of great service."

The men moved away from the computer and gathered in a far corner of the room. "Let us hope we are in time," the old man whispered.

Chapter 43

Over morning coffee, Randall appeared nervous but jubilant. He took a sip, savoring it, and then announced that the final Shroud sequencing had been completed last night.

It was hard for Bender to read his emotions—an odd mixture of excitement and apprehension. Strickland's reaction was, as usual, inscrutable.

Randall explained that to save time, they had sequenced the minimum base pairs required for full-facial imaging. While such sequence coverage would not provide the ultimate degree of visual resolution, it was still within the range required for his forensic-imaging work.

The only remaining task was to consolidate the data from the past few weeks with the previously amassed Shroud sequences; then everything would be ready for the RES-5000 system.

Bender sat back, watching the flurry of activity. Randall transferred files from the various networked systems onto the RES system's disk drive, preparing for importation into the reanimation software. On the surface, the work seemed routine enough, but beneath that veneer there was palpable tension.

As he transferred the remaining files, Randall turned to her and explained, "The system first constructs an on-screen wire matrix of the subject's face, similar to those used in building 3-D computer graphics images for the movies. But those originate solely from the imagination or from preproduction sketches, while ours is driven by the raw genetic sequence data."

Bender found herself instinctively falling into note taking, while trying to keep eye contact with Randall.

"We begin with sequences that define the gross skeletal contours of the face," he said, "then work our way up to the finer granularity of musculature and, finally, to skin color and tone."

"If his day job doesn't pan out, there's always Hollywood," Strickland said, grinning.

Randall ignored the comment. "At the display level, we do a series of data renderings," he said, "first transforming the wire mesh framework to a tissue-like graphical covering. Then we mathematically round out the discrete elements into a fully blended face, and add skin tones and ambient lighting and shading. These last stages require massive computational throughput. As our imaging has gotten more sophisticated and realistic, we've had to network more and more systems together to do the calculations in parallel—otherwise, we'd be here all night. In the past, the final rendering stages really *did* take all night."

Randall paused, glancing over at Bender. After scribbling down a sentence, she nodded and he continued. "Beyond the hardwired aspects of the genome, there are phenotypic and environmental elements that also come into play, such as . . . ?" he asked, slipping into teaching mode.

"Um . . . age, lifestyle, and nutrition?" she speculated.

"Exactly," he said. "Depending on subject age, the system has to generate appropriate wrinkles and sags, along with age-appropriate hair color and texture. And the same is true for general skin tone and texture. Then there are more subtle phenotypic manifestations, like age spots and microcapillary prominence in the thinning skin of the elderly. And many of these variables are further affected and compounded by environmental factors like long-term exposure to the sun. So even the subject's occupation becomes a factor in the rendering."

Randall pulled up a command pallet on the screen of the RES-5000. It presented a series of fields for age, occupation, and country of residence, with pull-down values for each. "In this case, I'm leaving the presentation variables at their default values," he said. "We'll present the image in standard indoor lighting, which is what we generally do for our criminal work. I've defined the subject to be age thirty-three, with an occupation of 'outdoor laborer.' And I've configured the system to present head and facial hair in a style consistent with the Biblical time.

Randall closed the configuration window, pausing briefly to look at Bender, then at Strickland. Getting no further response, he turned back to the screen and hit the "Final Render" button.

"So what do we do now?" she asked.

"We wait," said Randall. He took off his glasses and rubbed his eyes. "Let's meet back here in an hour. That should give the system enough time."

As the two scientists gathered up their paperwork, Strickland made fleeting eye contact with Bender, but as was so often the case, she couldn't decipher the meaning. And when she looked back for Randall, he was heading out the door.

Chapter 44

The phone rang, and the reporter cradled the receiver on one shoulder while picking at the remnants of a maple-glazed donut.

"Hello?" he said.

"Is this *The Sword*?" a gravelly voice inquired.

"It is," said the reporter. "May I help you?"

"I have some news . . . which I believe will be of great interest to you."

The caller's sense of drama was a bit irritating, but the reporter grabbed a pen and a yellow notepad, tearing away to a new page. "May I ask who this is?" he said, taking a gulp of bad coffee.

"I am not at liberty to say."

"Okay, then tell me what you have—we'll worry about the rest later. Go ahead."

Chapter 45

Bender wandered out the main doors of the Ethnogenomics building. The drooping birches hung heavy with last night's snow, in air so clear she felt she could reach out and touch the hills beyond.

She caught herself obsessively checking the time, not wanting to report back late to the lab. If the reanimation image looked nothing like the Shroud, it would certainly be the end of her work here, and she would have significantly delayed her original book project. But she wouldn't regret having come. If nothing else, there was something irresistibly compelling about the creative dynamic between Strickland and Randall.

A lone blackbird soared low over the rooftops, its call echoing between the stone buildings. The bird was strikingly beautiful—the sheen of its jet-black wings with their bright scarlet epaulets in the winter light, the sweeping arc of its flight. It perched in a high treetop and stared down at her, and something made her stop to admire the creature. Then, just as suddenly as the bird had arrived, it leaped up from its branch and gathered speed over a patch of open ground, in a true line toward the east. It cawed repeatedly, and she watched until it became a black speck against the slate gray sky.

* * *

When she returned to the lab, Strickland and Randall were already there. Randall was making last-minute adjustments to the RES-5000. After several minutes, he finally looked up. "Everybody ready?" he asked. Sara nodded, not even glancing at Strickland.

Randall dimmed a bank of overhead lights, then returned to his chair and hit the display button on the computer console. And as they watched the large high-resolution display mounted on the wall, the image slowly resolved from the top down.

As the display process completed, Randall gasped. It was a dead ringer for the Shroud visage, and the skin tone was clearly that of a Middle Eastern man.

But there was something more. The face seemed indescribably beatific, almost luminous. And there was something remarkable in the eyes—a palpable sense of inner peace that somehow transcended the computer-generated likeness. Bender wondered if it was just her own mental construct, but when she looked from Randall to Strickland, they appeared similarly entranced.

For a long moment no one spoke.

"My God . . ." Randall murmured, finally.

Not wanting to influence the response, Bender said nothing, waiting for Strickland's reaction. He paced the room, staring at the image and thinking aloud. "We're right on the money in terms of corroborating our earlier findings," he said. "This is definitely a Middle Eastern male, and it clearly matches the image on the Shroud. As to any *otherworldly* aspects that Jordan might argue for, I think that's quite easily explained. We're operating on a minimum of sequence data here—the very *lack* of information is perhaps exactly what gives the impression of so much more. Also, from a psychological point of view, we're all heavily invested in this. It's quite natural to project heightened meaning and significance . . ."

Watching his eyes, Bender had the sense that not even he quite believed what he was saying.

"It's a basic survival mechanism," he continued. "The human mind *wants* to fill in the blanks of any given experience. You hear a tree branch cracking in the distance—it could just be a branch falling, or it could be an approaching saber-toothed cat. From an evolutionary standpoint, those who properly analyzed the sensory data were the ones who survived and reproduced. But those same survival instincts can also play tricks on us, giving the impression that there's something there, when there really isn't."

Randall, who had remained conspicuously silent throughout this monologue, said, "In the end, some things can never be completely explained by rote logic. The human equation will always contain a coefficient of mystery."

He turned away from the wall-mounted screen, back to the workstation keyboard, and began rapidly typing something into the system. Bender strained to see the console and realized that he had engaged the RES-5000's text-to-speech module—the feature that provided a synthesized voice approximation based on a subject's individual larynx and vocal cord physiology.

He clicked on the play button, and the room filled with a soft, mellifluous voice.

"I am the way and the truth and the life . . ."

The voice was mesmerizing, beyond anything previously witnessed from the device. Randall replayed the simulation, and they sat in rapt silence, staring at the glowing image before them.

Chapter 46

The sun had just set outside the laboratory window, its dull red glow bleeding into the gray winter sky. Randall proceeded to encrypt the data files and the rendered graphics files on the RES-5000, sharing with Strickland the digital keys necessary to access them.

"We've witnessed something extraordinary today," Randall said in a reverent near-whisper.

Strickland bristled at his friend's tone. "I'm not sure *what* we've witnessed, Jordan. Again, people believe what they want to believe, and then everything they see is proof. I'm far more interested in seeing where the data takes us."

"As far as I'm concerned, the data has already taken us somewhere," Randall said.

An expression of anger flashed across Strickland's face, then just as quickly faded. "Okay, we have a difference of opinion," he said. "It's been a long day. Did Sara leave?"

"Yes. She said to tell you good-bye. She wanted to get back to her place, to record her thoughts while they were still fresh in her mind."

* * *

Back at her apartment, Bender stared out the picture window, unable to concentrate, unable to marshal her thoughts. Her laptop was on but untouched.

She had gone into the RES-5000 viewing as the ultimate dispassionate observer—a reporter. Why had the image affected her so powerfully? And why had she left so abruptly?

It was the critical juncture for any journalist: knowing when to disengage from the action and begin reporting. There had no doubt been much to gain in observing Strickland's and Randall's comments and behavior after the viewing, and yet she had fled.

Chapter 47

Randall had already left for the evening, and Strickland was halfway out the door of the lab when he glanced up at the RES-5000's darkened screen. He paused a moment, then went back in, dimmed the lights, and booted up the system, entering the encryption key that Randall had given him. After unlocking the already rendered graphics files, he imported them into the display software.

Within seconds, the image was before him once more. And again it was mesmerizing, almost impossible to look away from. He reactivated the text-to-speech passage and sat transfixed, listening to the otherworldly voice.

Suddenly, in mid sentence, he heard an unfamiliar noise from across the room. Whirling his chair around, he found José Posada, the night janitor, holding a dust mop.

Strickland hurriedly grabbed the RES-5000's mouse, hit the stop button, then fumbled to hit "Quit Application." As the RES image vanished from the screen, he looked back at Posada. Strickland probed for any sign of comprehension or discovery, but the janitor's expression was even and friendly. He appeared oblivious to what had been on the screen.

"*Hola, señor Roberto,*" he said, holding up his RFID passkey. "I saw no light on. Is okay to come in?"

Strickland waved him in, the better to gauge any potential exposure.

"*¿Qué pasó?*" Posada said, smiling and going about his business in the lab.

Strickland noted the extra emphasis on "*pasó.*" He knew that it meant they were *compadres.*

They talked easily. Strickland had worked enough late evenings that they had become passing friends. Posada talked about his wife and children with such love and openness, exuded such a warmth and optimism about life, that it affected him powerfully. By contrast, over the course of their many conversations, Strickland realized that his own life was so internalized, there was virtually nothing that he was able, or willing, to share with Posada.

After several minutes, they had exhausted the usual topics of conversation. Strickland decided that Posada had registered nothing, and his unease began to pass.

"*Es muy tarde, señor Roberto,*" the janitor said, checking his watch. "You should get home—*¡ándele!* Maybe if you have woman to go home to . . . ," he added, smiling.

Strickland smiled back, a little surprised at his own wistfulness. "Maybe you're right, José. I guess I'd better start looking!"

Posada's face suddenly became serious. "Don' wait for what is important, *señor.* No joke. Our time, *aquí,*" he said, running his hand level along the plane of the earth, "it is short."

Chapter 48

Strickland drove home in a daze. A full moon bathed the passing snowdrifts in silver light. His winter tires hissed and rumbled on the wet pavement, creating a low, hypnotic drone.

Unable to sleep, he padded into the living room and stared out at the swimming pool below. Long since drained and covered for the winter, it was now blanketed in several inches of snow.

He channel surfed, looking for something to help him nod out, or something that felt right for the moment, the way *Beckett* had been. But there was nothing.

While flipping through the channels, he fumbled the remote and inadvertently hit the *ANT* button, switching the TV receiver to a nonexistent external antenna. The screen unexpectedly filled with swirling digital snow, sparking a childhood recollection. Before the era of continuous multichannel cable, most stations went off the air around midnight, but before doing so, they played the national anthem, with a fluttering American flag in the background. And then, as if the world had suddenly come to an end, the image would vanish, replaced by the electronic snow and hiss of static.

There was something strangely compelling about such dead air, perhaps because it was so foreign in the current mediascape. Sitting in the dark, Strickland turned up the sound and propped his bare feet on the coffee table. He focused on the swirling digital confetti—it danced and spun, forming internal rivers that reminded him of the cytoplasmic streaming within a cell. He began to see complex patterns and colors flashing past in the randomness, and he heard barely perceptible words within the digital whispering. But these impressions were created and extinguished so fleetingly, he wasn't quite sure they ever existed. He sat in a trance, surrendering to the hypnotic light and the rushing sound.

Chapter 49

Sara Bender slept fitfully, awakening every few hours. At dawn she made coffee and finally began typing a summary of yesterday's events.

But reading back over the account, she saw that it failed to capture the essence of what had occurred in the lab. The reality was almost too intimate for journalism. And however she worded or reworded it, her descriptions paled in comparison to what the three of them had actually witnessed.

At 7:00 A.M., she grabbed a muffin and a second cup of coffee at the bakery down the street, then caught the Metro to the NIH, hoping to get there before either Strickland or Randall. But she found Strickland already hard at work, hunched over a workstation and downloading a series of software packages. Seeing her come in, he offered a perfunctory wave. Sara had hoped to engage him, to get a sense of his reaction to yesterday's unveiling, but he was even more remote than usual.

"So what's up?" she asked, to break the silence.

"Downloading some new genomic search-and-analysis facilities," he replied, typing in a Web URL. He seemed to be twisting uncomfortably in his chair. Then he stretched his arms high over his head, arching his back.

"Back stiff?" she asked.

"Fell asleep on the couch last night."

"What time did you and Jordan call it quits?" she asked, still hoping to take the conversation somewhere deeper.

"He left around six thirty; I left a bit later."

Good. Maybe she hadn't missed that much.

Strickland continued pecking away at the workstation keyboard, downloading more software, and sensing no further conversation in the offing, she decided to grab another cup of coffee from the break room. On the way back to the lab, she found herself walking in stride with Randall.

"Morning!" he said, smiling.

"Hello, Jordan," she said.

"So, what's on the agenda today? Where do we take it from here?"

"That's the big question," he said. "At this point, Bob and I really need to clarify our goals, and that'll take some discussion."

Strickland acknowledged Randall's arrival with a nod. Sara waited for someone to speak, but with the three of them together again, it became glaringly obvious how the dynamic had changed. It was as if a bomb had gone off the day before and nothing was the same.

Strickland hit a key at the workstation, executing another software download.

"Bob, if you don't mind, I think we need to sit down and review what happened yesterday," Randall said, "as well as discuss our course of action going forward."

Strickland looked up from the workstation screen. "I *am* sitting down, Jordan," he said. "And isn't our plan of action fairly obvious?"

"No, it's not," Randall said. "And by the way, what exactly are you downloading and installing?"

Some open-source genomic analysis engines. ChromOlogy, HelicoHunter, GeneSeeker, OrderFinder . . ."

"But those are all still at the beta release stage," Randall noted. "They'll be crashing every hour on the hour until the bugs are worked out. Why on earth would we want to saddle ourselves with that kind of software?"

"They're offering faster whole-genome cross-comparison and analyses, as well as delving into pseudogenes, antisense genes, and microRNAs."

"True. Still . . ."

"And they also provide for large-scale in-silico translation," Strickland continued, "spitting out the proteins coded for by given sequences, as well as offering 3-D display of the various proteomic configurations. We don't currently have that level of functionality in our packages, and we're going to need it."

"For what?" Randall asked.

"To explain what we saw yesterday."

Bender noted Randall's sudden intensity. "And what *did* we see yesterday?" he asked.

Finally, we're getting down to it, she thought.

"I don't know," Strickland said. "But that's what I intend to find out."

Chapter 50

The debate raged through the morning. Sara struggled to get down all the arguments and counterarguments. At one point, Strickland glowered at her—the equivalent of waving the camera away during a heated moment in a documentary.

Finally, during a lull in the exchange, Randall touched his chin, carefully weighing his words. "My feelings have admittedly been somewhat murky," he said, "both before and after the imaging. But the more we've talked about this, the clearer things have become." He paused for a long moment. "Bob, you said in the past that you'd know when we'd gone far enough with this study, and that you'd never 'hit the wall.' Well, we each have a wall. And last night I saw mine very clearly." Randall paused again. "It's time to stop," he said. "We've gone far enough."

"Jordan, are you *crazy*!" Strickland exclaimed. "We're potentially on the verge of something amazing. I don't claim to know what that is. But I can't deny there's something truly out of the ordinary here, and I want to know more."

"But where and when will you find what you're looking for?" Randall asked, a trace of anger rising in his voice.

"In the data! In the sequences! It's all there; we just have to know where to look, and then be able to interpret what we find."

"Bullshit!" Randall exploded.

The outburst was so unexpected and out of character, it hit Bender like a slap in the face.

"You're never going to find what you're looking for 'in the data,'" Randall continued, "because it's somewhere else!"

Strickland seemed momentarily stunned, and Sara realized she had never seen him at a loss for words.

"They said the same thing about Einstein," Strickland said. "That whatever had allowed him to make his astounding conceptual breakthroughs lay impenetrably within the synaptic gaps."

Strickland turned to Sara, as if seeking her support. "And for a while, that assessment seemed true," he continued. "Postmortem analyses of his brain found nothing unusual. But they were simply lacking the necessary tools. In the late nineties, using MRI scans, they found that his visuospatial and mathematical logic regions, in the inferior parietal lobe, were abnormally large. And his glial cells were unusually concentrated, permitting greater neural interconnection—which can provide more cross-referencing of information, and greater leaps of insight."

"And this told us *what* that furthered the advancement of physics or expanded on Einstein's basic theories?" Randall interjected.

"Nothing," Strickland admitted. "But who can say it won't? Maybe that analysis will one day help us identify future Einsteins, so we can better nurture them—so they don't waste their best years working in a patent office, for God's sake."

"Some might argue that working in a patent office gave Einstein the freedom to daydream, to perform thought experiments, and, ultimately, to turn established physics on its ear," Randall countered. "Maybe he couldn't have done all that within the confines of a demanding job in academia, teaching classes and pursuing tenure."

"Touché," Strickland said. Another lull enveloped the room. Suddenly turning to Bender, Strickland said, "So, what does the reporter have to say?"

Caught off guard, she put down her pen. She had been in observational mode up to this point, never expecting to be put on the spot. It was as if Strickland was looking for allies wherever he could find them.

"I . . . have to admit that what we witnessed yesterday was, to put it mildly, unlike anything I've seen before," she said. "What it was—or is—I can't really say. But I agree that it was something extraordinary—something I'm barely able to put my finger on."

"I agree," Strickland said. "Even the agnostic reporter believes that we need to know more."

Bender looked at Strickland and then Randall, wondering where things would go next.

"Jordan, I've never claimed to know where this study would lead us," he continued. "Like any scientific endeavor, we follow the trail and see where we end up. It's what we *do*! Don't *you* want to see where it takes us?"

Randall paused. "I may *want* to know, but I don't *have* to know," he said.

"Why the hell not?" challenged Strickland. "What makes you so damn sure!"

"This is exactly what concerns me," Randall said, his voice filled with emotion. "I worry that you're in search of something you'll never find—at least, not in this way. And I worry about the greater repercussions of that search. Much as you might claim otherwise, we can't divorce ourselves from the consequences of our actions. And for that reason, I stand by my decision: we have to stop."

Sara waited for something more from Strickland. But the two men simply stared at each other—not in defiance, but with a sense of sadness and resignation. Finally, Strickland turned back to the workstation keyboard. His latest analysis tool's download had just completed. In silence, he double-clicked on the "Install" icon.

Randall turned and left the room.

Chapter 51

Several days later, Bender watched from a distance as Strickland manipulated a three-dimensional graphic on the workstation screen, slowly rotating a protein in space—first clockwise, then counterclockwise. He clicked the mouse, and a second protein of contrasting color was superimposed on the first. Small areas at the periphery of the two shapes stood out as strikingly different.

Strickland donned a headset with goggles and again manipulated the joystick. Randall had previously described the equipment to Sara. The goggles contained tiny lasers in primary colors, which projected images directly onto the retina. The computer-generated images were each slightly altered in perspective, and beamed separately into each eye. The resulting effect was the vivid illusion of a three-dimensional object hovering in space some three feet before the viewer.

Bender moved closer to the workstation. Strickland began removing the goggles, then started—he had been so immersed in the work that he clearly hadn't realized she was here. "Oh, hello—want to take a look?" he asked, offering her the device.

"Sure," she said, putting it on and adjusting it to her head.

The image was momentarily disorienting. Although her brain told her she was wearing a bulky headset, her eyes told her she was gazing into the depths of something otherworldly and three-dimensional. It took a moment to reconcile this rift in the fabric of her reality, but after a few seconds, the illusion became seamless. She marveled at the shimmering multicolored molecule, slowly rotating like an alien structure in the blackness of space.

"Wow, this is beautiful!" she exclaimed. "What is it?"

"It's the *GNE* protein, which is deficient in anyone with a gene mutation associated with HIBM, a disease specific to people of Middle Eastern descent."

"So, have you found anything new on the Shroud front?" she asked, pulling off the headset.

"Nothing new to report, actually. At this point, I'm just testing the infrastructure: the new search engines, the control and manipulation hardware, and the display facilities. I'm not really the computer ace around here—that's Jordan's domain." He paused. "But I'm making do the best

I can. To be honest, I don't even know what I'm looking for in the data. In the latter stages of the Human Genome Project, we at least had a basic research paradigm: you sought out human populations with some well-defined disease process, tried to find a gene mutation unique to that group, figured out what protein the mutation coded for—or failed to code for—and then tried to discover what that protein did. Here I'm not tracking a disease, or even some quantifiable phenotypic trait. I'm trying to figure out what characteristics defined a unique individual. And I'm not even sure I can define what makes up that uniqueness."

Over the course of the afternoon, Sara found Strickland more open than she had seen him in weeks. It reminded her of the day they had bumped into each other in Georgetown. He could be utterly charming under the right circumstances, she thought. It occurred to her that without Randall in the picture, he needed someone to confide in. And since, in her trade, access was everything, this new dynamic presented unexpected opportunities. But it also caused her to let down her guard.

"By the way," she said during an especially lively exchange, "with the weather letting up a bit lately, I'm back to my regular jogging schedule. If you happen to be at the Hirshhorn some weekend, feel free to give me a buzz—it's a quick run over to Dean & Deluca's."

"Will do," Strickland said as he continued making adjustments to the workstation setup. "Sounds good," he added, donning the 3-D goggles once more.

But from his tone, Sara knew it would never happen.

Chapter 52

Mary Randall began loading the evening dishes into the washer. Both children had gone to their rooms to do homework.

Jordan continued clearing the table, but his mind seemed to be elsewhere. She had seen him like this many times before, so distracted by his work that the outside world ceased to exist. From years of experience, she knew when to give him space.

A small portrait of Jesus hung on the wall next to their dining room table. It was the only sign of their faith in the house. Mary had come from a family that believed in worshiping the Lord openly and often, but Jordan had always been more unassuming. He didn't feel it was his place to proselytize, particularly among scientists, many of whom were either agnostic or ardently atheist. "A journey has many paths," he had told her. "We've chosen ours, and we should let others do the same."

Jordan's attitudes about faith had bothered her at first, resulting in many spirited arguments, but in time she had come to respect her husband's openness and tolerance. He could sometimes be hot-tempered, but he had a bigger heart and deeper integrity than any man she had ever known.

As Mary scraped the stuck rice from the casserole dish, she watched her husband out of the corner of her eye. His path was not easy: a strong sense of faith, complicated by a powerful scientific curiosity. But these complexities were part of what made her love and respect him. She hated to see him so troubled, but when he excused himself to go up to his study, she intuitively knew to let him be alone.

Randall closed the door and fell heavily into his office chair, his arms hanging at his sides. On an impulse, he switched off the desk lamp to welcome the cool solace of the dark. A misted half-moon shone through the diaphanous curtains, bathing the room in pale silver light. Randall suddenly felt tears welling up, and almost involuntarily, he fell to his knees, folding his hands together.

"Lord, I don't often do this," he whispered. "I like to think you have more important things to deal with. But I need your help." He stared up into the darkness, his hands tightening. "I don't know what do to. Please guide me . . . show me the way."

Chapter 53

The assembled men waited for the last of their number to arrive. They had again gathered in the seldom-used basement room in the Palace of the Holy Office. Vestments rustled as the men shuffled and shifted nervously from foot to foot.

The last member slipped quietly into the room, and on his arrival, all stood a little more erect. Closing the door behind him, the man twisted the brass lock.

"I will make this brief," he said, in a gruff, wheezing voice. "I want to congratulate you all on your work. As you know, we are in the process of thwarting a dark and dangerous enterprise—one that threatens everything that we, and true believers everywhere, hold dear. The operation is now under way, and our efforts will soon bear fruit."

The elder bowed his head, and the others followed his lead. "May God be with us," he rasped.

"May God be with us," they chorused.

And he unlocked the door and was gone.

Chapter 54

Strickland finished his breakfast while leafing through the Sunday *New York Times*. Weeks had passed in the lab, and he had followed every lead, every conceptual path. There had been some intriguing possibilities, but so far, they all had led nowhere.

He thought back to the early examinations of Einstein's brain and wondered whether his analytical tools were simply too primitive to reveal what he was looking for. Clearly, there were unique aspects to the sequences. But the uniqueness, if it was of any consequence, seemed beyond current understanding. Even using the open-source analysis engines, the interactions were simply too complex and too poorly understood. He had hoped for some kind of revelation, a kernel of insight within the static of the Shroud's billions of nucleotides.

He poured another cup of coffee just as his father's antique clock began chiming from the mantel. Beneath the timepiece stood a framed black-and-white portrait of the elder Strickland. It had been taken in the man's early thirties, at the beginning of his medical career.

Dr. Robert Strickland had been an anachronism in Saranac Lake, a small community in upstate New York. He continued making house calls in an era when few physicians did, and he rarely turned a patient away, even at night or on weekends. But as a result, he gradually became a stranger to his own family. Strickland remembered hearing his mother tell a neighbor woman, "Beyond his commitment to medicine, I don't really understand what makes him tick." And young Robert Jr. often felt the same way.

He vividly remembered being driven to junior high school one morning by his father—an extremely rare event. His mother was suffering from "exhaustion" and was unable to get out of bed. On the drive, he and his father talked briefly about a radio-controlled model airplane they were building together. But then the boy realized he had no idea what to say next. He sat quietly during the long drive, taking in his father's odd metallic odor.

Strickland folded the newspaper, sucked down the last of his morning coffee, and pulled back the curtain to gaze out the breakfast nook window. It was a beautiful winter day, with the outdoor thermometer showing 53 degrees. On the spur of the moment, he decided to take a motorcycle ride through the surrounding woods. It had been weeks since this was even a remote possibility. Minutes later, he hit the ignition and was rewarded with the soft, low rumble of the big 1,200cc engine.

Clearing the suburbs and rising up into the hills, Strickland leaned in hard and accelerated through the winding back roads. The air was crisp and bracing, the highways snow-scrubbed and bone dry—perfect for high-speed maneuvering.

It felt good to be outdoors. There was something viscerally pleasing about the smell of trees, bark, forest duff, and the hint of wood smoke in the air. Maybe it was genetic memory, he pondered—earth, air, fire, and water: the prescientific elements of the universe, and the necessities of life.

Strickland hit a straightaway lined by towering white poplars, their long, narrow shadows striping the road in the low winter sun. He took the approaching turn more slowly as the sun momentarily blinded him. Suddenly, an oncoming vehicle appeared in his lane—the driver was attempting to pass but couldn't get back in.

Strickland gripped the handbrake and stepped on the brake pedal. The antilock system started chattering, and the bike oscillated wildly from side to side. He fought for control and headed for the shoulder, and as he came to a skidding halt on a patch of moldering leaves and mud, the rust-red Ford pickup screeched around the bend and was gone.

He sat there for a long moment, arms resting on the handlebars, chest heaving. In the instant the truck had passed, he had caught a glimpse of the driver's face—he looked remarkably like Strickland's father.

Chapter 55

Sara tossed her sweats into the hamper, still breathing hard from the long Sunday morning jog. She had taken the usual route, ending up on M Street. It was a leisurely day, with nothing of any consequence on her calendar, so she had stopped at Dean & Deluca's for a latte with steamed milk and a chocolate croissant. Her best friend, back in Manhattan, maintained that an increased craving for sweets and caffeine was a red flag that a woman was having boyfriend problems. But Sara wasn't buying it. She and Tom had some serious issues, that much was true, but she would still love coffee and chocolate even if they were floating in marital bliss.

She showered, then decided to catch up on her work notes. It was amazing how a little breather seemed to slow the passing of time. She had first learned the technique in college. When dealing with an overwhelming workload or a nearly impossible deadline, if she just chucked it all and took a few hours off, there was suddenly more than enough time. *Relativity at work.* She smiled. It sounded like something Strickland might suggest.

As she booted up the laptop and reviewed her notes, she began thinking about Randall. In recent days she had barely seen him. He had essentially disengaged from the Shroud project and was now dividing his time among the other projects in the lab, and she had no idea how to gauge where things would go next. At first she had been interested solely in the research, but now it was also the researchers themselves that she found so compelling. Strickland and Randall presented a fascinating contrast in personality and philosophy, and with this recent chill between them, that contrast might be all she would get. She resigned herself to the possibility that the entire enterprise might implode, yielding only an article about two interesting men of science.

As she brewed a cup of black tea, she thought again of her girlfriend's chocolate-and-caffeine theory. She tried calling Tom but got voice mail. Fighting the urge, she didn't try his cell.

In her e-mail in-box, she found a message from her editor, Ron. He asked how things were going, said everyone missed her, and mentioned that if her book "happens to wrap up ahead of schedule," he had some tantalizing assignments in the pipe—ones he had been saving for her. Sara thanked him, saying how much she missed everyone—and Manhattan.

Chapter 56

Strickland continued his analysis of the Shroud data but found that he was quickly running out of options. For several weeks, he had been examining non–protein-coding "dark matter" regions of the genome. The term referred to genomic control regions named after the "dark matter" of the cosmos.

Cosmologists had once assumed that the universe was composed primarily of stars, planets, and diffuse gases, with the vacuum of space making up most of what remained. This seemed intuitively and visually obvious. But after precise twentieth-century analyses of rotating galaxies, and the application of Kepler's laws for such rotating bodies, it became clear that the mass of these galaxies was far greater than could be predicted based on any known matter. This proposed "dark matter" was currently detectable only by its various gravitational influences, yet it was estimated to make up six times the mass of the directly observable universe. In addition, discoveries in the 1990s showed that the expansion of the universe was actually accelerating over time, as if everything was being pushed apart by some mysterious force. Whether this "dark energy" was an inherent property of space, an unknown energy field, or something that required an entirely new theory of gravity to account for it was still a matter of debate. But as in the "terra incognita" of ancient maps, there were clearly forces and masses out there that we could neither see nor directly measure, yet which composed the largest portion of the universe.

In a similar vein, geneticists had once proclaimed that most of the human genome was simply the dross of evolution—nonfunctional remnants of our genetic past. And for more than half a century, this central dogma of molecular genetics held: that DNA made RNA, and RNA made protein. The DNA was "transcribed" into RNA, and the RNA was "translated" into protein.

Since only a small portion of the genome actively coded for proteins, it seemed reasonable to assume that the rest was of little consequence—except for the inconvenient fact that this "inconsequential" portion made up over 90 percent of the genome.

But Strickland mused that nature rarely wastes energy or resources. And, more importantly, the early assumptions simply didn't match the data. Genetic diseases and traits were discovered that defied the normal laws of genetic inheritance. Also, there was no clear correlation between protein-coding genes and an organism's ultimate complexity. Rice plants were found to possess more protein-coding genes than humans did. Clearly, on a fundamental level, something was missing from the picture. But there *was* a clear correlation between organism complexity and *non*–protein-coding DNA.

Little by little, genomic researchers came to realize that the mechanics of the genome were far more complex than they had imagined. Like the dark matter of the cosmos, the non–protein-coding portion of the genome *was* in fact playing an essential role. Such entities as pseudogenes, antisense RNA, and riboswitches were discovered, which, though not involved explicitly in the production of proteins, nonetheless exerted control over sequences that did.

Thus, an entirely new "epigenetic" layer of information was uncovered within the genome. And ultimately, the entire definition of a functional genetic sequence was broadened to include anything that was transcribed into RNA.

Same as it ever was, thought Strickland. Whether it was the Copernican revolution, evolution, relativity, or quantum mechanics, the path of science was filled with disruptive paradigm shifts. As he adjusted the analysis parameters on HelicoHunter, Strickland thought of an often-spoken adage of science—"today's heresy is tomorrow's orthodoxy."

Chapter 57

Sara Bender hovered in the lab's open doorway, watching Strickland from a distance. She had become such a familiar part of the landscape that few even noticed her comings and goings. "Habituation," Strickland once called it, explaining, "with sufficient familiarity, a given external stimulus begins to be treated by the brain as inconsequential background noise, neither threatening nor novel."

As usual, Strickland was staring into a computer monitor. On the screen, a series of colored bars of varying thickness and hue ran at angles from bottom to top. HelicoHunter found sequence "alignments"—the matches—between two genomes and displayed them using different colors to denote various ranges of alignment size, while the width of each bar indicated the relative size of the sequence match within that particular color's range. The angle of the bars varied according to the location of the sequence match between the two genomes.

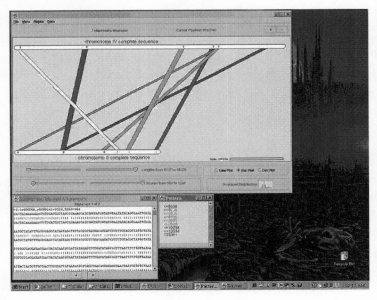

Using the mouse, Strickland was moving the onscreen sliders back and forth, making new bars of color materialize, and melting others away. He peered intently at the image, scribbling notes on the pad beside him. As he made minor adjustments to one of the sliders, the entire screen froze. Bender watched as he moved the mouse from side to side, getting no response.

"God damn it!" he shouted, slamming a fist down on the table.

Bender remained frozen in the doorway, not wanting to add to his frustration, but with his concentration now broken, he noticed her standing there.

"I guess I have to expect this," he said, turning toward her. "Jordan warned me about the buggy state of these applications. He's sometimes shielded me from the downside of technology."

"I'm convinced that machines have a malicious side," Bender said, smiling. "They seem to know the worst possible time to fail."

She turned as Randall entered the lab, trailed by several researchers. He looked suddenly ill at ease. "Oh, sorry," he said. "I've been searching all over for some notes—finally realized I left them in here."

Sara tried to make eye contact with him, to gauge the state of their relationship, but he never glanced her way, and before she could say anything, he and his train of postdocs were gone.

"As you can see, Ms. Bender," Strickland said, "here at the Ethnogenomics Center we're just one big happy family."

Chapter 58

In a quiet conference room down the hall from Strickland and Randall's offices, Bender had opened her laptop and was updating the past week's notes. Re-reading what she had written, she considered how Randall's perspective had kept the investigation on an even keel. With him gone, she wasn't quite sure how to relate to Strickland.

Pausing to glance at her watch, she realized that she had been at it over an hour and a half. She saved the file, closed the laptop, and went in search of Strickland. Not surprisingly, she found him still at the workstation, wrestling with the HelicoHunter program. She stood quietly in the corner, out of his line of sight.

An all-new pattern of colored bars was now arrayed on the screen. Sara glanced at Strickland's pad of paper and realized he had scribbled a good five pages of notes since she left. Again he began fine-tuning the onscreen sliders and noting the latest results. Then the screen froze again.

"Damn it!" he snarled, hurling the pad of paper across the room.

Bender knew how maddening lost work could be. She thought back to her colleague's stolen laptop.

Strickland looked up and, seeing her, smiled sheepishly at his outburst.

"What'd I tell you?" she said. "technology's evil side."

Strickland picked up the paperwork. Returning to the desk, he moved the mouse again in the vain hope that the system had somehow healed itself.

"Maybe it's time to take a break," Bender said, feeling almost motherly. "Sometimes you just have to step away, let the bad juju dissipate."

Strickland smiled. "Maybe you're right," he said. He checked his watch. "Wanna grab some lunch?"

"I'd love to."

Walking to Strickland's car, Bender told him a story from her college days in New York, and they soon discovered they had frequented the same dive bar, though at different times.

"Was Bruno still the bartender at the ZamZam during your era?" Strickland asked.

"Of course. He was an icon. What would a weekend night be without getting insulted by Bruno? If it wasn't the way you were dressed, the drink you had ordered, or your selection on the jukebox, he'd find *something* you weren't doing right. His abuse became almost an institution. But then the place got written up in *Zagat,* and that was the beginning of the end. The theater crowd even started coming in."

"Wow, amazing," Strickland said, laughing. "Imagine going out of your way to drink at a place like that."

In the distance, Bender spotted Connie Franklin coming out of the administration building, hurrying toward the parking lot while fishing in her purse. After her initial tour with Franklin, Bender had welcomed the prospect of a woman friend during her time in D.C. They had often crossed paths since that time, but the encounters always felt forced and strained.

As their paths began to converge, Franklin looked up and saw them and, unnoticed by Strickland, veered down an alternate path to the parking lot, as if to avoid a face-to-face encounter.

Chapter 59

As they arrived back at the lab, Bender had just set down her purse and the takeout bag from the restaurant when Randall walked in and tossed a printout from a Web page onto the desk between them.

"If you didn't have reason to stop before, you do now," he said.

The document banner read, THE SWORD—MAY THE TRUTH PREVAIL. Below this was a graphic of a gleaming metal cross in the shape of a sword, followed by bold red text proclaiming, "I did not come to bring peace, but a sword. —*Jesus Christ.*"

"A congregant from my church sent me this," Randall explained.

Sara and Strickland scanned down the text of the newsletter.

> ALERT: We have received reliable information that U.S. government labs are actively engaged in genetic analysis of blood samples taken from the Shroud of Turin—manipulating the very DNA of our savior, the Son of Man.

> And make no mistake about their true agenda. This is yet another attack on our faith by the world of science, attempting to discredit the miracle of Jesus' life and his resurrection.

> The scientific community already seeks to create new life only to destroy it—with the false promise of alleviating suffering and disease. And now this. Where will it end? Will they go from merely playing God to attempting to *create* God?"

"Shit," Strickland muttered.

"This is exactly what I've been dreading," said Randall.

"How did it get out?" Strickland wondered aloud. "Who knew this level of detail—other than top-level Vatican representatives, Director Burnham, and the three of us?" He was looking at Bender.

"Do you honestly think I'd jeopardize a story like this by leaking it to the *press*?" she said, bristling with indignation. "Much less to a fly-by-night online newsletter?"

"Maybe you decided to stir the pot—make things a little more interesting for your book," Strickland said.

"I don't need to 'stir the pot,' Robert. You do a stellar job of that with no help from me. Besides, you *know* me better than that. I signed an NDA, for God's sake. And you've read up on me enough to know I've gone to the mat—risked *jail*—to protect my sources."

Strickland's tone eased. "I know," he said. "I didn't seriously suspect you, but I had to ask."

"Thanks for the vote of confidence," Sara said.

Strickland turned his attention back to the printout. "This Web site seems in the crackpot realm. Maybe it won't go much further than their small readership."

"I wish," Randall said. "But the person who sent it to me said they have an online readership of over four million."

Chapter 60

Strickland spent another late night in the lab, making some halfhearted runs on HelicoHunter, then on ChromOlogy, checking various unexplored alignments in the Shroud data. But his mind wasn't in it.

There was a knock at the door.

"Who is it?" Strickland asked without opening it.

"José."

"*Hola, José, un momento, por favor.*"

Strickland opened the door, and José Posada entered the lab with his mop, bucket, and a large plastic trash bin on wheels.

"*Señor Roberto, ¿qué paso?*" Posada called out.

"*Todo bien,*" Strickland replied.

"Now you are always locked in this room," Posada said. "You need to get away sometime."

"You're probably right, but . . ." He gestured at the stack of paperwork beside him.

"You must love what you do, to work so hard," the janitor said.

"Actually, I do," Strickland acknowledged.

"I hope one of my sons can be a scientist, maybe even a *médico* like you," Posada said. "But maybe they can work only during the day!"

Strickland laughed. "Most doctors work during the day, so that shouldn't be a problem. But your daughters could also become doctors—I think women are sometimes better at the job. If you want to give the kids a tour of the place sometime, let me know. When I was a boy, my father once let me spend the day at his clinic. Things like that can plant a powerful seed."

"Thank you, señor Roberto," Posada said. "I appreciate it."

Suddenly serious, Strickland said, "José, have you spoken with anyone recently about our work here? Anyone at all?"

Posada's brow furrowed in thought. "Yes," he said, hesitantly. "A friendly man, say he worked for the NIH, want to write about the people here. He talked to me in the parking lot."

"What exactly did you tell him?"

"How much I like working here, how nice everyone is—especially you and señor Randall."

"Thank you, I appreciate that," Strickland said. He tried not to let the encounter seem like an interrogation—both to ease Posada's obvious anxiety and to encourage the flow of information. "Anything else?"

Posada paused, looking Strickland in the eye. "He ask me if I am a man of God. I say yes, but I think, why ask such a question? He said your work here is very important: cure disease, make the world better—almost like God himself. Then he ask me if you are a man of God, too."

"And what did you say?"

Posada hesitated. "I told him you *are* a man of God—I saw you watching the face of Jesus on a computer late one night."

Posada looked worriedly at Strickland. "*Hay problema, señor Roberto?*" he asked.

"No, everything's fine," Strickland said, patting him on the shoulder. "Thanks for telling me."

Chapter 61

As Bender entered the lab the next morning, she found Strickland once again viewing the Shroud image on the RES-5000 screen. He almost knocked over a cup of tea as he moved to halt the display process.

"It's okay," she said. "I've caught men looking at far more incriminating things on their computers."

But Strickland was in too somber a mood to crack a smile. Sara gazed up at the high-resolution image. "I have to admit, it's just as powerful the second time around," she said.

"I agree," Strickland said.

"What do you think your analysis will uncover?" she asked him.

"I really don't know. But for the first time, I'm beginning to question what we're doing here."

Perhaps he caught something in her look, because he quickly added, "Don't get me wrong. I don't share all of Jordan's concerns—that we're somehow 'ethically challenged' in what we do. And I know that the understanding of disease processes is incredibly important work. But I find myself wondering whether there's something bigger I should be focused on—bigger than I'd even considered."

When she didn't respond, he said, "Can I confess something to you?"

"Of course," she said.

"Since Jordan's departure from the project, it sometimes feels like I'm lost in space—out in the void on my own. And with everything that's going on right now, that's a tough place to be."

Sensing from his tone that there was more, Bender waited.

"Remember when we discussed epigenetic regions of the genome—pseudogenes, antisense RNA, and riboswitches?"

"How could I forget?" she said. My learning curve was a vertical line then."

"I've come to suspect that the key to the Shroud may lie in those regions. I've been working on extensive new sequencing," he continued, "well beyond the data we gathered for the RES-5000 imaging. I've been at it now for weeks, ever since Jordan pulled out of the study."

"I hate to stand in for Jordan," Bender said, "but where will it all end? You readily admit that you're not even sure what you're looking for. So how will you know when you've found it?"

"That's a valid question, and I'm not sure I can answer it," Strickland said, sounding more somber than ever. "This is a vague path, I admit."

She saw his eyes suddenly cut across the room. With the speed of a striking snake, his hand darted out and hit the "Quit Application" button on the RES-5000. The image from the Shroud data collapsed from the screen as the door swung open.

Randall entered the room. "Good morning," he said with forced geniality. "Don't mean to interrupt." He gathered up some manuals next to one of the workstations, then left as abruptly as he had entered.

"Please don't mention what we just discussed to Jordan," Strickland said after the door closed. "I don't want to create any further friction."

She looked into his eyes for a hint at the depth of collusion he seemed to be suggesting. She tried to recall the specifics of her NDA. To the best of her recollection, it dictated nondisclosure outside of the study participants, but not secrecy *between* them. Never in her wildest imagination had she anticipated the project fracturing into estranged camps. She didn't feel at all comfortable with the ethical bind that Strickland's confession seemed to create. Sara nodded at his request, but said nothing.

Chapter 62

As Randall had predicted, it didn't take long for the mainstream media to pick up on the online story. While no major news source had yet corroborated or disproved *The Sword's* allegations, they were more than happy to report on the public reaction to them.

The newsletter item initially generated scattered small protests around the country, which snowballed into local television coverage, which filtered up to the national arena. A week after Randall walked in with the newsletter, the first large-scale protest gatherings began.

As Strickland was walking to a budgetary meeting, he spotted a throng of about fifty protestors in front of the NIH administrative offices. Thankfully, they hadn't yet zeroed in on any specific building or person.

The temperature hovered near freezing, and the group stood huddled in a tight circle, patting their gloved hands together, sipping coffee from thermoses. Several held homemade signs, which they pumped rhythmically in the air. One sign pictured the head of Jesus attached to the body of a dinosaur, with a circle and a slash through it, and a caption that read, NO JURASSIC JESUS!

Meanwhile, other sympathetic protest movements had piggybacked onto the gathering. A sign protesting genetic modification of foods pictured Mr. Potato Head, with a green face covered in stitches, and steel electrodes protruding from the neck, and the words STOP FRANKENFOODS NOW!"

Strickland walked briskly past the group, with a benign facial expression of neither animosity nor support.

* * *

When Strickland returned from the meeting, his assistant handed him a FedEx envelope. The sender, a business address in Langley, Virginia, was not one he recognized. The envelope was marked "Personal and Confidential."

Inside was a single envelope of fine parchment, and inside that, a one-page communiqué from the Vatican's chief science attaché, Dr. Enrico Rutigliano.

Dear Dr. Strickland,

Hopefully, recent media attention has been the result of conjecture and misunderstanding on the part of various fringe elements. While the charter of your investigation was intentionally broad and open-ended, certainly you must understand that explicit manipulation of genetic material from the sample—particularly within the realm of cloning sciences—would be strictly forbidden by the Holy See. Please immediately provide us with a detailed account of your research activities to date, as well as your findings.

Sincerely,
Enrico Giuseppe Rutigliano Ph.D., Chief Vatican Science Adviser

CC: Dr. Daniel Burnham, Director, NIH

Chapter 63

The young man hung up the phone, hurriedly logged out of the computer system, and reshelved the programming manual he had been consulting. The gruff voice on the other end of the line was familiar and not one to be kept waiting.

As he walked, he reviewed the rough sketch of a map he had made during the conversation. As a first-time visitor inside the Palace of the Holy Office, he was soon required to show a Vatican picture ID and have his thumbprint scanned. After navigating a labyrinth of marble hallways, he arrived at a dark basement room whose heavy wooden door was unmarked.

He knocked softly, and after a short wait, the door opened and a lone figure inside waved him in.

The dimly lit room had a musty smell befitting the scowling old man who sat back down in the far corner. Before him, on a bare wooden table, sat a desktop computer plugged into a nearby wall jack.

The old man explained that he would like help setting up an e-mail account on a free Web-based service.

"But, sir," the young man explained, "it would be much more convenient in the long run to set up a Vatican account for you. It would use our domain name, and you'd be on the high-speed intranet. Also, we keep archives of such correspondences, so you can retrieve things later if need be."

The elder shook his head and reiterated his request.

The young man began the registration process on the Web e-mail service. Why had the old man chosen such an antiquated system? Perhaps he liked the keyboard. This one looked something like the IBM Selectric typewriter the young man's grandfather had owned, right down to the curved return key.

At the end of the registration process, the Web site asked for a user ID.

"CristoVerita," rasped the elder.

The requested user ID was unique, and the system accepted it without modification.

Even so, the elder waved his hand dismissively, indicating that the process was taking far too long.

The young man clicked the "Finish" button. "The account is in place," he said.

"Now, how do I send a message?" the old man snapped.

The young man was beginning to lose patience, but he kept an even tone. Opening a message window, he said, "You enter the recipient address here, and down below is the subject line. Below that, you type the actual message. When you're done, click here, on the send button."

Realizing how unfamiliar the old man was with the technology, he decided to stay a few minutes longer, to avoid being summoned back the minute he returned to his office.

The elder looked at him with a vague sense of irritation and disdain. "I require some privacy now," he said, inhaling heavily, "to collect my thoughts. I'm writing to a dear friend who has been very ill."

Relieved, the young man nodded and excused himself, closing the door and finding himself back out in the marble hallway.

* * *

The old man entered the e-mail address of his recipient, "editor. thesword@gmail.com" and put on the subject line "Research Question." In the text box, he typed, "The researcher in question is: Dr. Robert Allen Strickland."

He gazed at the screen for a moment, then sent the message.

Chapter 64

Bender entered the lab and smoothed down her disheveled hair. "Whew! I had to park in the overflow lot, then make my way through the protester gauntlet. Those people are really getting out of control. Screaming in someone's face isn't exactly the way to win converts."

"When people travel too far down a narrow philosophical path," Strickland said, "it gets harder and harder to see beyond the dogma. Soon they have to start excluding any contradictory data or opinions, whether those have to do with religion, genetics, or anything else."

The distant roar of a crowd drew Bender's attention to the office window. In a gap between two buildings, she could see the group of protesters in front of the NIH administrative building, chanting in unison and pumping and waving their signs. "The emotion out there reminds me of antiabortion rallies I've covered," she said.

"Yeah," he said. "Both issues involve similar philosophical and moral terrain. The problem is when people go too far in pushing their beliefs. In the same way that there have been attacks on abortion clinics and their workers, there are now 'ecoterrorists,' assaulting researchers and vandalizing genetically modified crop sites."

Bender looked out the window at the assembled crowd below. Beyond the protesters, an array of dark clouds cast a dappled mosaic of light across the NIH campus. She turned to Strickland, about to speak, but found that he was again immersed in the analysis software. She watched him work for a minute, then quietly picked up her pack and left the room.

Chapter 65

As Strickland approached the Ethnogenomics building, he passed a group of protesters. The loudest of the group held a sign that read, "STOP RACIST RESEARCH! BENEATH OUR SKIN, WE'RE ALL THE SAME!" Another sign showed two identical images of Jesus, with a circled slash through them. The caption read, "NO CLONING CHRIST!"

NIH security and the Maryland State Police had already formed a safety perimeter around the building. Hoping to avoid any confrontations, NIH staff had been instructed to be as conciliatory as possible.

As Strickland entered the building through a back entrance, he ran into Bender. "I suppose it was only a matter of time before they zeroed in on us," he said.

"How do you think that happened?"

"I'd rather not get into it just now," he said, grimly, stowing his coat and bag. He shook his head in disbelief at the protesters, still visible through the blinds.

"So much of what they're concerned about is totally in the realm of science fiction," he said. "There's an amazing chasm between the reality of science, in terms of possibility and agenda, and the public's perception."

They walked together to his office, where he sat down heavily at his desk and began sifting listlessly through a pile of new phone messages. "All right," he sighed. "A mob with burning torches outside my door, and a pile of bureaucratic bullshit to deal with—welcome to my nightmare."

* * *

That afternoon, George poked his head into the lab. "This just came in," he said. "It requires a signed receipt from you."

The moment his assistant had left, Strickland tore open the FedEx mailer, sent from a now-familiar business address in Langley. Inside, he found a cream-colored envelope sealed with a blob of red wax bearing the imprint of the crossed keys of St. Peter:

Dear Dr. Strickland,

While many here remain in support of your investigation, you must appreciate that this endeavor has been controversial from its inception. Sadly, recent media attention has left us no alternative but to act.

It is with regret that we require the return of the sample material, and the cessation of any further research on it.

Please submit a full report of your findings within 90 days of receipt of this letter. Representatives of the Holy See will arrive at 10:30 AM on the morning of February 17 to collect the sample.

Sincerely,
Enrico Giuseppe Rutigliano Ph.D., Chief Vatican Science Adviser

CC: Dr. Daniel Burnham, Director, NIH

Strickland clenched his jaw. Returning the letter to its envelope, he locked it in his desk drawer.

Chapter 66

Randall had resolved not to be there when the Vatican representatives came to collect the Shroud sample. But as the time drew near, he found himself drawn to the lab. The protesters outside were making it increasingly difficult to get any work done, anyway. Deliveries were stalled, and some staff had even been threatened while making their way through the crowd. The NIH's legal department filed injunctions against the protesters, but several sympathetic legal advocacy groups had filed counter motions.

Randall had always led a quiet researcher's life, and he carefully evaluated every project to make sure it didn't violate any of his core beliefs. As he stared out the office window, he wondered how things had gotten so far out of control. Last Sunday even the minister at his church had commented on the controversy. Randall imagined rows of accusing eyes cutting over at him during the sermon.

And reading the protesters' signs, he couldn't help but sympathize with at least some of their sentiments. He, too, revered the Scriptures as inspired by God. But too many people seemed happy to accept a comforting and nuance-free vision of the world—one that required discounting, perhaps even attacking, anything that threatened it. Biblical literalism was an impossible stance for a person of science. A literal reading of Genesis would lead to the theoretical collapse of almost every field of modern science, including physics, chemistry, biology, cosmology, and geology. And the "End Times," with its Rapture and its scorpion-tailed locusts descending from the sky, seemed like something out of a drug-induced nightmare. Some literalists even went so far as to argue that Satan had placed fossils on earth in order to test our faith.

* * *

Randall checked his watch—10:25 AM. He found his feet winding their way to the lab. As he entered the room, he made momentary eye contact with Strickland and then Bender. She smiled briefly, looking genuinely pleased to see him. Across the room stood two Vatican representatives, both dressed in plain dark suits. The stout older man commanded his younger companion in gruff, heavily accented English, and the young man gently lowered the Plexiglas enclosure back into its custom-padded briefcase.

Randall noticed the scowl on the older man's face, and his shallow breathing. His loathing for the lab and everything it represented was palpable.

By contrast, the younger man seemed calm and focused. His eyes were gentle and inquisitive. He endured the sometimes rude dictates of his superior with an unusual sense of relaxed detachment. He glanced at Randall as he secured the Shroud box into the briefcase, and as he locked the case, Randall noticed that he wore a gold ring with the image of an oak tree etched into its polished surface.

Chapter 67

The sample was gone. And so, in a roundabout way, Randall's prayers had been answered. And although the protesters remained, the process of winding things down had clearly begun. Randall guessed that NIH management and the Vatican would soon issue a joint press release corroborating the general nature of the work, and the fact that it had ended.

He began setting priorities for the lab's long-neglected roster of research projects. But in the course of reviewing the monthly departmental expenditures, an unfamiliar and particularly costly entry stood out. Randall flipped through the sheaf of papers, looking for the purchasing details. As he read through a yellow billing document, his eyes narrowed. He dialed the phone number listed on the paper.

"Hello, this is Dr. Jordan Randall, at the NIH. I'd like to check on a recent shipment to the Ethnogenomics Department."

He read off the purchase order number and the item identifiers. His brow furrowed as he scribbled down a series of notes. "All right," he said. "Thank you."

Randall stormed into the lab, where he found Strickland and Bender engaged in casual conversation.

"Bob, I need to have a word with you," he said in a controlled voice. "I was just going over the monthly expenditures and discovered this order from Geniac. Why would we need DNA chips tailored to sequences specific to the Middle East? And why such an extensive set of chips? There are over five thousand genes in this shipment. As department codirector, I'm supposed to be kept in the loop on such major acquisitions."

Strickland paused. "I've . . . been sequencing the remainder of the Shroud genome," he said.

"Are you out of your *mind*!" Randall exclaimed. "How long has this been going on?"

"Uh . . . about five weeks," admitted Strickland. "I knew I could speed the process by confirming known regions with the chips, and then sequencing any areas that contained unexpected SNPs or mutations."

"What the hell did you think the Vatican's recall of this sample was all *about*?" Randall all but shouted. "They clearly stated in their letter that we were to 'cease any further research on the sample.'"

"I'm not engaged in research per se, and I'm no longer using the sample," Strickland said.

"Don't pull that semantic crap with me!" Randall roared.

"Look Jordan," Strickland said, "I don't expect you to understand this or approve of it. That's why I tried to shield you from it."

"*Shield* me from it? Look out the window! Turn on the television! Do you realize the jeopardy, both personal and professional, that this puts us in—that it puts *me* in? *Damn it*, Bob!"

"I'm sorry if I betrayed your confidence." Strickland paused, as if to gather his thoughts. "I truly want you to understand where I'm coming from. You've read countless histories of the Shroud. Remember the picture taken in 1898—where the photographic negative produced a *positive* image of the figure on the Shroud? That image has captivated generations since, and sparked amazing discoveries about the Shroud, which are still ongoing."

Strickland rose from his chair and began pacing the room. "We all saw something extraordinary on the RES system," he said. "What if that imaging was a second phase to what began in 1898? The Church just barely allowed this study to occur. You weren't in on the negotiations, so you don't know how close it came to falling through. What if something should happen to the Shroud? It's nearly been destroyed countless times throughout history. I merely want to save its most valuable legacy—the DNA sequences stored on it. Would you have wanted Einstein's brain to be discarded after he died? Wouldn't *you* have fought to preserve that? What I'm doing isn't that different. Let others decide what to do with the data after the fact. I just want to make sure it isn't lost to the ages."

As usual, Strickland's arguments were persuasive, but Randall had already steeled himself against them. His old friend had a healthy ego, and professional glory had always played at least some part in his actions. Presenting himself as merely a passive caretaker and archivist of the Shroud data was self-deluded at best, and disingenuous at worst.

Randall turned to Sara. "Did you know about this?"

She nodded. "But if it's any consolation, I didn't approve of it either."

He shook his head in disbelief, his anger rising once more. "*Damn it*, Bob! I can't and won't be a party to this. I simply *won't*!"

Turning, he knocked over a wastebasket, then kicked it out of his way and stormed out of the office.

Chapter 68

"I'm sorry it turned out like this," Strickland said after Randall's tempestuous departure. "But I was fairly sure he'd react that way, which is why I kept it from him as long as I could."

"To be honest, I'm just glad it's out in the open," Bender replied. "I never felt comfortable being the sole confidante in what you were doing, particularly given my observer's role here."

He stared back at her. "So you also disagree with what I'm trying to do?"

"I think this undertaking has many motivations," she said carefully. "And many potential repercussions—including some you won't acknowledge."

"So, you're suggesting I'm not being entirely honest with myself?" he said.

Bender considered this. "Maybe."

Strickland was silent. When he finally spoke, his words were measured but pointed. "I suppose we've all done things without fully comprehending our deeper motivations," he said. "Who knows what factors led you to force your way, uninvited, into this study. In some circles, the way you managed it might even be called blackmail. But I'm sure you saw it very differently at the time."

Bender looked back at him as if she had been slapped. "I'm . . . sorry you feel that way," she said. "But I think I can remedy that situation." She felt the tears welling up as she began gathering her paperwork from a nearby desk. "You've already driven Jordan from your life. I may as well be next."

"Sara, wait," he said, grabbing her arm. She pulled away from him as someone knocked on the door, and George came in.

"Dr. Strickland, can I see you in private?" he said, his voice filled with urgency. I—"

"Not now!" Strickland snapped.

"I'm sorry, sir, but this one *can't* wait!"

Bender used the distraction to grab her coat and shoulder bag and slip out of the room.

Strickland turned back to his assistant, his eyes fiery. "All right.

What is it?" he barked.

George lowered his voice. "There's a man on the phone who says he's planted a bomb in the building. It's set to go off within the hour. He insisted on talking to you personally. I've already called NIH security, and they're patching in the FBI. They've asked that you keep him on the line for as long as possible. The caller ID shows a blocked number—it's probably been rerouted somehow."

George led Strickland to the phone and handed him the receiver.

"This is Dr. Strickland," he said. "What can I do for you?"

"I'm sure there's nothing you can do for me," said a hushed voice. "I just wanted you to know what *we're* going to do: blow you and your whole satanic enterprise off the face of the earth."

Strickland tried to stall. "I sympathize with how upset you are," he said. "Let's talk about your concerns. I'm more than willing to answer any questions you may have about genomic research. I think if people better understood our work, they'd come to appreciate what we're—"

"Don't patronize me!" the caller snarled. "I understand your work very well. And we're going to put a stop to it."

The voice sounded strangely electronic, with the odd harmonics and overtones that told Strickland it was being digitally altered to mask the caller's identity. Before he could say anything else, the line went dead.

Almost immediately, the other extension rang. George picked it up. "They couldn't trace it," he reported, looking over at Strickland.

The bomb squad ultimately evacuated the building and swept every inch, but no explosives were found.

Strickland wondered afterward whether the call had been intended simply to disrupt their operations, or had been a test to assess their vulnerabilities.

Chapter 69

The protests continued. Meanwhile, for nearly a week, both the NIH and the Vatican were the scenes of in-house battles over how to proceed. Finally, they each issued press releases reiterating that the Vatican was now in full possession of all materials related to the Shroud of Turin, intimating that any cause for controversy was now past. But both camps left the question of actual genetic analysis or manipulation glaringly unaddressed.

Sara Bender watched the evening news over dinner, as they profiled an odd new group calling itself Neoteric. The Neoterics had mobilized a candlelight vigil numbering in the thousands. The group's followers wore hooded iridescent robes of a holographic Mylar material, giving them a monklike aura but with a futuristic patina. Gathered in San Francisco's Golden Gate Park, they held bioluminescent candlesticks, chanting in Gregorian tones. The light from their wands rose into the night, casting the assembled faces in an unearthly glow.

Rather than *protesting* what had allegedly occurred at the NIH, the Neoterics saw recent events as welcome harbingers of a new era. They disagreed, a spokesperson said, not with the basic precepts and beliefs of the world's great religions, but with the modern-day implementation of those belief systems.

While there seemed to be no central organization or hierarchy of leadership in Neoteric, they did provide a brief charter statement. In a nutshell, the group painted most traditional religious institutions as having strayed far from the basic teachings of their spiritual founders. Neoteric, by contrast, favored the "open source" paradigm of the software world. In their statement, they advocated "a nonacquisitive, inclusive, and decentralized spirituality, without rigid authoritarian hierarchies or controlling and moralistic dogma."

As the TV camera panned across the assembled throng, Bender saw a montage of signs held aloft. One depicted a homeless person who looked like conventional depictions of Jesus, being ordered away from the steps of a church by a coifed and tailored televangelist. Another pictured a priest, a rabbi, and an imam feasting together in the back of a convertible superstretch limousine. But the best ones, she thought, read, "Neoteric...The Human Race, Version 2.0," and "Neoteric = Transcendence + Compassion. What more do we need?"

The assemblage seemed to be a loose confederation of cyber twenty-somethings and New Age enthusiasts. The obvious intent of the network television coverage was to present the group as a band of kooks. But Sara saw it very differently. Having flirted with the speed metal and trance music scenes during her teens, she often found herself in sympathy with the primal energy of such movements. Thank goodness for the young and the young at heart, she thought. Without a youthful sense of righteous indignation coupled with a healthy dose of naïveté, who would ever lead the charge for any real change?

The news story ultimately flashed up a picture of Strickland, obviously taken some years earlier, when he had no beard and rather longer hair.

Seeing Strickland's picture, Bender realized that she felt increasingly estranged from him, particularly after yesterday's encounter. He was obviously a brilliant man, but lately she had begun to wonder whether his inner demons might render him incapable of ever manifesting his true potential. His life seemed tragically flawed.

The news story ended, and she gazed out the window at the winter landscape below. A dead leaf fell from a tree and landed on the windowsill outside her living room. Desiccated and brown, it was soon dusted in a delicate layer of new snow. She sat watching as more snow slowly enveloped the leaf in a soft, white cocoon.

Chapter 70

As the days passed, the media circus surrounding the Shroud continued to gather steam. Bender watched on the evening news as a robed Neoteric engaged in debate with a man holding a sign proclaiming: "The End Times Have Begun." The man, red-faced and screaming, edged ever closer to the Neoteric.

The phone rang, and she fumbled with the TV remote, searching for the mute button. "Hello? Oh, hi, Ron!" she said. "No, not at all. Yeah, this is a good time to talk."

Since her arrival at the NIH, the D.C. area had become ground zero for a cultural, religious, and scientific maelstrom. It was now clear to Ron what she had been doing with her time in Bethesda.

She cradled the phone between shoulder and ear and began jotting down key words and phrases from their conversation, circling some, underlining others.

"Ron, are you *crazy*?" she said. "Look at the evening news. You think I'm going to abandon a story like this in midstream and take another assignment?"

"I'm not asking you to *abandon* it," he replied, "merely to alter your perspective. The current circus will hold the public interest for a few more weeks; then the cameras will move on."

Bender glanced back at the muted television screen. A nearly naked man in a loincloth had been lashed to a large, rough-hewn wooden cross and was now being hoisted into the air. The cameras pulled in for a tight shot, strategically framing an American flag in the background.

"Sara, I'm proposing something far bigger and more encompassing than the geek show of the week: the growing extremist movements in the major religions, the widening schism between science and religion, global holy wars, religious hyper-morality, the 'new religion' of scientific atheism, movie-based mythic spirituality, and more. I see a potential philosophical and cultural tipping point that few are addressing in depth or properly synthesizing."

Sara sighed, smiling despite herself at his persistence and energy. When she was a little girl, she and her sister used to watch Saturday morning cartoons with their father. At a key point, toward the end of every adventure, her father would say, "Look, the whole place is breaking up!"

As she grew older, Sara learned that there was indeed a pattern and commonality to each story—a mythic structure. But the most important aspect of the story, she came to recognize, was never about the place breaking up. The real insights came in the aftermath—when the characters picked up the pieces, ruminated on what had occurred, and assembled something new.

As Ron continued his pitch, Sara realized that her father had been right: the whole place *was* breaking up—both then and now. And maybe it *was* time to step out of the eye of the hurricane and see what was happening out on the periphery.

"Tell me you'll at least think about it," her editor urged.

Sara gazed back at the TV screen. The followers of the man on the cross had just placed a crown of thorns on his head, and the Jesus impersonator cocked his head to one side, mugging for the camera.

"Okay, I'll think about it," she said.

Chapter 71

Randall finished filling out the paperwork, then signed and dated it, sealed the envelope, and dropped it in the interdepartmental mailbox.

Next he called the director of SEW. "John, I just wanted you to know that I've finalized the arrangements on my end. I have a three-month sabbatical, so I'll be at the Society's disposal the entire time—no more squeezing in projects here and there." . . . "Yes, I have a number of ideas, but I'm also open to suggestions on where I can be most effective." He doodled nervously on a pad of paper. "I agree, recent developments *do* emphasize the need for what we've long been discussing. But I want to tell you up front that I won't be doing any interviews. I want my contributions to be purely academic and behind the scenes."

Randall's brow furrowed slightly at the commentary on the other end. "Cutting-edge science always runs the risk of going too far," he replied. "But we were operating with the full authority of the Vatican. The fact that the media has succeeded in spinning the study into something it never was—and perhaps never could be—is beyond our control." He began doodling again, the figures increasingly sharp and angular. "Exactly," he replied. "At the request of the Vatican, the sample has been returned. We're finalizing our work, and a report will be submitted in the near future. I'm leaving that phase to my colleague, so this seemed like the perfect time to take a breather and devote more time to SEW."

He paused, listening, and the tension in his face began to ease. "I'm looking forward to it, too," he said. "We'll talk soon!"

Through the blinds into the corridor, he saw Strickland passing by. Scrambling to open the door, he said, "Bob, could I have a moment?"

Strickland raised his eyebrows, clearly surprised by the sudden break in their silence. "Um, sure," he said, retracing his steps back to Randall's office.

The two men sat facing each other across Randall's desk. "What can I do for you?" Strickland asked.

"I just wanted you to hear this directly from me, before you get formal notification from the NIH: I'm taking a three-month sabbatical, beginning next week."

Strickland took a moment to digest the news. "But . . . you're not due for a sabbatical until next year."

"That's true, but I've requested it early, and Burnham's signed off on it."

"I'm . . . I'm sorry it's come to this, Jordan. I don't know what to say."

"At this point, I don't know what either of us *can* say." He sensed the questions going through Strickland's mind. "Don't worry," he said. "I won't say anything to anyone beyond the fact that the sample has been returned and the study formally completed."

"Thank you," Strickland said, though he still looked troubled.

"I'm not just doing it for you," Randall explained. "Frankly, it would have disastrous consequences to do otherwise. But I can no longer have any part in this. If you intend to continue sequencing in any way, shape, or form, I don't want to know about it."

Strickland nodded, his expression grim. "What will you do while you're away?" he asked.

"I'm planning to work full-time with SEW, to help set their lobbying priorities and put together various position papers. They need someone with my background to bring greater coherence and structure to the agenda. Also, there are some internal schisms cropping up that need attention."

"Well, good luck," said Strickland. "Sounds like important work."

Randall wondered if he was only imagining a slightly dismissive tone. "I believe it is," he replied. "But then, importance is always subjective."

The two men fell into another long silence. Randall stood, and Strickland followed his lead. Then Randall impulsively reached out and hugged Strickland.

"Take care of yourself, Bob," he said. "And be careful."

Strickland stiffened momentarily, then returned the embrace.

* * *

Randall's newly expanded association with SEW was clearly seen as a PR coup for the organization—a defector from perhaps the most controversial of all scientific endeavors. Within the week, they had issued an official press release, welcoming their newest full-time "advisory board member."

Randall watched the eleven o'clock news as a SEW spokeswoman discussed his move. "Dr. Randall's long-time commitment to the ethical application of genomic technologies makes him a valued addition to our board. We welcome his expertise and input as we seek to stem the reckless disregard for human values sometimes found in the realms of genomic research."

Switching off the television, Randall wearily made his way to bed. He spooned up next to Mary, but she was already sound asleep.

Chapter 72

The meeting had been entered into Strickland's online calendar, but for redundancy, George had also placed an appointment slip on his computer keyboard. "Daniel Burnham's office—2:00 P.M."

Arriving at the appointed time, Strickland was ushered into the spacious wood-paneled office. Dr. Burnham stood, and they shook hands over his polished L-shaped walnut desk.

Strickland hadn't been face to face with Burnham for many months, since the arrival of the Shroud sample. In truth, he preferred it that way. There was an unspoken belief in the research community that those who rose to the highest levels of management had gone over to the dark side, a place of deal making and compromise. And there was the corollary assumption that it was a raw thirst for power that led them there in the first place. One of Strickland's colleagues called it the "Oppenheimer syndrome." Access to the seat of power had always been a heady lure away from the lab bench.

As they exchanged pleasantries, Strickland marveled at Burnham's almost impenetrable sense of affability. In most encounters, it was easy to see through a veil of feigned cordiality, down to a person's motivating core. But Burnham's warmth and geniality presented a nearly seamless illusion, with any hidden agendas or subtexts lying inscrutably out of reach.

Strickland knew for a fact that the man could be ruthless, yet there seemed no trace of it in his face, not even in his eyes.

"It's getting pretty wild out there," Burnham said, looking out at the winter trees.

Strickland nodded in agreement.

"I'm sorry it's come to this," said Burnham. "This has been a truly unique and exciting project." He rubbed his index finger against his thumb. It was a tiny gesture, and the only sign of inner turmoil.

"Security notified me of the bomb threat last week," he continued. "They're still investigating, but I'm afraid we don't have any solid leads." He opened a manila folder on his desk and began leafing through a stack of papers. Strickland spotted the crossed keys of the Vatican on one. He recognized from the wording that it was the letter requesting return of the Shroud sample.

The director suddenly looked up at Strickland. "Do you believe in predestination?"

Strickland was momentarily taken aback, unsure how to respond. He wondered whether the comment was intended to put him at ease or throw him off. Or was Burnham so filled with imperial entitlement that he felt free to express any fleeting thought passing through his head?

"I can't conceive of any known mechanism for it," Strickland said, "but life sometimes does feel as if powerful themes are playing out, I'll say that much."

"I agree. Cause and effect are elusive concepts in quantum theory. The philosophical ramifications are endlessly fascinating."

Strickland wondered where the man was headed. But then he began shuffling papers from the folder again. This was vintage Burnham: as focused as a laser one moment, then scattered the next—but always with an agenda.

"The sample has been returned," Burnham said, reviewing the facts aloud, "and the Vatican has explicitly requested that we cease further study."

Strickland nodded in affirmation.

"Even so," Burnham added, "we continue to be a lightning rod for protest and controversy. It's putting a strain on the resources of the entire campus. Wouldn't you agree?" he said, looking up.

"Yes, I suppose it is," Strickland said.

"And it's not only straining our infrastructure, but potentially putting us at great risk. I'm not sure if you're aware of this, but the NIH administration building received a bomb threat three days ago."

"I hadn't heard that," Strickland said, frowning.

Burnham's eyes narrowed. "I'm reluctant to make this decision, given the importance of your department's other investigations. But we need to act quickly to defuse this. My only option, given where we are right now, is to shut down the Ethnogenomics Center, at least for several weeks. It will give the entire situation some time to cool off."

Burnham closed the folder on his desk. "I'll leave it up to you to inform your staff and find temporary placements for them. You have until the end of next week to wrap up ongoing tasks. If there are any sequencing operations that can't be cleanly suspended by then, notify me and we'll try to farm them out to other departments."

Strickland nodded, his mind racing. It was clear from the man's expression that there was no possibility of changing his mind.

"Thank you for dropping by," Burnham said, implicitly ending the meeting. His parting tone seemed to say that they had just had a casual and pleasant exchange and would likely be seeing each other for lunch sometime soon. It was a demeanor that had undoubtedly been honed through myriad encounters with Capitol Hill politicians and bureaucrats.

Chapter 73

The story was dying; Bender could feel it in her gut now. And with that realization, she found herself looking forward to being back in Manhattan and working on the proposed article series for Ron.

In the end, her editor was proposing a series in the same conceptual vein as her book. She might even be able to repackage the pieces as chapters—it would practically amount to paid research.

Just as Sara had resolved to make the call accepting the proposal, Strickland entered the lab. It was clear from his expression that something big had happened.

"Are you okay?" she asked.

"They're shutting us down," he said.

"Who?"

"The NIH, God damn it! I just got back from the director's office." Slumping into a chair, he stared out the window.

"I'm sorry, Robert," she said, instinctively reaching out to touch his arm. But he pulled away.

Chapter 74

Strickland worked late into the night, decrypting the data files one by one, analyzing the completed regions and those that remained. The computer monitors cast a ghostly light across the darkened lab. He liked it this way when he was analyzing data—it helped him to shut out distractions

He opened a spreadsheet used to track his work of the past weeks, including time frames and projected completion dates. As he adjusted the figures, a faint smile came over him. Factoring in the sequences derived using the DNA chips, he was significantly further along than he had supposed. And including the weekend, nine days still remained before the shutdown.

He might just make it.

Chapter 75

Long-stemmed roses arrived by courier to Bender's apartment. *News travels fast,* she thought. She couldn't quite suppress a smile as she tore open the attached card.

She had only made the call to Ron last night, but she knew that he and Tom worked out at the same gym on the upper West Side.

> *Dear Babe,*
>
> *A little bird told me that you'll soon be returning to the nest. I can't tell you how much I've missed you! Looking forward to being together again—and starting over.*
>
> *Love always,*
> *Tom*

She lowered her face into the fleshy red petals, taking in the luscious scent. Funny how some men seemed to have a sixth sense warning them when a woman was reevaluating her options. Looking back at all the times she had allowed a man to manipulate her feelings with flowers, she had to wonder what made such a simple gesture so compelling. Perhaps flowers resonated as a symbol of fertility, or simply reminded her of the beauty of nature. Whatever the mechanism, it still worked.

Chapter 76

Bender struggled to find a way to break the news to Strickland. She had already given notice on her apartment in Georgetown and was busy scanning documents and consolidating information onto her laptop.

The impending departmental shutdown had fired Strickland with a fevered urgency. Every time she dropped by the lab, day or night, there he was. She couldn't help but wonder what was going on, but her knowledge of his recent activities had put her in an ethical bind, and she had resolved not to ask questions—better just to stay out of the loop. Strickland's activities were violating explicit directives from the Vatican and thus were unethical at the very least, and quite possibly illegal, and she had the intuitive sense that he was simply wandering down one blind alley after another.

Meanwhile, their unpredictable relationship had settled into a broader personal estrangement, and at some point she realized she had endured more than enough of Strickland's mercurial personality. Connie Franklin's minefield analogy popped into her head. As her return to Manhattan neared, she felt more and more certain about the decision. She genuinely didn't want to hurt him, though he was sure to feel like the last man on a sinking ship.

Summoning her will, she walked into the lab and pulled up a chair next to Strickland's workstation. "I'm leaving Washington at the end of next week," she said.

Pulling his attention away from the computer monitor, he looked at her. "For how long?"

"Permanently," she said. "I'm going back to Manhattan."

He seemed to have trouble digesting the news. "If this is about what I said the other day, about forcing your way into the Shroud project, I'm truly sorry. I've been under a lot of stress, and I clearly overreacted."

"It's not about that," she said. "It's about a lot of things—I've been considering this for a while now."

"Guess I can't blame you," he said, looking out at the protesters who had gathered yet again outside. "This is all getting a bit old. The study's been shut down. It's yesterday's news."

"My decision has been building for some time," she reiterated. "My editor has offered me the opportunity to write a series of in-depth pieces about exactly what's been boiling up here these past weeks—the impact of genomic research on society at large, and the growing schism between religion and science."

"Sounds like fascinating stuff," he said. "And writing a book is admittedly a daunting undertaking. An article series is something you know."

"I'm really just taking a break from the book," she said, her irritation growing. "It's true that I miss reporting, but that doesn't mean—"

"You don't have to convince me," he interrupted. "It's always a matter of interpretation whether someone's moving *away* from something or *toward* something else."

Sara finally exploded. "Look around you, Robert! Look at your life! Did it ever occur to you that maybe it's *you* that people are moving away from? Jordan, me, the Vatican, the whole frigging NIH?"

In his expression of profound hurt, she saw the face of a small boy.

"Robert . . . I'm sorry," she said, moving toward him. But he turned away from her, and abruptly left the room.

Chapter 77

Strickland stared out the window of his study. The predawn sky was a luminous sheet of gray. Unable to get back to sleep after waking from a dream, he had tossed and turned for nearly an hour before finally getting up, making a cup of tea, and settling into the leather chair at his desk.

In the dream, he had been back in medical school, walking briskly along a pathway outside the hospital. In the distance he spotted a patient on a gurney, apparently abandoned. Rushing forward, he had looked at the woman's gaunt face to find that it was his mother. She looked up at him, her dark eyes dazed and imploring.

He quickly checked her vitals, to find her pulse weak and thready. He looked around frantically. The traffic was heavy and there was no crosswalk and no traffic light, but he had to get her across the street to the ER entrance.

Strickland began wheeling her across the pitted and potholed street, wending his way through the bumper-to-bumper traffic, with cars honking and drivers shaking fists. Suddenly, though he was still in hospital scrubs, he was a boy again. The gurney became heavier and heavier, nearly impossible to maneuver across the rutted street. His mother had lost consciousness by that time, and he could see that she was fading fast. The ER entrance was there before him, but it might as well have been across the country.

And then he awoke.

His father hadn't known she had been taking the pills, though perhaps he should have. And looking back at her sometimes erratic behavior, Strickland wondered whether she might have been mildly bipolar and perhaps self-medicating.

She had traveled to neighboring towns to get the prescriptions, knowing how tight-knit a small town medical community could be. In those days, "mother's little helpers" were handed out like gumdrops, often without strong enough warnings against mixing with alcohol. Yet, the same women seeking such pharmaceutical relief—from unfulfilling lives or troubled marriages—were often also abusing alcohol.

After her death, Strickland's father entered into a state of denial, burying himself even deeper in his work. And on the home front it was every man for himself, with Robert and his sister left to their own devices.

His sister turned to her girlfriends. Robert, in high school, channeled his grief into athletics, dirt bikes, and substance abuse of his own.

Strickland sipped his tea and gazed out at the moonlit winter landscape. The day his mother died, he didn't cry, any more than would a stone. His father forced him to see a therapist, who proved to be a rigid, arrogant Freudian. Even at fifteen, Robert thought the emphasis on symbolism and metaphor was off base. He considered himself too scientifically sophisticated for such hocus-pocus. Moreover, he didn't feel that he needed or wanted to change—he had the world pegged. After several sessions, he refused to return.

The experience permanently soured him on psychotherapy, though in looking back, he had to admit that his relationships, particularly with women, had traced a familiar arc. There were definitely subtle mechanisms at work that seemed beyond the reach of his conscious mind.

Chapter 78

The protesters continued their siege of the Ethnogenomics building, and Strickland couldn't help but wonder whether some of the throng came from the outreach of various organized religious groups. He noticed several men in suits who seemed to be directing the activities—handing out signs and carefully videotaping the events.

Large-scale protests had now taken place in New York, Boston, Los Angeles, and San Francisco. And oddly, every time, the Neoterics were also there. They continued to promote the idea that recent developments surrounding the Shroud were all part of "a bloodless spiritual revolution," the supposed next phase in mankind's evolution. In San Francisco, they proclaimed this "the Winter of Love."

Meanwhile, a number of fundamentalist Christian groups portrayed Strickland and anyone siding with him as tools of Satan. One group went so far as to declare, "Any means necessary would be justified in ending this insult to God!"

* * *

Bender decided to stay away from the lab for a few days to arrange her belongings and finish packing. It felt good to be out of the fray, away from everyone and everything.

In sorting through her research materials, she discovered several stacks of books and journal articles on loan from Strickland. Later in the day, she headed into Bethesda to drop them off. While refiling some of the papers in a research bay, she suddenly realized that Strickland was standing nearby.

"Haven't seen you for a few days," he said. He sipped a cup of coffee, as if to hide his awkwardness. "I'm sorry about my behavior the other day. I've felt under attack from all sides, which has sharpened my tongue. But . . . I can understand your decision, on many levels. The short-term situation here looks like more of the same—going back to New York is probably the right move."

Bender nodded.

"I've really enjoyed our time together," Strickland continued. "I can honestly say that you've brought something valuable . . . important . . . to this study—perspectives that might not have come to light otherwise. I just wanted you to know that."

Bender looked up at him, softening a bit. "Thanks," she said.

"I don't pay compliments very often. But you have a rare combination of intelligence, insight, and grit."

She smiled, silently accepting his words.

He paused, still obviously ill at ease. "Look, before you get away, I was wondering if you'd like to grab a bite some evening—sort of a farewell get-together?"

Bender thought back to their first encounter, and her suggestion of continuing the discussion over dinner. Had her motivations been entirely straightforward back then?

Pulling her hair back out of her eyes, she looked up from the stack of paperwork. "I suspect that things are going to be pretty hectic during the next few days," she said, "for both of us. I'm sure you have a lot to wrap up, and so do I. Let's just play it by ear and see if we both end up having the time."

Strickland nodded and headed back to the lab.

Chapter 79

Bender made several trips to and from her car that afternoon, returning books and journals to the Ethnogenomics library and moving her belongings out of the lab. As she approached the rear entrance of the building, an angry group of protesters suddenly confronted her.

"You can run, but you can't hide, 'cause we've got God on our side," they chanted in unison. They seemed jubilant at having cornered an actual Ethnogenomics scientist.

Bender looked around, recognizing her vulnerability. She was alone, and the crowd was getting bolder and more unruly by the minute. She tightened her grip on the box of books, ready to run if necessary.

"Look, I don't work here," she said. "I'm just visiting." She pulled her access badge out of her purse, and passed it over the reader, preparing to enter.

"Is that why you have a badge, and why you're sneaking in the back way?" a man said, reaching out and grabbing her roughly by the arm.

As her box of books fell to the ground, Bender felt a wave of panic. She had been in enough war zones to know what could happen when a mob mentality took over. Another hand grabbed at her shoulder, spinning her off balance. She fell to the ground. The crowd began to move in.

Suddenly, she felt her attacker release her arm and fall backward. He came down hard on the pavement.

Out of nowhere, Strickland was standing over her. He angrily shoved a second man back, and made clear to the crowd that anyone pursuing the attack would pay dearly. Someone stepped forward and snapped a picture before disappearing into the crowd.

Strickland helped Bender up and gathered her books, and together they slipped through the back door.

Chapter 80

The next day, Bender came back to the lab for one last sweep, to make sure she had left nothing behind. She bumped into Strickland in the hallway.

"I wanted to thank you again for saving me out there," she said.

"No problem," he replied. "When people act like animals, you sometimes have to treat them as such. It's a bit like confronting a snarling dog—you make clear who's the boss, and it'll usually back down."

"But what if those men *hadn't* backed down?" she said.

"Then they would have had a very bad day," he said.

Despite his good-natured grin, she had a feeling that he meant it. She smiled at his bravado. "Well, anyway, I'm glad you came along when you did. By the way, I'm actually moving faster than I expected. I'm leaving for New York on Monday, but if the dinner offer's still on the table, I could be free Saturday evening."

She saw his face brighten. "Great," he said. "I'll pick you up at seven."

Chapter 81

Jason Newcomb stood in his small second-story Rome apartment, staring out at the towering monument to Vittorio Emanuele, its floodlit white marble columns looming like an apparition in the night sky. He never tired of the view.

It was after midnight, but motor scooters and cars still moved like shoals of fish around the traffic circle down the block. In the distance, he heard the *dee-dah, dee-dah, dee-dah* of an approaching ambulance. The ghostly glow of its blue beacon flashed across stone walls as it speeded past.

Unable to sleep, at the mercy of street noise and caffeine, he sat down at his computer and brought up the CNN Web site to check the world news. A small photograph caught his eye, and he moved closer to the screen. Suddenly wide-awake, he launched his e-mail program.

> To: Sara.Bender@nyt.com
> From: Jason.Newcomb@vatican.va
> Subject: Big Bang.
>
> Hey, Sara,
>
> I just checked CNN.com, and there you were, about to be attacked by protesters at the NIH! Are you OK?
>
> Is the NIH doc really doing what they say? I've even heard rumblings about it here, although everyone's fairly tight lipped. Is this what brought you to D.C.?
>
> Please be careful, Sara. Having been in this milieu for the better part of a year, I've seen the spectrum of where religious belief can go—from beauty and transcendence to bitter divisiveness, and all the way down to hatred and murderous violence. Everything, supposedly, "in the name of God." We think of ourselves as rational creatures, but time and time again I see scant evidence of it. Too often, we take strongly held feelings and beliefs and then try to use God to justify them.
>
> Remember the movie *Dr. Strangelove,* where the U.S. general loses it and sets off World War III? He came to believe that fluoridation

of water was a Communist plot, designed to sap us of our "precious bodily fluids." He told another character in the movie that he had come to the realization "during the physical act of love," but had fortunately been able to "properly interpret those feelings."

The things I hear being attributed to God sometimes sound just as nutty. We're far too irrational, but also far too intelligent, for our own good—a dangerous admixture of beast and brains. Yet, most us can't even see it. And I think that's the real quandary of the human experience.

Well, I've bent your cyber-ear long enough (I'm on a caffeine high). I should probably get to bed—long day ahead.

I miss you, Sara. Take care of yourself!

XOXO, Jason

Chapter 82

Strickland stared up at the bedroom ceiling. It had been snowing for days, overtaxing the infrastructure of the entire D.C. area. The limited fleet of snowplows was working around the clock, and the walkways of his condominium complex were in dire need of shoveling.

An outdoor security light cast shadows of drifting snow across his bedroom wall, like tiny flitting moths. Closing his eyes, Strickland imagined that he could somehow hear the soft gathering of their mass—singly negligible, but combining into something powerful and new.

In high school, he had read an odd short story titled "Silent Snow, Secret Snow," about a young boy's growing conviction that his world was slowly being consumed by a gathering snow that no one else could perceive. At first, it had seemed a beautiful and comforting secret, there for him alone. But it gradually became an obsession that overwhelmed his every thought and experience until, in the end, there was nothing but the idea of the swirling snow.

Strickland's mind continued to flit from one thing to the next. He resisted the temptation to get up and log on to the Ethnogenomics Center's sequencing database. Envisioning the lab spreadsheet, he mentally checked off the milestones. If he could sustain this pace, he would complete the sequencing before the lab officially shut down.

* * *

When he awoke at dawn, the sun was shining, illuminating the glittering expanse of snow beyond the condominium complex. Strickland felt better than he had in weeks, as if a veil of gloom had been lifted. Perhaps it was the change in weather.

It was still early—time enough for a real breakfast. He drove over to the local market to pick up some eggs and bagels. As he returned, the phone began to ring, and he rushed to grab it.

There was someone on the line, but they said nothing. The caller ID was blocked. Strickland said hello once more, then hung up.

The calls had been happening for several weeks now, sometimes within minutes of his stepping inside the door.

Chapter 83

Strickland sifted through various sport coats and ties, trying to settle on the best ensemble for dinner. "Dressing the part" had never been a priority for him. In medical school and during his early days at the NIH, he had made a point of being antifashion: T-shirts, jeans, and motorcycle boots.

Once, during his residency, he had taken advantage of some downtime between patients to grab a few hours' sleep in the physician cot room. (Seventy-two hour shifts with little or no rest were an open invitation to deadly mistakes.) After about an hour, his pager had gone off. Unshaven and groggy, he headed down the hall to grab a cup of coffee. But he had neglected to put on his white coat. Hospital security stopped him, assuming he was a wandering indigent ER patient. When he flashed his hospital badge, the amazed officer simply shook his head. Since becoming the head of the Ethnogenomics Center, he had made a halfhearted stab at buying appropriate clothes for NIH management meetings and press events, but never felt quite comfortable in them.

He finally settled on some casual slacks, white shirt, dark brown tie, and tweed sportcoat. It was the standard dressy-casual academic's outfit and would surely pass muster at the Hay-Adams.

He wondered how Sara would dress, and what it would say about how she viewed the evening. But he wasn't even sure how *he* viewed the evening. Self-analysis had never been his forte. Maybe the failing came from his father, whether by example or by genetics.

* * *

On the drive into D.C., Strickland suddenly got the feeling that he was being followed. He had seen the same Ford sedan, with one headlight slightly askew, in his rearview mirror for miles.

He changed lanes, sometimes signaling as if he might exit from the highway. After several such maneuvers, it became clear that whatever he did, the Ford did, though it was all very low-key and always from a considerable distance. Satisfied that he wasn't imagining things, he continued toward D.C.

As he approached the Key Bridge off-ramp to Georgetown, he gradually started picking up speed—from sixty to seventy, to seventy-five.

At each increase, the sedan matched his speed.

Checking the mirror, he saw that the sedan was about four length's back. Spotting a perfect set of openings to the right, he swung hard across several lanes, just making the Roosevelt Bridge off-ramp. The Ford, unable to react in time, shot past.

Chapter 84

Bender raced through the apartment, tossing aside this skirt and that blouse, searching for her last unpacked pair of panty hose. She had considered shaving her legs but decided against it—after all, it was just a date; it wasn't as if she were going to spend the night.

But she had to admit that her impression of Strickland had subtly shifted in the past few days. She hated to consider the notion, but had his saving her from the mob of protesters had a subliminal effect? Was the whole gender thing really so primitive and simplistic—cavemen rescuing women from their brutish brethren, followed by the inevitable surrender?

After trying on several different outfits with her only pair of heels, Bender finally settled on a dark blue dress as the only reasonable match. In Manhattan, she regularly attended formal events with Tom. But in spite of her high-end wardrobe, there was still a place in her heart for old black leather jackets like the ones she had worn to CBGB back in college.

The phone rang as she fastened an ankle strap. Automatically she moved to get it, then hesitated and let the machine kick in.

"Hey, babe," said Tom, "just wanted to say hi, see if you got the flowers . . ." Sara glanced at the clock on the wall. Strickland was supposed to pick her up in ten minutes. If she stopped to talk with Tom, she'd never be ready in time. And she still needed to put on lipstick. She stood next to the phone, resisting the urge to pick it up. "Okay, I guess you're out," he said finally. "I'll try you in the morning. I love you!"

Resolving to e-mail Tom when she got home, Sara fastened the other ankle strap, then checked her hair in the mirror. Once again it seemed to be either feast or famine where men were concerned.

Applying lipstick, then a hint of eyeliner, she stepped back to inspect the full effect. *Not bad.* As Springsteen said, ". . . A little touch-up and a little paint . . ."

There were still a few minutes left before Strickland was due to arrive. Booting up her laptop, she launched the e-mail program and noticed a recent message from Jason entitled "Big Bang." Ignoring the in-box, she started a quick e-mail to Tom. But one sentence into it, the doorbell rang, so she put the laptop into sleep mode, grabbed her coat and purse, and headed downstairs.

Chapter 85

Driving to the restaurant, Strickland seemed distracted, constantly checking the rearview mirror.

"What's up?" she finally asked him. "Are you leading some kind of double life—an international man of mystery?"

"No, everything's fine," he said. He looked over at her and smiled. "I'm glad you could make it tonight."

When they arrived at the Hay-Adams, there was already a long line for valet parking, so he dropped her off in front, then parked in an adjacent lot.

The Lafayette Room's maître d' led them to a small candlelit table in the corner—intimate but with a spacious view of the floodlit Washington Monument. Ever the reporter, Bender surveyed the other diners in the room. At a nearby table, a portly older gentleman with dewlaps and bushy graying eyebrows held court over a group of men and women who seemed to hang on his every word. Turning her attention back to Strickland, she decided he could use a little work in the wardrobe department—particularly in comparison with the other diners. Tom's tailor could work wonders for him.

They started out with wine and hors d'oeuvres. But the dynamic between them felt strained and uncomfortable, like a bad blind date in college. She looked into Strickland's face, probing for some sense of what he was thinking and what they were really doing here. He returned her gaze, a faint smile raising the corners of his mouth.

It was the curse of women, she thought—reading too much into a relationship. But she remembered enough of her biology training to realize that there must be some evolutionary reward for any behavior that persisted through the ages. In this case, though, she couldn't imagine what that reward might be.

Chapter 86

The waiter refilled their glasses, and Bender basked in the glow of the fine red Bordeaux. Strickland had started to relax and seemed more like the man she had bumped into at an M Street gallery months ago. The conversation moved from Buddhism to E. O. Wilson's sociobiology (and the inherent incompatibilities between men and women), to the biological motivations for war and romantic love. The connections he was able to draw between seemingly unrelated topics were amazing and fun.

Suddenly, the conversation reached a natural lull. Had it come any earlier, it might have felt strained and uncomfortable, but now they both simply took it in. Strickland looked at Bender and smiled. She held his gaze for a long moment as he poured the remainder of the wine into their glasses and offered a toast.

"To the smartest, most mysterious . . . and sometimes most irritating woman I've ever known," he said, gently clinking his glass against hers. "I'm really going to miss you."

"Thanks. The feeling is mutual—on all counts," she said, smiling.

"Touché," he said, laughing. The waiter brought the bill, and Strickland signed the charge slip. As they walked out into the night air, he put his arm around her waist. "Thanks again for coming. I really enjoyed it."

"Me, too," she said, surrendering slightly to his embrace.

But as she moved toward him, her heel caught in a crack in the sidewalk, rolling her ankle outward. "Owww!" she gasped, almost collapsing on him from the pain. "Damn!" she said, trying to walk on but quickly realizing that she couldn't.

The valet parking line had subsided, and the young men in bow ties lingered in front with little to do. Strickland eyed the parking lot. Even though it was only a hundred yards away, it was clearly too far under the circumstances. He pulled one of the valets aside and offered him a tip to retrieve the car.

"Are you okay?" he asked, returning to Bender's side.

"Yeah, I think so."

"We should get some ice on that. Looks like a wicked sprain, and it's always possible you fractured the talus. I can arrange an X-ray in the morning."

Strickland began to say something else, but as Bender looked at him, the words suddenly evaporated and everything kicked into slow motion. From the corner of her eye, she saw an enormous flash of fire from the nearby parking lot; then a concussion wave knocked them both to the ground. Strickland covered her with his body as bits of debris rained down around them.

The ringing in her ears drowned out all sound. Nothing moved for several seconds. Then Strickland stood and helped her to her feet. She shivered uncontrollably in the cold night air. The area where Strickland's car had been parked was engulfed in flames.

III

Chapter 87

Strickland looked up and down the street, his heart pounding. The parking lot attendant was obviously dead, and flames billowed from the cars nearest Strickland's. Sirens were already wailing in the distance.

An older woman who had been standing nearby was lying flat on her back, but began to stir. Strickland helped her sit up and quickly performed a basic medical workup, first asking her name, the date, and where she was. Satisfied with the responses, he asked her if anything hurt. Then he did a quick check for broken bones, internal injuries, or obvious wounds. Satisfied that she wasn't seriously injured, he turned to Bender. "We've got to get out of here," he said.

A cab approached from the end of the block, trolling for after-dinner patrons. As it neared, the driver gaped at the still burning shells of cars in the lot. He hesitated, and was about to drive away when Strickland stepped into the street.

"Pull over!" he commanded, staring the man in the eyes. The driver complied, and he yanked open the back door.

"Holy shit!" said the cabbie. "What happened?"

"I'm not sure," Strickland said, helping Bender hop one-legged into the car. He slid in after her and slammed the door. "Dumbarton and Thirtieth."

The cabbie adjusted his rearview mirror as he pulled away from the curb. "Hey, you're that Jesus-cloning guy, right?"

"No . . . but I've been asked that before," Strickland said. "We must look alike." He turned to look out the rear window. A half minute later, he checked again, while the cabbie shot him glances in the mirror.

Several minutes later, as they neared Bender's block, Strickland suddenly pointed out a town house. "This is it," he said. "Twenty-eight fifty-three Dumbarton."

"I thought you said Dumbarton and *Thirtieth*."

"I had it wrong," Strickland said, looking up at the street sign. "It's Twenty-eighth."

"This is—" Bender began, but he grabbed her arm and helped her out of the car.

He pulled out his wallet and slapped a fifty into the cabbie's hand. "Keep the change."

"Hey, thanks!" the cabbie said as he pulled away.

Strickland hoped the tip might buy some loyalty in the form of forgetfulness if anyone started asking questions.

"You realize this isn't my block," Bender said as the cab drove off.

"I do."

"And you also realize that my place is nearly two blocks away and that I may have a broken ankle?"

"That, too. Here, lean on me," he said, as they started up the street.

Chapter 88

Bender winced in pain as she attempted to climb the stairs of her apartment. "This isn't going to work," Strickland muttered.

He lifted her in his arms, making his way up the long flight. She heard his breathing deepen from the effort as they neared the top. But she was relieved to be off her feet and to have the pain subside.

Gently setting her down on the couch, he unstrapped her shoe and wiggled it off the already swollen foot. He probed with his fingers, then rotated the foot carefully in different directions. "Tell me if any of this hurts," he said.

"Ow!" she yelped as he moved it left to right.

"Sorry," Strickland said. He tried the same movement again, but more gently. His brow furrowed slightly. "I don't think anything's broken. It's likely just a sprain, though you could have some torn ligaments, and there's the possibility of what's called an avulsion, where a sudden trauma tears loose a sliver of bone. Either way, we can play it by ear for now and just keep the foot immobilized."

He went into the kitchen, and Bender heard cabinets opening, then rifling in the freezer.

"Here," he said, returning with a bag of frozen peas. "Mold this around the side of your ankle. Got any Tylenol or ibuprofen? That'll help keep the swelling down and reduce the pain."

"In the bathroom medicine chest," she said.

Strickland came back with two capsules and a glass of water.

"I don't think you can charge for a house call if you're the one that brought me here," she said, trying to lighten the mood.

With almost a smile, he eased a pillow under her foot, elevating it slightly. Then he grabbed the television remote. Switching on the local late news, he landed in the middle of live coverage at the scene of the explosion. In the distance, he saw the smoking wreckage of his car, with firefighters rolling up their hoses and preparing to leave. The camera panned back as an on-site reporter spoke to the studio anchor. The woman cupped her earphone, straining to hear him over the street noise.

"That's right, Hal," she said. "At present we have one confirmed fatality. The destroyed vehicle was registered to Dr. Robert Strickland, a researcher with the National Institutes of Health and an expert on ethnic differences in genetic makeup. He and his lab have recently been embroiled in controversy. Several weeks ago, a confidential source charged that the Vatican had enlisted Strickland and the NIH to perform genetic analyses on purported bloodstains from the Shroud of Turin—to shed light on the garment's age and origin."

More police cars arrived at the scene, briefly drowning out the reporter's voice. She cupped her hand to her ear again, then continued.

"As a result of his findings, or due to internal struggles within the Vatican, the sample was reportedly withdrawn before Strickland's analysis was complete. Since that time, a number of religious Web sites have made accusations that Strickland and his department might have been investigating the possibility of cloning using the blood samples—something that most experts deny is even a possibility given current technologies. Nevertheless, the story seems to have acquired a life of its own."

An off-camera assistant ushered a uniformed police officer in front of the camera. The reporter touched her earphone while listening intently, then said, "We have Commander Pete Farmer with us, who is in charge of the crime scene. Commander, is there any information as to the fate of Dr. Robert Strickland?"

"No bodies have been found in the wreckage," said the square-jawed officer. "Only the body of a parking lot attendant, who was found nearby."

In the background, a fire chief could be seen gesturing to the officer. "I'm sorry," he said. "Afraid I have to go."

The reporter thanked him, resuming her synopsis of the situation. "Eyewitnesses have reported someone matching Dr. Strickland's description dining at the Hay-Adams Hotel restaurant this evening with a woman. Several days ago, a news crew filmed Dr. Strickland rescuing a woman from a group of violent protestors outside the NIH. The woman was later identified as Sara Bender, a reporter for the *New York Times,* who has interviewed Strickland extensively as part of a book she's writing on the field of genetics."

Twin photographs of Strickland and Sara appeared alongside the live video.

"Could Ms. Bender have been the woman with Strickland this

evening?" the studio anchor queried. "And if so, where are they now?"

"We have no further information about them at this time," said the reporter.

Chapter 89

Strickland stared at their pictures on the television screen. "I was afraid of this," he said. "Now we're both in jeopardy."

"What do you mean?" Bender asked.

"Tonight they were only trying to get to *me*. But now you'll be viewed as another way to do that." He paused. "Also, I may have been followed when I was on the Beltway earlier, heading to your apartment."

"Well, thanks for not telling me—and putting us both at risk," she said.

"I was pretty sure I lost them, but apparently not." He looked suddenly grim. "We can't stay here tonight. We have to get out of town— maybe out of the *country*."

"I . . . I can't do that," she said.

Strickland glanced again at the smoldering remains of his car on the television screen. "It may be the only rational choice."

Bender looked down at the bag of frozen peas saddled over her ankle. "What about my foot?"

"We'll give it another hour on the cold pack and give the ibuprofen some time to work. Got a stretch bandage anywhere? We'll need to immobilize it as much as possible."

"In the bathroom drawer. I tweaked my foot running a few weeks ago—stepped in a gopher hole."

"So, does clumsiness run in the family?" he asked, grinning.

It felt good, somehow reassuring, to see him smile. But she was also beginning to appreciate the gravity of their situation. Just then her cell phone began ringing. She sat up, straining to reach her purse.

"Don't answer it," Strickland said. "Too easy for someone to trace."

But Bender had already grabbed the phone by the time his words registered. Checking the display, she said, "It's Tom."

"All the more reason," he said. "Answering could put him at risk, too."

The phone stopped ringing, but a minute later a text message appeared on the screen: "R U OK?" Bender resisted the impulse to respond. She wanted to text Tom, and say, *Hell no, I'm not okay. Come get me out of this!*

The studio anchor appeared again on the screen, looking distracted by information coming through his earpiece. Strickland unmuted the sound. "This just in," the anchor said. "A group calling itself the Army of the Lord has reportedly taken responsibility for the bombing of Dr. Robert Strickland's car earlier this evening. In an e-mail communiqué, the previously unknown organization has stated that it, quote, 'will use any and all means necessary to stop those who would disobey the will of God by defiling the sanctity of our Lord, Jesus Christ.'"

Bender stared back at Strickland and sighed. "Okay . . . what do you suggest?"

Chapter 90

Strickland once again shifted into command mode, pacing back and forth in the small living room of Sara's apartment. "We need to change our look as much as possible," he said. "I'll need a razor—the beard has to go. Do you have any hair dye? We'll both need that."

"I don't," she said, "but there's a mom-and-pop market just down the street."

"Good. We'll also need some cash—as much as possible. This has to be our last blip on the radar screen before we go to black. Will they let you cash checks there?"

"Sure, I do it all the time," she said.

"After that, we'll each max out our ATM withdrawals for the day—preferably at someplace other than the store."

"There's an ATM down the street from the market," she said. "Also, I just got the deposit back from my apartment. I asked them to give it to me in cash. It's a habit I got into while covering war zones—always having ready cash in the event of an emergency."

"Perfect."

Bender rubbed her eyes. With the stress of the day's events, and her throbbing ankle, she could feel her mental powers turning to mush.

Strickland seemed to perceive her flagging energy. "We've got a long night ahead of us," he said, turning on her coffeemaker and grabbing two large mugs from the cabinet. "Do you have any extra clothes that aren't already packed and shipped?"

"Yeah, a few things—enough for several days. But what about you?" she asked.

"I don't need any clothes."

She gave him an incredulous look. "I'd say you do."

"I'll buy them when we get where we're going," he said. "We can't risk going by my place. Whoever these people are, they're bound to know where I live—it may already be staked out."

"Okay, whatever," she said, slowly coming to terms with this antithesis to Tom's microplanned travel itineraries.

"Hmm, I just remembered," she added. "I bought two shirts and a pair of slacks for Tom as a gift. You two are about the same height and build."

She limped over to a suitcase and opened it. "I was going to give them to him when he came to D.C., but somehow the visit never happened."

Strickland looked at the tags on the shirts and slacks. "They're my size—right on the money."

Bender sat on the bed as he stowed the extra clothes in a large gym bag. The coffeemaker in the kitchen began beeping, and she stood up, momentarily forgetting about her foot. "Ay-y!" she groaned, almost collapsing from the pain.

Strickland caught her in mid fall. "Here," he said, putting his arm around her shoulder and guiding her back to the couch. Then he filled the two mugs with strong coffee.

"I'm not sure I can get all the way to the store," Bender said. "But they know me pretty well there. Why don't I call and ask if you can cash a check for yourself and one for me. I'll give you my ID and ATM card."

She made the call, explaining that she had twisted an ankle and that a friend would be stopping by. The owner said it was fine.

But a few minutes after Strickland went out the door, the phone rang. "Hey, Sara, Rafiq. Your friend is here to cash the checks," he said, lowering his voice. "Rest assured, he is not listening. . . . I just want to make sure you're okay."

"Everything's fine, Rafiq," she said. "It's sweet of you to look out for me. I appreciate it."

* * *

Fifteen minutes later, Strickland was back with the money and supplies.

"I figured we needed something fairly far from our natural colors," he said. "'Sandy blonde' for you, and 'auburn-brown' for me."

"Okay, I see your point," she said. "I just never imagined myself as a blonde."

"All the more reason to go that route—probably no one else has, either."

She nodded. The caffeine was beginning to kick in, and she felt a new surge of energy. "Can you help me to the bathroom?" she asked.

"Sure," he said, putting his arm around her waist.

While applying the hair-coloring gel, Bender marveled at how, just a few hours earlier, she had resolved not to shave her legs for what was going to be a simple dinner out. Now here she was, dying her hair, with Strickland in the next room planning a plane trip to God knew where.

After a quick shower, she towel-dried her hair and paused to look in the mirror. With the new hair color, it was almost like looking into the face of a stranger. It amazed her how superficial the assessment of "self" could be.

Still staring at the image in the mirror, she decided to take the transformation one step further. She stuck her head back in the shower, wet her hair again, and took a comb and scissors from the drawer. Her roommate in college had been a hair stylist on the side and taught her some of the basics.

She settled on an easy cut without much layering: an ear-length bob. When she had finished, she barely recognized herself. And stranger still, she not only looked completely different, she also *felt* different.

"Wow!" Strickland said as she limped back out into the living room. "I'm Bob. Nice to meet you."

He, too, was transformed. Bender stared at him, her mind racing. For a second she couldn't place it. Then it hit her: the beard was gone.

"I picked up a razor at the store," he explained.

"I think I like you this way," she mused. "You look younger, and a little less, I don't know . . . *menacing.*"

He frowned slightly. "Menacing is good," he said, managing to keep a straight face. "Okay, now it's my turn." And he went into the bathroom with a package of hair color rinse in hand.

When he returned ten minutes later, she had to admit that the transformation was complete—she might have passed him on the street without even recognizing him.

Chapter 91

"Next we have to figure out plane tickets," Strickland said. "I think the safest way is to buy them online. But we'll need a credit card, and I'm reluctant to use either of ours—that would serve as a direct connect between us and where we're headed."

"By the way," Bender said, trying to suppress her annoyance at being left out of the decision-making process, "where *are* we headed?"

He looked momentarily confused, as if this detail should have been self-evident. "Um . . . Belize."

"Why Belize

"It's exotic and off the beaten track. If you were looking for someone on the run, you'd probably come up with Belize only by throwing a dart at the map—and it's not much bigger than the dart. Plus, I went there once on vacation, so I know something about the area. And, it's beautiful."

"Okay . . . ," she said, her voice laden with doubt. "At this point, I don't have any better suggestions. But aren't you forgetting another important element in this whole plan—over and above the credit card issue? We've changed our looks, but how do we change our names? I don't have a passport with me in D.C., and I can't imagine you brought one to dinner. And even if we did, they'd have our real names on them—and pictures that don't look a thing like us."

"True," he said, obviously mulling over this unforeseen obstacle. That he hadn't already considered such a major point was both satisfying and a little frightening to her.

"I have an idea," Bender said, "though I don't much like it. My cousin Todd is a computer science grad student at George Mason. When I was researching an article about the hacker underground, his name came up over and over as a master manipulator of digital information. I don't ask too many questions about what he does with his free time, but he lives awfully well for a doctoral student."

"Sounds like he might be our guy," Strickland said. "But we're going to need this stuff tonight."

"Todd's almost always home, glued to his computer," she said. "If anyone can deliver this on short notice, he's our guy. I don't know if the quality of his work will get past all the TSA's fancy scanners, but it's not as if we have a lot of options right now."

"True," he said, sitting down at her laptop and logging on to the Web. "I can establish a secure connection through an NIH system; then you can try an instant message from there."

* * *

As Sara had predicted, Todd was at his computer. And having just seen the news coverage, he was frantic to know whether she was all right.

"I'm fine," she typed back. "But we have to move fast. If you can get us passports and D.C. driver's licenses, you may just save our lives."

"Not to worry," he typed back. "One of my specialty areas. I'll need two digital photos. And give me the maximum resolution your camera offers. I can size them and dirty up the resolution to match typical government systems."

Bender and Strickland posed hurriedly for each other in front of her bare living room wall. Then she uploaded the photos to Todd.

"Got 'em!" he typed back. "Give me two hours. I'll have to involve a friend—he's a wiz on the paper, binding, and laminating end. Oh, and by the way, should you be apprehended, the secretary will disavow any knowledge of your actions."

"Thanks!" she typed back. "I needed that."

"I'll be by soon," Todd typed. "Sit tight."

Chapter 92

Two and a half hours later, Todd was standing at Bender's door. His henna-dyed hair was cut short on the sides and pulled back on top into a long ponytail.

"Sorry for the delay," he said, kissing her on the cheek. "The traffic was gnarly—I got caught in a cross-town presidential motorcade." He held up a padded mailer. "But we did it."

"You're a god, cousin!" Bender said, hugging him.

Todd tossed his leather jacket onto a chair, then turned to shake hands with Strickland. The two men sized each other up. It was an interesting juxtaposition, Sara thought: a rebel of the past meeting one from the present.

"I think you're going to like this," he said, opening the envelope and arraying its contents on the dining room table.

Strickland flipped through the passports—already weathered and stamped for various international destinations. "Pre-aged," he said, admiringly, noting the creases and worn edges. "Impressive work."

"Yeah, my friend has a machine that roughs them up, even adds a bit of grime."

"You're an artist, kid," Strickland said, holding up the licenses to the light and examining the embedded holograms. "Hope you're this good at staying out of jail."

As Strickland inspected the licenses further, he suddenly focused on the names. "Harold Michael Miller and Denise Ann Wheeler—how did you come up with those?"

Todd grinned. "Just what came to me from looking at the pics. I calls 'em as I sees 'em."

"By the way, what do we owe you?" Bender asked.

"It's on the house—family rate."

She kissed him on the cheek. "You are a lifesaver."

"One last favor," Strickland said, obviously warming to Todd. "Do you mind if we employ you for a little money-laundering operation?"

"Um, meaning . . . ?"

"We need to buy some plane tickets online. And we're hoping to use your credit card, then pay you back by check—with a bonus, of course."

"What destitute grad student could refuse?" said Todd. "So, where are you guys headed?"

"We—" Bender began.

"I think you'll be safer not knowing," Strickland cut in.

"Given what I've just delivered, I completely understand 'need to know' and 'plausible deniability.'"

"Spoken like a D.C. insider," Strickland said, grinning.

Todd handed Strickland his VISA card to buy the tickets. "Oops, almost forgot," he said. "Speaking of money laundering, I brought you guys something else that may come in handy."

He pulled out an unusually thick credit card with an intricate metallic pattern on its face. "It's a *smart* cash card," he said, responding to their puzzled looks. "You use them like credit cards but load them with cash online."

"Impressive," Strickland said. "I've used those for data storage, but never for e-cash."

"Welcome to the future," Todd said as he unraveled a computer cable and a small card-reading device. "I plug the access port into your computer; then I can load cash on it using my or your bank's Web site."

"I think it would be safer to use yours," Strickland said. "Again, we can write you a check."

"That's cool. I use these things all the time in my business—cybercash on delivery. It beats wondering whether the client's check is good—present company excluded, of course."

"You have a business?" asked Strickland. "I thought you were in grad school."

"You can't exactly live on a TA's salary these days. The biz grew out of a few spec projects, which we won't get into. Through word of mouth, other customers started beating a path to my door."

"Like us," said Strickland.

"Precisely." Todd accessed the card via the desktop icon and was soon connected to his bank's site. "How much do you need?"

"I think three thousand should do it," Strickland said, "along with the cash we already have."

Todd checked the screen again and frowned. "Um, how's two thousand sound? It's all I have."

"Then it's perfect," Strickland said. "It's enough to buy us a certain period of invisibility. If anyone's looking for us, hopefully they'll give up after a week or two."

Bender began writing the checks for Todd, then added an extra thousand to the total. He beamed. "Thanks, now I can turn up the thermostat." He began disconnecting and gathering up his equipment. "Well, I'd better let you guys get to it," he said. "Don't do anything I wouldn't do."

"That leaves us plenty of latitude," Strickland said, smiling.

Bender hugged him again. "Bye, honey," she said. "Thanks *so* much."

"Stay well," he called from the foyer. "And watch your back."

Chapter 93

While still connected through the NIH computer system, Strickland accessed an online reservation site and began ordering their airline tickets, using their new names along with the credit card information supplied by Todd.

"We need to get out of the country tonight," he said, scanning the flight possibilities on the laptop screen. "Dulles gives us the most options."

"I agree," Bender said, looking over Strickland's shoulder.

He confirmed the online reservation. "Okay, I've got us on a red-eye leaving at 1:30 A.M., with a brief stopover in Miami, arriving in Belize at 7:10 A.M., local time."

"Okay," Bender said, feeling exhaustion beginning to edge in around the caffeine. "But what about my foot, and getting to the gate?"

Strickland began printing out their boarding passes. "I've noted in the reservations that we'll need a wheelchair to take you to the gate. That may speed us through any lines, and it may even help us in terms of security scrutiny."

"Even so, one thirty only leaves us two and a half hours before the flight."

"Exactly—we need to get moving."

* * *

Strickland called for a cab. Ten minutes later they heard a tap on a car horn, and there it was, idling out front. Bender breathed a sigh of relief. Maybe the worst was over.

He helped her down the stairs and into the cab, and minutes later they were crossing the Potomac on the Channel Bridge, hugging the river along Washington Parkway. Sara looked over at Strickland, trying to gauge his mood. He seemed neither relaxed nor agitated—inscrutable. Suddenly, he pulled out his wallet and began rifling through the stack of credit cards.

"What's up?" she asked.

"Um, nothing," he said, continuing to examine the cards one at a time. Finally, he slipped the wallet in his pocket and fell back into his reverie.

As they approached the junction to highway 495, which would take them to Dulles, Strickland leaned forward and said to the driver, "We need to make a detour through Rockville."

"You're the boss," said the cabbie, changing lanes and heading north, back across the river.

"Are you out of your *mind*!" Sara hissed in his ear. "What on earth are you doing?"

Leaning close to her, he murmured in a voice at once calm and commanding, "There are vitally important papers at my place—pertaining to the study. I can't let them get in the wrong hands."

"It's too dangerous," she whispered. "They could be staking you out—you said so yourself."

"It's a risk we'll have to take," he said in a tone that ended the discussion.

Bender sat back with her arms folded, then leaned in again and whispered, "I hope you know what you're doing."

Strickland gazed out the window in silence, and she glanced up to see the cab driver watching them in the rearview mirror. From his curious but mischievous expression, he clearly thought they were having a lovers' quarrel.

As they merged onto Highway 270 toward Rockville, Strickland looked out the rear window. "Driver, could you get in the slow lane? The lady is feeling carsick."

Bender looked at him, mystified.

The driver complied without responding, though he was beginning to look annoyed.

"What's going on now?" Bender whispered.

"I thought we were being followed."

"And?"

"Coincidence, I think. They just pulled off."

"She's feeling better now," Strickland said to the driver. "We can get back in the fast lane.

Bender saw the driver almost imperceptibly shake his head as he changed lanes once more.

By the time they finally arrived at Strickland's condo, her nerves were screaming. According to her calculations, they would just barely make the flight.

Strickland's condo complex was situated in a small wooded grove, giving it a secluded feel despite its being so near the main highway. Under any other circumstances, she would have loved to get a look inside.

"I'll be right back," he told the cabbie. "Keep the engine running."

Just as Strickland got out, a sharp *bang* echoed from across the street. Bender flinched, adrenaline coursing through her as she scanned the dark terrain. Finally, she spotted someone revving an old racing-green Triumph TR6 sports car across the street. The engine backfired again as the car rattled to life.

A cold moon shone in silver patches on the concrete walkway to the condominium. Strickland fumbled with the keys, then quickly felt his way in the dark to his office. Flicking on a small desk lamp, he went to a stack of books on the top shelf and retrieved a hidden key. Unlocking the desk drawer, he grabbed a sheaf of papers, stashing them in a nearby leather folio. Finally, from the back of the drawer, he extracted a single credit card, placing it in a separate compartment of his wallet.

He flicked out the light and was halfway out of the office when he turned, taking in the shadowy room once more. Through the window, he saw the full moon, haloed in mist. Just then the cab driver tapped his horn twice, and Strickland hurried to the door.

Chapter 94

They made it to Dulles just minutes before the check-in deadline, thanks to the cab driver, who had maneuvered around a logjam caused by some late-night roadwork, speeding for a quarter mile along the klieg-lit shoulder.

The caffeine was beginning to wear off, and Sara felt exhausted. But she knew that airport security might be the most perilous part of their trip. After all, they were attempting international travel with forged passports, and there was the real possibility they could end up in jail after an all-night interrogation session. They might even precipitate a shutdown of the entire airport.

As the cab driver unloaded their bags, Strickland handed him an extra forty. The curiosity in the man's eyes persisted. "Good luck on your journey, my friend," he said.

Happily, there were no lines inside the terminal. Strickland handed the ticket agent their computer-printed boarding passes, along with their passports. The man scanned the boarding passes and handed them back. "Have a nice trip," he said, barely looking up.

An airline employee brought a wheelchair, and Strickland got Bender settled into it. Then, just as they started through the electric doors into the terminal, the ticket agent came dashing after them. "Ms. Wheeler! Ms. Wheeler!"

It took a split second for either of them to respond to her new name, and by then the agent had caught up to them. "I'm sorry," he said, panting, "but you dropped your boarding pass."

"Oh, thanks so much," she said, doing her best to hide her sudden panic.

They entered the metal-detector queue and were once again asked for their boarding passes and passports. Bender avoided eye contact with Strickland, fearing that it might somehow betray them. Strickland seemed to conclude the same, and casually checked his watch.

The screener inspected Bender's passport picture, then looked up at her face. He seemed to pause for a moment, and her breath caught. Then he handed back her documents and asked whether she was able to walk through the metal detector archway. She limped the ten feet through the detector, and then they brought her wheelchair around as Strickland breezed through after her.

As he wheeled her away, Bender murmured, "We made it."

"Never had any doubts," he replied. But she could see from his expression that this was far from true.

Chapter 95

Over the cruising drone of the jet engines, Strickland absentmindedly thumbed through the in-flight magazine. He had been so deep in thought, he hadn't noticed how quiet Bender was, and looking over, found her sound asleep beside him. He draped a blanket over her and glanced around the cabin. The plane was barely two-thirds full and most of the other passengers were also asleep. He gazed out at the dark, cloudless sky and the moonlight shimmering on the black ocean. After a few minutes, he took the phone from the seat back in front of him and inserted the cash card Todd had given him. Waiting for the system to approve the card, he looked around once more to make sure everyone nearby was asleep, and then punched in a number.

"Hey, it's me," he said. "No, everything's fine. I'm en route now. I'll arrive sometime after dawn." Cradling the phone against his shoulder, he jotted on a notepad. "Okay, that makes sense," he said, still writing. "I should be able to hire someone to get me there. . . . No, I don't think so, but thanks for the offer—I have reservations at a hotel tonight. I'll be in touch sometime tomorrow . . . Okay, will do," he said, and ended the call.

Bender stirred in her sleep, muttering something incomprehensible, and the blanket slid off her shoulders. Strickland leaned over and tucked it back in around her, then went back to staring out the window into the darkness below until sleep finally took him.

Chapter 96

Bender woke with a start as the tires bumped down on the runway. She turned and saw Strickland beside her, reading a magazine.

"Don't you ever sleep?" she asked, yawning.

"Someone has to mind the store," he said.

She looked past him and stared out the window at Belize City Airport, bathed in the first gray light of dawn.

"Welcome to Belize," the flight attendant announced in Caribbean-accented English.

Bender repositioned herself, surprised to find her foot noticeably less painful. Gingerly she rotated and flexed it this way and that.

"The best thing was to be off it for a while," Strickland said. "And if you can move it like that, I suspect you don't have a fracture after all."

They gathered their luggage at the baggage carousel and called for a cab. While they waited, Bender sat on a bench near the curb, Strickland standing by her side.

A cool, moist breeze blew in from the north. Since they landed, the dawn light had morphed into a flaming orange and magenta sunrise. The air was thick with the scent of vibrant flowers drooping from the branches above them.

Bender turned to the fragrant breeze, letting it wash over her. The adrenaline-charged sense of foreboding seemed to lift a bit with the night's rest and a new and exotic environment. She began to relax.

A stocky man with a wiry mustache approached them from the sidewalk. "Excuse me, mon," he said. "Can ye tell me where is the Hotel El Dorado?" He seemed open and friendly, but it struck her as odd that someone who looked and sounded like a local should be asking them for directions.

"We're visiting," Strickland said. "Afraid we can't be of much—"

A taller man who also looked like a local walked past them, looking the other way, and bumped into Strickland hard enough to make him stagger.

"Oh, 'scuse me, sah!" he said.

From her perch on the curb, Bender registered the events that followed as if in slow motion. With the deftness of a magician, the second man passed his hand over Strickland's back pocket, lifting the wallet out with two fingers. The first man had been a decoy, and now both were walking quickly away in opposite directions.

Strickland understood immediately what had happened, and after checking his pocket with his hand, he streaked off after the pickpocket. Within a block, he had caught up with the thief and landed a hard punch to his kidney, then another to the ribs. With a look of alarm and pain, the man dropped the wallet. Then, recovering his wits, he ran off down a row of whitewashed storefronts, soon blending in with the early-morning shoppers.

Strickland put the recovered wallet in the back pocket of his slacks, buttoned it into place, and, breathing heavily, went back to where Sara was sitting. By the time he reached her, a small crowd had gathered at the curb.

"Everything's fine," he said, reassuring the curious onlookers. "Nothing to worry about."

He took Bender's arm. "We have to get out of here," he whispered. "Before the police come."

"I can't believe what you did to that guy!" she whispered. "I was afraid you were going to kill him!"

"He had half our money and my ID," Strickland growled. "Not a good position to be in down here."

"But would you hurt someone—maybe even break a rib—over *that*?"

Strickland was barely listening. As they moved up the street from the scene of the disturbance, he took the wallet out and began rifling through the contents. When he found an American Express card, still in its separate zippered compartment, he seemed satisfied.

Something about the card looked oddly familiar to Sara. "Can I see that?" she asked.

"Why?"

"I'd just like to take a look."

"I'd rather not," he said.

"Unless you want me to walk out on you right now, you'll let me see that card!"

"Okay, here—relax," he said, handing it to her.

At first glance, it appeared to be a standard-issue American Express card. But on closer inspection, it was nearly three times the thickness of a normal credit card and not at all like the cash card Todd had given them.

Suddenly, it all came back. Jordan Randall had shown her one of these in the lab—an ultrahigh-capacity smart card for secure storage of digital data. Such cards even possessed a built-in "poison pill" function, so that any unauthorized attempt to access its contents would cause it to self-purge its memory.

She looked at the name etched into the card's surface: Richard K. Deckard.

"It's a disguised data card, from the Hong Kong black market," Strickland said matter-of-factly.

Whether it was his feigned nonchalance or something about the look in his eyes, she couldn't say, but something about the exchange betrayed the card's true purpose. The pieces of the puzzle fell into place.

"Oh, my God!" Bender said with rising rage. "You've really done it, haven't you? You completed the sequencing. This trip had nothing to do with our safety, and *everything* to do with the data. In the cab, you suddenly realized you didn't have the card, and that's why we had to go back to your condo. You put our lives at risk, all for this data!"

Strickland just stared back at her. "I need that card back," he said.

"God *damn* it, Bob!" she said, handing it to him and limping away.

Chapter 97

Sara was almost too angry and exhausted to think. Instinct told her to get away from Strickland and the maelstrom swirling around him, but she also recognized that they were still in danger and that, for now, he was the safest port in a building storm.

They flagged down a cab, and Strickland gave the address of their hotel. The driver turned and flashed several gold-capped teeth. "Si, señior," he said.

They rode in silence through the bustling early morning traffic, along rows of towering coco palms. A few minutes later they pulled up in front of a palatial Victorian colonial-style building—a three-story wooden structure encircled by a broad veranda and beginning to show its age.

A porter in a white suit took their bags, and the cab driver escorted them to the front desk. Strickland tipped the driver generously and thanked him.

"Would you like a king bed, or two twins?" asked the ruddy-faced desk clerk.

"We'll need separate rooms," Bender interrupted.

"May I see your credit card, please?" the man asked.

Strickland slid his passport and the smart cash card forward. The man examined the card, his brow furrowing.

"It's a cash card," Strickland noted. "It has two thousand U.S. dollars on it."

The man swiped the card and smiled. "Yes sir, that is fine," he said. "While it does have sufficient funds for your expected stay, we still require a credit card—we need a means of covering any potential damage to the rooms."

"I can assure you, we won't be damaging the rooms," Strickland said. "We aren't big drinkers or fighters."

The man looked back, unconvinced.

"Look, it's been a long night getting here," Strickland said. "We're on a business trip, and we've been instructed by our corporate office to use this card for all expenditures, for accounting purposes."

But the clerk stood firm.

Strickland leaned closer over the counter. "While it's true that *I'm* here on business," he said, "the lady with me is not . . . my usual companion. So I'd like to keep my stay here off the record."

The clerk glanced at Bender. Furious, she moved away from the desk, unwilling to endure the man's gaze.

Strickland reached into his pocket, then deftly folded a hundred-dollar bill into a hotel brochure. "I'd like to offer a small token of my appreciation for your understanding," he said, sliding the brochure forward. "It's a pleasure to be staying with you."

The clerk looked intently at Strickland. "Very good, sir," he said, slipping the brochure into his breast pocket. He reswiped the smart card and finalized the check-in process, marking a hotel map with their room locations. As he handed Strickland the two key cards, he glanced over at Bender once more.

Once they were in the elevator, she hissed, "How *dare* you present me as your concubine!"

"Look, I was trying to save our asses!" Strickland said. "You should be glad I'm fast on my feet. It worked didn't it? I know how men think—I am one. And I guessed that he'd feel a certain sense of identification with my position."

"You're not *in* that position," she huffed.

They got off the elevator, and when they reached their adjoining rooms, Bender swiped her key card in the door and disappeared into the room without a word.

Chapter 98

Bender stirred in the darkened room, momentarily disoriented by her unfamiliar surroundings, which smelled faintly of lilacs. Slowly regaining her bearings, she got out of bed. She pulled back the heavy red curtains to behold a breathtaking expanse of aquamarine sea. Billowing frigates of white cloud drifted across a dazzling blue sky. She checked the antique wall clock: 2:35 P.M. Muffled horns of midafternoon traffic rose above the low hum of the air conditioner.

On her way to the bathroom, she found that her foot had stiffened and was again swollen and tender—too much walking since the flight. She combed her hair and checked herself in the mirror. She looked like hell— eyes puffy and red.

She thought again of the data card, and her anger toward Strickland flared anew. After showering and dressing, she headed to his room. She knocked, and there was a brief rustling inside, then a pause—he must be checking the peephole—before the door finally opened.

"Good morning—or afternoon," he said, with what seemed like genuine calm good nature.

It was apparent that he had been up for some time. A half-empty cup of coffee lay on the table, alongside a large unfolded map.

"At the risk of repeating myself, don't you ever sleep?"

"I got some sleep," he said. "How'd you sleep?"

"As well as could be expected under the circumstances," she said, not smiling. "So, what's on the agenda for today—a little sightseeing?"

Strickland's television was tuned to CNN. He glanced over at the screen.

"A group calling itself the Army of the Lord has claimed responsibility for the attempt on Dr. Robert Strickland's life," the announcer said. "Strickland's car was bombed Friday night outside a popular Washington, D.C., area restaurant, killing a restaurant worker. In a communiqué received by a conservative religious Web site, the mysterious group has stated that Strickland 'can run, but he can't hide' and that they will 'put an end to his work by whatever means necessary.'"

"Turn it off!" Bender almost shouted.

"This confirms we made the right choice coming here," Strickland said. "We'll be safe for the time being. No one knows where we are."

"But it's just a matter of time," Bender replied. "We've made mistakes—most glaringly, you beating the crap out of that guy at the airport in front of a dozen witnesses."

"That was unfortunate but unavoidable."

"No, it wasn't unavoidable," she snapped. "It's part of a pattern—of putting your life *and mine* at risk in your pursuit of God knows what." She paused. "This is insanity, and I want out."

Strickland looked at her and sighed. "Obviously, you're free to go," he said in a tone of genuine concern. "But from what we've just seen, I would urge you to stay with me a bit longer, for your own safety."

"I didn't hear *my* name on that broadcast. I think they've forgotten all about me."

"Maybe so," he replied. "But do you really want to take that chance? I suspect the media has a much shorter attention span than these fanatics."

She just glared at him in response.

"Look, I'm sorry if you feel that I misled you," he said. "Whether you believe it or not, this trip *was* about our safety. And when I said there were vital papers that I couldn't let fall into the wrong hands, I was telling the truth—at least in a general sense. Papers are filled with information, as is a card of genomic data."

"Don't pull that semantic bullshit with me!" Bender snapped. "The bottom line is, you've lost all objectivity, at the risk of your own well-being—and mine!"

"Even if that's true," he replied solemnly, "I'm now looking out most diligently for our well-being. You have to trust me on that much, at least in the short term."

"Okay, then, what's your plan?" she said, folding her arms. "At the prices they charge here, assuming we don't start using our own credit cards, we're good for another five days at best. What are we going to do after that—beachcomb?"

"Not to worry Strickland said. "I've got it covered."

"Not *worry*? I'd have to be crazy not to worry."

He looked at her unfazed. "Our first order of business is to charter a boat."

"What on earth for?" she asked

"I've arranged for us to stay with someone," he explained. "Off the mainland."

"You have friends down here?"

"More like a colleague," he said. "We'll . . . be staying at his lab."

A wave of realization washed over Bender, then a whole new rush of anger. "I don't *believe* this shit!" she said. "You've flown us two thousand miles to hide out with *Manfred freaking Tellison*?"

Chapter 99

In the inner atrium of their hotel, Bender and Strickland sat at a small, deserted café. "Tellison was a logical choice," Strickland said. "We had to get out of D.C.—out of the whole damn country, in fact—and we needed a remote and secure location."

"I realize that, but . . . *Tellison*?"

A waiter brought Bender a fresh fish salad, but she just picked at it.

"You can condemn his ethics all you like," Strickland continued. "You can even question his methods. But you can't argue with his results. He's doing things down here that would have been unimaginable even two years ago."

"I don't give a damn what he's doing down here," she said. "And the fact that you do tells me more than I want to know about your motives."

Dr. Manfred "Manny" Tellison was a genetic researcher whose methods, lifestyle, and sheer genius had earned him notoriety that bordered on the mythic. Bender had interviewed him by phone in the early research stage of her book. The ethical issues so hotly debated by Strickland and Randall never even appeared on the man's radar screen. Some referred to him as "the new Timothy Leary," and as with psychedelic guru of the sixties, Tellison's life story was a roller coaster ride between academia and bohemia, with wild tales of success and excess scattered across the globe.

He had graduated from Stanford Medical School at twenty-one. Shortly thereafter, he had toured with the Grateful Dead, supposedly hired as a watchdog to keep the band's leader, Jerry Garcia, on the straight and narrow. But rumors flew fast and furiously that Tellison was, in reality, the group's "Dr. Feel Good."

In the late 1990s, he became fascinated with genetic research, briefly working as a fellow with the Human Genome Project's sequencing center at Washington University in St. Louis. But he found government and academic work too pedestrian, and soon jumped ship to company hop among the San Francisco Bay Area's more avant-garde biotech startups.

Ultimately, through venture capital contacts developed during his Bay Area days, Tellison got funding to start his own research facility. He chose Belize, not only for its tropical beauty but also for its lack of governmental restrictions.

After starting out on a shoestring budget, he soon attracted powerful silent investors, including a variety of questionable international consortia. His technologies and techniques came into their own with the successful cloning of various domestic animal species, which spawned a chain of pet-cloning boutiques around the world. But by that time, Tellison had already moved on to more cutting-edge research areas—including the rumored development of human cloning technologies.

According to the tabloids, during the final year of Jerry Garcia's life, Tellison contacted the Dead, suggesting that they "plan for the future" by archiving Garcia's DNA.

In the end, Bender had come away with nothing but disdain for the man. She viewed Tellison as dangerously childlike, manipulating the building blocks of life as if they were Lego toys, with apparently no thought to the consequences.

"Does he even know we're coming?" she asked Strickland, as she downed the last of her coffee.

"Oh, he knows. I called him from a pay phone near your local convenience store in D.C., when I was getting cash. Then I firmed things up during the flight, while you were sleeping."

"Gee, thanks for keeping me in the loop."

"As you may recall, we didn't have a lot of time for reflection or lengthy decision making. I had to go with someone who understands the importance of what we have, and how to best protect it."

"The man is a carnival barker in a lab coat," Bender hissed.

"He's offering sanctuary and security—and we're not really in a position to turn that down right now."

Chapter 100

As they made their way along the creaking planks of the small dock, Bender thought of the many war zones she had covered, often having to place her life in the hands of men whose only recommendation was a vague aura of trustworthiness. And here she was, doing it again.

She and Strickland had avoided the main docks near downtown, instead hiring a cab to take them to the outskirts of the city, where they hoped to find the nautical equivalent of her cousin Todd. Bender spoke enough Spanish that she was able to extract a recommendation from a group of local fishermen who were busy sorting their morning catch.

"*Sí—Eduardo!*" said one, motioning them toward a wooden boat with peeling paint at the far end of the tiny marina. "*¡A él le gustan los turistas!*" he added, chuckling.

They traversed a maze of rickety gangplanks leading to Eduardo's slip. As they neared, he pulled the bill of his cap down, shielding his gaze from the sun. He was old, and his features were distinctly Indian—weathered bronze face, sharp nose, and sparse white stubble on the chin.

"*¿Es usted Eduardo?*" Sara asked.

"*Sí,*" the man replied, giving them a wary look.

"We need to hire a boat," Strickland said, forgetting even to attempt Spanish.

"Where to?" the man replied.

Strickland offered the handwritten notes he'd scrawled during his phone conversation with Tellison.

The old man examined the notes, then looked his two potential fares over once more, sighed, and motioned them aboard. The boat heaved against its thick hemp hawser as swells rolled in from the gathering wind. Still a bit unsteady from her sprain, Bender nearly caught her foot between the shifting hull and the dock, but the nimble old man pulled her up with a surprisingly powerful grip.

After ushering them into the boat's partially enclosed cabin, Eduardo spread the notes on a small fold-down table and studied them, occasionally eyeing his passengers. From a wooden recess he pulled out a weathered nautical map, and using a marlinspike as a pointer, he drew an imaginary line along a small chain of islets situated next to a much larger mass, labeled "Ambergris Caye." As he reviewed the notes, his brow suddenly furrowed in apparent confusion. But then he noticed Strickland's scrawled latitude-longitude coordinates. "Ah, GPS—*bueno,*" he mumbled, moving the marlinspike with renewed certainty.

Turning his back to them, he began flipping various toggle switches on the boat's control panel.

"*¿Cuánto?*" Bender said anxiously, hoping to stop him before it was too late.

He turned again, probing them with his eyes. Something about his bearing was disarming. She smiled, and he smiled back almost imperceptibly.

"Fifty U.S. dollars," he answered gruffly, turning to fire up the diesel engine.

It was clear to both of them that they would find no better deal without hours of searching. And in their captain's mind, the journey had already begun. He motioned for Strickland to cast off the rope as he throttled up the engine.

They soon cleared the docks and pushed out to the open sea. Off to their northeast, a thicket of dark clouds loomed, and the ocean's earlier turquoise brilliance began fading to steel gray.

As they moved away from the sheltered cove, the bow lurched up at each gathering swell, then plunged back into the following trough. The roar of the full-throttled engine made conversation difficult, and spray from a glancing swell occasionally blasted completely over the bow. And yet, even with a storm on the way, the breeze felt distinctly tropical.

Bender glanced over at Strickland, scanning the horizon with hawklike intensity. At the helm, Eduardo checked a small handheld GPS device before turning hard to the north. On the horizon, as the boat crested each swell, she could see a chain of small, thicketed cays, with a much larger island lying in the distance beyond. Noticing Bender watch him, Eduardo pointed to the larger isle's dark silhouette. "Ambergris Caye!" he yelled over the engine's roar.

Chapter 101

Since news of the restaurant explosion first aired, Jordan Randall had tried every communication path he could think of to reach Strickland or Bender—to no avail. In response to his many phone calls and e-mails, there had been nothing but silence. It was as if they had vanished from the earth.

As he flipped nervously through the TV channels, a discussion panel show featuring the Shroud controversy caught his eye. A well-known fundamentalist preacher held forth on the recent events surrounding Strickland. The man was so vehement and self-righteous, it was almost more than Randall could bear. But he was desperate for any clues as to where the two might be—or whether they were even still alive.

"Tragic as this violence has been," said the televangelist, staring into the camera, "it pales in comparison to the blasphemous activities of Dr. Strickland and researchers like him." The minister left a pregnant pause—here was a man clearly accustomed to hearing his followers chime in with a dramatic "Amen!" His chubby pink cheeks gave him a cherubic quality, but his message was all fire and brimstone. "In the end, Dr. Strickland has only himself to blame for whatever fate may have befallen him."

"I hope you aren't suggesting that if anything has happened to Dr. Strickland, he deserved it!" said the shocked female host.

"I don't need to pass judgment—God will do it for me," the preacher said. "I merely refer your viewers to the words of the Bible and remind them that we each reap what we sow upon this earth."

At that point, the host switched her attention to Carol Armistead, a media liaison for SEW. Randall had met Armistead several times, though he didn't know her well.

"First of all," said the host, "let me clarify that the jury is still out regarding the exact nature of Dr. Strickland's work. Neither the NIH nor the Vatican has released any details as to his specific research activities. But given that uncertainty, Ms. Armistead, do you agree with Reverend Sumner that *any* genetic analysis of important religious artifacts—particularly during these times of bitter divide between the religious and scientific communities—invites great controversy and possibly even personal danger?"

"We don't believe that engaging in scientific or medical research should ever put someone's life at risk, no matter how heated or controversial the subject," Armistead replied. "On the other hand, our organization has long dedicated itself to acting as a catalyst in building public and government consensus on just such controversies. We believe in limiting certain research activities, but only until viable public policy can be formulated. As your viewers may know, Dr. Jordan Randall, a senior SEW board member, is one of Dr. Strickland's colleagues and participated in the early stages of the NIH's analysis for the Vatican. And yet, he is also a Christian and a proud advocate for ethical review and public debate in the realm of scientific research. My point is that cutting-edge research and a cautious ethical path needn't be opposing goals."

The televangelist interrupted, turning again to the camera. "Having their kind guarding our ethics and morals is like putting the fox in charge of the henhouse," he said. "And if they think folks are going to stand by while they defile the very body of our Savior, they have another thing coming. What they're doing is a blasphemy against God almighty! He is a just God, but he is also a God who smites his foes when they—"

The camera cut away from the minister, pulling in tight on the show's host. "I'm sorry, Reverend, she said, but that's all the time we have tonight. I want to thank you both for being here."

Chapter 102

After several course adjustments, a small, craggy island came into view, almost hidden among the reefs and atolls surrounding Ambergris Caye.

In this semiprotected area, the waters were much calmer. Broad shafts of sunlight broke through the cloud cover, painting the sea in scattered luminous patches. Bender glanced over at Eduardo, and he looked back at her with his same mysterious gaze. Beneath his weathered face and gruff exterior, his eyes felt kind and wise. In the brief time they had been with him, Sara felt as if a pall had somehow lifted.

As they neared the island, Bender noticed an array of one-story palm-thatched buildings. But as they drew closer, she saw that these tropical adornments were merely a facade. The buildings were actually fortified and bunkerlike, with high razor-wire fences marking the perimeter. Along the docks, yellow and black warning signs, in both Spanish and English, declared: DANGER! PRIVATE PROPERTY. DO NOT ENTER."

Eduardo noted the signs, and his brow furrowed. Nearing the shore, he throttled down the engine, slowing their approach as he maneuvered alongside the concrete docks. He cut the engine, then looked at Bender with concern.

"This the place you wanted?" he asked.

"I think so."

As Eduardo secured the boat, a lithe, athletic-looking man in his late forties descended a winding stone path. Flanking him were two burly men wearing matching bomber jackets.

Bender immediately recognized Tellison from his images in the media. He wore a Hawaiian shirt, cream-colored drawstring pants, and open-toe leather sandals. His sun-bleached hair hung down to his shoulders, and although his face had been weathered by the elements and the years, his eyes still held a boyish sparkle.

"Welcome!" he said. "We've been tracking your progress on radar for the last fifteen minutes or so. This isn't the easiest place to find, but then, that's the way I like it."

As they disembarked, Bender saw Eduardo glance warily at Tellison. She nodded reassuringly at the old man, wanting him to feel free to go. Tellison offered his hand to her as she stepped onto the dock, and

Strickland followed.

"Thanks again for having us on such short notice," he said.

"My pleasure." Their host smiled. "I have to say, for someone who believes in working behind the scenes, making his scientific discoveries quietly and without fanfare, you've become the man of the moment. I've been watching the news. So far, they have you headed for either Fiji, Mexico, or Morocco."

"Believe me, this is the last thing I had in mind," Strickland said.

Noticing Eduardo's continued presence, Tellison asked, "*¿Hay algo más que puedo hacer para usted, me amigo?*"

"*Gracias, no,*" Eduardo said. Then he glanced at Bender. She smiled and nodded once more, and he finally revved up the boat's engine. The boat pulled away and began churning back out to sea.

"The beauty of our location," Tellison boasted, "is that we're situated behind several other islands in the chain, which shields us from the sea lanes. If a ship heads here, it's a safe bet they've gone out of their way to do so. That gives us a bit of forewarning before any visitors arrive."

As they made their way up the stone path to the main compound, Sara noted that Tellison's two companions always stuck close to him. Beneath the left shoulder of each man's jacket, she noticed the telltale bulge of what was surely a weapon.

"How many people do you have staffing the island?" she asked.

"As many as necessary, and not one person more," Tellison said, winking. "Actually, it varies over time, depending on our current area of focus. It's not always so easy to vet people properly for this kind of work. It's, as they say, '*controversial.*' But in spite of our remote location, I manage to get the people I need." He glanced over at Strickland. "The right salary and no living expenses often does the trick."

They reached a fork in the trail, and Tellison directed them to the left, along a narrow, winding footpath. This soon led to a row of whitewashed, modern Aegean-style cottages situated on a panoramic rise set with coco palms, night-blooming cereus, and pink-blossomed frangipani.

"Anyway, getting back to your question," he said, "at one time, in the stages leading up to PetClone, I had over sixty people on the island. Acquiring the land was expensive, and our operational overhead was high, to say nothing of the equipment. But I had investors who recognized the potential of what we were doing. And that paid off in spades—not only in terms of our work here, but also in property value. The island's now worth many times what I paid for it, particularly since Belize has become a high-end resort destination. And that's also worked greatly to our advantage. Once we got the animal cloning technology down, clients could come here on holiday—with Fido or Mouser on its deathbed, or even with nothing more than a frozen tissue sample. A few months later, I'd ship them a genetic duplicate of their beloved pet. And with the money I made selling my shares of PetClone—which you may have read about—I'm now financially independent. It's such a *drag* having to answer to a corporate board. And they weren't always people of the highest moral caliber," he added, grinning. "But now I'm free to move back into pure research, and phase two."

"And that would be . . . ?" Bender asked.

"Always keep them guessing. For now, that will have to serve as the teaser. Then, depending on the nature of your visit, you may eventually learn more," he said, abruptly serious.

They paused before the largest and grandest of the cottages. "I saved the VIP suite for the two of you. It's housed some A-list paparazzi bait."

Bender hoisted her bag higher on her shoulder. "We'll be needing separate rooms."

"That can easily be arranged," Tellison replied, cocking an eyebrow at Strickland. "The cottages on either side are nearly as spacious, but without the kitchen and rec room. The doors are open."

When Bender and Strickland returned from stowing their bags in their cottages, Bender was surprised to see that Tellison's bodyguards had departed. Obviously, she and Strickland had passed some implicit security screening.

"By the way, the cottage is beautiful," she said.

Tellison smiled. "Thanks. I thought you might like it. Come, I'll show you around."

As they strolled along the cobbled walkway, breathing in the scent of tropical flowers, Tellison pointed out various details of the compound and the surrounding terrain. "In the distance, you can see the coast of Belize City, and then to the right is Ambergris Caye. And over the rise, is our main set of buildings, including the various labs, a state-of-the-art IT infrastructure, and even a gourmet kitchen. Oh, and getting back to your original question," he said to Bender, "now that we're no longer a commercial cloning facility, I've scaled way back on staff. I still have the necessary security, and a rotating skeleton crew of techies. Everyone gets shore leave, but in shifts. The work is increasingly automated, using sequencing and assembly bots." He glanced at Strickland. "They'll no doubt be using those in Bob's lab a few years from now. It takes the government boys and girls a while to catch up to the bleeding edge."

Strickland offered no response.

"I tried to lure Bob over to the dark side when we first started up here," Tellison said, "but I just couldn't win out over that shining castle on a hill that is the NIH." Turning to Bender, he said, "When I saw you and Bob on the newscast, your name seemed somehow familiar."

"I interviewed you once—on the phone," she replied.

"Oh, right, of course! I remember now. I have to say, you're even lovelier than I imagined back then—and I had a good imagination. The current news photos don't really capture you."

She gave him a sphinx-like smile. "Thank you . . . I think."

Chapter 103

In dramatic contrast to the guest cottages, the main compound featured high-tech industrial decor: brushed metal, luminous pine, buffed and polished concrete, and white LED spotlights. Strickland was most interested in the lab portion of the building, but Tellison clearly enjoyed showing off the entire facility.

"I've long been a fan of Scandinavian design," Tellison said. "Ever since a trip to Europe I took just out of med school. Of course, having hit Amsterdam first," he said with an impish grin, "I barely made it further north."

Strickland scanned the spacious, high-ceilinged room. The very existence of the compound was a staggering financial and technological statement. While he considered himself Tellison's intellectual peer, he had long since admitted to himself that he was neither businessman nor politician. And an enterprise of this scope and magnitude required both those skill sets and more.

"Before we enter the lab areas," Tellison said, "I have to program you both into the security system."

Next to a steel-framed touch screen embedded in the wall was a pulsing electronic eye. Strickland had noticed the devices positioned outside every door in the facility. As Tellison stood erect before the embedded sensor, a pulse of red light shot from the device into his eye.

"Retinal biometrics," he explained to Bender.

He engaged several menus on the touch screen, and a mellifluous synthesized voice said, "Administrative access requires additional voice-pat recognition. Begin now."

"Tellison," he said, crisply.

"Approved, Dr. Tellison," the voice replied after a momentary pause.

He entered Strickland's name via the onscreen keyboard, then asked him to step forward. Strickland had been retinally scanned before, and he positioned his eye before the device.

Tellison hit the scan button, and another burst of light flashed from the device. Strickland's field of vision in one eye turned momentarily to crimson, and "Scan successful" appeared on the display.

Then it was Bender's turn. She hesitated for a moment, then moved forward and looked into the device. Another crimson flash.

"That's all there is to it," Tellison proclaimed. "You're good to go. I've given you both all-access clearance, except for the embryo and sequencing rooms—you'll need an escort for those areas."

Bender blinked her scanned eye several times, testing her vision.

"It's a harmless level of intensity," Tellison said, "particularly with such a brief burst."

"So, what exactly happened?" she asked, falling into reporter mode.

"The eye scan stores a digital representation of the capillary patterns in your retina, It's more reliable than a fingerprint. That image is now associated with your name in the system. From now on, you just put your face within a few inches of the security eye outside any door of the compound. It senses your presence, delivers a brief scan of laser light, and determines who you are. If you're authorized for that area, the door unlocks."

"And if you're not authorized?" Bender asked.

"That's also configurable. The outcome varies—anything from the door not opening to all hell breaking loose."

"Pretty impressive tech," she said. "I've read about such systems but never actually used one."

"They're virtually foolproof," Tellison said. "You couldn't get around it even if you removed someone's eye and tried to use it to gain access."

Bender shuddered at the mental image.

"The system detects the pulse in retinal capillaries, he explained. "And in the labs, you can't force someone with access to let you in, since the doors allow only one entry at a time. Of course, someone with an escort-level clearance can bring in two ret-pats at a time. That's what we'll do for the sequencing and embryo areas. Would you like to see them?"

Strickland nodded, trying not to betray his eagerness.

"As you can see, we've made a lot of changes since the last time you were here," he said to Strickland as they neared the end of the main foyer. "We were pretty bare-bones."

Bender stopped in her tracks. "Since the *last time* you were here?"

she said, eying Strickland.

Clearly realizing he had struck a nerve, Tellison explained, "I said we've made a lot of upgrades since the previous time Bob visited, just after I established the facility."

Strickland started to offer an explanation, but she cut him off. "At every turn, I find that you're withholding information and keeping me in the dark," she said, her voice seething with anger. Then she stormed out of the room.

"Looks like you've snagged a live one," said Tellison, obviously enjoying the fireworks. "Women with some fire are typically keepers. You know what they say, 'crazy in the head, crazy in bed.' So how'd you manage to turn her against you so soon?"

Strickland sighed. "It's complicated."

Chapter 104

Tellison led Strickland into an aluminum-paneled room filled with vertical banks of sequencing bots. Strickland prodded him for details on the functionality and work flow, and in response Tellison activated one of the dormant machines, cycling it through its various modes.

The facilities were at least a half-step beyond the leading edge of genomic science. Strickland had seen most of the basic functionalities before, but the elegance, compactness, and parallel-processing throughput were beyond anything to be found at the NIH or any other lab he had ever visited.

Tellison seemed to read his mind. "The government procurement bureaucracy is like an ocean liner," he said. "It's one of the reasons I finally jumped ship. It can take years to change course, in a world where paradigms and technologies are turning over by the month. Since divesting from PetClone, I have complete control, with absolutely no interference or oversight." He grinned. "And you know how much I love control."

Though each lab room was numbered, few gave any clue to their purpose. If you didn't know where you were going and what you were looking for, it would quickly become apparent to those who did.

Tellison led Strickland into a room about ten feet square. Strangely, there were no tables or chairs inside. At the center of the space, embedded in the floor, was a white ceramic basin about two feet in diameter. Mounted within the basin was what appeared to be a complex optical apparatus.

Tellison dimmed the lights and engaged a wall-mounted control panel. "Watch this," he whispered.

The optical device buzzed to life, firing three laser beams upward. The intense red, green, and blue columns entered into the complex of lenses and emerged as a stunningly realistic three-dimensional color figure—of a small, not particularly attractive Pekinese dog.

"Damn!" exclaimed Tellison. "There goes my demo. Somehow this got left behind as the default data."

"Nevertheless, *very* impressive," Strickland mused, moving around the room to view the image from all angles. He found that if he stood on his toes or crouched down, the illusion began to distort and then disintegrated altogether.

"I knew you'd test the envelope," Tellison said. "As you've no doubt guessed, it's the basic functionality of genomic reanimation, but taken into the holographic realm. It's fine to be able to rotate something in space on a flat screen, but this facility provides a full-size corporeal representation. Here—let me bring up something that really takes it out for a spin."

Tellison accessed the control panel and began loading a new data file. The buzz of the lasers fell silent, and the dog's image evaporated. He keyed a new sequence into the device, and the lasers fired back to life, producing the image of a man. At first it was pixelated and indistinct, but then it suddenly came into sharp focus.

It was an image of Tellison, and though it was ghostlike and translucent, Strickland felt that he could almost reach out and touch the shimmering strands of hair.

"Oh, man, Jordan would kill to get his hands on this! The resolution is incredible. Who developed it?"

"It uses an amalgamation of open-source technologies, just like in the software world," Tellison explained. "I've tapped into developers on the Net, from all over the world. They're like neurons in an ever-growing, self-wiring supraorgan. And in many instances, they're not even interested in compensation. But I believe in giving credit where it's due. I've signed a hefty long-term licensing agreement with the recently formed RES consortium, the global body charged with the development and exchange of such technologies. No doubt your partner Randall's aware of them. But the federal procurement bureaucracy probably makes it hard for him to tap into their resources."

Strickland stood mesmerized. He moved around the room, examining the image from various perspectives.

"This device obviously uses the RES 5000 as a jumping-off point," Tellison said, "but they've taken it quite a bit further, wouldn't you say?"

"I would most definitely agree," Strickland said, feeling both stunned and envious.

Tellison paused, and it was suddenly clear that the demonstration had been leading up to something. "So, did you bring the data?" he asked casually.

"What data?" Strickland replied, pokerfaced.

"You know what I mean."

"There is no data. I didn't complete the process."

"Listen, man, don't even try to tell me you came all the way down here just to hide out from the religious crazies. There are plenty of places you could have gone for that, and much closer to home."

"That's exactly what I'm telling you," Strickland insisted. "I—we—came here for our safety and for your hospitality."

"Okay, whatever," Tellison said, shutting down the RES imaging device. "I won't ask again. When you're ready, let me know."

Strickland remained silent.

Tellison seemed oddly unfazed by his lack of success. "Before we end the tour, do you want to see the assembly bot room?" he asked.

"Definitely," Strickland said. "I'm curious to see how far you've gotten in that realm."

"We can, of course, assemble custom genes or even construct small, entirely synthetic chromosomes," Tellison noted as they entered the bot room. "But I wanted to take the process to its logical conclusion: automating the assembly of an entire set of functioning chromosomes, from the ground up and solely from the base-pair data on a computer."

"And how far have you gone with it?" Strickland asked, scanning the banks of equipment.

"All the way. In goes the base-pair data, and out come the chromosomes. We started with mice and have worked our way up to cats and dogs."

"But *how*?" Strickland probed. "The technical hurdles are staggering!"

"I can't get into too many specifics," Tellison said, with a wink. "After all, on a certain level, you're the competition. But I will tell you that my process is essentially the reverse of the 'shotgun' method employed during the Human Genome Project. Here, instead of breaking the genome into small pieces and then sequencing each piece, we *build* small strands and then assemble those myriad strands into ever larger strands. By performing this process in parallel, millions of times over, we can speed the completion time exponentially."

"But how long does all that take?" Strickland asked.

"When we first started out, many months. But practice makes perfect. The technology's been improving by leaps and bounds over the past two years. I can now assemble an entire genome in a matter of weeks."

"Including a *human* genome?"

Tellison nodded. "Just recently."

Strickland was stunned. "Is this what you referred to as phase two?"

His host smiled.

Chapter 105

On a whim, Strickland engaged the retinal scanner outside Bender's cottage. A moment later, the screen displayed ACCESS APPROVED, and the door latch clicked softly open. He chalked it up to a tip of the hat from Tellison and wondered whether Sara had similar access to his unit. But even if she did, he concluded, she would never have tested it.

The door latched shut again. He assumed that the access attempt had been logged somewhere, but hoped Bender hadn't heard the mechanism.

He knocked on the door. After a long silence, she finally answered.

"How could you lie to me?" she said. "Not just once, but over and over again!"

"I didn't lie to you. Maybe I left out a few salient details, but there were no explicit lies."

"Again, semantics!" she said. "In my book, intentional acts of omission are still lies. And more importantly, why did you feel you had to mislead me about your relationship with Tellison?"

"First of all, there is no relationship," he insisted. "What I presented to you was essentially the truth. Had I told you the *literal* truth, there's every reason to believe you would have read something into it that wasn't there—at a time when we couldn't afford indecision. The reality is, I *have* been here before, shortly after Tellison first took possession of the island. We had crossed paths numerous times professionally, and we were curious enough about each other that he offered to fly me down here for the weekend. Believe me, he was more interested in me than I was in him. I'll grant you, I was curious about his facility, but I had no intention of signing on with him. For God's sake, I was already a department head at the NIH. Do you think I'd blow that off for a risky venture like his?"

She looked back at him with narrowed eyes. "I never know *what* men are capable of," she said. "You're an unpredictable, alien species. I'd just like to hear again why we've come to this place."

"We're here because it was the safest refuge I could come up with on short notice—both for the data and for ourselves," he said peevishly. "Our lives were in imminent danger. And we should be grateful that such a refuge was made available."

Bender sighed and turned away. She stared out the cottage window at the turquoise expanse below, her mood beginning to soften. "So, what have you seen so far?"

"You wouldn't believe the facilities he has, the technologies he's using," Strickland gushed. "The sophistication is staggering."

"I stand by my original assessment," she said, stiffening once more. "The man's a huckster—a carnie in a lab coat—or a Hawaiian shirt, in this case. At least one of us has to maintain an objective sense of who and what we're dealing with."

"I don't buy such simplistic portrayals," Strickland countered. "People are capable of wildly divergent acts, from crimes against humanity to transcendent feats of creativity. Von Braun headed up the Nazi missile program during World War Two, but he was later instrumental in sending America to the moon."

"All the more reason why women have sometimes had to lash men to the masts when the sirens begin to sing," she said. "Call it simplistic if you will, but all your example tells me is that men go with the 'challenge,' regardless of whether it's for good or evil. And as we've all seen, if not properly directed, such challenges have sometimes run the risk of global destruction."

"That's an awfully cynical and overly dramatic view," Strickland replied.

"It's just reality."

Chapter 106

Jordan Randall sat nervously in the green room of CNN's D.C. broadcast center. With him were representatives from several religious groups, a spokeswoman for the ACLU, and Roderick Kern, an increasingly influential member of SEW.

Randall had long viewed SEW as a coalition of like-minded academics and researchers, devoting a few spare hours a month to causes of shared interest and concern. But in recent months, Kern, a bioethicist and former Episcopalian minister, had forged alliances with a wide array of fundamentalist religious groups. While these groups appeared to share many of SEW's core concerns, Randall had begun to detect fractures within the coalition. He perceived in these new associates a different agenda from that of the original membership. But Kern explained this shift as merely an attempt to make the organization more inclusive—more "big-tent," as he called it.

A number of the new members belonged to an Episcopalian splinter faction, formed in response to the church's consecration of several openly gay bishops. And they seemed intent on using the controversy surrounding Strickland's work as a vehicle for tying bioethics to various hot-button religious and moral issues.

As a testament to SEW's shifting power base and to the man's growing influence, Kern had been chosen as the group's official representative on the television panel. Randall had initially accepted CNN's invitation to participate in the discussion, wanting primarily to clarify his own involvement with the Shroud project and with SEW. But at the news of Kern's participation, he had attempted to bail out, claiming a "scheduling conflict."

To his amazement, he received a phone call from Kern himself, lobbying him to appear on the show. "This is an opportunity for everyone to set the record straight," Kern argued, "to be very clear about what we believe and why. I think it will be educational for all concerned, and I would welcome your participation."

In the end, Randall concluded that it was his duty to appear. If he didn't, it might appear that he had something to hide. And without his input on these controversies, the opinions expressed by SEW might seem to be his own by association.

Now, sipping a cup of bitter coffee in the station's green room, he felt increasingly nervous and alone. Kern sat on the opposite side of the room, engaged in animated discussion with a fundamentalist minister. During a pause in the exchange, Kern perceived Randall's gaze and offered back a media-ready smile.

Randall wondered whether Strickland might watch the program somewhere, and imagined what would be going through his mind. Just then, a bubbly young assistant poked her head in and announced that they would be moving onto the set in five minutes. A makeup man came in and touched up their faces.

As they made their way into the studio, a producer asked to speak with Randall privately. "I don't mean to alarm you, Dr. Randall," he whispered, "but our legal department requires me to inform you that we've received several threatening calls directed at you. You're entirely safe inside the facility. And on your way out, we'll have security escort you to your car."

"Thanks for letting me know," Randall said, and he felt his jaw clench.

"Okay, let's get started," the producer said.

Chapter 107

Tellison had given Bender and Strickland free run of the island's facilities, encouraging them to swim and relax. But the more they experienced of the compound, the more eerily deserted the place seemed.

"This place has a strange vibe," Bender said as a lab tech scurried past, gingerly carrying a lunchbox-size embryo-cryo container in each hand. "It almost seems as if Tellison has instructed the staff not to speak to us—or even make eye contact."

"That's entirely possible," Strickland said. "Manny has always been a stickler for privacy, sometimes bordering on paranoia. Maybe he picked it up during his biotech start-up days in California."

Bender had begun to realize that her flip characterization of Tellison as carnival barker was off the mark. In truth, he was a skilled politician and entrepreneur, as well as a brilliant research scientist. Money at the level of this facility didn't just manifest out of the ethers—it took a lot of charisma and talent to make that happen. Tellison was a formidable player, she realized—at whatever game he chose. And with such players, there was always an endgame in mind.

* * *

Later that afternoon, Strickland invited Bender for a stroll on a nearby stretch of white sand beach. She accepted the offer, in spite of their recent heated encounter over Tellison. The calming tropical breeze had worked its magic on her.

After wandering and talking for some time, they paused at a rock outcropping to watch a glorious sunset in the making. "It's amazing how simple light breaking through the clouds can be so satisfying?" she said.

"I agree," said Strickland. "Evolutionary biologists would probably say it's part of our genetic memory," he continued, ever the scientist. "Clement weather has always signaled bountiful times, so it resonates positively with us at a visceral level. Certainly that's the case with the sound of running water, indicating that it's fresh and potable, or the crackling of a fire, signaling warmth and cooked food. But why would a cloud-filled sunset be any more pleasing than one that's clear, or . . ."

Bender put her finger gently to his lips and pointed out to sea, and they watched in silence as the brilliant red-orange ball slipped beneath a blue-green horizon. They sat for a long time, listening to the breeze whisper through the overhanging palms.

Chapter 108

As they returned to the main compound from the beach, they passed by the entertainment room, where they found Tellison lounging with his feet propped up, watching the evening news.

"Come on in," he beckoned. "I just got here myself. After a hard day's work, I like to see what kind of crazy shit is going down in the world—oh, and please, dig in." He pointed to a tray laden with flat bread, sliced vegetables, and hummus dip. "I grew to love this stuff during a vacation on Mykonos," he said, dipping a carrot stick. "But I mix in chopped mango to give it a local flavor."

They arrayed themselves around the wall-mounted TV display as Tellison turned up the volume. A news update appeared concerning Strickland. The Vatican, after keeping a low profile for many weeks, had finally taken a stand on the controversy surrounding the Shroud. The pope issued an encyclical to all bishops, officially condemning "any research that might desecrate the holy vestment of the Shroud of Turin or the sacred blood of our Savior, Jesus Christ." In an attempt to cover all possible eventualities, the document further stated, "Even if the worst fears of some were to be realized, such a desecration would be merely human and would not *in any way* possess the divine spirit of Jesus Christ."

But the directive had done little to stem the controversy. The news piece on Strickland was followed by a story about the growing Neoteric movement. The group had organized a two-day assemblage on the Washington Mall, which had already attracted tens of thousands. The coverage showed a sea of glowing bioluminescent wands, the now familiar icon of the group.

But the Neoterics were not alone in the throng. Various sects of Buddhists, Hindus, Jews, Muslims, and even atheists had organized their own countergatherings to protest what they considered an insulting Christian-centric filter used when discussing the controversy.

A fundamentalist Christian group in the crowd carried signs reading, "Beware of False Idols!" and "Prepare for Finals—Read the Bible!" The television coverage featured several of these sign carriers engaged in heated debate with a cluster of Neoterics. The fundamentalists were poking their fingers into the robed figures while reciting scripture. One of the fundamentalists, angered at a particular Neoteric's passivity, shoved him backward, causing him to fall to the ground. Within seconds, a full-scale melee had erupted. The police, who had been standing by on the sidelines, were soon drawn into the fray. Scripture signs and lume-wands and, eventually, police batons began flying.

Bender was horrified at the turn of events, but Tellison watched with an almost childlike glee. "This is great!" he said, leaning forward. "It's like a fucking movie! Nothing like the peace and love of spiritual bliss, I always say. The funny thing is, these fundamentalists are the new Romans, but they can't even see it."

"Same-old, same-old," Strickland said. "Fear causes a banding together against a perceived common enemy. It's a visceral, tribalistic response hardwired into us. But if space aliens were to invade tomorrow, you can be sure all these groups would come together against the newer common 'evil.'"

"Precisely," Tellison said. "Lower animals are locked into their tribal associations—typically defined by species and geography. But the human territorial impulse is more fluid and can morph in response to changing circumstances."

"But even though human responses are more plastic and varied, there are so many similarities to animal behavior," Strickland said. "I remember a study where biologists in England took a flock of birds from the trees of a particular village, drove them a hundred miles away, and then set them loose. They settled into their new habitat but were soon recognized by the local birds of the same species as 'outsiders'—because of their 'foreign' song. Within hours, the two groups were squabbling in the trees. Given those results, it's not hard to understand the human ethnic and territorial skirmishes we see scattered around the globe."

"But with our higher cognitive functions, we can rationalize deep-seated aggression toward outsiders," Tellison added. "Plus, it's more of a shifting, more cerebral sand, based on geography, ethnicity, politics, economics, religion, or even hobbies like gun ownership. On the other hand, even in lower animals there's sometimes a brief window of malleability as to who or what you bond with, as seen with Konrad Lorenz's ducklings."

"I remember that from one of my biology classes," Bender interjected. "The guy who hatched ducklings and then pretended to be their mother. He established that there was a brief period of time, an 'imprinting window,' when the ducklings came to recognize their 'mother.'"

"Yup," said Tellison. "And since there were no other animals around at the time, Lorenz became the mother. I used to tell Jerry Garcia he was like the mother duck to all those little Deadhead ducklings. It was like a new virtual tribe, formed through an imprinting window opened up by the mass ingestion of psychedelic drugs, along with the bonding experience of a shared community of music. He was like the Pied Piper—which is maybe just a parable form of the same phenomenon."

"Interesting theory," said Strickland. "Maybe you should apply for a study grant."

"I could certainly come up with some interesting experiments," Tellison replied, smiling.

Chapter 109

Strickland crept into the RES room, fearful that he might be discovered at any moment. Unsure how to operate the device, he did his best to repeat the activation sequences used by Tellison.

To his amazement, the control panel's operation proved completely intuitive, with no security measures guarding it. He plugged the counterfeit American Express data card into a port on the side of the desk, and the card's indicator light flashed as the Shroud genomic data was accessed. Then a low hum filled the room as the lasers shot to life, firing their multicolored shafts of light up into the darkened space.

The three grainy columns of color swirled together in a dazzling rainbow-hued helix before finally materializing into the body of Jesus. Strickland stared at the visage, awestruck. Once again the hair appeared so lifelike, he wanted to reach out and touch it. But in the course of trying, he found that the image perpetually kept its back to him. At first, it had seemed a coincidence. But as he moved around the room, the image rotated, too, as if to prevent him from ever seeing its face. He tried moving faster, but it matched him at every turn.

Then he had an idea, recalled from his days playing high school football: he bolted in one direction, then darted back the opposite way. Amazingly, the ruse worked!

But to his horror, the shimmering face was Tellison's—with a frightening look of malevolence in its eyes. The rigidity of the body made it appear trapped—levitated against its will, as if held in some invisible cage. Horrified by the image, Strickland turned away. But after briefly looking away, he found that he couldn't keep his eyes averted. Looking up again, he discovered, to his even greater horror, that his own face had replaced Tellison's. It, too, looked dark and malevolent.

* * *

Strickland awoke, momentarily disoriented. Looking around the dimly lit room, he realized that he was in his cottage on Tellison's island. Outside, the first light of dawn was gathering on the pearl gray horizon. The palms were bent back, their fronds fluttering in the morning breeze. It looked as if a storm was on the way.

As he crunched along the gravel path leading up to the main compound, he heard squawking in the trees above: two parrots wrestling over a palm nut.

Inside the building, he found Tellison finishing his breakfast. An open manila folder, containing what looked like lab data, lay beside him on the table. Seeing Strickland, Tellison restacked the pages and closed the folder.

"Ah, another early riser," he said. "Let me get you a cup of coffee."

"Thanks. Sounds good."

"I've always had trouble sleeping," Tellison said.

Strickland smiled and nodded.

"But that's not always such a bad thing," his host continued. "Insomnia sometimes spawns my best creative insights, in that transitional state between sleep and wakefulness. Know what I mean?"

"I do," Strickland said. "Been there many times." He took a sip of the coffee. "Man, this is great stuff!"

"Belize grown—it's something in the soil."

Strickland glanced over at the folder on the table. "Already hard at work, I see."

"Yup, more of phase two. I'd tell you more, but . . . you know."

Strickland smiled again. "I still can't get over the holographic RES facility."

"Glad you liked it. But it's much more than just eye candy or something to merely corroborate already sequenced and understood data. In some instances, the imagery can actually be *predictive*."

Strickland set down his cup. "Meaning?"

"I've been able to discern previously unknown or undetected phenotypic manifestations of a genome merely by analyzing the RES imagery. If a picture is worth a thousand words, it's also worth a few million base pairs."

"But how's that possible? The imaging apparatus can only display what's already known about the sequences and then programmed into the rendering logic."

"Yes and no," Tellison replied. "In some cases the truth hides in the *interactions* between the various genes and their regulatory sequences.

Strickland stared back at him. "For example . . . ?"

"I discovered a previously unknown mechanism for a rare form of rosacea. It involved interactions between so many different genes, and in such a complex regulatory web, that it would have been opaque to the rule sets programmed into the underlying software. It only became apparent *visually*. And that was particularly true with . . ."

But Strickland had stopped listening. He was lost in thought.

Chapter 110

Strickland interrupted Tellison in mid sentence. "I have the data."

The statement didn't immediately register, and Tellison continued with his exposition on the RES imaging facility. "This particular variant of rosacea was diagnosed . . . um, what did you just say?"

"I have the data," Strickland repeated.

Tellison moved his plate and cup to one side. "Tell me more."

For a moment, neither man spoke. Finally, Strickland opened his wallet and held out the data card.

Tellison held up the device admiringly. "Nice hardware," he said. "What's the capacity?"

"Fifty gig—enough for multiple genomes and proteomes."

"My, my, just what the doctor ordered."

* * *

Entering the RES room evoked the eerie mood of Strickland's dream once more—the same sense of foreboding. Tellison activated the RES apparatus, and he watched the process more carefully this time. The sequence of events, of course, was nothing like in the dream.

"I'm assuming the card is password protected," said Tellison.

Strickland nodded.

"I'll tell you when I need it." Inserting the card into a slot alongside the control panel, he entered an additional series of commands. "Okay, you're up," he said.

He turned his back as Strickland poised his fingers over the on-screen keyboard. "How do I know there isn't a keystroke-capturing function, so you'll have the password after I type it in?" he asked.

Tellison looked mildly hurt. "If you like, when we're done I'll loan you a laptop so you can reset the password on the card. And if the laptop is a worry, just toss it off a cliff once you're done. But at a certain point, we're going to have to trust one another."

Strickland looked him in the eye for a moment, then began typing. When he had finished, Tellison entered a number of additional commands.

"Ah," he said, "I see you have the card configured so that it can only be accessed as a peripheral device—no data can be copied from it.

No worries—the RES facility can operate directly from the card, so there's no need to move the data to local disk."

Tellison dimmed the lights, hit the final okay button, and motioned for them to stand off in one corner. A high-voltage hum filled the room as the lasers fired up into the darkness. The three intensely colored beams swirled together as one, melding into a column of pure white light. Suddenly, the amorphous glow materialized into the hazy figure of a man.

Strickland stopped breathing for a moment as the image sharpened into focus. The figure was every bit as awe-inspiring as it had been in Bethesda, but it was now life-size and three-dimensional. Also, due to the now complete set of sequence data, the entire body was displayed. Out of deference to the subject, Tellison had programmed a period-specific robe.

Except for the hum of the high-powered lasers, the room fell totally silent. The two men moved about the space, examining the image from every angle. Strickland reached out to the face, his hand passing through the ghostly image.

The facial features contained such intimate detail, there was the genuine sense of a living person hovering before them. And as in Bethesda, it was a dead ringer for the Shroud image.

"This is *unbelievable,*" Strickland said in a hushed voice.

The room's access panel suddenly engaged. "Sara Bender," the automated voice announced. "Grant access?"

"Once the RES system is engaged, no one can enter without explicit approval," Tellison explained.

"Tellison," he spoke to the system.

"Voice-pat approved, Dr. Tellison," replied the voice.

"Grant access."

"Access granted," the system confirmed.

The door's lock snapped open, and Bender peered in around the corner, spotting first Tellison, then Strickland.

"Hope I'm not interrupting," she said. "One of your assistants told me you guys were . . ." She stopped dead as she registered the ghostly image hovering in the center of the room. "My God!" she exclaimed.

"A billion people seem to think so," said Tellison.

Sara cut her eyes over at Strickland.

"This isn't what you think," he said.

"No? Then what is it?"

"It's the obvious next step," Strickland said.

"Next *step*?" Bender gasped. "You're serious, aren't you!"

"This could be the key," he explained. "The analytical tool I was searching for in Bethesda, to finally understand the data."

"Exactly," Tellison mused, continuing to examine the image as if he were appraising a show horse. "This is data with real *possibilities*."

Stunned, she looked back at him, then turned to Strickland. "I don't feel good about this—about any of it," she said, and left the room.

"I'll go talk with her," Strickland said.

"Best of luck, my friend," Tellison said, not taking his eyes off the image.

Chapter 111

Strickland tried Bender's cottage first, but there was no answer. Following the path back to the main compound, he spotted her on the beach below and made his way down the trail.

"So much for 'hiding out and protecting the data!'" she said as he caught up to her.

"As I've already said, that's why I came here. But things have changed. His RES facility could potentially show me what I couldn't discern in Bethesda."

Bender wrapped her arms around herself against the cool, blustery wind. "Robert, I don't think you even *know* what drives you."

"Does anyone entirely?" he replied. "Look, I don't expect you to approve of every decision I make. But like it or not, we're in this together, and we should try to make the best of it. Here," he said, taking off his windbreaker. She put it on and stared in silence at the set of breakers rolling in, her brow furrowed in thought.

"On some level, I guess I understand your conflict," she said at last. "I realize now that I bolted after the first RES imaging in Bethesda. And here I am, doing it again. Maybe there's something about this whole thing that's just too overwhelming. I've always considered myself an atheist, or at best an agnostic. But when a phenomenon like this is staring you in the face, it brings out all kinds of subconscious feelings."

"You're not alone in that," Strickland said.

"And maybe I'm also reacting to Tellison," she added. "I worry about his motives. I feel like he'd do almost anything to achieve his ends— whatever they might be. He's clearly sacrificed lab animals by the score."

"But what research arm of the biological sciences hasn't?" Strickland countered.

"True. But I'd be surprised if he wasn't willing to extend that notion . . . maybe even to humans. I sometimes get sucked in by his charisma, but in more sober moments, I realize I don't trust his methods, and I don't trust *him*. He's the antithesis of Jordan. And I miss having that moral and ethical rudder in the mix."

"I know what you mean," Strickland said. "For all of our friction and squabbling, there's something calming and truly spiritual about Jordan.

Some people claim to be 'religious,' but beneath that pious exterior, they can be complete hypocrites. With Jordan, you can really *feel* his sense of faith. It's at the very core of his being. Me, on the other hand . . . well, I can't honestly say I've experienced that. I've been interested in spirituality for a long time, and I've meditated since I was in college. But beyond brief moments of transcendence and a vague sense of inner peace, I can't say I've ever really felt 'touched by God.' I can perceive it on a certain level, but I can't feel it *inside,* not the way Jordan seems to."

"Maybe I'm missing a chip or something," she said. "I've just never been able to tune in to those frequencies."

"Well, that analogy might not be so far off base," Strickland said. "Brain studies increasingly demonstrate that some people are actually physiologically predisposed to a heightened sense of spirituality. Those who experience profound spiritual yearnings seem to have measurable differences in the brain's temporal lobe, and differences in certain monoamine neurotransmitter levels. But is having a sense of the divine just a matter of being preconfigured for belief, or do brain physiology and chemistry somehow act as an antenna, a receiver, for a phenomenon that is real but simply imperceptible to many?"

"Yeah, I've read a little about that," Bender said. "Fascinating stuff. Maybe I can get a neuro plug-in someday and tune in to what Jordan is experiencing."

He laughed. "I might join you. On the other hand, maybe you've just never heard a message that resonates with the wiring you came with."

"Maybe so. What frequency do you think Tellison's on?"

"I'd say he's on his own unique wavelength. Out there all by himself."

Bender paused. "I worry about what he might have planned . . . or might suggest. Some of these religious fanatics already consider it a fait accompli—who's to say they're wrong? But I guess if Jordan were here, the question he'd ask would be, 'Assuming it were possible, would you actually consider making a clone from the data?'"

"No," Strickland replied without any hesitation. "And I told Tellison as much. I'm interested in the data and how it manifests—the phenotype. But that's as far as it goes. There's a wealth of data to be explored, assuming we have the necessary tools. And that may very well be the case now. But the consequences of going any further would be far too serious."

Bender seemed to be digesting his remarks, probing his face for any deeper feelings.

"Hell, I'm still open to the question of whose DNA this really is," he added. "But even assuming that Jesus *was* what some people say, that the Shroud *was* his burial cloth, and that this *is* his actual genetic data, a clone of him would still be only a man—a genetic twin, with its own personality and psychological makeup. Like countless identical twins throughout human history. That's what all these fundamentalist extremists seem to be missing in the whole debate."

"Yeah, that's what the pope says, too," she agreed. "But I guess the Neoterics might say, if you build it, he will come."

Strickland was looking back at her, but his eyes again had that faraway look.

Chapter 112

That evening, Tellison asked Bender and Strickland to join him in the entertainment room. They arrived to find him scrolling through the video server's on-screen menu. "I saw this on the schedule a few nights ago and recorded it," he said. "I knew you'd both be interested."

He hit the play button, and Jordan Randall appeared on the screen, seated in a semicircle with six other men. The moderator was speaking.

". . . Tonight's show focuses on the controversy surrounding recent genetic research on the Shroud of Turin, the disappearance of genomic researcher Robert Strickland, and the broader topic raised by this controversy: the growing schism between science and religion."

As Strickland and Bender sat down to watch, the avuncular moderator began introducing the various panel members.

"Dr. Randall, let's begin with you," said the host. "You've worked with Dr. Strickland for decades, and you also participated in the early stages of the Shroud research. But you are known to be a man of faith, as well as an advocate of careful ethical balance in scientific endeavors. Do you see any of these roles as potentially in conflict?"

Randall appeared unsure about which camera to face. "Not at all," he began tentatively. "I like to think that I don't fear the unknown—either in the sciences or in the realm of religion. In these two worlds, since ancient times, change has always been the norm. But institutions consistently lag the advances of individuals, and therein lies the problem. Galileo considered himself a religious man, but church authorities refused even to look in his telescope, fearing what they might see and how it might impact their beliefs. I don't subscribe to any belief system, whether scientific or religious, that is based in fear and ignorance. I believe in seeking the truth, in an ever-evolving sense of that word. And let the chips fall where they may."

"Dr. Randall," said a representative from the United Atheists/Agnostics Coalition, "I couldn't help but see the irony in your use of the term 'evolve.' Let me ask you this: if a scientific discovery were to come along that seemed to refute everything you believe, in a religious sense, how would you deal with that? And which side would you then choose: science or religion?" The man grinned confidently.

"My beliefs don't require me to take sides," Randall said. "My religious and scientific beliefs are resilient enough to endlessly accommodate one another. For me, they're really just two sides of the same coin. I see each new scientific discovery, such as those resulting from the Human Genome Project, as ever greater evidence of God's handiwork. And I see the human hunger to comprehend this handiwork as part of God's greater plan."

"But what if some complete paradigm shift in the sciences were to call into question the very *existence* of God?" the moderator asked. "What then?"

"This has been predicted, and feared by some, for centuries," said Randall, gaining confidence with every exchange. "But I really don't see it coming to pass. For me, God is everything and, therefore, never quite knowable by the human mind. And science, with every new threshold it crosses, has found this 'everything' to be indeed infinite. We once thought we'd find the 'end of the earth.' Then we thought we'd find the end of the universe. We once thought we'd find the ultimate stuff of matter—hence the word 'atom,' from the Greek word meaning 'indivisible.' But atoms proved to be made up of protons, neutrons, and electrons. And those particles in turn proved to be made up of a seemingly endless array of smaller particles. And then the smallest subatomic particles proved to be—at least under certain circumstances—not particles at all but energy waves. No, I don't believe we'll ever know enough about the universe to question the existence of its creator."

"Well and good," the UAAC representative countered, "but at least these are testable phenomena, and the theories can be refined and revised. How, though, do we conduct empirical tests on the existence of *God*?"

"Again, God is never entirely knowable," Randall admitted. "But we can sense his—or her, or its—presence in myriad ways: feelings of transcendence during prayer or meditation, the miracle of a newborn baby, the epiphany of scientific insight, or the rapture brought about by music, art, and poetry. God is there in all these things, and more."

"Nicely put, Jordan!" Sara remarked.

"I have to say, I always viewed this guy as your Boy Scout sidekick," said Tellison. "Robin to your Dark Knight. But he runs a little deeper than I imagined."

Strickland said nothing, focusing all his attention on the panel discussion.

"But what if all these feelings and emotions, these seemingly concrete moments of transcendence, are little more than neurochemical artifacts of the human brain, refined over the eons for our evolutionary benefit?" the moderator asked.

"Perhaps they *do* exist for that purpose," Randall admitted. "But even that doesn't negate the existence of God. Quantum Theory tells us there is often a duality to things. Light behaves as either a wave or a particle, depending on your observational perspective at any given moment. I might similarly argue that the rapture experienced while listening to a symphony is both a stress reduction mechanism at work *and* a gift from the Almighty. After all, sound is simply modulated waves of air impinging on our eardrums. It is the human mind—or, some would say, soul—that translates those vibrations into a moment of musical bliss."

"So what you're basically saying," the UAAC representative said, "is that any evidence that seems to argue *against* the existence of God is also evidence *for* the existence of God. In debate, that's called 'begging the question.'"

"We can obviously pursue this topic all evening," the moderator interrupted, shuffling his stack of notes. "Dr. Randall, let's shift gears a bit and discuss the more specific topic of the controversy surrounding research on the Shroud of Turin."

"Gladly," said Randall. "As a member of SEW, as well as in my capacity as director of technology at the NIH's department of Ethnogenomics, I've always striven to guide any scientific endeavor along a careful and ethical path. . . ."

The fundamentalist minister on the panel, James Thornton, interrupted. "On that note, perhaps this evening is as good a time as any for Dr. Randall to finally disclose the true nature of his department's activities where the Shroud is concerned."

Thornton opened a sheaf of papers and donned a pair of half-frame reading glasses. A smug look solidified on his face as he read: "According to purchase order records we have obtained, Doctors Strickland and Randall, at a date by which the Vatican had already explicitly directed that they 'cease any and all research on the Shroud,' ordered what are often referred to as DNA chips, from a biotechnology firm in Sunnyvale, California."

"And this is incriminating in what sense exactly?" Randall countered. "We deal with such chips all the time in our work. We're a genetics lab—it's what we *do*."

Thornton further scanned his paperwork. "The chips in question were specific to genes found only in people of Middle Eastern descent. Given the timing, and the research being conducted, that would seem rather, um, coincidental, wouldn't you agree?"

Randall looked suddenly ill at ease.

"Dr. Randall, why don't you simply admit, here and now, what your true activities have been. In short, tell us: what did you know, and when did you know it?"

"Reverend Thornton, this is not a tribunal," Randall said dryly. "The specifics of my research are between the NIH and the Vatican. I have only my employer and my God to answer to for my actions. And even if what you are insinuating had some actual basis, I might note that such information is, in the end, only data. We are years, perhaps even decades, from being able to produce a clone—much less a *human* clone—from dried blood that is hundreds, even thousands, of years old."

"This sort of intellectualization and semantic parsing is exactly what our ministry has warned against," said Thornton. "Apostate Christians falling away from adherence to the true message of the scriptures. They are capable of rationalizing almost any behavior or belief. *We* believe that one must either obey God's laws *as written* or suffer his ultimate wrath!"

Randall turned back to Thornton. A fire seemed to rise in him. "I might just as easily argue, Reverend, that the true *apostasy* occurs when belief is carried to such extremes that it runs contrary to the most basic tenets of a group's original faith and philosophies: charity, love, brotherhood, and oneness with God. Given the hateful tenor of so many of their pronouncements, the Savior himself would surely hesitate to join many of today's ministries that preach so sanctimoniously in his name."

"Go, Jordan!" Bender cheered.

Thornton looked as if he might come up swinging at Randall, and Randall looked as if he might welcome the possibility.

"This is outrageous!" the evangelist spluttered. "How *dare* you speak to me in that way!"

Wisely, the moderator intervened. "Gentlemen, we have a number of topics to cover tonight, so we'll have to move on. Dr. Kern, this exchange brings to light an important related topic. Many past supporters of your organization, Scientists for an Ethical World, have recently accused it of becoming overly politicized, with a distinctly religious tone and fervor. How do you respond to such criticisms?"

"As Dr. Randall has pointed out," said Kern, "religion and science have long been at odds. But throughout human history, religious groups have often been a voice of moderation, compassion, and ethics. So it stands to reason that an organization like SEW, whose very purpose is to bring the voice of ethics and compassion into the sciences, would want to avail itself of such religious voices."

"And we might also note that religious groups have historically been a voice of repression, hatred, violence, xenophobia, and intolerance," noted the UAAC representative.

"Jesus tells us very clearly in the scriptures," Thornton interjected, his voice rising, "'I am the vine and you are the branches. If a man remains in me and I in him, he will bear much fruit. If anyone does not remain in me, he is like a branch that is thrown away and withers; such branches are picked up, thrown into the fire, and burned!'"

"Which is exactly what they did to the so-called *witches* in Salem," the UAAC representative quipped. "So much for 'love thy neighbor.'"

Thornton scowled back, apparently marshaling his words for another salvo. But the moderator interrupted once again. "Gentlemen, I'm afraid our time is up. These discussions could go on—and undoubtedly will. I'd like to thank you all for being with us tonight."

The stage lights faded, and Tellison switched off the recording. "Now, *that's* entertainment!" he said, clearly energized. "Your boy *skewered* those yahoos. I like a man who knows how to push buttons." When Strickland didn't respond, he added, "But there's one thing he misrepresented."

"What's that?" Strickland asked.

"He claimed that we were years, even decades, away from being able to produce a clone from dried blood, but that's not really true."

His two guests looked at him.

"Phase two . . . point five," said Tellison, smiling.

Chapter 113

Since arriving on the island, Strickland found that his dreams had become both more frequent and more vivid. He wondered whether it might have something to do with the gentle sounds of sea and wind—perhaps inducing brain states conducive to dreaming. In comparison, Rockville seemed almost *too* quiet.

He had been dreaming again about Lester, the first patient to die while under his care. By the time he got involved in the case, Lester was in end-stage lung cancer—never an easy way to go. A medical directive kept them from doing much beyond palliative care. But Strickland found himself inexplicably drawn to the elderly patient. There was a riveting quality, almost a radiance, about him that drew Strickland to spend his downtime at the old man's bedside.

Between coughing fits, Lester mesmerized the young student doctor with ribald tales from his life. He had been a P-51 Mustang fighter pilot during World War II and had later explored and mapped the Pantanal wetlands of Brazil. But beyond these stories of adventure, the old man's face and eyes conveyed a sense of inner peace that resonated powerfully with Strickland.

As Lester lay dying, Strickland held his hand, wondering what would come of all this man had been, all he had known. He felt the thready pulse at the old pilot's wrist and knew it wouldn't be long.

As if sensing these thoughts, Lester looked up and asked Strickland what he thought would happen to him when he died. Strickland looked back, suddenly feeling as if he were being given a pop quiz.

"I don't know," he finally replied.

Lester just smiled.

Strickland had always considered himself emotionally controlled, hardened against the vagaries of life. But when Lester's hand finally went limp, he felt desolate. The attending physician eventually found him in the medical students' lounge. "It never gets any easier," he told Strickland, "but you just somehow learn to live with it."

Chapter 114

Bender and Strickland once again gathered to watch the evening news with Tellison. An obviously unbalanced man, claiming that the end times were near, had immolated himself at the front gates of the White House. The Secret Service had wrestled him to the ground and eventually extinguished the flames, but he was in critical condition at a Washington area burn unit.

Meanwhile, a religious sect had emerged that melded many of the beliefs of the Neoterics with those of existing UFO cults. The group, who referred to themselves as the Biogens, claimed that aliens from another galaxy had first planted the seeds of humanoid DNA on earth, and that this had been part of the Biblical "Creation" referred to in the scriptures. Extrapolating from this premise, they viewed Strickland's purported work as the prophesied Second Coming.

On a blustery winter evening beneath the St. Louis arch, the Biogens erected a large wooden crucifix with the crossbeam entwined in a spiraling neon double helix. When a local evangelical church group heard about the event, they quickly mobilized a countergathering. What began as scattered verbal sparring between the two groups soon escalated into outright violence. Wild punches were thrown from both sides. One man tried to tear down the Biogen cross but succeeded only in shattering the neon tubes. Sparks shot out of the structure into the twilit snow, sending zealots from both sides scrambling for cover. The cross, left unsupported, crashed to the ground.

"My God," Bender said, horrified, "this has to stop! We have to intervene."

"How, exactly?" said Strickland. "If we denied it, they'd never believe us anyway. And the mere act of communication would send these same wackos homing in on us like cruise missiles."

"Which is exactly why you *should* move ahead," said Tellison.

Both Bender and Strickland turned to him for an explanation.

"They think you've done it anyway," he said. "You're already on third—why not steal home? Give me free access to the data—the ability to upload it off the card—and I can have a blastula ready for implantation within a matter of weeks."

Strickland gaped at him. "That's not going to happen," he said.

"Come on," Tellison chided. "Be honest with yourself. Don't tell me you came all the way down here just to hang out with moi. This might be the most important thing either of us will—or won't—do in our entire careers. You're the one who always said the role of the scientist is to push the envelope and then let the chips fall where they may. Well, those chips are already in the air, big-time. You might as well break some new ground as part of the bargain."

"There is no bargain," Strickland said, his face set. "Not with you or anyone else." He hit the off switch on the television and stalked out of the room.

Tellison raised an impish eyebrow at Bender. "Pushing buttons is how you get beneath the surface. But he's got an especially tough hide."

Chapter 115

When he awoke the next morning, Strickland felt an overpowering desire to get away—from Bender, Tellison, and the entire compound. Maybe Bender had been right: perhaps the RES image of the Shroud had affected both of them more profoundly than either was willing to admit.

A couple of days ago, Tellison had mentioned a spectacular coral cove just beyond the small stretch of beach where Strickland and Bender sometimes walked together. And Tellison had apparently picked up on his interest. The next day, Strickland found a mesh bag containing a mask, snorkel, and fins at the front door of his cottage.

The morning was clear and unseasonably warm, and as he gazed out the cottage window, Strickland impulsively decided to give the cove a try. He grabbed the diving gear and wended his way down the overgrown trail to the beach, hoping not to be spotted by either Tellison or Sara. If only for a few hours, he wanted to be alone.

* * *

He had first tried snorkeling ten years ago. Marian, who had just finished a grueling economic forecasting project, insisted that they celebrate with a week at the Ritz-Carlton Kapalua on Maui.

They had gone to the island several years earlier on their honeymoon. Being on a tighter budget back then, they had stayed in a little clapboard bungalow about a mile down the road from the resort. Looking back, Strickland preferred almost everything about that more Spartan bungalow setting. The opulence of the Kapalua resort hadn't been his thing. He felt uncomfortable being pampered and serviced at every turn, and he couldn't help but wonder what the employees in the hallways were really thinking as they uttered all those effusive "aloha's" and "mahalo's" to their well-heeled guests.

By the time of the second trip, he and Marian hadn't been getting along for a year or two. It was clear that she had suggested the Maui vacation as both a celebration of her business success and a last-gasp effort to rekindle their marriage. They both wanted to believe that returning to a place where they had experienced such bliss might somehow stoke the fires again.

The first evening, they had sat out on the veranda sipping wine, a beautiful tropical sunset ablaze before them. "To us," Marian had said, clinking her glass against his.

Beyond the veranda, a young couple were making out in the surf, their bodies intertwined as they passionately caressed in the warm sea. Strickland and Marian had made small talk, attempting to ignore the couple, but it felt as if they were gazing back in time at themselves as they once had been. The vision brought home just how far apart they had drifted. They sipped their wine in silence, gazing out at the setting sun.

The unexpected upside of the trip, however, had been his introduction to snorkeling. Marian had gotten up early to take advantage of the hotel's in-house scuba lesson. For her, the greater the complexity and challenge of an endeavor, the greater its appeal. But Strickland had preferred the simplicity of a mask and snorkel, and the freedom of moving about free and unencumbered.

When he first entered the water that day, the explosion of color and light was overwhelming. It wasn't just the visual cornucopia that struck him so; it was the visceral realization that life somehow *wanted* to emerge, in whatever forms it could conjure.

He had watched the interplay between various schools of fish, and tried to imagine their reality. It seemed an existence of profound beauty, intermingled with moments of pure terror. It was a life spent hunting for food while avoiding *being* food, where split-second decisions made all the difference.

Before leaving the island, he and Marian had attended a stage production based on the Polynesian legends. Using modern dance, acrobatics, and traditional drumming, the play presented a sweeping history of Hawaii—from the mythic creation of the islands to the emergence of the volcano goddess and her brother the shark god, to the arrival of the white man. The play presented Hawaii as a native culture rich in reverence for life and nature. The main character's eyes filled with awe as he witnessed the miracle of the demigod Maui pulling the islands up from the depths of the ocean.

Intrigued by the play, Strickland later read more about the history of the islands. It wasn't a pretty picture. The Hawaiian experience had been a microcosm of the historical interplay between Western civilization and native peoples wherever it found them. European explorers had spread out across the globe, bringing with them horrific diseases, a rigid, moralistic work ethic, and "one true religion" that had no room for local spiritual beliefs.

Captain Cook, he read, had at first been revered by the Hawaiian natives as a god. But from there, the even greater god of commerce arrived. With the support of various Western interests, King Kamehameha brutally consolidated his power over the other tribal leaders. And when the bloodletting was done, and this unknowing puppet had served his purpose, the corporations swept in and took over.

* * *

Not much had changed in the succeeding two and a half centuries, Strickland reflected as he sat at the edge of the cove and pulled on his flippers. He gazed out at the mainland of Belize. It seemed a safe bet that this region had suffered a similarly violent colonial past.

But why? he wondered. Why was it all so primitive? Perhaps biological evolution was simply too slow to keep pace with human social evolution. Our basic behavior patterns lagged woefully behind our raw intellectual capabilities. Behavior seemed fixed at a level better suited to battling saber-toothed cats than reaching for the stars. An evolutionary leap was long overdue.

Strickland felt as if he were slipping into a tepid bath. After swimming some seventy-five yards, he floated out over a steep, rocky ledge. It was like soaring off the edge of a cliff, and he felt almost as if he might fall through the invisible medium supporting him and crash onto the coral-crusted seafloor

As he focused on his breathing, his eyes began to adjust, and the aquamarine light morphed into a stunning array of every imaginable hue. In a strange yet oddly familiar feeling, he seemed at one with the creatures around him. Every nook teemed with life—urchins and anemones, parrot fish, puffers and silver needlefish, octopuses and eels.

Hovering over a bed of luminescent-green brain coral, he marveled at its amazing likeness to cerebral cortical reticulations. The advantage of the structure, whether for neurons or for microscopic animals, was clearly the same: maximal surface area within a compact space. It was the same evolutionary directive served by chromatin, the compacted form of DNA, which allowed several meters of genetic material to be contained within a vessel the size of a single cell. Everywhere you looked, the same principles were on display.

The dancing patterns of light suddenly seemed filled with meaning. It was as if they contained a slowly repeating message. But perhaps this was merely what humans were wired for: making sense out of chaos, and sometimes going overboard in the process.

During his medical training, Strickland had completed a psych rotation at a local county hospital. While there, he encountered a young man manifesting the early stages of schizophrenia. Wildly hallucinating, the patient perceived spectral colors when looking at white lights—as if viewing the world through a prism. He obsessively dribbled his spittle on hot lightbulbs and then stared at the rainbow hues of steam he saw rising up—certain that the cure for cancer was contained within the patterns.

"Why won't you people *listen* to me!" the young man had screamed. "Don't you realize what this could mean to you?" Frustrated by a perceived lack of understanding and validation, he leaped on Strickland and had to be forcibly restrained and sedated. At the time, Strickland viewed the incident through the lens of his traditional medical training: the meaningless rantings of early-stage schizophrenia. But years later, he couldn't help but wonder whether the patterns of spittle evaporating from a lightbulb might in fact contain some hidden truths—able to trigger profound insights in the properly prepared mind.

He shifted his focus back to the explosion of color around him. A large, iridescent-blue fish trolled past, its sides covered in black glyphlike patterns. Strickland paddled with one hand, rotating his body in order to gain a better view. As he stared into the creature's large golden eye, he realized that it was now also observing him.

He marveled again at the evolution of consciousness—the juxtaposition between this instinctive, predatory underwater existence and the seemingly inquisitive, sentient creature floating before him. How had it all begun, and where was it all heading?

Chapter 116

That evening, Strickland sat in the darkness of his cottage, surf pounding outside the open window. A knock came at the door, but he made no move to answer it.

"Robert, are you all right?" Bender asked. "I haven't seen you all day. If you're in there, call me, okay? I'm also leaving a note."

Strickland listened as her footsteps faded into the night. He stared at the softly glowing digital clock on the wall. How odd it seemed, compared to the antiques he had experimented with as a boy. Coursing electrons and glowing displays had replaced the gears, springs, and hands of his childhood. The two entities were utterly different yet somehow the same, one a digital-era re-creation of the other.

After sitting silently for another half hour, he finally decided to retrieve Sara's note and let her know he was back in the compound. As he stepped outside to get the message, the glowing red security eye near the door caught his attention. It suddenly transported him back to the cove and the iridescent blue fish with its probing golden eye. The retinal scanning device seemed momentarily alive as he stared into its pulsing red depths.

Just as he reentered the cottage, note in hand, the digital clock on the wall struck 9:00 P.M. Despite its electronic origin, the chime was an almost exact re-creation of his grandfather clock back in Rockville. The low, droning tone faded back into the distant whoosh and sigh of the surf.

But there in the darkness, Strickland's eyes were suddenly wild and alive. He dropped Sara's unread note on the bed and raced out of the cottage. When he arrived at her door, he frantically positioned his eye against the sensor outside. Unwilling to wait for the access sequence to complete, he pounded at the door.

Sara opened it, startled by the wild look in his eyes. "My God, Robert!" she said. "What's wrong? Are you all right?"

"No—I mean, yes!" he stammered, his words tumbling over each other in the effort to keep up with his train of thought. He sat down in the rattan chair before her. "We have to move ahead," he announced.

"With what?" she asked, mystified.

"Letting Tellison perform the DNA assembly. I understand it now," he said, still catching his breath. "This is what we're *supposed* to do."

"Robert, are you out of your *mind*?" she said.

"Did you ever read Arthur C. Clarke's *2001*?" he asked, ignoring the question.

"No, but I saw the movie. What does—"

"The movie doesn't do it," he interrupted. "Most people who saw it completely missed this point, but there was a wonderful conceptual symmetry to the existence of the monolith on the moon. It was placed there as a *timing* device. Whoever put it there knew that the very act of being able to *get* to the moon, to find the monolith in the first place, ensured that we'd be ready for the next step in our evolution as a race. It was a cosmic stumbling block, a test."

"And this has what to do with the Shroud?" she asked, still baffled.

"Don't you see!" he continued. "Maybe this is the same thing. You made it fall into place when you said, 'If you build it, he will come.' What if the human body described by this DNA *is* a vessel, an antenna—almost like an organic version of the RES system? You create a biological entity, but then it becomes something more—*much* more. Maybe, at some conceptual level, this *is* the Second Coming—whatever the hell that may mean. And maybe we're the agents destined to make that happen."

Sara sat there, stunned. "This is all getting too weird for me."

"No. Look. What if the Shroud is like the monolith? It was left behind for a purpose—again, as a timing mechanism. It's been sitting there for over two thousand years, waiting for this exact moment in history, when we're finally able to do what we were *meant* to do. I don't claim to know what's supposed to happen, but maybe we're not playing God—maybe God is playing *us*!"

"Robert, every mad bomber, religious zealot, and megalomaniac throughout history has thought that he or she was somehow an instrument of God. And that's exactly what the crazies who tried to kill us were telling themselves."

Chapter 117

Bender sat next to Strickland in Tellison's lab. The bombshell had been dropped.

"Maybe this is looking a gift horse in the mouth," Tellison said, "but the obvious question is, why now?"

Strickland paused. "Let's just say that after long and careful consideration, I've decided it's the right path."

Tellison frowned. "That's it? That's all you're going to give me?"

Strickland glanced at the lab's glowing security eye. "Some things are better left unexplained—or perhaps are beyond explanation."

"Okay," said Tellison. "I guess, if it's some personal epiphany that you'd rather not share, I can live with that. I'm glad to have you on board." He smiled and stuck out his hand.

Strickland hesitated, then shook it.

"Okay, let me fill you in on what needs to happen next," Tellison began, clearly energized. "Our first order of business is the data. It was fine to operate from the smart card for the RES-X system. But we'll now be doing a full chromosome assembly—on the order of three billion base pairs. To finish this in any reasonable time, we'll need significant levels of parallel processing. To achieve that, the assembly bots need local disk access to the data." He paused. "And that means . . ."

Strickland opened his wallet and handed over the smart card.

Tellison inserted the card into a receptacle in the assembly bot's control server. "Once I have the data copied onto the server's hard disk, it can be transferred through network connections to the local hard drives of the various bot systems."

The server monitor flashed a message requesting the smart card's access password. "I'm going to need the password," said Tellison.

Strickland scooted forward in his chair. "Assuming you don't already have it," he noted, positioning his fingers on the keyboard.

Tellison bristled. "Again, this is too important an endeavor for either of us to be harboring any mistrust. I don't operate like that."

He turned away from the keyboard as Strickland entered the password. But Bender recognized this act of discretion for the eyewash that it was. Within seconds, the data download would begin, and the password would mean nothing.

"Great," Tellison said as the process began. "Let me give you both a big-picture overview of what's in store. First, I'll need to evaluate whether we have all the necessary sequence data. The system will also go through everything and verify it. Assuming all the data is in place, we shift into high gear. The first step will be a massive base-pair assembly. As I explained, this occurs in smaller segments, which are then joined together into larger strands—a technique I've perfected that's basically the reverse of the 'shotgun' approach used during the latter phases of the Human Genome Project."

"Can you give a quick overview of the process?" Bender asked.

"Sure. Rather than laboriously trying to sequence enormous strands of DNA, the HGP approach was to chemically chop them up, sequence those smaller strands using massive parallel processing, and then figure out how those sequences all fit together in the original larger strands. That was called the 'shotgun' approach. Here, we essentially do the reverse—but driven by the Shroud data. We build the smaller strands, also using massive parallel processing, then assemble those smaller strands into ever-larger strands, until we're finally at the full chromosome level."

Sara pulled out a pocket notepad and began jotting down portions of what he was saying.

"As we proceed, I'll fill you both in on whatever I can," Tellison said, eyeing the notepad. "But some of what I do will be proprietary in nature. My original partnerships and licenses don't allow me to divulge certain procedures and techniques, even if you were to sign NDAs."

"Understood," Strickland said.

"Once we've assembled a full component of chromosomes with proper chromatin folding, I'll insert them into an egg that's had its nuclear material removed. The egg, with a full set of chromosomes rather than the half set it originally possessed, will then be chemically stimulated to begin dividing, as if it had been fertilized. Once the embryo has reached approximately the sixty-four-cell stage, it will be ready for implantation—and gestation."

Bender stared at Tellison, struck by his matter-of-fact discussion of such a groundbreaking endeavor. "So, you're able to assemble entirely functional artificial human genomes?" she asked.

"Yes. It's an extension of the artificial chromosome technologies perfected some years back and used as gene vectors. It's the same basic science but carried out on a much larger scale. I plan to assemble three complete sets of the Shroud genome, in anticipation of any possible genetic errors. So there will be three final embryos—I have plenty of frozen eggs left over from past work."

"You've already performed successful human cloning?" Bender asked in amazement.

Tellison just smiled. "Proprietary information," he said.

"But if you're using existing human eggs," she said, "then the embryo that results is still going to possess the donor woman's mitochondrial DNA, true?'

Tellison turned to Strickland. "She's pretty good," he noted. "I can see why you like her."

He turned back to Bender. "That's correct. But there's no clinical evidence that mitochondrial DNA plays a significant role in a given entity's genetic uniqueness."

"Perhaps not," Bender replied. "But in a situation like this, can you afford to leave such a variable up in the air?"

"There's essentially no alternative," Tellison replied. "We can't afford to disrupt the cytoplasm to any major degree. And it would be virtually impossible to excise the existent mitochondria. Plus, even my lab isn't capable of replicating and inserting new mtDNA. In the end, we'll have to take it on faith that the nuclear DNA is sufficient."

Bender jotted down his words. "Interesting wording, coming from you," she said, with a wry smile.

"We all have contradictory aspects," he said, enjoying the sparring. "In some, the contradictions are just better hidden." He turned from Bender to Strickland, waiting for any further comments or questions. "Well, that's about all I have to offer at this point," he said. "Again, as we move ahead, I'll fill you both in wherever I can—proprietary agreements permitting. Most of what's going to happen is pretty straightforward, at least at the big-picture level. The devil, as always, is in the details."

Chapter 118

"Let's go for a walk on the beach," Bender suggested as she and Strickland headed back to their rooms.

He looked at her as if probing for some agenda, then said, "Sure."

They threaded their way down the meandering stone path from the cottages, then strolled aimlessly in silence along the expansive white sand shoreline. The tide was out, revealing a teeming world of littoral life forms. Large brown crabs scuttled from rock to rock as a low fog swirled along the coast, casting a haze over the choppy gray waters.

Bender found herself torn. On a certain level, she had always believed that cloning would be the ultimate grand finale to this story. But now that it seemed imminent, she found the whole thing somehow repellent. Her rational mind told her it was the story of a lifetime, but her intuitive side, which she had often subverted, felt that it was wrong.

"Don't you wonder whether we're being too hasty in this?" she finally said. "Shouldn't we be asking more questions—both of Tellison and of ourselves?"

Strickland smiled, and his lack of defensiveness surprised her. "I *don't* have any doubts about the path I'm taking," he said. "It just feels right somehow. I know that sounds crazy, but I've never been more certain of what I was doing."

"I have to say, she replied, "decisions prefaced that way have led to some of the most disastrous outcomes in history."

"I know. I recognize that, and I see the logical contradictions. I don't claim to be some divinely guided instrument, if that's what you're suggesting. But there's a sense of synchronicity to these recent events, or a 'flow,' as some might characterize it. I realize now, as you had suspected, that there *was* more than just a desire for refuge drawing me here. I sensed, at least subliminally, that Tellison's technologies might give me a better understanding of the Shroud sequences—perhaps offering some kernel of insight that had eluded me in Bethesda. Looking back, only the facilities of the NIH were capable of sequencing highly fractured DNA from a two-thousand-year-old blood sample. And now only Tellison's lab has the ability to actually 'rebuild' that DNA from the Shroud data. In each instance, we've found ourselves at the perfect place, at the perfect time."

"Playing the devil's advocate," Bender said, "you yourself pointed out that the human mind *wants* to find meaning in any given experience or sequence of events. It filters for it. You said we're programmed to fill in the blanks. So how do you know you're not doing that right now?"

"I don't," he admitted. "But it doesn't feel that way—in the strongest sense I can imagine. And for now, that's enough." He smiled slightly. "Call it what you will."

"Some might call it 'faith.'"

He looked back at her with the same smile. "Who knew?"

"I'm curious," she said, continuing to probe him, "why didn't you let Tellison in on what prompted you to move ahead?"

"I know him," Strickland said. "At least, I know him well enough to recognize that nothing I could say would change his worldview. He once said we're simply apes with unusually large cerebral cortexes. And on a certain level, of course, that's true. But that's only one way of looking at things." He paused, leading Sara around a large cluster of tide pools, and then back to the waterline. "Many years ago," he continued, "I had a talk with Tellison about drugs. From his stories, it was clear that he'd popped psychedelics like jellybeans at one time in his life. And it was also clear that he viewed them as little more than a chemical roller coaster—a thrill ride for our overdeveloped brains. Meanwhile, I had a friend in high school who later went on to take psychedelics, and for him it was the catalyst for a profound spiritual transformation—a window into the divine. It always struck me as odd that two people could experience the same thing in such vastly different ways. I knew I'd be wasting my breath to go into my own thoughts and motivations. You think *you* have no spiritual antenna. He's back in the preradio era. If I've learned anything, it's that matters of faith and belief don't occur at the level of logic. You can't *debate* someone into believing in a higher power. To a certain extent, either you do or you don't. And when that change occurs, it's never the result of some cognitive process—it emerges from a profound life experience or as a matter of the heart."

Bender stood quietly between the tidal pools and the sea, taking it all in. She had always considered herself a nonbeliever. But as they talked, she realized that she was also light-years away from Tellison's reductionist worldview.

"Let's assume for a moment you're right," she posed, "that this is all somehow *meant* to be. What happens after the clone? And, more importantly, who's going to carry it? I didn't dare pose questions like that to Tellison. Maybe I didn't want to hear the answers."

"I can't answer them, either," Strickland admitted. "To be honest, I'm sort of operating on instinct. It's all new territory."

They stood silently, watching a set of waves crash into the rocky headland up the beach from the tide pools, spraying salt mist into the air. A crab came scuttling toward them, within inches of their feet; then, perhaps sensing their presence, it sidestepped and disappeared under a pocked and barnacled boulder.

"It's amazing what's revealed once the tide pulls back," Bender said.

"Yeah. "I had a college friend who went into marine biology. At the time, spending one's life studying crabs and starfish seemed a bit odd to me. But now he's one of the deepest and most thoughtful people I know. He almost reminds me of the ferryman in *Siddhartha*—uncovering the wonders of existence while engaged in what some might see as the most mundane of activities."

"I read that in high school," said Sara. "I loved the ferryman character—coming to know the river's every current and eddy until it became almost a revelatory voice."

They stopped walking again and gazed out to sea. "I went snorkeling again yesterday," Strickland said, "and found myself transfixed by a cluster of tiny jellyfish. Columns of light came down through the cloud cover, illuminating the details of their inner structure—like the way they're lit in the display at the National Aquarium in D.C. I was suddenly mesmerized by the beauty and complexity of creatures that, superficially, appear as little more than pulsing gelatinous blobs."

Bender found herself captivated by his imagery. "It's funny," she said. "I also find them incredibly beautiful, almost jewellike."

"Exactly," he said. "And looking at that school of jellies, I realized it's not hard to imagine simple organisms diversifying and becoming more complex. But to imagine those creatures somehow spawning from basic organic molecules sort of boggles the mind."

"Yeah," she said, "but then, isn't that bordering on the whole

'Intelligent Design' idea?"

"Don't get me wrong," he replied. "I'm a firm believer in evolution. But looking at those jellies, it just seemed *miraculous* somehow, whatever the explanation. It was as if the mysterious nature of life was more evident when viewed at such an elementary level. How the hell did simple organic molecules coalesce in such amazing ways and then learn how to reproduce themselves? It's like the wind etching the components of a clock from sheer rock and then tossing those components together into a functioning timepiece. I'm not saying I know how it happened, or what forces caused it, but it's miraculous nonetheless."

"Compelling analogy," she agreed.

"The conundrum of consciousness and self-awareness is equally mysterious," Strickland continued. "Many theorists have proposed that with sufficient networking and processing power, future supercomputers will somehow become sentient, capable of looking out at the world with a sense of wonder, pathos, pain, and love. But at what point will that happen, and how? They say 'God is in the gaps,' and science is steadily shrinking or filling those gaps. First the gods were in charge of the sea and the elements. Then they were in charge of the heavens. What's next? The god of neurotransmitters?"

Bender watched a small school of flying fish launch themselves out of one swell and zip into the next, either chasing or being chased. "The other day on the beach, when we talked about spirituality, you hinted at a few things in terms of your own beliefs, but I was doing most of the talking. I often get a sense of what you *reject*, but not so much on what you believe in."

Strickland looked back at her, his face troubled. "That's a good question," he said. "It's, you might say, a work in progress. I'm not sure I can really pin it down. But I can't help but think—no, *feel*—that there's something more out there, beyond all this." He swept his arm toward the horizon.

She looked out in the direction of Strickland's gesture, then back at him, and held his gaze for a long moment. Then, stepping toward him, she took his head gently in her hands and kissed him on the lips.

Chapter 119

Bender awoke the next morning feeling as if she were emerging from a fog. Rubbing her eyes, she wondered whether the kiss on the beach had really happened. On the walk back, Strickland had seemed unusually subdued. And when they parted, he just waved and said, "See ya."

As she dressed, a computerized call on the bedside phone directed her to a breakfast meeting with Tellison and Strickland.

"We're moving ahead in earnest," said Tellison as he entered the small conference room. "The assembly bots will soon be operating full-bore, so you're going to be seeing a lot less of me for a while. We're shooting for a four-week completion date, which is ambitious because there's a hell of a lot to manage. And you're going to be seeing a bit *more* of the technical staff. I've canceled all scheduled shore leave and pulled some of the contingency technicians back onto the island. They'll have a lot to do, so don't be offended if they might seem aloof in passing—it's part of the culture I've put in place." And with that he was gone, leaving her in an uneasy silence with Strickland.

"I guess at this point we're just island phantoms," said Strickland, finally. "Well, I'm off to finish up *Zen and the Art of Motorcycle Maintenance*." He stood up, smiled inscrutably, and left.

* * *

Several days into the project, Bender awoke in the middle of the night. After tossing and turning for an hour, she decided to head up to the main compound and make herself a snack.

Pinholes of starlight shone through the black dome of sky as she crunched along the winding pathways overhung with ferns and big-leafed tropical plants. Listening to the waves break on the rocks below, she realized that she had become so attuned to her surroundings, she could tell the tides simply from the sound of the waves.

In the kitchen, she steeped a bag of chamomile tea and sat by the window, gazing out through her reflection into the darkness.

"Can't sleep, either?" asked a familiar voice. She turned to find Tellison padding into the room, wearing cotton drawstring pants and no shirt. He was tanned and well built and seemed to enjoy having her see him this way.

"No," she said, smiling. "It's become more of a problem as I get older."

He looked at her. "Older? What are you, twenty-nine?"

"Twenty-nine works," she said, laughing. She took a sip of tea, glanced up at him again, and found herself involuntarily averting her eyes from his bare torso.

Sitting down across the small round table from her, he said, "So, is the cottage comfortable?"

"Yeah, wonderful, actually," she said, brushing a wisp of hair back from her eyes.

"Glad to hear it," he replied. "My designer was right: most people seem to like them—though my tastes lean in other directions."

"So your place looks different inside?" she asked, distractedly.

"Very," he said. "Would you like to see it?"

"No, that's all r—"

"Oh, come on," he said. "It's worth seeing, I guarantee it."

Bender paused, but he was already walking, so she followed him, a little reluctantly, down the dimly lit paneled corridor. As they approached an unmarked door, Tellison allowed the entry eye to scan his retina. A moment later, the latch snapped open.

The room was spacious and ultramodern: a mix of paneled walnut and brushed chrome, with subtle Japanese touches. In the corner, a fountain gurgled from a small grove of live bamboo down onto a bed of smooth gray pebbles.

"When I was just out of college, I took a trip to Japan," he said, walking over to the fountain. "It was as if I'd come home to a place I'd never been before—genetic memory, some might say."

Bender noticed several mounted photographs on the living room wall. In one, Tellison stood beside a beaming Jerry Garcia before the Great Pyramid of Cheops. Another photo pictured him with a young woman, standing in the snow before St. Louis's Gateway Arch.

"My girlfriend, back in the Human Genome Project days," he explained. When Bender said nothing, he added, "My life hasn't been very conducive to long-term relationships."

"Do you get lonely here?" she asked.

"Sometimes. But it's the life I've chosen. Once in a while, I go to the mainland to 'work out the kinks,' as they say, but I try to keep a low a profile. In general, the locals I meet don't know who I am."

Her eyes narrowed almost imperceptibly.

"I gather you don't approve," he said.

"It doesn't really matter what I think," she replied.

"I actually haven't partied in town for quite some time," he said, still gazing at the photos. "Increasingly, I worry about the security aspects. The local intellectuals refer to my workers as 'Moreaus,' as in *The Island of Doctor Moreau*. They say I'm like the mad scientist in the H. G. Wells book, who constructed hideous artificial life forms. Of course, it's all blather. I suppose I should be flattered that they see me as larger than life."

"Well, thanks for the tour," Bender said. "I should finish my tea and try to get a few hours' sleep."

Tellison followed her back to the kitchen. "So, what's the story with you and Bob?" he asked. "Are you guys an item? I can't quite sort it out. Reminds me of my days with the Dead. Some of the couples in that scene were so low-key, you couldn't always tell who was with who."

Bender took another sip of her tea, but it had gone cold. "Bob and I are just colleagues . . . I suppose," she said. "Maybe you should ask him."

"Hmm, maybe *you* should ask him."

In reply, she took her mug to the sink, poured it out and rinsed it.

"Well, let me know when you guys figure it out," he added. "And next time you can't sleep, give me a buzz. Maybe we can go for a walk on the beach."

"Thanks for the offer," she replied icily.

Chapter 120

The days flew by, yet Bender felt an oddly heightened sense of awareness. Even though not much actually *happened* each day, she could have described the day's events in fine detail.

In Bethesda, during a similarly intense period of lab work, she had spent her days engaged with Strickland and Randall and then processing and transcribing the information dumps. But in this setting, other than occasional high-level briefings from Tellison, they lived in an information void.

Bender spent her time either walking on the beach or exploring Tellison's extensive library—reveling in books that she had either promised herself to read one day or hadn't read since high school. And she found surprising new meaning even in the books she knew. Golding's *Lord of the Flies,* for instance, revealed insights into sociobiology that had completely eluded her in younger days.

Her perspective on so many things seemed to be shifting. She had seen much of the world, whether on vacation or on assignment, but there had always been an agenda. On assignment, the goal had been to gather as much information as possible, often under stressful and dangerous circumstances. On vacation, the goal had been to decompress and unwind as quickly as possible, in anticipation of the next work assignment. But here on the island, time just passed.

Bender had no idea what was running through Strickland's mind, but she sensed a tranquility in him that she had not seen before. He carried himself differently, with greater ease. Occasionally, he disappeared for hours or even entire days. She sometimes saw him wandering leisurely on the beach. Other times, who knew where he went?

This period of slowing down allowed her to recognize for the first time just how frantic her old life had been. And for what? Had she truly been happy? Occasionally but not that often, she had to admit. Had she been truly fulfilled? Again, occasionally, just after completing an assignment. But after that brief high wore off, she would find herself pacing like a caged panther or a junkie in search of her next fix.

After dinner one evening, she and Strickland again sat watching the news. Events out there had begun to seem otherworldly, like images from a realm they no longer inhabited.

Network news stations, hoping to keep the Strickland story alive, would seize on the flimsiest rumors of his whereabouts. And occasionally, a religious leader, feeling his own press coverage beginning to flag, would damn Strickland anew for having "turned to the forces of darkness." Such teasers barely even registered on Bender's radar screen anymore.

But as a new image suddenly flashed onto the television screen, she jerked forward and grabbed the remote. Her boyfriend, Tom, stood somberly before a group of reporters, reading from a prepared statement.

"Sara and I have been together for many years," he said. "I know her, and I know how she would react under almost any circumstance. Given that she has been missing now for many weeks with no apparent word to anyone, I have to assume that she is not a willing participant in the events at hand."

Tom peered intently into the cameras. "Wherever you are, Sara, all I ask is that you let me know that you're all right . . ." His voice began to crack, and he turned from the cameras.

Tears welled up in Sara's eyes. She hated to admit how rarely she had thought about Tom in the past weeks. It seemed a lifetime ago that she had last been with him. But seeing him in such pain tugged at her in ways she couldn't have predicted. She looked over at Strickland. "I have to get a message to him," she said.

Strickland nodded in assent.

Chapter 121

Tellison led Sara and Strickland to a workspace with a computer. "I'm a soft touch when it comes to damsels in distress, or I'd never go along with this," he said, sitting down at the keyboard. "We need an Internet e-mail server that's geographically and logically removed from us. Fortunately, I've had accounts at universities all over the world, and systems administrators are often pretty sloppy about deleting them. Let's try the Max Planck Institute of Molecular Genetics, in Berlin—I did some consulting there a few years back."

Tellison directed himself to a remote IP address, and a logon prompt appeared on the screen. "On second thought," he muttered, "I'd better not use one of my accounts. There's usually an installation account called simply "Maintenance." Many times it's not configured properly when the system is first set up. The default password is typically the same as the user ID—let's try that."

Tellison typed in "Maintenance" for the user ID and again for the password, and the system replied, INVALID PASSWORD. "Hmmm, they're not as sloppy as I'd hoped," he said. "Wait a minute—what was I thinking? Let's try it in German. He typed "*Kontenpflege*" as the password and then hit the return. "Bingo!" he said, as the system offered a prompt. "Now, as an extra security measure, I'm going to leapfrog to another system. I've also done work at the Pasteur Institute in Paris—let's hop over there."

Using another IP address dredged up from memory, he typed "Telnet 164.192.63.33." The system immediately presented a Unix prompt.

"Incredible. We've apparently landed in an active session—a glitch that happens once in a blue moon if a user fails to log out and just shuts down the workstation. There's a window of just a few seconds where you can grab that session—and here we are."

Tellison typed the Unix query "WhoAmI," and the system replied, "Root." "Whoever left this session open should be shot and then hanged— the most powerful account on the system is now ours for the taking. Lucky for them we only want to do e-mail."

"You're an excellent hacker, among other things," said Bender.

"Thanks," he replied, grinning. He brought up the Unix mail software and scooted his chair away from the screen. "All yours," he said.

Bender sat before the screen and rested her hands on the keyboard. She hesitated. Finally, she typed Tom's e-mail address, and then entered "I'm OK" on the subject line. Pausing, she looked over at Strickland and Tellison. They moved away as she continued to type:

Dear Tom,

I feel terrible for causing you so much worry. I'm honestly fine. Things have been chaotic, but I'm safe and well. For everyone's safety, I can't tell you anything more right now. I'll be in touch when I can.

Thinking of you,
Bubbles.

She read through the message. Admittedly, it was brief—almost formal. But she couldn't bring herself to sign it "With love." More and more, she felt estranged from her previous life and everyone in it. She wondered whether it might be a subtle variation on the Stockholm syndrome, in which people under confined duress began to bond with their captors.

Chapter 122

When Bender had finished typing, Strickland moved closer to the screen. As she prepared to hit "Send," he noted the signature line.

"*Bubbles?*" he said.

She gave him an annoyed look. "It's code, so he'll know for certain that it's me and that I'm not acting under duress. It was my sorority nickname, having to do with a certain alcoholic beverage I favored."

"You were in a *sorority*? Hmm, that explains a lot, I guess."

"Oh, get off your high horse," she muttered. "I joined for professional, networking purposes."

"Yeah, hence the moniker 'Bubbles.'"

As Bender was about to object further, Strickland turned to Tellison. "Since we're on this system in Paris, I'd like to hop over to the NIH and check my e-mail there. At that level of redirection, it should be safe enough."

"Everybody needs their fix," Tellison replied. "For the record, I think this is a bad idea, but if you make it quick and don't send any replies, we'll probably be okay."

Strickland sat down at the keyboard, and with Tellison's multiple redirections still in place, he used the Telnet command to reach the Ethnogenomics e-mail server in Bethesda. To his surprise, he found that even with his department officially locked down and his whereabouts unknown, his e-mail account was still active. So much for government security, he reflected.

After so many weeks away, Strickland found an avalanche of messages in his in-box. He scanned down the list. Most were blanket NIH advisories, with very few directed specifically to him. But two messages jumped out: one from Jordan Randall and the other from his old friend Mark Altman.

The e-mail from Randall was already many weeks old: "*Bob, I'm praying that both you and Sara are safe. Please contact me whenever you're able! Much love, Jordan.*"

The signature line seized Strickland at a gut level. Jordan had rarely expressed himself so openly, and he felt an overwhelming desire to reply. But he agreed with Tellison on staying under the radar. He closed the message window and moved on.

The message from his friend Altman had been sent more recently. Strickland noted that it had been posted in the middle of the night:

Hey Man,

Who knows when you'll see this, but I somehow have the sense that you're OK. I've been thinking about you a lot lately, and wanted to get this down while it's still swimming around in my head.

The more I look at the world, the more I sense something new taking shape—and maybe in a big way. I'm not entirely sure what I mean by that just yet, but I'll tell you more as I figure it out. It has to do with spirituality and technology. Bear with me on this, because I may ramble a bit (it's late). I've been thinking that we humans, at a tribal level, are like a super-immunological system. We react viscerally to any perceived "outsiders." But that sense of "otherness" is forever shifting. In more primitive times, people rarely traveled more than a few miles from where they were born. But the horse, the boat, the train, and the airplane changed all that, mingling cultures beyond anything seen before. Marco Polo, the conquistadors, etc., were like injections of foreign antigens (to use an analogy from your world), with wildly unpredictable results. In the worst cases, they brought plague, enslavement, and destruction of indigenous cultures. But in the modern era, the concept of tribe has become more nebulous and virtual—defined by far more than just geography or ethnicity.

It occurs to me that as we move beyond demarcations based on ethnicity or geography, the Internet is slowly serving to desensitize us to the shock of exposure to these new virtual cultures and tribes. True, the Net is sometimes used as a tool for negativity—by hate groups, with videos of beheadings, etc. But I suspect that's just the initial exposure phase. Ultimately, it can't help but acclimatize us to new groups and ways of thinking—and promote more harmonious intermingling. Orwell had it wrong. Technology isn't a tool of oppression and darkness. It's increasingly proving to be the antidote to such things. The enemy of oppression is free-flowing information, and that's what the Internet is all about. And I can't help but think there's going to be some spiritual component to this evolution as well.

It just hasn't manifested yet.

Well, I hope I'm not just talking to myself here, and that you'll eventually see this and respond. I'll be interested to get your thoughts.

Eyes Wide...
Mark

Strickland closed the window without responding, then killed the remote network session.

"Good," said Tellison. "I think that should be your last contact with the Internet. I don't want the crazies who are after you knocking at my door."

Chapter 123

Bender and Strickland monitored the U.S. news channels for the next several evenings, hoping to determine whether Tom had received the message. In a brief segment, Tom was shown leaving his Manhattan apartment building. He was wearing a suit and looked rested and upbeat. A female reporter shoved a microphone in his face as he made his way along the sidewalk.

"Any news from Sara Bender?"

"No comment," he replied. "But have a nice day."

The reporter attempted a follow-up question, but Tom jumped in a cab and speeded away.

"Good," Bender said. "He got it."

Tellison wandered by. "I need to take a break," he said, rubbing his eyes. "Mind if I join you for a few minutes?"

"Please do," said Strickland, moving over to make room on the sofa in front of the giant flat-screen TV.

As Tellison settled in, the coverage switched to another gathering of Neoterics, and the usual cast of opposing protest groups. "I see nothing much has changed since I last checked in with the real world," Tellison said, shaking his head.

True to form, the televised gathering soon turned ugly when a protestor in one group inadvertently jostled someone in another. Shouting erupted between the various groups, and a Mylar-robed Neoteric was pushed to the ground. A pack mentality quickly set in. It was difficult to hear what was being said over the din of the crowd, but as the Neoteric got up, grimacing in pain, the angry group appeared to be shouting obscenities at him. One of the attackers held up a Bible and began quoting from the scriptures. A paint balloon suddenly splattered in the self-styled preacher's face. The violence quickly spread, and even the cameraman was drawn into the melee; then the remote image went black.

"This reminds me of the period just after 9/11," said Tellison, "when Sikhs were being beaten, even killed, because they wore turbans—wrong hat on the wrong turf. On the other hand, even the Deadheads were a manifestation of tribalism on some level, with their own culture and customs, their own deity in the form of Garcia, and various pharmaceutical sacraments. But at least they didn't go around pummeling nonbelievers."

"The 60s movement was arguably a super-tribe," noted Bender, "an amalgamation of environmentalists, women's rights advocates, anti-war and civil rights activists, etc.—bound together by their alienation from the established order, and unified by a common tribal music. There was an openness for sure, better than most tribes—but still a tribe."

"The animal kingdom seems to be hardwired for such tribalistic behavior," said Tellison, "whether we like it or not. When I was a kid, my mother bought me an ant farm. I went straight to the library and checked out a picture book on ants. The notion of a queen at the top of the social hierarchy was fascinating. After observing my ants for several days, I got the bright idea of finding a queen to rule the colony. I finally located one in a nearby anthill and, naively, added her to my little ant world. A few hours later I came back, expecting her to have whipped the place into shape. But there was nothing left of her but the wings—the workers sensed that she was an outsider, and devoured her. I guess we need to keep that principle in mind the next time we try to install a leader in some culture we barely understand."

Tellison glanced up at a televised replay of the Neoteric being knocked down. "That's why I've never liked organized religion," he said. "Too often it's used as a tribalistic tool for manipulating and controlling the small-minded and the disenfranchised, to mobilize them against perceived outsiders."

"That's a rather sweeping statement," said Strickland. "A little facile, don't you think?"

"Sometimes the simplest explanation is the correct one," Tellison said.

* * *

Jordan Randall sat in the darkness of his study, watching the news coverage of the Neoteric being brutalized by the angry mob.

"My God . . . ," he whispered to himself. No longer able to watch, he switched to another news channel, but it offered little solace. A splinter faction within SEW, made up of religious hard-liners brought in by Kern, was announcing that it had broken away from the parent organization.

"Desperate times call for desperate measures," read a spokesperson for the new group, his eyes fiery and intense. "We can no longer sit idly by while apostates threaten our faith and our very existence. We will do whatever we must to stop this menace, and we urge all men and women of true faith to join us in this quest. Let us leave no place of refuge from the light of righteousness, no hiding place from the judgment that God calls down upon them!"

* * *

On the other side of the Atlantic, in an opulent wood-paneled room, a group of robed men watched this same pronouncement being made. An older man with a sallow, gaunt face switched off the television and turned to the assemblage.

"Gentlemen," he rasped, "our work is nearly complete. The enterprise is in motion."

Chapter 124

Tellison again summoned Bender and Strickland to the lab. Because of the intense work flow, they had seen little of him in the past few days.

There was a noticeable increase in security around the facility. An assistant ushered them into the room.

"We've reached a milestone," Tellison said, his tone more formal than usual. "As promised, I wanted to give you both an update."

As Bender pulled out her notebook, he said, "My basic strategy is a combination of techniques perfected during the development of artificial chromosomes. These designer chromosomes were originally intended as a better means of inserting new genes into living cells." He spoke directly to Bender, who was writing furiously. "Artificial chromosomes allow for the targeted insertion of multiple genes. Before this breakthrough, viral-vector gene therapy often resulted in insertion at random sites, partial functionality, or even corruption of the host DNA. So that's been part of our tool kit here. But we're not just interested in building a single, small chromosome. We're building a full set—all forty-six. That's a Herculean task—the difference between constructing an outhouse and a hundred-story high-rise. But the basic techniques I'm using have been refined and perfected by researchers over the course of decades. That's why science is so powerful—we build on the foundational genius of researchers before us."

Tellison's brief note of humility surprised Bender. He further surprised her by pacing the flow of information to accommodate her note taking. "Chromosomes consist not only of tens of thousands of genes," he continued, "but also specialized elements that are essential to their structure, stability, and function. Telomeres, which consist of DNA and protein, are located at the ends of the chromosomes, protecting them from damage. Centromeres are specialized regions in the middle that are essential to proper chromosome distribution during cell division. Human centromeres consist of large segments of highly repetitive DNA, called alpha satellite DNA."

Tellison paused briefly to let Bender catch up. "Early attempts at creating artificial human chromosomes failed because they lacked the proper centromeres," he continued. "They finally succeeded by synthesizing arrays of alpha satellite DNA. That centromeric DNA, along with telomeres and genomic DNA, was introduced into human cells. Amazingly, once inside the cells, these independent building blocks came together to form miniature chromosomes. On closer analysis, these mini chromosomes demonstrated normal centromeric activity, genetic stability, and gene expression through repeated cell divisions."

"So, they just *worked*," Bender said. "That's incredible!"

"Well, it took many, many attempts, with just the right chemical agents to coax the process along," Tellison replied. "But nevertheless, I agree—it *is* incredible. We don't have to understand every detail and mechanism along the way. On a certain level, it's a self-assembling system. So, getting back to the construction analogy, our high-rise building is now complete. Our next step is to—"

"I just want to make sure I understood you," Bender interrupted. "You've now assembled the entire Shroud genome from the data on the card? *All* the chromosomes?"

"That's correct," Tellison said, obviously pleased with himself.

"Wow!" Bender said, putting down her pen. "That's huge!" She turned to Strickland, who appeared just as stunned.

"Of course, that's really only half the battle," Tellison continued. "We now have to get them into a cell so they can replicate. To do that, we'll need to use a whole other realm of cloning-specific technologies. In the big picture, there isn't much difference between inserting chromosomes from a donor cell into an egg and inserting artificially constructed chromosomes. The important thing in both cases is that the chromosomes look, at a chemical level, like those found in an egg, so they can act appropriately."

Tellison saw Bender's look of confusion. "The DNA of already differentiated cells, like skin cells or nerve cells, is compacted and stored differently from that of an egg—an oocyte. And that's because the genome in each type of cell plays a very different role. In the egg, it will differentiate into an entire organism and therefore needs the full complement of its DNA. In a skin cell, on the other hand, it's already become what it's going to be, and so it has nonrelevant portions of its genome protected by various inhibitory and regulatory structures. So we have to make sure that the chromatin folding occurs such that the cell biochemically *thinks* it's an egg. But because these chromosomes were built from scratch, they're inherently free of any inhibitory structures that would be present in already differentiated cells, such as a nerve cell or a blood cell. So the chromatin modeling phase, where we make sure the chromosomes are folded properly, is relatively straightforward—just a matter of using the proper chemical reagents. Also, the cytoplasm surrounding the nucleus plays a vital role, so it's key that we leave everything in the donor egg, other than its original genetic material, intact. The trickiest phase will be removing the donor egg's chromosomes and then inserting the Shroud chromosomes. The slightest error at this stage can leave the cell damaged and functionally compromised, dooming the entire undertaking. I'll discuss the process in greater detail when we get to it."

Tellison paused as Bender scribbled in her notebook. "We'll begin the chromosome insertion phase tomorrow, which you're both welcome to observe," he said. "Any questions?"

Bender said nothing, trying to digest it all.

"Just one," Strickland said. "Who's going to be the implantation subject once the embryos are ready?"

"Not a problem," said Tellison. "In vitro surrogates are available all over the world. Some wealthy women can't, or don't want to, bear their own children. So we have a network of local women who are willing to fill that role. They've done it before, and this procedure will seem no different to them. Rest assured," he said, "when the time comes, we'll have a subject in place."

Chapter 125

After the meeting, Bender told Strickland she needed some time alone to flesh out her notes. "This is vital material," she explained. "I want to make sure I got it all down."

But once they parted, she headed to the beach. Picking up a piece of sun-bleached driftwood, she dragged it in the sand, drawing a thin line as she wandered along.

Though she always tried to maintain her reporter's objectivity on events surrounding the Shroud, she found herself strangely affected by what she had heard and what still lay ahead. It reminded her of how jangled she had felt after viewing the Shroud RES image in Bethesda.

A tern cried overhead, dived down, and flew low along the beach, as if following the line she had traced in the sand.

A low evening fog had rolled in, and the sunset glowed as if from behind a veil. Through the mist, she spotted a lone figure walking toward her in the distance. She recognized Strickland's body language long before she could actually make out his face.

"I guess you had the same idea," he said when he caught up to her. "A little time for reflection."

She smiled. "Exactly. If you want to be alone, I'll understand."

"No, I'm glad you're here," he said.

They stood quietly side by side, gazing out at the misted sea.

After last week's kiss on the beach, Bender wondered whether she had pushed their relationship beyond its natural limits, so she was surprised when Strickland moved closer and took her hand. She leaned toward him, their bodies touching, only to feel him tense almost imperceptibly.

She looked into his eyes. "You seem to withdraw anytime someone gets close," she said, doing her best not to sound confrontational. "I've seen it a few times now—even Jordan mentioned it. What's going on?"

His face tightened, then seemed to soften as if by force of will. "Part of it is that I've always been focused on my work," he said.

Again she looked into his eyes, demanding more. "And the rest?"

"There have been certain incidents . . . especially in my early life. I really don't want to get into the details, but the bottom line is, my pulling away has nothing to do with anything you've ever said or done."

She gazed at him in silence for a few moments.

He returned her gaze and then sighed. "I'm sorry if I've hurt you along the way," he said. "If I didn't care so much about you, I would have ended our association a long time ago. The truth is, my life has often felt like a chaotic, unsolvable puzzle. But now the pieces are mysteriously falling into place, and you play a very big part in that."

"It's funny," she said. "I've been feeling the same way lately. I—"

Before she could finish, Strickland took her in his arms and kissed her. He pulled off her windbreaker and then his own. Bender wrapped her arms around his neck, and they sank slowly down onto the sand.

Chapter 126

The next morning, Tellison left a voice mail saying that chromosome insertion was to begin at 10:00 A.M. sharp.

Bender met Strickland in the hallway, and he kissed her.

"Good morning," he said. "Sleep well?"

"Better than I have in a long time. Where did you disappear to?"

"I went for a run on the beach," he explained.

Tellison emerged from a neighboring room. "Good, I'm glad you're both on time," he said. "We have a lot to do."

After escorting them into the embryology lab down the hall, Tellison donned disposable surgical scrubs and cap, and had them do the same. Then he scrubbed in as if preparing for surgery. He seemed calm but intensely focused. After reviewing a laminated checklist, he began activating a panel of electrical switches.

A single petri dish was positioned on a large lab bench surrounded by robotic arms and probes, all directed downward at the dish. As the automata came to life, servomotors hummed, and the mechanical arms performed a self-test sequence to orient themselves. A large flat-panel monitor powered up, displaying an enormous image of the petri dish.

"The enucleation/renucleation bot—I call it the enuke-renuke—uses a high-res camera to direct a series of micropipettes," Tellison explained. "Pattern recognition software allows the system to direct the pipettes more accurately and delicately than would be possible with most human control." He glanced at Strickland, then Bender. "Everybody ready?" He positioned his finger above an illuminated red switch. "Okay . . . here we go."

Bender watched as the floating egg was targeted from three directions by the micropipettes. A barely perceptible servomotor drone could be heard as the probes delicately maneuvered into position. The translucent egg moved from side to side in the tiny currents of the culture media, as if trying to elude capture. Then the automata closed-in, pinning the egg and holding it steadily in place. The cell remained motionless, its seaweedlike corona undulating in the growth medium.

Bender suddenly had the sense of a helpless creature being seized by a predator, like a fly caught in a spider's web.

"Got it!" Watching through virtual-reality goggles that gave him a

3-D view of the microscopic drama unfolding, Tellison flexed and relaxed his fingers in the metal rings of a device that would let him manually override the procedure if necessary. His foot moved into position over a pedal switch on the floor. "Here comes the piezo," he said as the hollow-pointed pipette approached the egg's outer membrane. "It acts like a tiny drill."

The automata maneuvered the piezo slowly into position, applying gradual pressure against the cell membrane, slowly depressing it, like a pencil eraser pressed against the surface of a balloon. But the membrane remained stubbornly intact.

"A little more pressure," Tellison coaxed, as if somehow verbally directing his machines. "There!" he said as the tool finally penetrated to the egg's interior.

"Don't worry," he assured his audience. "The cell membrane will close once we pull out. Next we apply the permeabilization reagent to the nuclear membrane. It will make the membrane temporarily porous so we can remove the native DNA and replace it with the Shroud DNA. But we can't just go in like gangbusters—there's too much risk of wreaking cellular havoc. And once we add the reagent, we have just five minutes to swap out the genetic material before the nuclear membrane begins to resolidify."

The egg remained motionless, held firmly in place, as the piezo penetrated deep into the cell body, finally reaching the nuclear membrane. The permeabilization reagent oozed out of the probe, and a portion of the membrane seemed to become diaphanous and ghostlike.

"Okay, here we go," said Tellison. A digital timer automatically appeared in the upper right quadrant of the display screen. As the probe neared the center of the nucleus, ultraviolet light suddenly bathed the cell, casting it in a deep-purple glow. "This helps us better visualize the DNA," Tellison explained, "but we can't keep it on too long, for fear of damaging the nucleotides."

With the UV light clearly delineating the egg's chromosomes, the piezo edged closer to the chromosome bundle until it nearly made contact. Then, quite suddenly, the edge of one chromosome was sucked into the probe's interior, followed by the others, some in groups, others singly. Soon the egg's nucleus was an empty vessel.

"Got 'em!" Tellison exclaimed, and the UV light automatically switched off.

He checked the timer display, which continued counting down from five minutes. "Two thirty-five remaining," he murmured.

Okay," he said, "now we pull out and bring in a new piezo containing the Shroud DNA."

The first probe pulled out of the nucleus and then out of the cell membrane, and the puncture point partially sealed, remaining barely visible. The second piezo approached the egg's membrane.

"This is the moon-landing part of the procedure," Tellison said. "A bit like threading a needle with boxing gloves on—only harder. We can't afford to poke more than one hole in the cell membrane, so we have to find exactly the same entry point. Even trickier, we also need to penetrate the nuclear membrane in the same general vicinity as before, where it's still most porous from the reagent."

Bender heard the drone of the servomechanism as the automata attempted to direct the second piezo into the original entry site. But the device was having trouble finding the spot. The motors whined as the probe approached, paused, pulled back, and reapproached. The process repeated several times as the computer software searched for the previous entry point.

Bender watched Tellison, marveling that he could appear so relaxed yet supremely focused.

The probe made two more approaches, without success.

"Shit!" Tellison muttered. "Okay, showtime." he said, tightening his fingers in the array of rings.

As Tellison took control of the process, the piezo suddenly seemed more fluid, almost alive, in its movements. It moved slowly toward the now barely perceptible original entry point in the cell membrane, paused for a moment, and then moved effortlessly through the cell wall and into the cytoplasm.

"Bulls-eye," Tellison said softly.

"Nice work," Strickland whispered.

The piezo next moved into the still permeable nucleus, stopping within the empty space that had once held the chromosomes.

"Okay, here we go," Tellison said, depressing the foot pedal. He briefly reengaged the UV light, and Bender saw the Shroud DNA emerge from the micropipette like a bundle of dark snakes flushed from a drainpipe. A moment later, the UV light snapped off, and the snakes were all but invisible.

"Just wanted to make sure they were perfectly positioned," said Tellison.

He began maneuvering the piezo back out of the nucleus, through the cytoplasm, and then out of the cell membrane. "We're out!" he said, exhaling.

Bender took a deep breath, suddenly registering the pounding of her heart. She checked the timer display: seventeen seconds remaining.

"Okay, folks, that's it," said Tellison. "You've seen what happens. Now I have to repeat the performance two more times to make sure we have sufficient backup embryos. I'll do those without an audience."

Bender began gathering up her notes.

"After we give the eggs some time to recover from the enuke-renuke," he added, "we'll activate them chemically, to simulate fertilization. That's the 'virgin birth' part of the process," he said, winking.

Bender looked over at Strickland for some clue to his feelings about what they had just witnessed. But as was so often the case, she couldn't read him at all.

Chapter 127

Later, over coffee, Tellison explained to them that the embryos would be left to divide for several days so he could gauge their "genetic integrity." During this critical phase of cellular division, it was essential that they be untouched and undisturbed. After five days, each embryo should be at the blastocyst stage, and roughly the size of a period on a page. At that point, transfer into a human subject would be optimal.

Bender didn't see Tellison for several days following the lab procedure. After so much time, she was beginning to think that perhaps the process had failed and he had gone into seclusion. But then she finally ran into him in the kitchen, and he seemed in an unusually good mood.

"I know you're wondering," he said, "so I'll give you the good news. Things are going swimmingly. All three embryos are dividing right on schedule, and there's virtually no cellular fracturing in any of them. Using the scale from the in vitro fertilization world, they're all A grade."

"That's wonderful news!" Bender said, smiling.

Against her will, she felt herself softening toward the man, particularly after watching the enuke-renuke procedure. Despite his flippant demeanor, he was clearly a brilliant, dedicated scientist. Nevertheless, she questioned the endeavor on so many levels that she found herself secretly hoping it might fail.

"Would you like to see them?" Tellison asked, interrupting her reverie.

"I thought they couldn't be disturbed."

"We're already past the critical phase," he said, "particularly given their excellent grades. I have a camera positioned over the petri dish. It's simply a matter of switching it on, using ambient light—nothing invasive about it."

"Okay, then, sure."

She followed him down the long series of hallways leading to the embryology wing.

A lone incubation chamber sat unceremoniously on a lab bench. Its ventilation fan hummed quietly, and the digital display showed thirty-seven degrees Celsius. An embedded keypad combination lock on the side of the box gave the only hint that something important lay within.

Tellison dimmed an overhead light, then flipped a switch on a wall-mounted control panel. Projected on the screen, the three spherical embryos floated in a pinkish nutrient solution.

"Oh, they're beautiful!" Bender exclaimed. "They almost look like clumps of pearls."

"Good analogy," Tellison said. "In a similar sense, we've taken an inert substance, hidden it inside a living entity, and it's been transformed into something luminous and quite mysterious—a true metamorphosis."

"You know, you sometimes surprise me," Bender said.

He paused before responding, then looked into her eyes. "The ability to alter people's lives—and maybe even the world—is what drew me to medicine in the first place."

She waited for a sarcastic quip or stinger, but none followed.

"My mother died of breast cancer when I was thirteen," he said. "Not even Bob knows that. He and I both have that in common: losing our mothers at an early age."

"I'm so sorry," Bender replied.

"Don't be. I've dealt with it . . . maybe not always in the best way. I daresay she wouldn't approve of *everything* I've done with my life, but I like to think, on the whole, that I've done more good than harm and that she'd be proud of me."

"I think she would."

Chapter 128

After the many weeks of round-the-clock production work and grueling shifts by the island's staff, the sequencing work and chromosome insertion had all come to fruition: the embryos were stable and dividing regularly. Tellison mentioned to Bender that he had encouraged all nonessential employees to take long-overdue shore leave, with bonuses.

But even with the remaining skeleton crew, an aggressive new phase of preparations was clearly underway. Surgical supplies were delivered to a procedure room with a medical exam table at its center, complete with stirrup footrests.

"Will you have anyone assist in the embryo transfer?" Bender asked him.

"No. The automata allow me to work alone. And I'd just as soon keep it that way. When I first began planning my own facility, I toured various IVF clinics. I saw numerous failures as a result of poor sterile technique or just simple procedural errors. This way, I'll have only myself to blame if something goes wrong."

Bender noticed several of the island's security staff fueling a boat down at the docks. She assumed this was in preparation for transporting the "implantation subject," as Tellison called her.

She felt a visceral pain at the thought of a local woman carrying one of these embryos to term—without a clue to what she had become involved in, or the dangers she might be facing. But at this point the process seemed like an unstoppable juggernaut. In a matter of days it would be done, with unknown consequences. She wondered if this was how it felt before the first atomic bomb test in New Mexico: an eerie mixture of routine banality and supreme anticipation.

That evening, Bender and Strickland again watched the news. Thankfully, there had been no further mention of Tom. Her e-mail clearly had served its purpose, and the news media seemed to be respecting Tom's obvious desire for privacy.

But the splinter group from SEW continued its denunciation of Strickland and all other "apostates of the Word." And the brush of their condemnation was making ever broader strokes. They now portrayed Randall as similarly "fallen" for his "indisputable hand in the dark art of genetic heresy."

Thankfully, the trail of Strickland and Bender had grown cold, except for an unsubstantiated sighting in Fez, Morocco, and a reported hasty retreat into the medina.

Bored, Strickland muted the volume. But seconds after he did, a breaking story interrupted the video signal. A photo of Tom flashed up on the screen. The coverage suddenly switched to a live camera in Manhattan. Bender's eyes filled with horror. Intense red and blue police lights washed across the entrance of her New York apartment building, and yellow crime scene tape blocked all access to the building.

Bender bolted forward. She grabbed the remote and turned up the volume. ". . . live-in boyfriend of Sara Bender was found murdered this evening in their Manhattan apartment."

"No! Oh, God, no!" Bender screamed.

". . . Neighbors reported sounds of a struggle and alerted authorities," the reporter continued. "While robbery does not appear to have been the motive, investigators haven't ruled it out. Apparently, some computer equipment has been damaged or stolen. Authorities refuse to speculate whether the murder could in any way be related to Ms. Bender or her association with Dr. Robert Strickland."

Bender rocked in place on the couch, sobbing, then bolted from the room. Strickland followed her, but she turned against him in fury.

"This is all your fault!" she screamed, nearly falling to the ground in her anguish. "This whole fucking mess has been wrong from the beginning, but you just couldn't let it go! You just couldn't, you . . . *bastard*!"

She tore out of the building, stumbling as she went. Strickland followed, vainly attempting to offer solace. But she turned on him again.

"Leave me alone!" she wailed, barely able to stand. "Don't you *dare* touch me!" And she staggered down the trail to her cottage.

Chapter 129

For several days, Strickland tried knocking at Bender's cottage, only to receive either a firm "Go away!" or no response at all. Distraught and emotionally drained, he confronted Tellison.

"We have to stop," he said. "Sara's right: it's gone too far. The consequences are simply too much."

Tellison stared back. "You were the driving force behind this thing," he said. "I may have suggested it at one point, but that was just a trial balloon. You're the one who said we had to do it. Now it's like a missile launch, and I'm afraid we've already passed the go/no-go point, and we're counting down."

Strickland flexed his jaw. "That's how some felt about the Manhattan Project and the bombing of Japan: it just '*had* to happen.'"

"That's your analogy, not mine."

Strickland eyed him. "What if I try to stop you?"

"I wouldn't go there," said Tellison.

"Are you threatening me?"

"No. Actually, you're threatening me. I'm merely protecting my property and my work—and, at this point, a huge investment. And I have staff and infrastructure in place to ensure that protection."

"You wouldn't even *have* this work if not for me!" Strickland said acidly.

"True, but no one coerced you to come here or to give me the data. I'm just working with that data now. That's how the sciences operate. I'll leave it to others to judge the outcome of my work."

"You fucking prick!" said Strickland, clenching his fist.

"What happened to Sara's boyfriend is unfortunate, but it doesn't change anything." Tellison turned and headed back to the lab. "Now, if you'll excuse me, I have work to do."

Chapter 130

Weeping uncontrollably, Bender fell to her knees and pounded the cottage floor until her hands throbbed.

What had she done? This entire time with Strickland, this entire *life,* now felt horribly wrong. She prayed that Tom was somehow at peace, that there was a place like heaven after all. She thought about making love with Strickland and was overwhelmed with guilt and remorse. Looking back on her life with Tom, she felt nothing but regret—for the missed opportunities, things left unsaid, moments taken for granted. They were all gone.

To dull her agony somehow, she turned her attention to the fanatics who, she imagined, had killed Tom. She viewed them now as worse than any predatory animal and wanted to hurt them the way they had hurt him. But beneath her anguish, she knew that any violence would only spawn more of the same.

A journalist friend, who had covered the Middle East for decades, once detailed a series of plots to blow up the Dome of the Rock. Those plotting on the Palestinian side saw it as a vehicle to energize their followers, who would see such an attack as the handiwork of the Israelis. And those plotting on the Israeli side saw it as a means of finally purging their holy site of Muslims—and, more importantly, as a means of bringing forth the prophesied Messiah.

The notion of one group believing themselves the chosen of God, above all others, had always seemed almost clinically delusional to Bender. But fanatics of all stripes operated from this same orientation of tribal superiority—their God was bigger, better, and truer than all others.

After one too many drinks in a Beirut bar, Bender's journalist friend had suggested that the destruction of the Dome might actually be a good thing—then, he theorized, both sides would be forced to face the reality of their beliefs. A Messiah would not appear in a cloud of light. A thousand-year reign of perfect peace would not occur. There would be only the deaths of countless innocents. But at least then, her friend had drunkenly maintained, mankind could move beyond the violence and dogma of its hidebound mythologies.

Bender's reverie about such needless loss of life inevitably led her back to Tom, and she fell onto the bed and began sobbing all over again.

She wanted somehow to end the pain, to transform this whole terrible chapter of her life.

And then, as if by a switch, a light came on.

Chapter 131

Bender dried her eyes and then showered for the first time in days. She couldn't remember how long she had been without sleep, yet she felt oddly energized.

Her path was clear. As in the Dome of the Rock scenario posed by her colleague, she resolved to become the instrument of a global cataclysm. She would shake these zealots to the core, in the most public way, and put a stop to this madness once and for all. Tom's death would not be in vain. She would force rationality and *reality* down the collective throat of this deranged world. And when nothing more earthshaking happened than simply the birth of a child, people could finally wake up. An application of global shock therapy would cure the condition once and for all.

"Are you out of your *mind*?" Strickland exploded at her announcement.

"I've never felt more certain of anything in my life," she replied. "Besides, I'll probably never have a baby any other way now—this might be my best chance." Her eyes filled with a manic light. "Also, it will be great publicity for my book. I can call it *Mother of God*." But her voice caught as she said it.

"This is insanity," Strickland said, turning to Tellison. "I forbid it."

"Stay out of this!" said Bender. She turned to Tellison. "If I have to, I'll force your hand on this. Either use me as the surrogate, or I'll blow the lid off the whole enterprise—who, what, and where."

"What makes you think I'd let you?" Tellison said evenly.

"Just try me."

Tellison paused. "I already had someone lined up," he said, "but I actually like this idea—on several levels. It has a certain conceptual symmetry."

"You can't be serious!" said Strickland.

"Frankly, a local woman poses far less security risk," Tellison mused. "They're more, shall we say, *malleable*. But I like the way Sara thinks. And as you well know, there's something to be said for having a smart loose canon working *for* you rather than against you." He paused, deep in thought. "Tell you what, let me do a little blood work on you. If you're at a viable point in your cycle, I might just take you up on this."

Chapter 132

Strickland followed Bender out of the lab. "Sara, I'm begging you, don't do this! It's all wrong."

"Stay out of my life!" she hissed. "It's been wrong from the start. Now I'm trying to make it right—and extract a shred of meaning and purpose from the mess you've made."

"You call this 'meaning and purpose'? It's more like going for the jugular."

But Bender kept walking.

"I deserve to have you at least *talk* to me!"

"You deserve nothing!" she said. "You've been manipulative and selfish from the moment I met you!"

"Talk about manipulative!" he raged. "You all but blackmailed your way into this project in the first place!"

"Fuck you, Robert!" she said, her eyes blazing. She turned and continued down the hall.

Strickland returned to the lab and confronted Tellison. "You can't let her do this," he said. "She's in no condition to offer informed consent."

"Um, that sort of thing isn't required down here," Tellison replied. "You knew what you were getting into when we agreed to move ahead. In the big picture, nothing's really changed."

"*Everything* has changed! You're proposing using a surrogate who's been emotionally traumatized and who is no longer in a rational state of mind! I'd question the ethics of someone who would even *consider* that."

"You're not the first person to question my ethics," Tellison said. "Sara's a big girl. You're not her husband or her father. She's made a decision—a proclamation, actually. And assuming her blood work checks out, I intend to abide by that decision."

The two men stared at each other, neither of them blinking, until finally Strickland turned and left the room.

Chapter 133

Strickland tried several times to dissuade Bender and Tellison, but to no avail. Bender seemed transformed by her grief—emotionally controlled, with an almost fevered sense of purpose and resolve. And to Strickland's dismay, her monthly cycle proved almost perfectly synchronized for the implantation of the embryos.

"By your luteinizing hormone level," Tellison said, scanning down her blood work report, "I'd estimate that you ovulated about five days ago. So the timing will be perfect if we proceed by tomorrow night."

She nodded solemnly.

That evening, Strickland sat in Tellison's media room, distractedly watching the news. Bender was nowhere to be found. He assumed that she was either engaged in last-minute preparations with Tellison or cloistered away in her cottage.

A picture of Tom flashed up on the television screen. Strickland leaned forward and turned up the sound. "In a rambling communiqué, a group identifying itself as the Army of the Lord has taken responsibility for the death of investment banker Tom Aruldoss," said the reporter. "This is the same group that earlier claimed responsibility for the bombing of Dr. Robert Strickland's car."

The reporter began reading from the group's statement: *"We view all life as sacred in the eyes of God. And while we regret the spilling of innocent blood, those we seek have brought these events upon themselves. We are servants of the Lord and, toward that end, answer only to his divine purpose, justice, and righteousness. Those who bow to him and serve him have nothing to fear."*

Bender walked by just then and caught a snippet of the broadcast. She seemed in a hurry, heading down the hall toward the embryology wing. But at the sight of Tom's image and the reading of the proclamation, she came back.

"You see?" she said. "These are people who can rationalize murder and then call it the will of God. Do you honestly think you can reason with that? They already think we've done it, so what have we got to lose?"

Chapter 134

Three men in dark suits walked into the San Francisco high-rise offices of Forensic Computer Investigations and announced themselves to the receptionist, who ushered them into the spacious office of one of the firm's principal investigators.

"As we indicated by phone," said the tall red-haired man who appeared to be in charge, "we represent a Fortune Two Hundred company that wishes to remain anonymous. We suspect that one of our employees is engaged in corporate espionage and is planning to sell company secrets to an offshore concern."

One of his associates snapped open an attaché case to reveal a computer disk drive. He handed it to the investigator, who examined the dented and slightly battered device.

"Your guy plays rough with his PC," said the investigator.

There was no response.

"We'd like you to track down the origin of a particular e-mail," the group's leader continued. "We need as much geographic and server-specific information as you can provide."

"Okay, let me plug this into one of our systems," said the cyberdetective. "Then you can show me the message in question."

Once the e-mail in-box was on the screen, the client directed the investigator to a brief message signed "Bubbles."

The detective examined the expanded transmission path of the message. "This appears to have come from a government system in France," he noted. "But it's possible the message was simply routed through that system. To know for certain, I'd need access to that system and any others that might have come into play along the way."

"And you can do that for us?" the man asked.

The investigator eyed the men. "Absolutely not," he said. "Unless you have an international warrant. Otherwise, I'd have to hack into them, and that's illegal."

The leader paused for a moment, his eyes severe. "Thank you for your expertise," he said in a controlled voice.

Later that day, the same trio entered a dilapidated warehouse on the outskirts of Oakland. The space was cold and bare but for a few rows of high-end workstations, racks of network routers, and a spiderweb of cables crisscrossing the floor.

Along the wall, cases of Red Bull and Mountain Dew were stacked in shrink-wrapped cartons. The workstation tables were littered with open soda cans, bags of chips, and discarded pizza boxes.

The three men in suits explained their objective to the tattooed young man who appeared to be in charge but looked as if he might still be a graduate student at Berkeley. He eyed the dark blue business suits with bemusement.

"So, you guys undertakers, or what?" he asked, draining the last of a Red Bull.

The men offered no response. The disk drive was presented, and the situation once again detailed.

"You realize, of course, that we'd have to hack into foreign government servers to get this information," the young man pointed out, examining the battered drive.

With an annoyed look, the leader gestured, and one of his associates produced a bound stack of hundred-dollar bills from a breast coat pocket and put it on the table.

The young man's eyes widened as he began improvising. "The hacking work is not a major problem," he noted. "It does, however, cause our *high-risk* rate to kick in."

"Understood," said the leader. "We are prepared to cover your fees."

"Okay," said the young man, smiling. He crumpled an empty Cheetos bag, tossed it into a trash bin along the wall, and dusted the bright orange powder from his fingertips. "Then I think we're in business. With any luck, I can have this for you by the close of business today."

They shook hands. Before the three men were out the warehouse door, the young hacker had swiveled back to his computer workstation, where he cracked a can of Mountain Dew and began keying commands.

* * *

It was nearly midnight when the three men returned to the warehouse. The hacker presented the trio with a printout detailing his findings. He had highlighted a series of system paths and gateways centered in both Paris and Berlin.

The men huddled together, examining the printout.

"But we didn't stop there," the young man said with obvious pride. "This message path proved to be masked by several additional layers of intermediate ISPs. We tweaked an experimental knowledge bot and finally tracked the originating message to Belize City. So that's where your guy is probably doing business."

The hacker leaned back in his chair, glorying in his success.

"May God bless you," said the group's leader, taking the printout and handing it to one of his subordinates.

"Um, okay, if you say so," said the young man.

One of the men handed him an envelope, then snapped open a briefcase and placed the disk drive inside.

The hacker fanned through the crisp packet of hundreds with a government-issue band reading "$5,000" wrapped around it. "Sweet!" he said as the three men turned to leave.

"Hey," he called out. "What's going to happen to this guy?"

The men continued walking.

Chapter 135

A pair of casually dressed men made their way among the fishermen and boats for hire on the outskirts of Belize City. The fishermen eyed them suspiciously. Although dressed for the tropics, they somehow seemed out of place.

The duo explained in broken Spanish that they were with the American FBI, and produced laminated picture badges as proof. They said they were pursuing an armed and dangerous couple, wanted for both robbery and murder. And they mentioned more than once that there was a reward for information leading to the couple's capture.

They presented digitally altered photographs of a man and a woman, with varying hairstyles and hair color. In some instances, the man had facial hair, and in others, none.

At first there were no takers. The fishermen shook their heads and glanced nervously at one another. Finally, one of the younger men took the bait and stepped forward.

"*¡Sí—con los Moreaus!*" said the man, pointing with conviction at photographs of a blonde Bender and a clean-shaven Strickland.

"What is a Moreau?" asked one of the men.

"The scientists," replied the young man.

"Can you take us to them?" he asked eagerly.

"Yes," the young man said.

Bundles of Belize dollars were soon produced, as both reward for the information, and payment for the boat passage.

The other fishermen quickly drifted away, fearful of both the boat's destination and its passengers. Among the group of fishermen was Eduardo. Fortunately, the young man had not identified him as the pilot who ferried Bender and Strickland to the island. Eduardo puffed at his cigar, watching the exchange of money from a distance. It was clear to him that these men were lying. He could feel it.

Chapter 136

Strickland went again to Tellison's lab, hoping somehow to talk him out of his plans. But it appeared that Tellison had meant what he said: the launch sequence was in place, and nothing short of an act of God was going to interrupt it.

At the center of the room stood a medical exam table, intended for Bender. A small wheeled metal side table was arrayed with sterile, wrapped medical instruments. And nearby was a portable incubation chamber containing the embryos.

A strange equanimity had settled in between the two men, as if they were military foes resigned to the inevitability of war. Tellison busied himself preparing the equipment, then noticed Strickland gazing at the incubation box.

"Would you like to see them?" he asked. "They're at the sixty-four-cell stage now."

Strickland hesitated, flooded with conflicting emotions.

"They're really quite beautiful," said Tellison. "And there's almost zero fracturing. Considering their superlative grade, I'll have to decide whether to insert one, two, or all three."

At Tellison's repeated urging, Strickland finally bent down over the microscope positioned above the incubation dish. He adjusted the focus until the blastocysts came into crystalline view; then he realized he had momentarily stopped breathing.

Strickland suddenly considered destroying the embryos. It would take only a swipe of his hand. But he knew that Tellison could always produce more. The data was out there now, beyond his control.

"I hope you understand the enormity of what you're doing," he said, looking up at Tellison.

Tellison was uncharacteristically solemn as he returned Strickland's gaze and nodded without a trace of irony.

Several hours later, Strickland returned to the lab. He wanted to confirm the exact time of the embryo transfer to Bender. He still hadn't made up his mind about being present and had no idea whether Bender would even allow it. After their night together, the idea of such clinical intimacy felt strange.

Just as Strickland approached the lab's security eye, an assistant came out of the room, loaded down with an armload of used medical packaging. Recognizing Strickland from numerous encounters, he held the door open with his elbow.

"Thanks," Strickland said.

As he entered the room, Tellison shot him an angry glance, and hurriedly finished placing several embryo vials into a liquid nitrogen storage vault in the far corner.

"What's going on?" Strickland asked, his suspicions aroused.

Tellison hesitated for a moment. "When the embryos were at the sixteen-cell stage, I teased off a few cells from each—'twinning,' if you will."

"What on earth for?"

"This is the culmination of a grueling cycle of work and years' worth of research," Tellison replied. "In the event that none of the primary embryos take, I'll still have these as backup, for possible later use."

Strickland stared back at him in horror.

Chapter 137

The embryo transfer was scheduled for 8:00 P.M. Strickland checked his watch—only four hours away.

Bender had sequestered herself in her cottage for most of the day, in preparation for what lay ahead. Strickland had tried to connect several times in the past few days, but she was cold and aloof and answered in monosyllables.

Heading back to his cottage, Strickland had never felt so alone. He was haunted by the implications of Tellison teasing off additional embryo cells for storage. But short of a physical assault on the lab, there was really nothing he could do.

Gazing down at the beach below, he felt suddenly drawn to the water. On an impulse, he decided to go snorkeling, in hopes that it might bring him some sort of clarity.

Slipping on his mask and fins, he waded in, letting the waves wash over him. The water felt unusually cool—initially shocking, but then somehow rejuvenating. As he drifted on the surface, the tide began to take him out. He focused on his breathing, on the idea of surrender, of being cast adrift. As he moved away from the shore, the water grew choppier and murky. Soon he could barely see the bottom.

The swells buffeted him from side to side, almost scraping him against an outcropping of jagged rocks. And the cool water, which at first had felt refreshing, soon left him shivering and drained.

He plowed through the chop, trying to warm up and work off a growing sense of anxiety. His chest heaved as he moved farther and farther from the shore, but the exertions brought none of the comforting, calming effect he had hoped for. Finally, he stopped and floated motionless— exhausted, cold, and supremely depressed.

Swimming back toward the shore, he felt as if the world had suddenly been drained of color. He thought back to the vibrancy he had once experienced in this place, and the strange iridescent blue fish he had encountered. But as the waves carried him back into the shallows, there were no fish, only silt and chop. He stood shivering and heaving from exhaustion, then slowly trudged through the surf to the shore.

Chapter 138

After shucking off his fins and toweling off, Strickland put on running sweats, but he stayed on the beach. Staring out to sea, he tried to imagine himself in another time, another world, far from everything that surrounded him now.

He sat in the lee of a large boulder to watch the gathering sunset. The rhythmic pounding of the waves was hypnotic, bringing with it the sense of transcendence that had evaded him while he was snorkeling. His mind gradually quieted. A brilliant tropical sunset reached out from the horizon, its rose light soon fading to deep purple, then dull gray.

A lone figure darted from behind the boulder, dodging a powerful breaking wave. "Shit! You scared me!" Bender exclaimed as she nearly fell on top of him.

"Sorry," he offered. "Just trying to gather my thoughts . . ."

"Same here," she said. "I'm sorry if I interrupted." And she turned to go.

"No, it's fine," Strickland said. "There's room enough for two. Just pretend you didn't see me."

Bender checked her watch. "Actually, I should probably get back."

Strickland glanced at his watch—the transfer procedure was less than two hours away.

"I should head back, too," he said. "Anyway, it's getting cold."

Bender offered no response.

They walked in silence, with Bender several paces ahead. Gulls hovered on the land breeze, diving down in twos and threes and squabbling over morsels on the rocks yet to be claimed by the rising tide.

"Sara, I need to tell you something," Strickland said, breaking the silence.

She stopped and turned.

"I'm sorry, if I . . ." His voice trailed off.

"What exactly are you sorry for?" she challenged.

"Everything," he said. "What's about to occur, what's already happened. And I'm sorry for my role in bringing you to this place—for leading you down this path."

"Don't be," she bristled. "I'm a grown woman, and I know what

I'm doing. Anyway, it's not as if you *led* me anywhere. In fact, I'm doing exactly what you yourself claimed was practically *destined* to occur." Irritation rose in her voice. "But now, inexplicably, you're arguing *against* the whole thing."

"I admit the contradiction," he said. "It once felt right, but it doesn't anymore. Things have changed—it's as simple as that."

"For God's sake, Robert," she snapped, "why don't you make up your mind for once! At least Tom knew who he was and what he stood for." Her voice began to catch. "And I respected that."

Strickland remained silent—beaten and emotionally spent.

But then something caught his attention—a distant movement in the high grasses behind Tellison's compound. For a moment, he thought it might be pelicans or several gulls.

Two figures emerged from the grass, both wearing military green camouflage and black knit ski masks. Things began to unfold in slow motion. To Strickland's horror, one man picked up a shoulder-fired missile launcher and began to take aim as the other slipped a large projectile into the hollow tube.

Before Strickland could speak, a missile hissed from the commando's shoulder. It streaked through the darkening sky, leaving a ragged corkscrew of smoke trailing behind. Bender turned at the sound, registering Strickland's look of shock.

"Robert, what was that? What's—"

Strickland jumped on her in mid-sentence, pulling her down behind a dune as a tremendous explosion rocked the compound. Through the grasses, he could see several other camouflaged figures. Another explosion shook the earth, then a third. Blast waves rattled their chests with each new assault.

Flickering orange firelight illuminated the dunes as the acrid smell of burned high explosive drifted on the breeze. Strickland heard more explosions, and then gunshots, coming from the direction of the docks.

Bender tried to rise to her knees to catch a better view, but Strickland forced her back down.

An eerie silence followed the assault. Then they heard voices and, soon, approaching footsteps. Strickland motioned to Bender, and they crawled on their bellies into a nearby clump of tall grass. The footsteps grew closer. Through the grass, Strickland could see camouflaged legs and sets of tromping boots.

The attackers searched the area for some time, then finally departed. Several minutes later, in the distance, an engine revved to life. In the firelight, Strickland spotted a small boat with a number of men on board. With running lights off, it maneuvered away from the docks and headed out to sea. The high-revving engine strained as the craft bounded on the waves, racing into the darkness.

Minutes later, there was only the wind in the grasses, and the gentle lapping of waves.

Chapter 139

Strickland and Bender staggered dumbstruck through the ruins of the compound. The explosions had twisted and uprooted the security fences, and most of the structures looked as if a wrecking ball had hit them.

They made their way to the main building and found half of it leveled by a direct hit. The residential portion, miraculously, was still standing, but there was no sign of Tellison.

After orienting themselves amid the smoking rubble, they located the assembly and embryology complex. The assembly bot lab was almost unrecognizable. The walls had caved in, exposing the neighboring embryology lab. On the floor they found Tellison, half buried in rubble, his face smeared in blood.

"Oh, dear God!" Bender gasped.

Rushing forward, Strickland checked for a carotid pulse but found none. "Go back to the main compound," he said. "There's a portable defibrillator in the admin wing, in a cabinet on the wall."

Stunned, Bender gazed at Tellison's lifeless body.

"Go!" Strickland shouted, and she turned and ran.

After clearing the smaller debris away, he braced himself and, in a surge of adrenaline, lifted the piece of wall still resting on Tellison's chest. Heaving until he got it vertical, he toppled it over onto a low pile of rubble, then quickly but gently tilted Tellison's head back and cleared the airway with his finger.

Bender returned with the defib-pack just as Strickland was putting his mouth over Tellison's. He gave two quick breaths, but the air gurgled out with a sickening wet sound. He ripped open Tellison's shirt to reveal a gaping chest wound.

Pulling the shirt back together, Strickland passed one hand over Tellison's eyes, closing the lids. Then he stood and moved toward Bender. Her eyes welled with tears, and when he took her in his arms, she rested her head on his shoulder and sobbed.

He surveyed the wreckage around them. The exam table, intended for Bender, had been destroyed along with the incubation chamber containing the embryos.

Strickland hugged her in silence for a long time. Suddenly, a sputtering came from the lab's control grid. A fountain of sparks shot out the side, and the room went dark. Bender held her ears as a Klaxon blared over the *whoop-whoop-whoop* of the alarms.

Apparently, the power outage had triggered a still-functioning battery-driven backup system. Flashing strobes bathed the room in an eerie crimson light.

Bender followed Strickland's gaze to the liquid nitrogen chamber, where Tellison had stored the extra embryos. The chamber was still intact, and the digital display read a perfect negative 196 degrees Celsius. Strickland waded through the rubble, toward the chamber.

"No more!" he shouted. "It's over!"

He looked at Bender, who was still trembling. She nodded, and with a broken two-by-four, he smashed the glass plate covering the emergency control panel, exposing two large power levers, then reached in and pulled them to the off position. The alarms died, and the digital temperature display on the liquid nitrogen chamber faded to black.

Chapter 140

Making their way through the rest of the ravaged compound, Strickland and Bender discovered nine other survivors. With the help of two who weren't badly injured, they dragged couches from the lobby out onto the lawn and set up a triage area.

A stout black woman appeared to have a mild concussion, though she became more lucid by the minute. Strickland checked her pupillary response, then did a cursory neuro workup; everything appeared normal.

For the several men with burns or minor shrapnel wounds, Strickland pried open a first-aid box on the lobby wall, then applied bandages and Steri-Strips. One scalp wound, though, was too deep for Steri-Strips. "I'm going to have to suture this," he whispered to Bender, glancing back at the lanky mestizo on the couch.

After searching the compound high and low, he found a small plastic sewing kit in a desk drawer. He grabbed a bottle of rum from the pantry.

"This is a nasty way to go," he told Bender while soaking the thread and needle in the alcohol, "but the mainland docs can pump him full of antibiotics afterward."

He explained to the injured man what was going to happen, gave him a slug of rum, then trickled some on the wound. At the man's grimaced nod, he went to work.

After stabilizing everyone, Strickland used a borrowed cell phone to call Heusner Memorial Hospital in Belize City. He detailed what had happened and the status of the injured but refused to give his name.

"We have to get out of here," he said to Bender after completing the call. "It's not safe for anyone as long as we're still on the island."

Bender, still numb, only nodded.

Fortunately, the compound's security systems had been designed with a catastrophic-override feature. Artificial intelligence software had determined that a compoundwide disaster had occurred, and all doors had automatically unlocked, at least for the time being.

"Robert, wait," Bender said, grabbing his upper arm. "Remember when Tellison said he gave himself a 'different look' when he went to the mainland?"

Without another word, they both ran to Tellison's living quarters, where they searched feverishly through his belongings. In the bathroom, they found a box containing various hair dyes.

"There's not much I can do," Strickland said. "I can't grow a beard overnight, and at my age, if I dyed my hair lighter, it would look bizarre. But *you* have a few more options."

He helped Bender cut her hair short—almost in a boy's cut. Then she selected a henna dye.

While waiting for her to shower, Strickland searched Tellison's living quarters. In the far wall of the bedroom, he discovered a barely perceptible narrow door. It was built flush with the surface of the wall and had no doorknob. He tried prying it open with his fingers, but it was impossible to get a good grip. Then he began probing the periphery of the opening, applying pressure at random spots, and suddenly it popped open.

Inside, he found a small, sparsely furnished office—apparently Tellison's inner sanctum. At the center of the room stood an antique wooden desk.

Using the chromed handle of a large letter opener, Strickland broke into each drawer. In one, he found a leather-bound journal chronicling Tellison's thoughts and activities during the entire Shroud project. In another, he found a flash memory stick with a backup date listed as two days ago. And at the back of a third drawer, he found a single envelope from a post office box in the Philippines. Postmarked just a week ago, it contained what appeared to be an invoice. The cover letter was brief and cryptic: *"Upon receipt of the embryos, intact and viable, US$20,000,000.00 (twenty million USD) will be deposited in the agreed-upon account."*

Strickland's eyes narrowed in anger. Returning the letter to its envelope, he placed it in the middle pages of the journal, tucked the book under his arm, and stashed the memory stick in his pocket.

When he returned to Bender, she was towel-drying her hair.

"We haven't got much time," he said. "Let's get back to our cottages, pick up whatever we absolutely need—and anything with our personal information—and head to the docks."

Bender nodded quietly. She seemed to be running on instinct and adrenaline.

Back at the cottages, they found Bender's room turned upside down. Her bags and belongings had been strewn everywhere. "God, what could they possibly have been looking for?" she said, amazed.

"They may not have known for certain themselves," Strickland said. "They obviously wanted to wipe out all possibility of further work on the Shroud data."

Bender wandered through the room, surveying the damage. Then her eyes widened.

"Oh, no . . . my notes!" she cried, making a beeline for the room safe hidden inside the closet. Frantically she punched in the code, and the lock snapped open. Inside, she found her gear, apparently untouched.

"Glad I decided to use the safe," she said. "And thank God they didn't torch the cottages."

"I need to check my room, too," Strickland said. "I'll be right back."

Next door, he found his room similarly ransacked. But the hidden safe was intact, and there inside lay the smart card. Picking the card up, he held it firmly in both hands. He tightened his grip on the device and was about to snap it in half. Then he looked down at Tellison's leather-bound journal, and his grip eased. He stowed the card in his wallet and put the journal in his duffel bag.

Chapter 141

Checking back at the triage area, Strickland and Bender learned that the black woman had used her cell phone to call her family on the Belize mainland. A local television channel had just aired a news item concerning the attack.

"Come on," Strickland said. "We don't have much time."

At the dock, they found Tellison's boats riddled with large-caliber bullet holes. Several of the vessels had burned to the waterline when their gas tanks ignited.

"This explains the explosions we heard from over here," Strickland said as they surveyed the destruction.

Along the wharf, they found the bodies of several security guards. Strickland turned them over, checking for survivors, but all were dead from gunshot wounds to the back or head. The safeties on their weapons were still set, meaning they had been taken utterly by surprise.

Bender surveyed the scene in numb silence. They found the melted wreckage of an inflatable boat, sill tied to the dock.

"Rigid inflatables," Strickland noted. "Used a lot by drug runners—nearly invisible to radar. That explains why Tellison's people didn't see these guys coming. They've even got an auxiliary battery-powered motor for silent approach. The explosions must have disabled this one, so they all escaped in the one inflatable."

Bender closed her eyes against the bodies and the charred wreckage.

"We have to get to the mainland somehow," Strickland said. "These people are obviously professionals. And it won't be long before the Belize City police arrive. At this point, I'm not sure who we can trust."

In the distance, they heard the sound of a fast-approaching boat.

"Get down," Strickland hissed.

They ducked behind a storage shed and peered around the wall as the boat slowed and moved parallel to the shore. An intense spotlight swept over the docks and paused on the still-smoldering ruins of several boats, then again on the lifeless bodies of the guards.

"Could be the police," Strickland whispered. "Or maybe it's a mop-up crew, checking for survivors and wanting to finish the job. Either way, we need to keep still."

Bender nodded. She peered again around the corner of the shed. The pilot of the boat seemed to be plotting his next move. She spotted the faint glow of a cigar at the helm.

After a long pause, a voice hesitantly called out from the boat, *"¿Señor . . . señorita?"*

The voice was hoarse and strained, but Bender recognized it instantly. She stood up.

"What are you *doing*?" Strickland whispered, trying to pull her back down.

Pushing his hand away, Bender walked forward into the light.

Chapter 142

Strickland stood up from his hiding place, shielding his eyes from the boat's blinding spotlight.

"*¡Señorita, señor!*" said Eduardo. "*Gracias a Dios.* Are you all right?"

"No," Bender said in a tremulous voice. "We need help."

They made their way along the dock toward the boat. "Eduardo, turn out your light!" she said.

The searchlight switched off, and the dock fell into darkness. Eduardo helped them into the boat, then stowed their bags.

"Can you take us to the mainland?" asked Strickland.

"Of course," the old man said. His eyes locked on to the bodies of Tellison's guards, their dark shapes just visible in the thin starlight. "What terrible thing has happened here?" he asked.

"There's been an attack on the island—that's all we know," said Strickland. "But we need to get away—now."

"Yes. It is a bad place. I feel it before."

Eduardo started the engines and threw the boat into reverse.

The boat came around in a hard left turn, and he kicked it up to full throttle. A moment later, they were speeding through the black channel waters toward the mainland, with embers from the smoldering compound rising behind them into the night.

Bender wanted to thank Eduardo, but he seemed busy enough with piloting the boat. He peered out at the horizon, making minor adjustments as they ran toward the lights of Belize City. After all she had just witnessed, she felt somehow calmed by the old man's presence, just as she had on the way out to the island—a passage that now felt like a distant dream.

While Strickland stood in the bow, deep in thought, Bender watched the approaching city lights rising from the dark waters. The scene looked so peaceful and beautiful. But she knew that Tellison's killers—and perhaps Tom's as well—were out there somewhere.

As they cleared the chain of smaller islands and entered the open channel, it became easier to spot approaching vessels, and the tension in Eduardo's stance eased.

Bender shivered in the night wind and had drifted into a numbed reverie when a pair of broad hands wrapped a coat around her. Eduardo's eyes were kind and strangely penetrating.

She smiled and thanked him but then glanced at the helm with concern.

"*Piloto automático,*" he said reassuringly.

"So what made you look for us?" she asked him.

"Men at the docks came asking," he replied. "I knew something was not right. I worried . . . you might need help. But I did not know how bad these men were," he said, looking back at the island. "If I did, I would have come sooner."

"I'm sorry we got you involved in all this," she said. "But you probably saved our lives. . . . Thank you."

He smiled and then returned to the helm, and she pulled the jacket tighter around her shoulders.

About forty minutes later, they motored up to the same docks where Strickland and Bender had first met Eduardo. It was late, and the area was entirely deserted.

Eduardo secured the boat, then fetched their bags. He helped them onto the dock but kept a wary eye.

"Please don't tell anyone that you picked us up," Strickland said, "or where you let us off."

"Yes, *señor,*" said Eduardo. "*Entiendo.*"

Eduardo shook Strickland's hand and then turned to Bender. He smiled warmly.

Bender hugged him. "I'll never forget you," she said.

"And I will always remember you," he replied, returning her embrace. "You will be safe, *señorita*—I feel it."

Strickland and Bender headed away from the docks, avoiding major thoroughfares. Given the late hour, there was almost no automobile traffic, and they encountered no one on foot.

Strickland once again seemed energized by the danger. "Our first order of business is to find a room," he said, "preferably off the beaten path. We need to stay away from anything mainstream. And we'll need international phone access. We can't risk using our cells. But I need to start making calls, first to a good friend who's a powerful attorney in D.C. We need expert advice on several fronts. I'm hoping he can get us federal protection, until we figure out who and what we're dealing with."

Bender waited until he had finished. "No," she said finally.

"What do you mean, 'no'?" he asked, mystified. "What part of it?"

"All of it."

Strickland just looked at her, dumbfounded.

"This is your path, Robert," she said, "not mine. I've been a reluctant passenger all along—with devastating results. Now, I want out. Besides, they're looking for a couple. No one's going to recognize me now. The minute we split up, we automatically draw a lot less attention. We're actually safer traveling separately."

Strickland said nothing, considering her words.

"Also," she continued, "I have a lot to figure out—Tom, you, me, and all that's happened here. The last thing I need is to be holed up in a safe house, surrounded by G-men playing cards."

"You're not being reasonable," he said. "It's far too dangerous for you to—"

"Robert, I'm not asking," she interrupted, boring into his eyes. "My mind is made up." She stared up at the star-filled sky. "Besides, I always intended to see this part of the world. It's been a weird path getting here, but maybe this is finally my time."

Strickland remained silent for a moment. "I can't let you do this," he said, but his tone was far less certain this time. "What if..."

Bender put her finger on his lips. "Robert, look within. You know what I'm saying is true. You said it yourself—*it's over*."

Strickland looked back at her but said nothing.

Bender slung her bag over one shoulder, gazed at him for a moment, then kissed him on the cheek and was gone.

Chapter 143

Strickland found a ramshackle hotel not far from the docks. The office was dark, and the clerk was already gone for the night. He pressed the buzzer a few times, until a middle-aged man with salt-and-pepper stubble emerged from a room in the back.

The cheaply paneled lobby smelled of bleach and cigarette butts. Strickland entered a name and address in the registration book, then paid in cash.

"Checkout, eleven," the man said in heavily accented English, barely even looking up. He put a heavy brass key on the worn countertop, then glanced at Strickland with a blank expression while flicking his cigarette ash into a rusted coffee can on the counter.

Before heading upstairs, Strickland ducked into the lobby phone booth and carefully closed the dark wooden door. After nervously surveying the lobby through the small pane of glass, he fumbled with a handful of coins and began dropping them into the phone. A minute later, he was narrating the events of the past twenty-four hours.

He listened for a while, then said, "Yeah, that was my thinking as well—seems like the best way to go at this point." He jotted down notes as he spoke. "Okay, with any luck, I'll see you tomorrow. Thanks for handling this, Jim. I really appreciate it."

Hanging up, he crossed the lobby and climbed a flight of worn wooden stairs. His room was small and smelled of mildew and insecticide. Stretching out on the narrow, sagging bed, he sighed with exhaustion. But sleep was slow to come. Nerves screaming, he lay there in a trance, watching the dance of passing headlights on the water-stained ceiling.

Finally, he drifted off into fitful sleep, but then a fight broke out in the next room. Rapid-fire Spanish, laced with profanities, erupted between a man and a woman, followed by the hard slamming of a door. He heard clattering high heels on the outdoor hallway. Moments later, someone began pounding at his door. At first, he ignored it, but the pounding continued. Strickland checked the small security chain and realized that it was next to useless. Then he cracked open the door.

"*¿Dónde estás, Estela?*" demanded a small, wiry man in shorts and a worn T-shirt. "*¿Dónde estás?*" he barked again. His eyes looked crazed.

Behind the flimsy door, Strickland said, *"No hay nadie aquí,"* gesturing to the dark interior of the room.

Like a dog distracted by a new noise, the man looked out to the street below, then turned and staggered away.

Strickland locked the door again, jamming the one chair in the room firmly up under the doorknob.

At first light, he dragged himself out of bed and looked at himself in the cracked bureau mirror. He looked like hell. He shaved, but that somehow made his eyes look even more sunken and dull.

Walking down the concrete hallway lined with empty liquor bottles and cigar butts, he hurried down the stairs and was relieved to find a cab rumbling and smoking in front of the hotel.

At the airport, he booked a seat on the first flight to Dulles, still using his forged ID. The screening agents, who seemed distracted and overworked, glanced at him and then at his passport.

An hour and a half later, he was in the air. The plane banked hard over Belize City. The air was crystal clear, and Strickland caught a glimpse of the distant chain of islands offshore—like a giant's stepping-stones heading out to sea. At the end of the chain, a wisp of dark smoke rose from what must have been Tellison's compound.

In the relative comfort and security of the plane, sleep finally came. And though he woke from time to time, momentarily disoriented, he quickly fell back into exhausted oblivion. The next thing he knew, the pilot announced that they were making their descent into Washington.

* * *

At the baggage carousel, Strickland's friend and attorney, James Needle, barely recognized him without his beard.

"But that's a good thing," Needle said. "If *I* don't even recognize you, no one else will, either. And you'll be relieved to know that the plan is in place," he said as they headed to his car. "I'm cleared to deliver you into federal custody."

"Thanks, Jim," said Strickland. "I'm so burned out, I don't know what else to say."

"Nothing else required," his friend replied. "Happily, the news coverage from Belize is vague at this point. I found brief mention of it on the CNN Web site, but it was presented as a possible 'industrial accident.' I have a feeling the officials in Belize are withholding information until they know more themselves."

Sitting in Needle's Mercedes in the cavernous parking structure at Dulles, Strickland unzipped his nylon travel bag and handed his friend a small package wrapped in brown paper.

"I'd like you to hold on to this for me," he said.

Their eyes locked. "Am I breaking any laws by taking possession of this material?" Needle asked.

"None that I'm aware of," Strickland replied with a weary smile. "But you're the lawyer." When this got him only a deadpan look, he said, "It contains Tellison's lab notes. I'd eventually like to review his methodologies and techniques, but I suspect the documents would bring up whole new lines of inquiry if the government examined them."

Needle took the package. "You realize I'll have to open this, much as I trust your integrity."

"Be my guest."

The lawyer opened the bundle and glanced through the journal, then examined the flash memory and the smart card. He looked back to Strickland, waiting for the rest of the story, but there was no further explanation.

"Okay, I won't ask," Needle said. "Clearly there's a lot of technical material here that I'm not qualified to evaluate. To reiterate, you'd simply like me to keep this safe somewhere."

"Precisely."

"Done."

Chapter 144

On the drive into Washington, Strickland felt as if he had just arrived from another planet. Hours ago, he had awakened to the squawking of blue and red macaws outside a dilapidated hotel in Belize. Now here they were in gridlocked traffic on the Leesburg Pike.

Needle drove them to a nondescript two-story office building in Falls Church, on the outskirts of the capital. It could easily have been a medical/professional building. A sign in the lobby read simply, United States Office of Internal Affairs.

A small, groaning elevator took them to the second floor, where two casually dressed agents met them. Neither wore identification, but both flashed government badges as they introduced themselves.

"Frank," the man said. "And Sue," the woman added as they shook hands with Strickland. Something about their delivery made him wonder whether these were really their names.

After introductions, the agents glanced at Needle, making clear that his role had ended.

"Thanks for everything, Jim," Strickland said wearily.

"We'll talk soon," said Needle, patting him on the shoulder.

* * *

Strickland was fingerprinted and photographed, then led through an initial debriefing interview, which was recorded on video. The two agents were more than respectful, always addressing him as "Dr. Strickland," and later even got him a take-out dinner from a nearby Chinese restaurant.

Afterward, he was escorted to a black SUV in the office building's underground garage. The agents explained that they would be transporting him to a "protection location."

Rush hour had long since passed, and the ride out of town was smooth and uneventful. Frank tuned in a classic rock station playing rather bland hits of the 1980s.

After several lane changes, he realized that his guides were making certain they weren't being followed. And at one point, as Frank turned to speak, Strickland noticed the bulge of a firearm beneath his sport coat.

They drove deep into the Virginia countryside, winding along progressively smaller highways, and by late evening the rural back roads were all but deserted. Checking in both directions for approaching headlights, Frank slowed at a small unmarked road. A rusted sign read, PRIVATE PROPERTY. NO TRESPASSING.

They bounced along the rutted dirt track for half a mile through a dense mix of pine and hardwoods, finally reaching a reinforced metal gate with a smart card reader attached to a flat-black steel post. Frank extracted a card from his breast pocket and inserted it into the reader, and the gate swung open. The SUV pulled into a small clearing with a quaint two-story farmhouse. The lights were on.

Stretching his legs, Strickland marveled at the dense, unbroken canopy overhead.

"It's one of our best locations," Frank said. "And with these woods, it's nearly invisible from the air."

The two agents surveyed the surrounding terrain as they walked toward the house, as if admiring a newly discovered bed-and-breakfast. But beneath their practiced casual air, Strickland sensed a heightened intensity and focus. They were clearly running through a mental checklist of security precautions.

Just then, the rotor *whop* of a low-flying helicopter sliced through the night air. As the craft banked sharply overhead, Strickland glimpsed the alternately strobing red and green lights through the trees.

"Move it!" Frank barked at Sue.

She grabbed Strickland roughly by the shoulder, almost shoving him along the stone trail leading to the dark side of the house.

Looking back, Strickland watched as Frank unholstered a pistol from beneath his jacket, crouching low beneath a tree and pointing the weapon skyward.

Huddled in the shadows with Strickland, Sue was already on a handheld communicator. "This is site eleven, repeat, site eleven. We have a low-altitude helicopter, need *immediate* identification! Do you copy?"

"Roger, site eleven," crackled a voice at the other end. "Copy, and checking now."

Through a small break in the trees, Strickland spotted the sleek copter fuselage silhouetted against the moonlit sky. It seemed to have slowed in its path and was now hovering almost directly overhead. Seeking a better vantage point, Frank ran low, gun in hand, to an adjacent clump of trees.

Sue's radio crackled briefly with static, but there was no response. As Frank took his new position, again targeting the craft, Sue drew out a pistol from inside her jacket, thumbing off the safety as she did. She scanned the surrounding terrain, glancing down the dark side yard.

The radio suddenly crackled back to life. "Site eleven, we have confirmation: flight plan filed, local residence, aircraft owned by CitiGroup. No perceived risk—repeat, *no* perceived risk."

"Shit," she sighed, holstering her weapon and switching off the radio. Frank soon rejoined them from the clearing.

"More and more Manhattan execs have discovered the area," she explained to Strickland, "for its beauty and proximity to D.C. They come by jet copter for some R and R at their country estate, then a little networking in D.C. Great for them, but a pain in the ass for us."

Frank holstered his weapon and swiped his smart card at the front door. "Okay," he said, "let's get some sleep."

Chapter 145

In the ensuing days at the safe house, Strickland fleshed out the details of what had transpired in Belize. Needle had coached him on what to expect from the debriefings, and how to respond.

"The feds are trying to keep you out of harm's way and return things to status quo," he had explained. "In the end, they don't really *want* any blockbuster revelations, so if possible, don't give them any."

Strickland told the agents that he and Bender had initially fled to the island as a safe haven. Later, hoping to continue his research, he had given Tellison access to the Shroud data. But once the information was in Tellison's systems, things spun out of his control. Tellison began actually assembling the Shroud DNA, using the sequences provided by Strickland. This was something Strickland hadn't even believed possible when he originally supplied the data. And while Tellison *had* taken the Shroud DNA assembly phase to completion, no cloning effort was ever fully realized. Moreover, Tellison's assembly work, and the data on his systems, were destroyed by the attack on the lab.

Needle's advice had been correct. His hosts seemed most interested in events surrounding the car bomb attack in D.C., and the decimation of Tellison's island. Thankfully, neither of them asked what had become of the unspecified data device used to bring the Shroud sequence data to Belize—the assumption seemed to be that any such device had been destroyed during the attack. And Strickland offered nothing to counter that notion.

After many days of interviewing, the agents began to assemble a chronological account of Strickland's activities, intended for his eventual signed approval. They also revealed that a field report from Belize corroborated the primary details of his account. After interviewing the surviving staff from Tellison's compound, the CIA and the local authorities in Belize concluded the obvious: that unknown assailants had invaded the island and bombarded it with rockets, intentionally or unintentionally causing Tellison's death. The island staff had spoken highly of Strickland's actions following the attack, some even calling him a hero.

And true to Bender's nightmare fantasies of federal custody, there were indeed a few late-night poker sessions. But the agents typically worked long hours—compiling their sessions with Strickland, filing reports, and trading encrypted wireless e-mail with Langley and D.C.

In many ways, the cottage *was* like a country bed-and-breakfast, complete with its own wicker-furnished sunroom and library. Over the course of his stay, Strickland pored through *Moby Dick* and *The Brothers Karamazov*—books he had always hoped to revisit.

But as the days wore on, he found himself thinking often of Bender. At one point, he asked Frank whether he could send an e-mail message— on the outside chance she might be accessing her account. But he was told that no outside contact of any kind was permitted during this phase. His isolation, they explained, was primarily for his own protection, but his attackers might also pose a national security threat—if his whereabouts became known, it could put others at risk as well.

In thinking about his new circumstances, Strickland realized that not much had changed—he was still on the run, still hiding out in an isolated compound, and still at the mercy of others. He just wanted to go home and have his old life back.

Chapter 146

Three weeks later

One blustery morning, Frank and Sue unceremoniously announced that Strickland's federal custody had been terminated. After he packed, the agents drove him from the wooded glen to James Needle's D.C. law office, where Strickland signed paperwork describing his activities before and after arriving in Belize. The documents included an agreement, reached by the Justice Department and the NIH, that placed Strickland under the supervision of an oversight committee for any government-funded research he might perform during the next two years.

Strickland looked to Needle before signing the oversight clause.

"If it were me, I'd sign it, Bob," Needle said. "All in all, I think it's a fair and equitable resolution. And most importantly, it protects you from any future prosecution."

The FBI revealed that it had been monitoring Strickland's condominium for the past several weeks and had detected no activity that would indicate a threat. Without mentioning any specifics, the agents told Strickland privately that they were closing in on a number of suspects in the death of Tom Aruldoss and the bombing of Strickland's car. None were believed to be located in the D.C. area.

Nevertheless, the Bureau offered to continue its surveillance of Strickland's home. He declined. As an alternative measure, he was given a handheld GPS-linked communicator that could summon an agent within five minutes. Then, after signing the documents at Needle's office, he was delivered back to his Rockville home.

Standing on the front porch, he watched the black SUV pull away and round the far corner. He turned and put his key in the door, wandering tentatively from room to room as if in a trance. The wind rustled through the hickory tree outside. Dappled golden sunlight fell across the framed photographs on the mantel: his niece, his sister, his father, and his mother.

Strickland gazed at the images, and for reasons he couldn't quite fathom, began to quietly cry.

Chapter 147

The next day, Randall arrived at Strickland's home with a turkey sausage pizza from Manny and Olga's, their favorite. When Strickland opened the door, his friend just stood there, as if viewing an apparition.

"Bob . . ." His voice cracked. Setting the pizza down inside, he threw his arms around Strickland.

"You are truly my dearest friend," Strickland said.

They both were quiet for a moment; then Strickland went to the kitchen and returned with two bottles of beer. In no time, they had fallen into familiar, easy conversation.

"Damn, this is good!" Strickland said. "I have to say, it's great to be home," he added, looking first at Randall and then around the living room. With broad smiles, they clinked their bottles together.

"Have you heard anything from Sara?" Randall asked him.

"Not yet," said Strickland, grimly. "I've tried sending several e-mails, but there's been no response. According to her editor at the *Times,* they haven't heard anything, either. I even asked some agents from the Bureau to find out what they could."

Randall seemed surprisingly unfazed by the news. "I can't explain it," he said, "but somehow I have the sense that she's doing fine."

"I hope you're right," said Strickland.

Chapter 148

One week later

Incognito without his beard, Strickland walked across the NIH campus to the Ethnogenomics Center. The cherry trees had just begun to blossom, and feathery cirrus clouds streaked the slate blue sky. On the abutting quad, a small group of die-hard protestors stood assembled, kept back by court order to a respectful hundred yards from the building's entrance. Nothing had changed, and yet he felt a strange sense of unreality, as if everything in the entire scene had been remade out of a different substance.

Strickland spent the morning getting an overview of the department's current projects. Thanks to Randall and a team of postdocs who had assisted in the bureaucratic heavy lifting during his absence, the center was running on all cylinders.

As Strickland navigated the halls, there were no questions, just smiles and handshakes. Even so, he sensed a certain distance in some of the interactions.

The NIH had done an admirable job of defusing tensions concerning the Shroud project. A press release stated, "*After an exhaustive internal investigation by the NIH, assisted by the FBI and CIA, it has been determined that no portion of the Shroud research project led to cloned entities based on data uncovered during the study. All known data from the Shroud investigation has either been purged from NIH systems, turned over to the Vatican, or destroyed during the attack in Belize.*"

The statement concluded by emphasizing the two-year oversight agreement signed by Strickland. It also mentioned the inclusion of members of several faith-based groups in the oversight committee.

Even so, Internet conspiracy blogs persisted, claiming that the United Nations was planning to use the Shroud data to develop a cross-faith cybernetic deity—all part of its master plan for a one-world government and religion. But the general public's obsession with the Shroud was gradually waning. Nothing cataclysmic had actually happened, and it became increasingly difficult to stoke the media fires. Little by little, end-time prophets began looking for other "signs" to fuel their passions and motivate their followers.

Chapter 149

Strickland gradually began to make headway against the piles of documents and administrative tasks that had accumulated during his sojourn in Belize. In his absence, Randall and the postdocs had structured operations to give greater local autonomy to each project lead. As a result, Strickland was still finding his place in the new order.

As he lugged a precarious stack of documents across the room, the phone rang. He managed to juggle the pile with one hand long enough to hit the speaker phone button.

"Yeah?" he barked.

"Um, Dr. Strickland?"

"Speaking," he said.

"This is Angela Patterson, Sara Bender's literary agent."

Strickland set down the papers and grabbed the receiver.

"Is Sara all right?" he blurted out.

"Yes, she's fine," the woman replied. "Sara wanted me to let you know that she's safe, and working hard on her book."

"That's great news!" he said, feeling his body relax. "Did she say where she was or how to reach her?"

"She's doing a lot of traveling, mostly in Central America. I don't know where she is at any given time. And she seems to prefer being off the communications grid—says she's getting a lot more work done that way."

"Do you know when she plans to return?"

"The last time I asked her that, she wasn't sure." The woman seemed to be waiting for him to signal the end of the call.

"All right," he said. "Thanks for the info."

Chapter 150

A week after their reunion, Randall entered Strickland's office. "My father-in-law died last night from a massive coronary," he said wearily. "To be honest, Mary's a basket case. She and her dad had a lot of unresolved issues, and now they'll stay that way, in limbo. Her mother was just barely able to take care of herself before, and now this. I'm going with Mary to Florida to help settle things, so I'm not sure how long I'll be gone."

"I'm really sorry, Jordan," Strickland said. "Take whatever time you need—we'll limp along. And tell Mary I'm thinking of her and the family."

Strickland spent the next morning going through voluminous piles of paperwork, trying to get up to speed on the department's new protocols and procedures. In the past, he had always reveled in his solitude, but being back at the NIH, with neither Randall nor Bender around, left him feeling strangely isolated.

That afternoon, George tapped on the door and poked his head in. "You have a visitor in the lobby."

Strickland's mind raced. "Who is it?"

"James Needle—says he has an appointment."

"Right. Send him up. Thanks."

A minute later, Strickland ushered Needle into his office and closed the door.

"Good to see you Jim," he said.

"You look tired," said Needle.

"I'm having some trouble adjusting to civilian life. A small taste of what it must be like to return from war—the things you've experienced are so intense, it's hard to get back in the swing of a normal existence."

"I understand. It'll probably take some time."

"Yeah, probably so."

"I've got your package," Needle said.

Opening his briefcase, he took out a heavy-gauge opaque plastic bag with a zip fastener along the side. Strickland's gaze was riveted to the package, but he said nothing.

"Everything's settled and finalized with the feds," Needle said. "Consider yourself a free man, except for that little two-year oversight business. So try to keep your nose clean from here on out. And don't leave town just yet, in case they have further questions."

A grin flickered across Strickland's face, but his mind was elsewhere.

Needle glanced at his watch. "I'm on a mad schedule today. Why don't you come into D.C. some evening soon, and we'll have dinner."

"Sounds good," Strickland said. "Thanks, Jim—for everything."

After Needle left, Strickland continued where he had left off on his computer. But after several minutes, he paused and glanced at the plastic bag on the table. Unzipping it, he dumped the notebook, flash memory, and smart card out on the table.

He stared at the worn smart card, then picked up Tellison's notebook. It still held the acrid smokiness of that day. A wave of emotion swept over him, and an image of the surprised look frozen on Tellison's face flashed through his mind. He could hear the sickening, wet wheeze of the chest wound when he had attempted CPR. It all came back with a visceral punch.

He pushed aside his office work and began paging through the notebook, trying to make sense of the scribbled abbreviations and arcane nomenclature. It was sometimes like hieroglyphics, but with repetition of terms and contextual clues, the entries and sequences of events slowly began to fall into place. Strickland made notes as he read, filling in the technical and chronological blanks in the narrative.

When he finally pulled himself away, it was nearly eight in the evening. He closed the lab book and was about to return the smart card to the plastic bag. Then he paused and checked the clock again.

He couldn't recall whether use of the facility had been explicitly addressed in his NIH oversight agreement. The document was so voluminous, and he had been so emotionally wrung out when he signed it, that he could easily have missed it.

The area around the RES-5000 room was practically deserted. He looked up and down the hall, then slipped into the room, locking the door behind him. After dimming the lights, he booted up the RES-5000, and to his surprise, the screen presented a login menu—a security measure apparently instituted in his absence.

His name was not on the list of authorized users, so he selected

Randall's. He tried Mary's maiden name as the password, then Randall's favorite rock group from their med school days (ZZ Top). Nothing worked. He wondered how many guesses he would be allowed before the system permanently locked him out.

"Oppenheimer," he murmured, and typed it in. After a momentary pause, the main menu appeared. Strickland smiled. Randall had chosen the perfect personification for this device: the man who lived the duality of everything science represented.

Strickland inserted the smart card containing the Shroud DNA data and began importing the information. Once completed, it would take several hours to render an image based on the data, but he just had to see it again. He set the file privileges so that only someone using Randall's login could access the data again.

Putting the card back in his lab coat pocket, his fingers felt an old photograph he had put there earlier in the day while cleaning his office. The snapshot was slightly faded, and torn at one corner. It showed Strickland and his high school pal Altman, posing together on their motorcycles. They had rolled their T-shirt sleeves up over their cigarette packs and were doing their best James Dean and Marlon Brando poses. But it wasn't their youthful bravado that captivated Strickland. It was the look in Altman's eyes—preternaturally wise and filled with a transcendent energy.

As he gazed at the photograph, Strickland suddenly realized that Altman's striking aura wasn't entirely due to his college drug experiences. The core of what he had become had always been there; Strickland had simply failed to perceive it before.

He was suddenly distracted from this reverie by the completion of the data-rendering process on the RES-5000. It should have taken hours longer. He checked for error messages, wondering if the process had somehow aborted. But then he remembered that Randall had mentioned installing a bank of parallel coprocessors that would speed computation times by a factor of ten.

After double-checking the latch on the lab door, he activated the display sequence. In the darkness, the Shroud image materialized on the large wall-mounted display. The visage shimmered with energy. Once again, Strickland stared in awe into the eyes of a sage imbued with indescribable mystery.

But what gave the image such awe-inspiring power? The figure was everything Strickland had remembered. But he realized now that the power of this image—its inner light—was not entirely unique. The old creased photo of Altman had been the key. There were similarities in the gaze. He hadn't registered it before, but it was clear to him now—the same seed existed in others as well, perhaps just waiting to be developed and nurtured.

IV

Chapter 151

Two months later

Strickland filled another set of packing boxes, then sealed them with tape. The task of vacating his office at the NIH seemed never-ending. Every niche and corner contained books, papers, and memorabilia. In a bottom drawer, he found his original job offer to Randall and, under it, Randall's acceptance letter. He put both in a folder of personal correspondence.

In spite of Strickland's many accomplishments and contributions, it was clear that upper management was relieved to see him go. His presence was a constant reminder of a chapter in NIH history that everyone would prefer to forget.

Director Burnham had offered a perfunctory pat on the back in response to his surprise announcement. "We'll be sorry to see you go, Bob," he said. "You've been an invaluable asset to the Institutes." But Strickland noted that there were no questions regarding what might change his mind.

He opened his briefcase and returned Tellison's lab notebook to a locked steel filing cabinet. In the intervening weeks, after countless rereadings, he had gradually made sense of most of the book's entries. Tellison's cloning technologies were staggering in their complexity and sophistication. And in the process of developing these procedures, he had made truly brilliant leaps in the basic understanding of genetic molecular biology.

Tellison had discovered new and vital roles for riboswitches, which were part of a wave of newly discovered epigenetic regulatory mechanisms. Riboswitches were small strands of folded RNA that became translated into protein only in the presence of a specific target chemical or protein. These "trigger" substances effectively turned on the genetic information contained within a given riboswitch. But Tellison had uncovered something far more important than the pervasive functionality of riboswitches: he had discovered an entirely new layer of epigenetic information.

The complexity and elegance of biological systems had long seemed to defy the small percentage of the genome devoted to actual protein production. Recently revealed epigenetic layers, illuminating a vast array of regulatory mechanisms, had helped explain the obvious complexity of the human organism. But the story seemed far from complete.

From the notebook, Strickland learned that Tellison had discovered an entirely separate epigenetic mechanism for storing information in DNA, based on "shifting the read frame." Reading any information, whether text or DNA, was based on knowing where to start and stop. It had long been recognized that palindromes existed in genomes, particularly within certain human cancers. These were genetic sequences that read the same way forward and backward. Perhaps the best-known text palindrome was "Madam, I'm Adam"—with the punctuation and spaces removed, the phrase said the same thing in either direction. No one knew exactly what function genetic palindromes served. But Tellison's discoveries went far beyond the relative simplicity of such anomalies. He had discovered instances where separately transcribed and translated genetic sequences were contained within the *same segment* of DNA. It was like burying multiple coded messages within seemingly mundane text. To access this secondary information, one need only know where to start and stop. For instance, the phrase, "I am one, yes," also contained the word "money" and the phrase "I am on." It was the same principle that led some to claim that coded prophesies were hidden within Biblical scripture.

Tellison's read-frame discoveries took the concept of epigenetics to an entirely new level. Who knew how many different layers of information lay buried within a given genetic sequence? Strickland suspected that if Tellison had made these discoveries under the auspices of a traditional academic institution, he likely would have been nominated for a Nobel Prize.

Now Strickland wondered what to *do* with the information. His instinct was to do nothing in the short term, then research what portions of the discoveries Tellison might have already submitted to scientific journals, and what portions he might have licensed or sold to private-sector companies. He decided that in the near future he would hire an attorney to contact Tellison's heirs, and ask permission to summarize the discoveries in appropriate journals, under Tellison's name.

He pulled the notebook from the filing cabinet and fanned through the hundreds of pages of now familiar text. While several loose ends within the journal continued to tug at him, at the same time it seemed like the ephemera of another lifetime—as did Strickland's own work at the NIH. If the director had asked him what they might do to change his mind, his answer would have been an unqualified "Nothing." He felt no ambivalence whatever about his decision.

It had also been odd to read about himself and Bender in Tellison's notes. To his amazement, the notebook also contained personal thoughts and observations.

"*There has to be something wrong with this guy if he hasn't made it with her,*" Tellison had scribbled shortly after their arrival on the island.

And maybe Tellison was right, he reflected. Maybe there *was* something wrong with him. The observation was just a step away from comments Randall had made in the past about Strickland's relationships with women.

In another section of the notes, Tellison had fantasized about Bender—apparently after a late-night snack with her in the compound. "*She's tightly wound,*" he noted, "*but beneath the surface, there's something sensual and untamed. Under the right circumstances, who knows?*"

The one remaining mystery in the notebook was Tellison's occasional cryptic references to "*the exogenous sequences.*" These entries seemed to have been unusually scribbled, as if in an intentional attempt to make them illegible to anyone but the writer. But what could he have been referring to?

Chapter 152

Step by step, the FBI and CIA mapped out the organizational hierarchy of the Army of the Lord. Even the most conservative American evangelical churches had strongly condemned the organization and its actions, and as a result, a series of anonymous tips concerning the group came pouring in.

Ironically, a teenage girl from the founder's church congregation delivered the decisive blow. Having frequently babysat for the family, she revealed that the founder had been amassing bomb-making materials and small arms on his rural compound. In an early-morning raid, ATF and FBI agents seized the site, arresting fourteen people without incident.

No one in the organization's inner circle would reveal specific plans for the cache of weapons recovered, but personal computers confiscated in the raid soon provided sufficient evidence to implicate Army of the Lord members in the bombing of Strickland's car as well as in the death of Bender's boyfriend, Thomas Aruldoss.

And when looking at the same punishment they had so eagerly meted out to others, the apprehended members quickly started talking. Soon those in the upper echelon were freely implicating one another in the effort to avoid the death penalty. The group's leader and three top lieutenants were ultimately given life sentences without the possibility of parole, and five others received sentences of thirty years.

After being decapitated, the Army of the Lord quickly imploded. Many of its harder-core members simply went into hiding, while others aligned themselves with less extreme groups. Several of the more moderate members had a change of heart and actively denounced organizations where "belief turns to extremism." One former member, a part-time St. Louis minister, delivered a fiery televised sermon in which he declared that his former group had been "cut from the same cloth as al-Qaeda," and urged that religious extremists of all faiths "take a long hard look at themselves."

Chapter 153

Strickland pulled another late-night marathon of filing and packing in his NIH office. As he took a break, he gazed at the locked cabinet where Tellison's notebook was stored. Despite all his efforts to let go, the document continued to exert an almost magnetic pull, and soon it was again open on the desk.

With repeated readings, he had become more and more familiar with Tellison's chaotic scrawling. Words and phrases that had once seemed indecipherable gradually fell into place. But the occasional references to the "exogenous sequences" continued to trouble him. He had already checked Tellison's flash memory device, but hadn't found any clues there. The data seemed to be part of a weekly backup process for Tellison's PC.

Checking the flash stick again, Strickland browsed through Tellison's "desktop" folder, a repository for work that had not yet been moved to other directories. The folder was sparsely populated: several to-do lists, notes on planned laboratory hardware upgrades, a series of graphics files, and a single encrypted file. The graphics files were labeled sequentially: *chimera_1.jpg*, *chimera_2.jpg*, *chimera_3.jpg*, *chimera_4.jpg*, and *chimera_5.jpg*.

When Strickland opened the first of the files, it appeared to be nothing more than a field of randomly recurring characters. After repeated readings, he failed to discern any technical meaning to the text, and it certainly made no poetic sense.

It had been a long day of packing. Strickland paused to remove his glasses and rub his eyes. Glancing at the desk clock, he saw that it was nearly 11:30 P.M., and decided to head home. Looking back at the on-screen text image, his vision fell momentarily out of focus. As it did, the words began to drift in his visual field, like rafts riding up over one another. Strickland reveled in the experience for a moment, imagining that he was floating in the familiar warm waters of his condominium pool, gazing at the glowing latticework of light.

Suddenly, a remarkable optical illusion emerged from the random sea of letters. He saw two overlapping rectangles, floating in 3-D above the plane of the background text.

He realized at once that the file was a crude stereogram—and that Tellison had intentionally processed the words to produce this effect. It was similar to a technique used in several of Strickland's premed textbooks as a means of visualizing three-dimensional organic molecules. If you crossed your eyes, two slightly different perspectives of a molecule would fuse together into a three-dimensional whole.

```
\vFGS\,h:Jw~!+½m:I\vFGS\,h:Jw~!+½m:I\vFGS\,h:Jw~!+½m:I\vFGS\,h:Jw~!+½m:I\vFGS\,h:Jw~!+½m:I\vF
Ulq:Pe$(+!*KbTw~EbUlq:Pe$(+!*KbTw~EbUlq:Pe$(+!*KbTw~EbUlq:Pe$(+!*KbTw~EbUlq:Pe$(+!*KbTw~EbUlq
|TkTVScI:X<bZJDd!,|TkTVScI:X<bZJDd!,|TkTVScI:X<bZJDd!,|TkTVScI:X<bZJDd!,|TkTVScI:X<bZJDd!,|Tk
~0":8QinHo_t4g?vEi~0":8QinH_t4g?vEi~0":8QinH_t4g?vEi~0":8QinH_t4g?vEi~0":8QQinH_t4g?vEi~0":8Q
n!Zi(aLi\_qwU%01^en!Zi(aLi\qwU%01^en!Zi(aLi\qwU%01^en!Zi(aLi\qwU%01^en!Zi(aaLi\qwU%01^en!Zi(a
pzy!'V>CPYS}({J];%pzy!'V>CPS}({J];%pzy!'V>CPS}({J];%pzy!'VV>CPS}({J];%pzy!'VV>CPS}({J];%pzy!'V
?b.Ugr\IE@00B5R?00?b.Ugr\IE@00B5R?00?b.Ugr\IE@00B5R?00?b.Ugr\IE@00B5R?00?b.Ugr\IE@00B5R?00?b.Ugr
n<86y;O$#\n4E<xvOYn<86y;O$#n4E<xvOYn<86y;O$#n4E<xvOYn<86y;O$#n4E<xvOYn<86y;O$#n4E<xvOYn<86y;
BnD<K91kRU{bCcmSt6BnD<K91kR{bCcmSt6BnD<K91kR{bCcmSt6BnD<K91kR{bCcmSt6BnD<K991kR{bCcmSt6BnD<K9
0o+FE@EOWSkX'Ms?hS0o+FE@EOWkX'Ms?hS0o+FE@EOWkX'Ms?hS0o+FE@EOWkX'Ms?hS0o+FE@EOWkX'Ms?hS0o+FE@
2*`4WPr&Jg3n\1q;<=2*`4WPr&J3n\1q;<=2*`4WPr&J3n1q;<=2*`4WPr&J3n1q;<=2*`4WPr&J3n1q;<=2*`4WPr&J3
>YR<Plm#nUb.G3j/mz>YR<Plm#nb.G3j/mz>YR<Plm#nb.3j/mz>YR<Plm#nb.3j/mz>YR<Plm#nb.3j/mz>YR<Plm#nb
wpfN\v/bto]^y&{z_CwpfN\v/bt]^y&{z_CwpfN\v/bt]^&{z_CwpfN\v/bt]^&{z_CwpfN\v/bt]^&{z_CwpfN\v/bt]
o,vP*T6'<tagSzBD}o,vP*T6'tagSzBD}o,vP*T6'taSzBD}o,vP*T6'taSzBD}o,vP*T6'taSzBD}o,vP*T6't
q,m`%}3~}yMv2Q4T}=q,m`%}3~}Mv2Q4T}=q,m`%}3~}Mv2Q4T}=q,m`%}3~|MvQ4T}=q,m`%}3~|MvQ4T}=q,m`%}3~|M
avut2r1~}P'oGX nR<avut2r1~}'oGX nR<avut2r1~}'oX nR<avut2r1~}'oX nR<avut2r1~}'oX nR<avut2r1~}'
TF0=96#"QQ<)xcc0'CTF0=96#"Q<)xcc0'CTF0=96#"Q<)cc0'CTF0=96#"Q<)cc0'CTF0=96#"Q<)cc0'CTF0=96#"Q<
[zL?]Fc$M?~8v}jt5^[zL?]Fc$M~8v}jt5^[zL?]Fc$M-8}jt5^[zL?]Fc$M-8}jt5^[zL?]Fc$M-8}jt5^[zL?]Fc$M-
h3in%,gk'~?s3=zUi h3in%,gk'?s3=zUi h3in%,gk'?s=zUi h3in%,gk'?s=zUi h3in%,gk'?s=zUi h3in%,gk'?
wf8i66dc]X-4!$R-rowf8i66dc]-4!$R-rowf8i66dc]-4$R-rowf8i66dc]-4$R-rowf8i66dc]-4$R-rowf8i66dc]-
4/6_+IdT_Lpf2:2%*k4/6_+IdT_pf2:2%*k4/6_+IdT_pf:2%*k4/6_+IdT_p:2%*k4/6_+IdT_p:2%*k4/6_+IdT_p
@R)Ld2%/1Rx?KWDDDi@R)Ld2%/1Rx?KWDDDi@R)Ld2%/1RKWDDDi@R)Ld2%/1RKWDDDi@R)Ld2%/1RKWDDDi@R)Ld2%/1
.>"er\{QwJusavKa"1.>"er\{QwJusavKa"1.>"er\{QwJavKa"1.>"er\{QwJavKa"1.>"er\{QwJavKa"1.>"er\{Qw
;nvOF+N$cZ|Vs~byEy;nvOF+N$cZ|Vs~byEy;nvOF+N$cZs~byEy;nvOF+N$cZs~byEy;nvOF+N$cZs~byEy;nvOF+N$c
5YzxWkvfEs5<G!P[+#5YzxWkvfEs5<G!P[+#5YzxWkvfEsG!P[+#5YzxWkvfEsG!P[+#5YzxWkvfEsG!P[+#5YzxWkvfE
>qeWiJEQRe_U c~-L >qeWiJEQRe_U c~-L >qeWiJEQRe c~-L >qeWiJEQRe c~-L >qeWiJEQRe c~-L >qeWiJEQR
PWm0}N>21CS8)QXih3PWm0}N>21CS8)QXih3PWm0}N>21C)QXih3PWm0}N>21C)QXih3PWm0}N>21C)QXih3PWm0}N>21
1Z4 M_zL~W"#0iY*hcl1Z4 M_zL~W"#0iY*hcl1Z4 M_zL~W"#0iY*hcl1Z4 M_zL~W"#0iY*hcl1Z4 M_zL~W"#0iY*hcl1Z4
oREG4.R76httF3!]DkoREG4.R76httF3!]DkoREG4.R76httF3!]DkoREG4.R76httF3!]DkoRE
uyKzR';%c8j]xsCi(~uyKzR';%c8j]xsCi(~uyKzR';%c8j]xsCi(~uyKzR';%c8j]xsCi(~uyK
HJ\,{Qp8WqG(fa;W):HJ\,{Qp8WqG(fa;W):HJ\,{Qp8WqG(fa;W):HJ\,{Qp8WqG(fa;W):HJ\
he>gOyNJ4_!'{e,~Ihe>gOyNJ4_!'{e,~Ihe>gOyNJ4_!'{e,~Ihe>gOyNJ4_!'{e,~Ihe>gOyNJ4_!'{e,~Ihe>
^X.t3J<KUK:\ifo&R1^X.t3J<KUK:\ifo&R1^X.t3J<KUK:\ifo&R1^X.t3J<KUK:\ifo&R1^X.t3J<KUK:\ifo&R1^X.
```

Strickland opened the second file in the series. The text itself was composed of variations on the genetic alphabet, ATCG, along with the repeated phrases "armored island" and "tiny monsters." When he again crossed his eyes, the text produced Tellison's initials, "M T," in large block letters, floating above the jumble of words.

Tellison had apparently been experimenting with a stereogram-generating software package. Each new file in the series proved more sophisticated than the last. And with each viewing, Strickland found it easier to experience the effect. It was almost as if his eyes now *intuited* what they needed to do.

In the last file of the series, it was harder to discern any stereographic effect. The words didn't seem to form a significantly larger body as they had before. Strickland momentarily spotted a single floating island of text, which obscured portions of the words beneath it. Then he lost his focus— or lack of it—and the text dissolved back into the sea of words.

Through force of will, he finally regained the desired slightly out-

```
_____I_____I_____I_____I_____I_____
=>ATCG*ArmoredI=>ATCG*ArmoredI=>ATCG*ArmoredI=>ATCG*ArmoredI=>ATCG*ArmoredI=>ATC
slands>TinyMonsslands>TinyMonsslands>TinyMonsslands>TinyMonsslands>TinyMonssland
ters!=>ATCG*Armters!=>ATCG*Armters!=>ATCG*Armters!=>ATCG*Armters!=>ATCG*Armters!
oredIslands>TinoredIslands>TinoredIslands>TinoredIslands>TinoredIslands>TinoredI
yMonsters!=>ATCyMonsters!=>ATCyMosters!!=>ATCyMoters!!!=>ACyMoters!!!!=>ACyMMoter
G*ArmoredIslandG*ArmoredIslandG*AmoredIsslandG*moredIsssladG*moredIsssladG**more
s>TinyMonsteers!s>TinyMonsters!s>TnyMonsters!sTnyMonstteer!sTnyMonsttteer!sTTnyMo
=>ATCG*ArmoredI=>ATCG*ArmoredI=>ACG*ArmooreedI>ACG*ArmooreedI>ACGArmoooreedI>ACGA
slands>TinyMonsslands>TinyMonsslads>TTnyMonnsladssTTnyyMonnsladsTTnyyyMonnsladsT
ters!=>ATCG*Armters!=>ATCG*Armter!=>AATG*Armter!!=AATGG*Armter!!AATGGG*Armter!!A
oredIslands>TinoredIslands>TinoreIslaand>TinoreeIsaandd>TinoreeIaanddd>TinoreeIa
yMonsters!=>ATCyMonsters!=>ATCyMosterrs!=ATCyMMostrrs!!=ATCyMMosrrs!!!=ATCyMMosr
G*ArmoredIslandG*ArmoredIslandG*AmoreedIslndGG*AmoeedIIslndGG*AmeedIIIslndGG*Ame
s>TinyMonsters!s>TinyMonsters!s>TnyMoonster!!s>Tnyoonsster!!s>Tnoonsssster!!s>Tno
=>ATCG*ArmoredI=>ATCG*ArmoredI=>ACG*AArmoredI=>ACGAArmmoredI=>ACAArmmmoredI=>ACA
slands>TinyMonsslands>TinyMonsslads>TTinyMonssladsTTinnyMonssladTTinnnyMonssladT
ters!=>ATCG*Armters!=>ATCG*Armter!=>ATCG*Armter!=>AATCCG*Armter!AATCCCG*Armter!A
oredIslands>TinoredIslands>TinoreIslaands>TinoreIsaandds>TinoreIaanddds>TinoreIa
yMonsters!=>ATCyMonsters!=>ATCyMosterrs!=>ATCyMostrrs!!=>ATCyMosrrs!!!=>ATCyMosr
G*ArmoredIslandG*ArmoredIslandG*ArmoredIslandG*ArmoredIslandG*ArmoredIslandG*Arm
s>TinyMonsters!s>TinyMonsters!s>TinyMonsters!s>TinyMonsters!s>TinyMonsters!s>Tin
=>ATCG*ArmoredI=>ATCG*ArmoredI=>ATCG*ArmoredI=>ATCG*ArmoredI=>ATCG*ArmoredI=>ATC
slands>TinyMonsslands>TinyMonsslands>TinyMonsslands>TinyMonsslands>TinyMonssland
ters!=>ATCG*Armters!=>ATCG*Armters!=>ATCG*Armters!=>ATCG*Armters!=>ATCG*Armters!
oredIslands>TinoredIslands>TinoredIslands>TinoredIslands>TinoredIslands>TinoredI
_____I_____I_____I_____I_____I_____
```

of-phase visual state. And there, above the sea of jumbled words, hovered the phrase "use: zyzzyva."

Strickland stared crosseyed at the odd message, long enough that anyone watching would have thought him deranged. What could it mean?

```
lude the as include the as include the as include the as include the as include
ute a right minute a right minute a right minute a right minute a right minute
wn year left down year left down year left down year left down year left down y
mpiler error compiler error compiler error compiler error compiler error compil
econd month i second month i second month i second month i second month i secon
using face her using face her using face her using face her using face her usin
they use: tart they use: tart the use: start the use: start the use: start the
it at zyzzyva pit at zyzzyva pit a zyzzyva spit a zyzzyva spit a zyzzyva spit a
lude the as include the as include the as include the as include the as include
ute a right minute a right minute a right minute a right minute a right minute
wn year left down year left down year left down year left down year left down y
mpiler error compiler error compiler error compiler error compiler error compil
econd month i second month i second month i second month i second month i secon
using face her using face her using face her using face her using face her usin
lude the as include the as include the as include the as include the as include
ute a right minute a right minute a right minute a right minute a right minute
wn year left down year left down year left down year left down year left down y
mpiler error compiler error compiler error compiler error compiler error compil
econd month i second month i second month i second month i second month i secon
using face her using face her using face her using face her using face her usin
```

Then he suddenly remembered the encrypted file in the desktop folder. Opening that folder again, he double-clicked on the file. When the system asked for an encryption key, he typed in "zyzzyva." Permission denied. Then he hit the caps key and typed in "ZYZZYVA," and the file opened.

It contained pages and pages of procedural notes referencing the "exogenous sequences." He flipped back through Tellison's notebook to the part comparing the cumulative sequence lengths with those on the smart card. Then he grabbed several sheets of blank paper and began furiously scribbling notes, cross-correlating Tellison's references to the actual sequence numbers of the embryos. The clincher was a seemingly innocuous reference in the notebook to the "Tel-1 sequence builds," and their subsequent incorporation into the Shroud DNA.

"The exogenous sequences," he whispered to himself.

* * *

Dawn came, and Strickland barely noticed as he pored over the notebook and the decrypted file, now and then leafing back through the pages of handwritten notes that he had scribbled during the night. Why had Tellison stored the encryption key in the stereogram? The man had a steel-trap memory, perhaps better than any Strickland had ever known. The only explanation was that he had left this trail for someone else to find—in one final and perhaps hastily executed gesture, he had wanted Strickland to know everything in the event of a worst-case scenario.

* * *

A soft knock came at the door, and Strickland raised his head from the desktop. He rubbed his blurry eyes and checked the clock: 9:06 A.M. The morning sun was already high outside his office window.

The knock came again. "Dr. Strickland?" It was George.

"Uh, yes," Strickland said, clearing his throat.

"Sorry to interrupt, but you have a visitor. It's Sara Bender."

"Shit!" Strickland muttered, scrambling to his feet and checking himself in a small mirror on the wall. He looked like hell.

"Um, tell her I'll be with her in a few minutes...I'm just finishing up with something."

Chapter 154

Strickland heard Bender chatting with George in the hall. He glanced around him; the office looked like a storage unit. After smoothing back his tousled hair with both hands, he buzzed George on the phone.

Bender came in, wearing a loose-fitting cotton print dress. Her hair had grown out a bit and was back to its natural dark brown. She looked radiant.

"Hey, stranger," she said, grinning. *"¿Qué tal?"*

Before he could react, she put down her shoulder bag and kissed him on the cheek. She looked around at the office, taking in the boxes and disarray, but didn't comment.

"I hope this isn't a bad time," she said.

"No, no, it's fine," he replied, feeling as frazzled as he looked.

Bender's eyes lit up. She extracted a massive bound manuscript from her bag and flopped it down on the table. The front page read simply, "The Shroud."

"It's only a draft," she said. "I was hoping you might take a look, to make sure I haven't made any glaring technical errors."

Strickland picked up the manuscript and skimmed the first paragraph, then leafed through the pages, pausing briefly on the section devoted to the first viewing of the Shroud data with the RES-5000 system. He also paused on the chapter detailing their arrival at Tellison's compound.

"Impressive," he said. "How on earth did you write it in just a few months?"

"I'd been working steadily during the entire project," she said. "And I regularly archived my work online. So the only new material had to do with our time in Belize. I wrote that in San Miguel de Allende over the past six weeks or so. Then it was just a matter of fitting all the disparate pieces together—sort of the shotgun method."

Strickland closed the manuscript. "I can't wait to read it. Congratulations!"

"Thanks." She was beaming.

There was a brief silence as their eyes met.

"I was *so* worried about you," he said.

"Didn't you get my message from Angela?"

"I did, and it helped . . . some."

"You're forgetting that I've dodged bullets and gone through minefields for a living. I'm a pretty tough girl."

"Yeah, I've seen you in action." Strickland smiled. "Even so . . ." He just gazed at her for a moment. "When did you get back?"

"A few weeks ago. I missed Tom's funeral while we were on the island, so I had some things to sort out. I had my own memorial for him last week. His family scattered his ashes off Long Island while I was away. So I sat on the beach at sunset, played some of his favorite music on a boom box, and read some of his favorite poetry. Afterward, at dusk, I burned the poems and watched the embers drift up into the sky."

Her eyes had a faraway look. "It was bittersweet, and strange, feeling so close to the infinite. I'm not really sure what I believe happens after we die. But I felt as if Tom and I were truly connected in that moment."

Strickland sighed. "I still blame myself."

"Don't," she said, dabbing at her eyes. "I've done a lot of thinking about this. No one could have predicted all that happened. Besides, you looked out for me when it really mattered, and Tom would have respected that."

"Thank you. I've been going over and over it. What you've just said means a lot to me." Strickland paused. "So . . . I'm surprised to see you back in D.C."

"I had some loose ends to tie up," she said. "As you may recall, I was in the process of moving out of my place when you and I took an impromptu Caribbean vacation. Fortunately, my landlady put my things in storage. Plus, there were a few geographic details in and around D.C. that I wanted to review for the book. . . . Also, there was someone I wanted to see."

Strickland smiled.

"So, enough about me," she said. "What's happening with you?"

"Pretty big news, I suppose," he said. "I'm leaving the NIH."

"From the looks of your office, I had a feeling something big was in the works."

"It is. I don't quite know how to verbalize it, but a *seed* was planted back in Belize, and during the past few months it's been steadily growing. . . ."

She leaned forward in her chair. "Tell me more."

After taking a moment to gather his thoughts, Strickland said, "Remember on the beach, when we were talking about being 'wired for God'?"

Bender nodded.

"I think the mistake most people make is expecting some sort of spiritual epiphany—a profound awakening, with shafts of light through the clouds, and trumpet fanfares. But I think it rarely happens that way. More often, it's a slow burn—smoldering embers that one day simply catch fire."

He stopped, groping for the right words, but Bender's eyes urged him on. "I can't quite put my finger on it," he said, "and I don't know exactly how it happened, but I can *feel* a presence now. Like I never have before. It's the strangest thing—we built it, and he *did* come. But not from the outside, from within."

"I'd like to hear more," she said.

"How much time have you got?"

"The whole afternoon."

Chapter 155

Strickland picked up Tellison's notebook and led Bender through the labyrinthine halls of the Ethnogenomics Center, stopping finally at the RES-5000 room. Glancing up and down the hallway as they approached the door, he hurried them both inside, then locked the door and booted up the RES-5000 system.

Bender looked around her. "It's so strange to be back here," she said. "It was only a few months ago, but it feels like eons."

"Yeah, same here. Pull up a chair."

They sat down, and he said, "I've been studying Tellison's lab notes ever since I got back."

"And what did you find?"

"It's impressive stuff—in some cases, staggeringly so. Remember when we discussed epigenetics?"

"Sure," Bender said. "Pseudogenes, antisense RNA, microRNAs, riboswitches . . ."

"You have a formidable memory," Strickland said.

She laughed. "Thanks. I'm a reporter, remember?"

"The thing is," he continued, "Tellison's work takes the science of epigenetics a quantum leap forward, particularly in his recognition of the importance of riboswitches in early gestational differentiation."

"But if this notebook was all about his work during our time on the island, why all the references to epigenetic discoveries?" she asked.

"My sequencing of the Shroud sample wasn't cut short by the car bombing in D.C.," Strickland replied. "I had everything I needed by that time—or so I thought. But through his cloning work, Tellison uncovered previously unrecognized epigenetic regions. And he learned that those regions are essential for early cellular differentiation to occur."

Bender looked baffled.

"In his notes, I found several cryptic references to 'exogenous sequences,' along with their specific chromosomal locations. Once I analyzed things more thoroughly, I realized those regions weren't in the data I had brought to the island on the smart card."

"Then where did they come from?"

"He called them the *Tel-1* sequences," Strickland said, looking intently at her.

"My God," she whispered. "Mixing in his own DNA—that's a truly scary notion."

"In the end, it wasn't much—less than .01 percent of the total genome. By our current understanding of genetics, it would still have been a genetic duplicate of whoever once lay beneath the Shroud of Turin. But it's enough to give you pause. And it made me think even more about how obsessed I had gotten with bringing a clone to fruition. I lost sight of the idea that the appearance of Jesus, or any great avatar, is a singular event in history, inextricable from the fabric of that time and place, and is carried forward in people's minds in ways that transcend the flesh and blood of any one person, no matter how divinely inspired they may have been. The avatar comes to live in the collective consciousness of millions of people, going forward seemingly indefinitely."

"Beautifully put. I agree completely."

"Through the whole endeavor, maybe, on some level, I didn't *want* to know how Tellison worked his magic—I just wanted to believe."

"Don't be too hard on yourself," Bender said. "I should tell you that I've engaged in some selective amnesia in the book—particularly about having volunteered to be the embryo implantation subject."

"Not a problem," said Strickland. "That's in keeping with the *selective* summary I gave to the feds. But what I've told you so far isn't all of it. Just before the attack on the compound, I caught Tellison teasing off cells from the cloned embryos. He claimed to be freezing them as backup, in case something went wrong with the primary incubation. But in his private office, I found an invoice from a firm in the Philippines, promising a payment of twenty million dollars U.S. in return for safe delivery of the embryos."

She shook her head and sighed. "The man was a world-class chaos generator."

"Tellison always pushed the envelope," Strickland mused, "in science and in ethics. Research compounds like his don't just appear out of the ethers. I'm sure he felt that a Faustian bargain here and there simply went with the territory."

"Do you think he actually delivered any embryos?" Bender asked.

"No, I don't. He stored the teased-off cells just hours before the attack. I can't imagine, in the bustle of that time, that he was able to organize the shipment. I suspect they died with him."

"I hope so," Bender said, giving him a worried look.

Strickland turned to the RES-5000 console and typed in an encryption key. "Which brings me to something I've been considering for a while."

Opening the encrypted data file, he clicked on the "Display" button. Bender froze as the Shroud image came to life on the wall-mounted RES panel.

"Bob . . . how? I thought the data had been destroyed!"

"I still have the smart card."

"But I thought you'd moved past all this."

"I have, but I wanted to see it one more time. As long as this data exists, someone will always be tempted," he said thoughtfully, as if convincing himself to take the final step.

Taking out his wallet, he removed the Shroud smart card and plugged it into the RES-5000. It immediately appeared as a device icon on the console screen.

He typed in "Select Smart Drive 1," and the smart card's icon highlighted and began flashing.

"Encryption key required for access to this device," replied a synthesized voice.

Strickland reeled off the string of characters: "03A5G7749P68M."

"Accepted," the system replied.

Pausing to center himself, he commanded, "Delete all data."

"This command will delete all data on device Smart Drive One," the system's voice warned. "Please confirm by saying 'Yes' within five seconds."

Hesitating, he looked over at Bender. She nodded.

"Yes," he commanded.

"Data from device Smart Drive 1 deleted," the system informed them a moment later.

"There's still one more loose end," Strickland noted. "The reanimation image that I just showed you came from a previously rendered file, which is still on the RES-5000."

Bender watched as he again commanded the system to delete the file. But at the final step, he paused, as if something in him couldn't quite let go. Bender's eyes locked on to his. His jaw tightened, and a moment later, the file was gone.

Chapter 156

Back in Strickland's office, Bender glanced again at the stacks of sealed moving boxes. "So . . . what's next?" she asked.

He smiled. "Remember that night on the beach, when we talked about the idea of a spiritual antenna?"

"Yeah, I do," she said. "It was a little out there, but fascinating."

"Well, I'd like to explore that sort of thing scientifically and see where it takes me. I've been in talks with Jordan. We're going to establish a research institute to investigate the biophysiology of spirituality."

Bender gave him a bemused look.

"I'm serious," he said. "Science is usually in the position of *challenging* spiritual belief. But we want to use the scientific method to explore the spiritual experience in a rigorous way, with none of the usual soft-science mumbo jumbo. What brain regions and neurotransmitters are involved in transcendent experiences? If there is a spiritual antenna, how does it work? Clearly, prayer and meditation can alter individual physiology, but can they also somehow affect the physical world at large? And can consciousness exist at some level *outside* of the brain? More than a handful of respectable studies seem to actually support these notions. We want to explore the principles involved—the physiological structures, the neurotransmitters, the physics."

She smiled at his boyish enthusiasm. "Amazing stuff."

"There's even federal money for this kind of work, if it's done the right way and by the right people," he continued. "We already have a preliminary group of test subjects lined up: Buddhist monks, Catholic priests, rabbis, and Muslim clerics."

Bender laughed. "Boy, the Vatican's going to love you guys."

"At this point, I think they'll be happy to have us concentrating on something more theoretical," Strickland said, gesturing toward a table covered with textbooks on clinical neuroanatomy, medical imaging, and neuropharmacology. "This will be a return to my broader medical roots. And our investigations will open up whole new hardware vistas for Jordan."

"I'm really happy for you," said Bender, touching his hand.

"The Shroud data set me on a new path, and I want to continue exploring it," he said. "But as I studied the RES image and really started contemplating it, I began to realize that what we perceived in the image is not unique. I've noticed a similar presence in other people—I just never recognized it before. I even sensed a certain aspect of what I'm talking about in that guy on the boat in Belize."

Bender smiled at the mention of Eduardo. "It's strange," she said, "I know exactly what you mean. There *was* something almost saintly in his gaze."

"So how do we quantify things like that and study them?" Strickland posed. "We still have to work that out. But the bottom line is, we have certain behaviors and tendencies for a reason. Nature doesn't waste resources. Opium and similar drugs affect us the way they do because we have neural receptors for them. But it wasn't until 1975 that researchers discovered exactly why. It turns out we produce naturally occurring analogues to those compounds—the endorphins, our own endogenous painkillers."

"But how's that related to spirituality?" she asked.

"Analogous to the endorphin receptors, our brains seem hardwired for transcendent experiences. Human beings have been seeking those experiences since the dawn of time—through prayer, chanting, meditation, drugs. That's why God *won't* go away, even after centuries of rational materialism. Some might argue that spiritual tendencies are simply survival mechanisms to help us to deal with the existential conundrum of our own mortality. But these are the kinds of questions and issues I want to explore. The interface between our inner and outer worlds is one of the last great frontiers of science. After all, everything we perceive—you, me, this room, the tulip tree out front—is really just a shared and agreed-upon cerebral construct. A bouquet of red roses is red only because our hard wiring agrees to call it that, based on a particular wavelength of reflected light."

"Gee, thanks for knocking all the romance out of a dozen roses," Bender said, grinning.

Chapter 157

An awkward silence filled the room. Strickland smiled wistfully at Bender, and she returned his gaze, each waiting for the other to make the next move.

"I've also been doing a lot of thinking about that night on the beach," said Bender. "I . . ." The tears welled up, and she couldn't continue. She looked at him, wiping one eye with the back of her hand, and tried to force a smile.

An eternity seemed to pass between them. Then something in Strickland finally gave. "I've missed you so much, Sara."

"I've missed you, too," she said, and all the tension poured out with her tears as they fell into each other's arms and kissed.

When they pulled away, she said, "There's something I have to tell you."

"You've taken a foreign assignment?" he asked, feeling a twinge of dread.

"No, that's not it," she said, smiling with sudden shyness. "Speaking of *seeds* being planted that night on the beach . . ."

Strickland's eyes widened—at first with disbelief, then with joy. He took her in his arms again.

"In Honduras, I started feeling sick to my stomach. At first, I thought it might have been something I ate. But by the time I got to Isla de las Mujeres, just the thought of certain foods started to make me ill. I finally picked up a test kit—three weeks ago in San Miguel de Allende."

"That's right," Strickland said, thinking back. "Tellison said you'd ovulated right around that night on the beach."

She pulled back from their embrace. "So, you're okay with this?"

"Much more than okay," he replied.

Chapter 158

One year later

Strickland called toward the open kitchen window, "Honey, could you bring some more buns when you get a chance?" More friends had shown up for the backyard barbecue than either of them anticipated, and he was surrounded by a hungry throng.

Through the window he saw Sara, juggling the baby in one arm and answering her cell phone. She was in deadline mode, and her editor had been calling daily. Even so, she managed a smile and gave Strickland the thumbs-up that more hamburger buns were on the way.

He turned his attention back to a group of friends standing in front of the grill. "Umm, where was I?" he said as he flipped salmon steaks and burgers and painted more olive oil on the strips of red pepper and zucchini. "Oh . . . when relativity and quantum physics came along, it changed the whole fabric of scientific inquiry. Newton had only *part* of the picture: simple actions and reactions. His universe was like a billiard table, and that worked fine—for a while. But it took twentieth-century paradigm shifts for physicists to begin imagining curved space, the relativity of time, solid matter having a wave component, black holes, and string theory. So maybe, when it comes to spiritual understanding, we're still in the Newtonian era."

He paused to offload a batch of grilled veggies.

"In addition to studying members of different faiths while they're engaged in meditation or devotional practices, we're also hoping to find subjects who have undergone some sort of life-changing spiritual or religious transformation," he added. "Of course, we'll need before-and-after data for that. But how many normal, healthy people have had brain scans? So experimental design will be challenging."

"I'm curious," said Brooks, an athletically built former colleague from the NIH. "Given your previous involvement with the Shroud of Turin study, do you see this endeavor as fulfilling some sort of *mission*? And if so, isn't that antithetical to hard science?"

"Our spiritual interests are certainly one motivation for the research," Strickland replied. "But that won't compromise our objectivity.

The funding charter requires rigorous double-blind experimental design. Any results we might come up with are worthless if the design is flawed. And rigorous study is what this is all about. Look at the advances that occurred in medicine once the scientific method was applied. Before that, our well-being was determined by demons and angels, ethers, humors, and the stars. What if we're in a similar state when it comes to spirituality? After all, the knowledge base has remained essentially unchanged since the early Middle Ages. Wouldn't it be ironic if modern scientific inquiry, the end result of rational materialism, somehow served to bring about a spiritual renaissance?"

"But aren't they mutually exclusive realms?" Brooks posed, ready to begin a verbal joust. "How can you scientifically investigate the intangible?"

"At one time, radio waves and magnetism would have been considered intangible," Strickland replied. "Maybe we're just not asking the right questions or using the right tools when it comes to spirituality. Science continually tries to unravel the nature of existence and our place in the universe. And aren't those the very same questions that the world's religions have been asking throughout history? Science and spirituality have traditionally been seen as mutually exclusive domains—often overtly fearful of each other. But maybe they're merely two sides of the same coin, like the particle/wave duality of light. Each may be a shadow of some greater truth."

"But the question remains," he said, "how do you study these phenomena?"

"That's one of our major challenges," Strickland admitted. "Far-out as it may seem, numerous studies have shown statistically significant results for prayer, or even just *intent,* being capable of altering the state of the physical world—from speeding the recovery phase of an illness, to altering the pH of a solution, to affecting the outcome of random event generators. And there are indications that this phenomenon could be *additive*, increasing in its effect depending upon the numbers involved. No one claims to understand the possible mechanisms involved, but the results, if consistently repeatable, are pretty intriguing. And with our increasing interconnectedness via the Internet, it's hard to say where it could all lead. The Institute of Noetic Sciences in California has been doing some fascinating research in the realm of how conscious intention seems to influence the physical world. And we have some ideas of our own that we plan to pursue."

He paused to cut into a slab of grilled salmon. It was ready, and he began serving it onto paper plates. "Some of the investigational areas we have in mind even enter into the realms of physics and cosmology," he continued. "Gravity appears intuitively obvious as a nebulous force holding us to the surface of the earth. But in reality, all matter seems to create an indentation in the fabric of space-time, drawing two bodies together with a force proportional to their mass. That's all pretty counterintuitive stuff. In a similar vein, we perceive time like a linear filmstrip. But many physicists now believe that it's more like a road with an infinite number of forks along the way—and, in some sense, all possible paths may exist simultaneously. In other words, there are myriad possible outcomes from moment to moment, but it takes consciousness and intent to collapse those possibilities down into a single outcome. And as strange as it might sound, some physicists even believe that quantum theory is consistent with the existence of an immortal soul, and that at the moment of death, our consciousness may be absorbed into a realm where time ceases to exist. In order to better explore such questions, we've recently added a particle physicist and a cosmologist to the project."

"When can we expect our first dispatch from the new frontier?" asked a tall red headed reporter friend of Sara's, as she sampled the just-grilled veggies put on her plate.

"We'll make our findings available for peer review," Strickland replied. "And whether we like it or not, the Neoterics and the online world seem to be taking quite an interest in our work. So we won't be wanting for disciples. I guess all we need now is a new gospel."

"It will be interesting to see how such revelations go down with the established faiths," she said. "Talk about a hot potato . . ."

Strickland paused. "This isn't about *us* versus *them*," he emphasized. "That's been the situation far too often. And I'm not suggesting that I have any answers. But I do have a lot of interesting questions, and I'm trying to develop my intuition without compromising scientific rigor. Any good investigator learns never to ignore the power of synchronicity. You all know the many scientific epiphanies that have come about during a dream state—from the ring structure of the benzene molecule to the organization of the chemical periodic table. Science and spirituality have been going down separate paths for too long. In reality, they should both be perpetual works in progress—a process, not an ultimate destination. Opponents of the theory of evolution like to point out that it's 'only a theory.' And they're right about that. But then, so is the theory of relativity. In reality, each may someday be overturned, to a greater or lesser degree, by a newer and better theory. But for now they offer the best explanations for what we observe. The only way to move forward—in either realm—is to stay open to what's out there. If the spiritual and scientific realms can cross-pollinate and begin building on each other's strengths, it may wake a sleeping giant."

Chapter 159

After distributing another batch of food from the grill, Strickland excused himself and crossed the yard toward the wine table. A tall, lean young man was walking in the same direction.

"Dr. Strickland, Roger Ambrose," the man said, extending a hand. His eyes projected a striking sense of inner calm. "My uncle Jordan has told me so much about you over the years, I feel as if I already know you."

Strickland's mind raced as he tried to place the name. Then he recalled the details: Jordan's brother's son, a recently appointed assistant professor of religion and an expert in religious iconography.

"Ah, yes, Roger!" Strickland said. "Jordan has also told me about you. Congratulations on your appointment at Duke. Weren't you also doing some work at the Vatican?"

"Exactly right," he said. "I had a year-long fellowship there—coincidentally, during the time you were working on the Shroud."

Strickland's face tightened ever so slightly.

"Not to worry," said Ambrose. "I'm on your side. But there *was* quite a reaction over there. You had to be in the midst of it to fully appreciate the hubbub."

Strickland smiled. "I can only imagine. But the Vatican is a fascinating place, political intrigues and all. I'm sure it was a time that will always loom large in your memory."

"Oh, most definitely. I actually had a chance to renew my fellowship there, but then the offer from Duke came along."

"Duke's a great institution."

Ambrose paused. "To be perfectly honest, I also came back to be closer to what you and Uncle Jordan are planning. The Neoteric blogs are all buzzing about it. I've been interested in the prospect of a convergence between science and spirituality for some time. I have an undergraduate degree in physics, and the work you and Jordan have in mind is exactly what I've wanted to see take root."

Strickland was caught off guard by what appeared to be a less-than-subtle job inquiry. But something about the young man drew him in. He said, "We may need occasional help from someone with your expertise in iconography. Feel free to contact either Jordan or me about that in a few months."

"Thanks, I definitely will," Ambrose replied. He lingered for a moment, then took a sip of wine, and as he did, his small gold signet ring caught Strickland's eye. It contained the etched image of a tree with dense, intertwining branches—the symbol of the Order of the Oak.

Ambrose caught Strickland's gaze "Are you familiar with the Order?" he asked.

"Somewhat," Strickland said.

"The original monks were a fascinating group," Ambrose explained. "They believed that certain religious icons served as catalysts to push us forward in our spiritual evolution. Their founder, Frère Jean, had a vision that commanded him to 'transport the Shroud to the valley beyond the blue hills'—where its true destiny lay. A few days later, invading troops burned the village to the ground. But Jean had already arranged for the Shroud's safe passage. Since that time, successive generations of members have continued to hone their intuition, guiding the Shroud along its intended path. Some questioned the most recent research decision, but in the end, the path of greater knowledge has always been shown to be the correct one."

Ambrose removed the ring from his finger, his eyes alive with energy. "If anyone should have this, I think it should be you," he said, offering the ring.

Strickland hesitated, but the young man's gaze convinced him. He accepted the signet and tried it on his right ring finger. It fit perfectly.

Chapter 160

Sara emerged from the rear of the house, carrying buns and a big bowl of potato salad.

Strickland walked up from behind and hugged her around the waist, and she turned and kissed him. But as she did, a look of worry flashed across his face.

"Where's Rose?" he asked.

"Calm down, Mr. Safety," she said. "Rosie's fine—just taking a nap. Judy's watching her. So we're both off duty for a while. Enjoy it while you can!"

Sara suddenly spotted Jordan Randall parting from a group across the lawn. She touched Strickland on the shoulder. "I've been wanting to talk to Jordan all day. I'll catch up with you later, okay?" She kissed him again and strode away.

"You know where to find me," Strickland said, returning to the grill.

Before Sara was halfway across the lawn, a young man had approached Randall and engaged him in conversation. The two seemed to know each other. Sara had so wanted to take advantage of this window while her daughter was napping. But just then, as if sensing her gaze, Randall glanced up and motioned her over.

"Sara!" he said. "I was hoping you'd get out of the house and join the party."

"Well, motherhood calls . . . and calls," she said, smiling.

Randall hugged her warmly. "Whatever you've been doing, don't stop—you look terrific."

"Just what a girl likes to hear," she said, playfully smoothing her dress over her hips.

"Oh, I'm sorry," Randall said, turning back to his guest. "Sara, meet my nephew, Roger Ambrose. He's starting an assistant professorship at Duke after a year's research at the Vatican. Roger, Sara Bender, Bob Strickland's wife."

"You're friends with Jason Newcomb, aren't you?" Ambrose asked.

"Why, yes," she replied in surprise.

"I knew him during my fellowship at the Vatican."

"That's great!" Sara said. "I *love* Jason. We've been friends since college. How's he doing?"

"I think his stay at the Vatican has turned out to be a watershed chapter in his life," the young man said.

"Oh, how so?" she asked.

"He found an important sense of community there—maybe even a sense of mission."

"Sounds intriguing," said Bender. "I really need to catch up with him. My communications with the outside world have dropped off some since motherhood."

"Sometimes our priorities change," said Ambrose. "And that can be a good thing." He suddenly checked his watch. "I'm afraid I have to run. I'll call you next week, Uncle Jordan."

"Please do," said Randall.

Ambrose turned back to Sara and shook her hand. His gaze was oddly penetrating. "It was a pleasure to finally meet you," he said.

"Likewise" she said, smiling.

After Ambrose left, Sara turned her attention back to Randall. "It's great to see you again, Jordan. I thought about you so many times in Belize. Without your steadying influence, everything seemed . . . I don't know, out of kilter."

"I'm just thankful you and Bob got through it all unscathed."

"To be honest, it was touch-and-go at times," she said

"I put together a group on the Internet, and we prayed for both of you every day."

"Thanks, Jordan, I really appreciate that," she replied.

"I'm just sorry we haven't seen more of each other in the past few months," he said. "There are so many details to be sorted out with this new enterprise. It's almost like setting up the Ethnogenomics Center all over again. And your whirlwind life as a writer and mother has kept you just as busy, it seems. By the way, Rose gets more beautiful by the day—a cherub in the flesh."

Sara smiled "I can't help but agree with you. She melts my heart."

They sat in silence for a few moments. Looking up, she saw Strickland crossing the lawn from one group of friends to another. Sara smiled, and he broke into a broad grin and waved.

"You and Bob seem very happy," Randall noted.

"Yeah, we are," she replied.

"It seems like Bob's been searching for a long time," Randall said, "and now he's found his path."

"I agree. He's as focused as ever, but there's also a sense of great calm."

They were silent for a moment.

"And what about you, Jordan?" she asked. "You've also been through a lot. How are you doing?"

Randall paused. "In the past, my place in the world seemed pretty well defined," he said. "I felt bad for people like Bob, who seemed tortured and always searching for something. But after my experience with SEW, and everything that happened during your time on the island, I began to reexamine almost every aspect of my life. I came to the conclusion that I no longer felt completely at home with the people and the beliefs I once considered my own. To be honest, it was a very difficult time. And deciding whether to join Bob in this new venture was equally tough. I'd followed him once before, and I didn't want to be the eternal Govinda, trailing Siddhartha at the expense of his own destiny. Also, at first blush, Bob's proposals sounded pretty far-out."

Sara nodded, smiling in agreement.

"But the more I listened, the more his ideas resonated for me. I realized that my personal and professional goals are totally in sync with the work Bob has in mind. In fact, this is more me than any work I've ever done."

Sara's sister, Judy, suddenly appeared, with Rose in her arms. The baby's face was red from crying, her mouth puckered in anticipation.

"Snack time!" Judy said.

"Thanks, sis," Sara said. Loosening the front of her blouse, she discreetly pulled it up at the bottom. "Excuse me, Jordan . . ."

"Feel free," he replied.

Rose moved into position, and as she began suckling in earnest, Sara beamed with serene contentment.

"I've already learned so much from the subjects we've been studying," Randall said, reacting to the moment. "There's something palpable in the nature of people who have had profound spiritual experiences. Their paths may have been different, but somehow they've all arrived at the same destination. I still consider myself a Christian, but I've increasingly come to realize that once you really *get it,* the belief system and the rituals of a given faith become less important. These people have been transformed—you can see it in their eyes."

They sat in silence as Rose nursed. Then Sara rebuttoned her blouse and propped the baby up on her lap. Rose looked up with searching eyes, then reached out with both arms as if to embrace the world. Wrapping a hand around each of the baby's tiny hands, she moved in close to kiss her. And as she glanced over at Randall, her lip trembled and her eyes filled with tears.

Chapter 161

Strickland awoke suddenly, thinking he had heard Rose whimpering from the other room. But it was a dream. He listened carefully; the house was utterly silent. Sara was sound asleep, her face softly illuminated by moonlight.

But he was now wide-awake. Since Rose's birth, he had grown accustomed to sleeping in shifts. It was almost a replay of his medical residency days. He slid quietly out of bed and covered Sara.

On the way to his study, he crept into the nursery. But in the semidarkness, he stubbed his toe on an end table. "Shit!" he muttered.

Rose began to whimper and toss in her crib. *No, no!* he thought, imagining everyone being awakened. The baby opened her eyes and stared up at him, and her mouth parted in a brief but perfect smile. He kissed her on the forehead, and a few seconds later she was fast asleep. He gazed at her in the dim glow of the night-light.

In his study, Strickland did an Internet search on the Order of the Oak. He clicked on a link near the top that referenced "the light within." The article offered a lengthy historical account of the group, along with a synthesis of certain aspects of the gnostic gospels. "According to the Gospel of Thomas," it read, "Jesus said that we all come from the same divine light, and that this is the true *Gospel*—the good news. And as Frère Jean stated in his own writings, 'those who have achieved this realization shall be known by their gaze.'" Strickland printed out the article, planning to read it in more detail later.

Next he checked for an e-mail from Randall, regarding several résumés that had arrived pertaining to their future research. Then he opened the message, intending to review the attached documents. Waiting for them to print, he scanned the rest of his in-box. There were several e-mails from friends and former associates, as well as the usual overload of spam. He was just about to delete a large block when a message near the bottom caught his eye. The subject line read, "You're an ass!" The sender was *motoguzzi@beliefweb.net*. Opening the message, he saw, to his delight, that it was from Mark Altman.

Hey Man,

Congratulations on your marriage, your daughter, and all else. Wow! Somehow I can't quite picture you changing diapers, but I guess stranger transformations have occurred in this world.

I read about your new foundation in the blogosphere. I always sensed you had something like this in you. And it looks like you've really created some waves (see: www.neoteric.net). Maybe our ultimate challenge as a race isn't about declining resources, weaponry, and war. Maybe it's about seeing past the tribalistic aspects of religious belief, to our essential spiritual core. If we get there, we can fix the other problems together.

I think a new global family is forming. And, like it or not, you're one of the founding members. Shine on, man!

Best always,
Mark

Strickland clicked on the embedded Neoteric web address, and a shimmering image of a many-limbed network materialized on the screen. Glowing, animated impulses of light flowed through the latticework and down to the central trunk, ending at a pulsing node near the bottom. Rhythmic electronic music accompanied the image. The overall effect was wonderfully hypnotic.

He clicked on a link marked "Mission Statement," and the network image faded to black, replaced by a block of golden text:

Advanced technologies nearly led to global destruction during the Cold War. Now a mad scramble to build nuclear weapons has emerged among developing nations. In response, developed nations contemplate economy-draining missile defense systems while engaging in ill-defined "wars against terror." These simplistic responses to ever shifting "evils" demonstrate the futility of a global vision driven by primitive tribal impulses.

Having reached the third millennium, we finally have the

technologies, agricultural resources, and social infrastructures necessary to bring about world peace. The only missing ingredient is our will. The ability to transcend the tooth-and-claw underpinnings of our basic nature is what separates us from the animal world. It is our most valuable gift. To realize our full potential, we must move beyond visceral, hardwired responses intended by nature for a far more primitive world.

The popularity of books and movies depicting mythic ethereal worlds demonstrates the ongoing desire for transcendent mystery and spiritual connection. Too often, established religions fail to meet these needs. They have become mired in xenophobia, rigid lifestyle dictates, and moralistic doctrine. The focus on compassion and a sense of wonder has fallen from their vision.

At the same time, science and spirituality appear to be converging, often posing the same questions that ancient wizards and seers once pondered when staring up at the night sky: "Why are we here, and what is our destiny?" From the big bang, to dark matter, to parallel universes, the sciences are increasingly finding that our world is a far more mysterious place than anyone could have imagined.

Science and religion have for too long been at odds. The union of scientific knowledge and spiritual intuition holds the key to our survival—by encouraging the recognition of our shared humanity and oneness of spirit. Genetic science demonstrates the narrow inconsequence of racial differences. And neuro-imaging has illuminated the universality of transcendent experience, regardless of religious belief system.

The exploration of consciousness and pursuit of the spirit is our destiny. It's time to awaken. This is our childhood's end.

~ Neoteric

Without glancing away from the glowing screen, Strickland moved the freshly printed résumés to the side and scooted his chair closer to the desk. He clicked on the "Beliefs" link, and the screen again went black, followed by more golden text:

1. Rigid sectarian belief systems prescribe unbending modes of behavior and dress and attempt to micromanage followers under the guise of morality. Yet they often fail to address the key goals of spirituality: compassion and cultivation of transcendent states. These values were almost certainly at the core of any given spiritual founder's philosophies and beliefs. How many wars and acts of aggression have been perpetrated throughout history, bolstered by a distorted notion of God's will? In reality, all religions tap into a common spiritual base. Sectarian notions of divine destiny run contrary to the stated teachings of almost all faiths.

2. We are part biology and part spirit. To some degree, we are animals, exhibiting many of the same behaviors and traits found throughout the animal kingdom. These traits lead us to compete for food, territory, and mates. Such hardwired tendencies were clearly beneficial in a world where survival was the prime directive.

Over the course of time, tribes extended to villages, villages to cities, and cities to nations. Modern social organizations offer security, identity, and shared resources. But in a global economy, where we are interconnected to within hours by air, minutes by nuclear missile, and milliseconds via the Internet, attitudes and perceptions must evolve. We are more than just sophisticated animals vying selfishly for resources. Most people have a spiritual predilection that yearns to be developed. In every society on earth, men and women search for this connection.

3. Recognizing the biological remnants of our past is essential to our survival as a species. In a study of territorial behavior, birds of a particular species were transplanted to a neighboring village where the same species thrived. The new location was only a few hundred miles away, but much further than the birds would ever have traveled of their own volition. The "outsider" birds were then released in the new village and quickly settled into the trees. Almost immediately, these outsiders were recognized as such by their foreign song and were set upon by the local birds. Vigorous squabbles erupted.

In similar circumstances of confronting outsiders, humans tend to apply a template of race, religion, national pride, and other rationalizations to justify feelings of animosity and aggression motivated by xenophobia. But at their core, most ethnic, religious, and territorial battles are little different, in origin or execution, from the squabbling of those birds in the trees. Such behaviors ultimately stem from hardwired biology that is directed toward ensuring access to resources, territory, and mating privileges.

These primitive tribal strategies are part of the evolutionary framework of animal behavior. But they are not beneficial for modern humans. We have the ability to feed everyone on earth. We have the means to solve disputes, justly and fairly, through world courts. And most importantly, we have the higher-brain functions necessary to subvert the primitive and counterproductive remnants of our animal heritage. The only missing ingredient is a willingness to rise above our biological baggage and foster respect for every individual.

Millions of people around the globe are oppressed by ethnic, tribal, religious, or nationalistic conflict. Political action is required to protect the innocent in such situations. But these conflicts are symptoms of a greater malaise. The better we understand root causes, the better we can become at solving the problems. While it is indisputable that economic disparity and racial or religious discrimination breed conflict, these inequities are the end result of our primitive impulses. The willingness to subjugate others, based   on economics, politics, or religion, is predicated on viewing that group as fundamentally different and apart from one's own tribe.

4. Science is the key to illuminating our shared humanity and our shared spirit. Data from the Human Genome Project has demonstrated how little we actually differ from one another when viewed at the genetic level. And brain studies have shown the physiological commonality of transcendent states achieved by devotees of diverse religions and faiths.

5. Science and spirituality appear to be reconverging. Centuries ago, the intermingled realms of scientific inquiry and religious study diverged down sharply disparate paths, eventually becoming mutually exclusive worlds. Science claimed the domain of secular, verifiable, and "worldly" phenomena. Its focus was the understanding and manipulation of physical existence. Religion became inwardly directed, seemingly nonverifiable, and distinctly "otherworldly." The afterlife, targeting what many believe awaits us beyond this world, became its focus.

But increasingly, these two domains have begun to look like approximations of the same basic truths. Recent discoveries in genetics and molecular biology have led to profound questions about the basic definition of life. Breakthroughs in computing and artificial intelligence have spawned new debate about the nature of consciousness. Modern physics offers a universe of relativistic time and multiple dimensions beyond those of the observable physical realm. And the search for extraterrestrial life and hospitable planets beyond the solar system has awakened our intuitive sense that we are neither alone nor unique.

In short, science and religion are once again asking the same basic questions about our existence and our universe. To better shed light on these questions, pragmatic scientific knowledge and the insights of spiritual intuition must be more effectively melded and utilized. Science and religion have for too long been at odds—it's time to leverage this emerging synchronicity.

6. Science is the key to taking our spiritual exploration and evolution to the next stage. Advanced imaging techniques are increasingly elucidating the physiological and biochemical mechanisms by which we experience spiritually transcendent states—an investigative discipline sometimes referred to as neurotheology.

Brain imaging studies have also demonstrated that meditation and contemplative prayer are a highly efficient means of achieving transcendent spiritual states. Nearly all religions place the pursuit of such divine unity at the core of their original belief system. And scientific research increasingly finds that the attainment of these states promotes physical health and general well-being.

But most meditative and prayer disciplines are thousands of years old and often require years of immersion and seclusion to reach the most profound states of mystical unity. We believe that technology can be tapped to more easily achieve transcendent meditative states—through real-time processing of brain activity using computers. Visual and auditory feedback tools can help spiritual practitioners of all faiths more effectively advance their meditative skills. Using data obtained from studies of practitioners across diverse faiths, the Neoterics are developing hardware and software systems directed toward this goal.

7. The universe is infinitely mysterious. And contrary to the assertion of Occam's razor, the simplest explanation is not always the correct one. The word "atom" is derived from the ancient Greek notion of the "uncuttable"—the final elementary particle. But since the discovery of protons, neutrons, and electrons, scores of subatomic particles have been identified, with no end in sight. It's impossible to predict the direction that future scientific inquiries may take. Staying open to new ideas is essential.

Quantum theory indicates that we live in an interactive universe, and that consciousness may be woven into the very fabric of existence, as surely as space and time. Some theorists believe that the universe exists because of consciousness and that the simple act of observation can affect both the future and the past, a phenomenon known as retrocausality. The quantum double-slit experiment and the Schrödinger's cat conundrum imply that (at the quantum level) reality is literally altered by our observations. Prayer and affirmation might even be cast in this same light.

Several theorists have gone as far as proposing that reality consists of a series of discrete moments in time, rather than a smooth, linear progression of events. The way these moments are navigated is believed to depend, to some degree, on our beliefs, observations, and intent. These notions seem completely counterintuitive, but so did Einstein's theories of relativity when they were first introduced.

Roughly 500 years ago, most scientists believed that the earth was the center of the universe, around which all other bodies revolved. And 150 years ago, the existence of radio waves was a topic of heated scientific debate. Who could blame scientists of that day— on any of these fronts? The truth could not have been deduced using the observational tools and methods of the era.

Gravity is now seen as a bending of the space-time continuum— a trough created by a body of a given mass. But what if consciousness creates a similar trough in a currently unknown continuum? Perhaps we all exist at a locus of physical and spiritual energy—what some have called an "assemblage point." Our current experience of reality may be funneled through a profoundly narrow porthole of perception that offers only a hint of the true picture. The spiritual component of existence may be no more apparent or quantifiable today than the space-time aspect of gravity would have been to Isaac Newton as he watched an apple fall from a tree.

8. Perhaps it is no coincidence that in the Gnostic Gospels, Thomas quoted Jesus as saying, "we are children of the light." This is yet another manifestation of the intersection between ancient spiritual truths and modern scientific discoveries. It was the unique qualities of light that led Einstein to formulate his theories of relativity, offering the first inkling that the observer occupied a central place in the fabric of the universe. And it was the particle/wave duality of light that subsequently led to the formulation of quantum theory, the new understanding that the universe consists of clouds of quantum possibilities, made manifest by conscious observation. More recently, with the discovery of quantum entanglement, where elementary particles have been shown to interact with one another, instantly and at great distances, there's growing evidence that the universe as a whole is capable of storing information—like an enormous quantum hologram.

Consciousness has even been shown to affect processes at the genetic level. The recently formulated science of epigenetics demonstrates a level of genetic control that can be influenced by human thought and experience, and that can alter genetic function within a single generation and even be passed onto subsequent generations.

9. Mainstream institutions will cling desperately to the status quo. Galileo risked imprisonment and death for his support of theories, proposed by Copernicus, that effectively obliterated the earth-centric view of the universe. Religious leaders of Galileo's day refused even to gaze into his telescope, where they could have seen for themselves that other planets had smaller bodies orbiting around them. They feared the loss of their worldview—and the loss of their power. Similar trepidation will be encountered in trying to extend viewpoints on the relationship between science and spirituality.

Some believe that states of spiritual transcendence are little more than neuroprocessing anomalies produced by the inhibition of certain brain centers, a disruption of neurotransmitters, or even a simple lack of oxygen. But all human perceptions and experiences, including those of the spirit, occur in the brain. The fact that a perception of light can be triggered by electrical stimulation of the brain does not negate the existence of light. In a similar vein, the fact that experiences of a spiritual nature may occur due to rare neurological conditions does not negate the potential reality of these spiritual states.

10. The Internet is vital for the dissemination of newfound knowledge, for the acceleration of our spiritual evolution, and to facilitate the additive potential of conscious intent. One reason for the Internet's profound impact is that it mirrors the way our brains store and access information: there is no discrete center of processing, and nodes are widely interconnected. This structure allows us to extend, associate, and correlate knowledge—globally and almost instantaneously. Some theorize that the Internet may actually be a protoglobal mind, an entelechy, with power and potential that far exceeds the sum of its parts.

Like all technologies, the Internet has positive and negative repercussions—it can disseminate both enlightenment and hatred. But in the long run, the scales tend to tip in the direction of enlightened thought. As with the experiment involving neighboring populations of birds, sudden forced proximity (even at a virtual level on the Internet) will lead to initial conflict. But in the long term, this unrestricted intermingling of thought will serve to promote coexistence. Such globally accessible systems tend to be consensus driven and self-purifying.

11. Women will become increasingly important to spiritual evolution. With biological hard wiring oriented more toward interconnection and nurturing and less toward combative survival strategies, women are essential to our transformation. Statistics show that men perpetrate 90 percent of violent crimes, and almost all wars are precipitated and fought by men. Even in the midst of hostilities, women often act as social buffers, tending to minimize tensions and alleviate conflict. This basic predilection and skill set should be more fully recognized and utilized.

During the conflicts in Afghanistan and Iraq, women have helped mitigate regional and tribal strife by aiding in the formation of new and more inclusive governments. And American women were pivotal in bringing abuses to light in a number of corporate and government scandals. Programmed by nature to facilitate cohesiveness and nurture the young, they are better able to step back from petty issues of competition and personal gain, to more clearly delineate right from wrong.

12. This is a global effort. The Neoteric movement is not a religion defined and prescribed from "on high." This is open-source spirituality—a community of seekers anxious to know the divine. Hone your intuition through contemplation, prayer, and meditation. Find your own path. Be aware of synchronistic events that may shape your destiny. We want to hear from you.

* * *

As Strickland finished reading the final page, the screen once again faded to black, and he suddenly became aware of the room around him: the whisper of the computer fan, and the call of an owl somewhere in the distance.

During his time in Belize, he had discounted the Neoterics as just another misguided cult—restless kids in search of the antiestablishment flavor of the month. But the points they made had resonated powerfully. Either he had changed or they had, or maybe he had misread them all along.

Strickland stepped out onto the balcony of his study. Overhead, it was still pitch black, but the first light of day glowed almost imperceptibly in the east. The morning was chilly and clear as ether; the Milky Way formed a vivid glowing swath across the center of the sky. He sat down cross-legged on the deck, zipped up his jacket, and gazed into the night.

Chapter 162

Strickland meditated on the deck for what seemed like minutes, but when he checked his watch, nearly a half hour had passed. He felt wonderfully rested and filled with energy. Inside, he found Rose and Sara snuggled in their beds, still sound asleep.

Grabbing the newspaper from the front porch, he caught the first glint of sun over the neighbors' fence and breathed in the sharp whiff of pine.

On his way to the breakfast nook, he checked his watch: 6:15 A.M. Sara and Rose would probably sleep for several more hours. There might be just enough time . . .

After a quick cup of coffee and a toasted bagel, he wheeled the bike out to the street, away from the house. He pressed the starter button and let it idle without revving the engine, so as not to wake anyone.

A few minutes later, he had cleared the suburban sprawl of Rockville. The early-morning weekend highways were nearly deserted. Heading south on 270, he throttled up to seventy-five. He hadn't ridden often since Rose's birth. He loved his new life, but it felt good to be back on the road with some time alone.

A little over an hour later, he was on Skyline Drive, climbing into the wooded beauty of Shenandoah National Park. As he made his way along the winding mountain passes, the foliage grew denser, with stands of chestnut, hickory, and poplar. Below him, to the west, sunlight glinted like fire along the winding Shenandoah River.

It felt like a lifetime since he had last taken this ride. So many things had changed. Glancing down at the oak tree image on the gold ring he now wore, he thought about the Neoteric e-mail from Altman and then recalled his encounter with Ambrose at the backyard barbecue. Altman and Ambrose were somehow spiritually related, in ways that he had just begun to perceive.

An enormous gray heron suddenly rose from a high treetop and swooped down through a narrow clearing in the trees. Strickland slowed his bike and caught a glimpse of the bird in profile. It arced into a long glide, as if attempting to match his speed and path. Then, just as he was about to catch up to it, the bird dropped into the river valley below and was obscured by the trees.

Strickland leaned through a sweeping turn, then emerged into a broad clearing. A stunning vista of the Blue Ridge Mountains and the river valley below opened before him. The brilliant sun cast dancing patterns on the distant river. A moment later, he spotted the heron again—a tiny speck now against the shimmering reflections.

He thought again of Ambrose and the Order of the Oak's prophecy about the Shroud's ultimate destiny "in the valley beyond the blue hills." Strickland gazed out at the bluish morning haze hanging over the mountains, and the winding valley beyond. A slight smile came to his lips. His eyes were alive as he guided the bike down a long straight expanse of road.

END

Authors' Note

The near future time frame of *The Shroud* has necessitated melding cutting-edge science with educated speculation. The basic concepts and plot elements adhere to the known laws of biology, chemistry, and physics, as well as currently viable theories regarding the authenticity of the Shroud of Turin. Certain artistic liberties have been taken, however, concerning historical groups charged with the protection of the Shroud of Turin.

The Shroud was influenced and inspired by Carl Sagan's *Contact*, which beautifully captured the sense of awe and wonder at the core of scientific exploration. Our goal has been to create an exciting tale, and to inspire speculation and discussion about science, spirituality, and the universe at large.

We look forward to hearing from you:
contact@theshroud.net

Made in the USA
Charleston, SC
03 July 2010